Praise for

The Elephant of Belfast

A National Bestseller

"In 1941, with Nazi bombs shattering Belfast, a young zookeeper rushed to save the elephant in her charge. Walsh's lovely debut spins this historical sliver into a vivid novel of redemption and mutual care."
—*The New York Times Book Review*

"Based on real events, this engrossing novel takes place a year into the Second World War. A three-year-old elephant named Violet arrives at Belfast's Bellevue Zoo, where Hettie Quin, a young zookeeper mourning the recent death of a sister, finds purpose and solace in caring for her . . . The novel vividly evokes the speed with which war makes the commonplace surreal, as Hettie and Violet become fugitives in a ruined city."
—*The New Yorker*

"Breathtaking . . . The setting may be historic, but the novel's shattering themes are sadly evergreen. In Walsh's retelling, it's heartening to remember that even through the worst sacrifices, love and courage can prevail."
—REBEKAH DENN, *The Christian Science Monitor*

"A charming debut around a little-known chapter of World War II—the German blitz of Belfast in a city already reeling from sectarian violence. But the real heart of this story centers around the love and devotion between Hettie and Violet, a twenty-year-old zookeeper and an orphaned three-year-old Indian elephant. While war rages on, Hettie will go to great lengths to protect Violet giving readers a riveting story of strength and survival, hope and resilience."
—*B&N Reads*, The Best
Historical Fiction Books to Read Right Now

"Offering a distinctive slant among this year's strong World War II novels."   —*Library Journal*

"Inspired by the true story of the 'elephant angel' of Belfast, Walsh's debut is a stirring tale of grief, loss, and survival against the chaotic backdrop of the war and the IRA's actions. The unique setting of Belfast during WWII makes this book stand out . . . Overall, fans of WWII fiction and historical fiction will enjoy this fresh take on the era."   —*Booklist*

"Walsh fictionalizes in her charming debut a little-known true story from WWII, that of a female Irish zookeeper and a 3,000-pound young elephant. The year is 1940 when 20-year-old Hettie Quin, a part-time zookeeper, waits at the Belfast docks for the arrival of Bellevue Zoo's latest attraction—a three-year-old elephant named Violet . . . Hettie's devotion to Violet forms the emotional core of this novel, which does an excellent job of recreating daily life in Belfast during WWII. Hettie and Violet's bond is one to treasure."   —*Publishers Weekly*

"Walsh delivers a turbulent portrait of life in a divided city . . . A unique perspective of a country at war and the lengths people will go for those they love."   —*Kirkus Reviews*

"*The Elephant of Belfast* knocked me flat and picked me up, not just once but many times over the course of S. Kirk Walsh's deeply satisfying telling. There's so much life in these pages, life as well as death—we're in wartime Belfast, dear reader, and the Luftwaffe is dropping bombs—that I couldn't help but feel changed by the end, experienced. Only the best novels do that, and the very fine *Elephant of Belfast* belongs in that rank."   —BEN FOUNTAIN, author of *Billy Lynn's Long Halftime Walk*

"This remarkable novel about the unexpected relationship between a woman and an elephant was inspired by true events that took place during the so-called Belfast Blitz in the 1940s, when Hitler attacked the capital of Northern Ireland. A vivid tale of resilience and loss, *The Elephant of Belfast* is ultimately about the transformative power of love and the surprising ability we humans have to find joy in the midst of heartache." —CHRISTINA BAKER KLINE, #1 *New York Times* bestselling author of *Orphan Train* and *The Exiles*

"*The Elephant of Belfast* boasts not one but two dauntless heroines: Hettie, a young Irish zookeeper, and Violet, a young Indian elephant. From their first meeting, Hettie is determined to protect Violet, and as dangers mount, we cannot help cheering on her devotion and her resourcefulness. Walsh has written a novel of deep affection and knife-edge suspense. A brilliant debut." —MARGOT LIVESEY, author of *The Boy in The Field*

"In S. Kirk Walsh's hands, the city of Belfast, its zoo, and the creatures who resided there during the Belfast Blitz come vividly and brilliantly alive. *The Elephant of Belfast* is impeccably researched and thrillingly suspenseful. I churned through the pages, anxious to know what became of Hettie Quin and Violet, the elephant in her charge: a heartbreaking animal heroine to rival Tarka the otter and the rabbits of *Watership Down*." —LOUISA HALL, author of *Trinity* and *Speak*

"*The Elephant of Belfast* is a lovely book about a fascinating piece of history, and its two heroines—animal and human—are enthralling and beautifully drawn. S. Kirk Walsh writes wonderfully about heartbreak both personal and historic." —ELIZABETH McCRACKEN, author of *The Souvenir Museum*

"A zoo in wartime Belfast and a young woman's fierce love for the elephant in her care come vividly to life in this beautiful, beguiling, and atmospheric debut novel." —DOMINIC SMITH, author of
The Last Painting of Sara de Vos

"An elephant, a young zookeeper, the city of Belfast, bombings, and an IRA member are the improbable characters in this captivating and intimately felt novel that tells the story of a young woman's uncommon devotion and courage under fire." —LILY TUCK, author of
Sisters and *The Double Life of Liliane*

The Elephant *of* Belfast

The Elephant
of Belfast

A Novel

S. Kirk Walsh

Counterpoint Berkeley, California

THE ELEPHANT OF BELFAST

The Library of Congress has cataloged the hardcover edition as follows:
Names: Walsh, S. Kirk, author.
Title: The elephant of Belfast : a novel / S. Kirk Walsh.
Description: First hardcover edition. | Berkeley, California : Counterpoint
    Press, 2020.
Identifiers: LCCN 2020017594| ISBN 9781640094000 (hardcover) | ISBN
    9781640094017 (ebook)
Subjects: LCSH: Belfast (Northern Ireland)—History—Bombardment,
    1941—Fiction. GSAFD: Historical fiction.
Classification: LCC PS3623.A366146 E44 2020 | DDC 813/.6—dc23
LC record available at https://lccn.loc.gov/2020017594

Paperback ISBN: 978-1-64009-511-3

Cover design by Alison Forner
Book design by Wah-Ming Chang

COUNTERPOINT
2560 Ninth Street, Suite 318
Berkeley, CA 94710
www.counterpointpress.com

Printed in the United States of America

10 9 8 7 6 5 4 3 2 1

With love, for Michael

&

in loving memory of my parents & my uncle Kirk

And I say, how lucky I was. I was only buried
alive a few hours, you know.

—EITHNE O'CONNOR,
Belfast Blitz survivor

The Elephant *of* Belfast

One

ON THAT MORNING OF OCTOBER 3, 1940, HETTIE QUIN KNEW
she was lucky to be there, at the docks of Belfast, assisting with the
elephant's arrival. One of the other zookeepers had come down with a
fever, and Ferris Poole had enlisted her help at the last minute. As she
stood next to Ferris at the edge of the crowd, Hettie steadied herself
after having sprinted down to the docks from the nearby tram stop;
her mother had made her tardy by requesting multiple chores around
the house before Hettie finally managed to slip out the door. As she
pushed sweaty strands of hair from her eyes, she took in the stunning
sight overhead—a young elephant being maneuvered through the air.
A crane and a system of chains and pulleys elevated the animal from
the deck of the moored steamship. The elephant's trunk coiled up and
then unfurled like an opening fist. There was a hollow trumpet call.
The crowd—women, men, children, sailors, dockworkers—let out a
collective gasp, their gazes following the orchestrated movements of the
hoisting operation. Hettie had never seen so many people at the docks:
It was as if British royalty or a famous screen actress were among the
steamer's passengers arriving that morning. The atmosphere felt festive,
bright with expectation.

Here was the three-year-old elephant. Here was her potential new charge at the zoo. Here was Violet. A local poacher had killed the animal's mother with poisoned arrows on a savanna in faraway Ceylon, and Mr. Christie, the owner of the Bellevue Zoo & Gardens, had bought the orphaned elephant for a good price from another animal trader in Ceylon. Standing next to Hettie, Ferris dropped his half-finished cigarette onto the ground and squared his shoulders for Violet's arrival. Mr. Wright, the head zookeeper, stood at the foot of the gangplank. Two reporters appeared by his side and scribbled in their notepads as Mr. Wright kept his gaze fixed on Violet. The elephant hovered, her feet hanging in midair, her flap-like ears pinned against her head. There was another collective sigh as she lifted her trunk and produced a high-pitched whistle. The elephant's cry tumbled over the crowd.

With his ramrod-straight posture and a subtle theatrical swing to his gait, Mr. Wright looked like a cross between a military general and a ringmaster. He wore a pair of jodhpurs, a brilliant red jacket, a fedora, and a pair of polished knee-high riding boots. Two rows of shiny brass buttons trailed down the front of his double-breasted coat, and a golden braid was threaded through the epaulets that rested on his shoulders. Several medals decorated the right side of his chest. Hettie had heard from one of the other zookeepers that Mr. Wright had fought at the Battle of Arras during World War I and saved more than a dozen men's lives. Mr. Wright was always dressed in this outfit, Hettie had noticed, regardless of whether he was training Wallace the lion with a crack of his whip or tossing silver-scaled herrings for the sea lions or greeting visitors at the zoo's front entrance.

The winch raised Violet higher. The machinery rasped and whined. The crowd grew silent. Gulls wheeled overhead. Violet uncoiled her trunk again and released another cry. A commotion stirred on the deck. Several men yelled at one another. The chain attached to the crane's neck tightened. Slowly the crane swiveled to one side and then began to rise. The air turned electric.

Mr. Christie stood at the top of the walkway, looking something like a campaigning politician, in a three-piece suit with a brilliant yellow scarf around his neck, its tasseled ends flying up in the breeze. He fervently shook hands with one of the ship's officers on deck, signed several sheets of paper, and walked down the ramp to greet Mr. Wright and his new elephant. Mr. Wright cleared away the crowd to make more room for Violet's imminent landing on the dock.

"Ferris," Mr. Wright yelled. "Miss Quin. Over here!"

"Yes, sir," she said, walking over to him and positioning herself next to Mr. Wright.

"Where have you been?" he asked curtly.

"My mum—" Hettie started to say, and then stopped.

"Take this," instructed Mr. Wright, handing her a metal bucket of carrots, the feathery tops brushing her hand. "Here she comes."

"Look," Ferris said, glancing over at Hettie. There was that familiar clear blue flash of Ferris's eyes, the dimple in the center of his left cheek. Hettie's hands pricked with perspiration. Ferris turned his attention to Violet. The crane groaned and wheezed as it continued lowering Violet to the ground. Hettie stood mesmerized by the strange sight of the elephant suspended, like an enormous anvil, in midair. The cranking of the winch was paused while the sailors on deck adjusted the controls and yelled at one another.

For a moment, Hettie was afraid the mechanism would fail and the elephant would come crashing onto the dock. Violet would break through the weathered planks, and multiple civilians would be injured, some might even drown. TRAGEDY STRIKES BELFAST DOCKS, the *Telegraph*'s headlines would read the following day. COUNTLESS IN-NOCENT CIVILIANS AND CHILDREN KILLED. The chains tightened and creaked. Two men cranked the winch on the ship's deck—and finally the animal's feet touched down onto the dock to a thunderous cheer. Violet shook her torso, sending a nimbus of dust and dirt from her skin. Mr. Christie walked over to Mr. Wright, his scarf fluttering as he took in the eager crowd.

A girl stood at her mother's knee, gaping up at the elephant, her small face open with wonder. A young couple in matching school uniforms tittered, the boy's lanky arm draped around the girl's shoulder. The crew on the neighboring oil tanker paused to take in the unusual sight. On the other adjacent vessel, a Royal Navy ship, the captain prematurely ended his drill instructions and allowed the men to peer over the ship's railing at the spectacle of Violet and the rest of the city below.

Belfast was alive with activity that morning. The hum of life and industry was everywhere. The docks, the streets, the factories. Lorries, cars, and buses streamed through major arteries of the city. Pedestrians hurried along the pavements to their jobs. At the York Street Flax Spinning Company, pairs of rubber-aproned women oversaw the electricity generators in the enginehouse, which drove the shafts of the machines that powered the spindles and looms that spun and wove the threads into cheap utility clothing and fabric for airplanes and other myriad purposes. Armies of men sat at their drafting desks at Short & Harland, sketching designs of Sunderland flying boats and Stirling bombers. The Linfield Football Club had begun its morning practice on its pitted playing field at Windsor Park, not far from the Lisburn Road. Dozens of Poor Clare nuns sang "How Great Is Our God" at their convent's chapel on the Cliftonville Road, their voices coalescing into one celestial sound that drifted beyond the chapel's stained-glass windows. To Hettie, it felt as if the entire city were awake and ready for Violet—and her auspicious arrival in Belfast. There was a freshness. An opportunity. Something was about to happen.

The crowd clapped and cheered for Violet as passengers filed down the ship's ramp. Hettie noticed the rolling dollies of luggage, steamer trunks, and bags being ferried down another plank that extended from the ship's belly. One man carried a terrarium with a hooded cobra pressed against the box's translucent sides, its thin tongue flicking against the glass. An elderly woman held a wired cage with a pair of chickens; a few loose feathers floated up like rings of smoke.

"Carrots, Miss Quin," Mr. Wright ordered. "Now."

Hettie handed him a pair of carrots, and he held them out for the elephant. Violet grabbed the carrots with the fingerlike end of her trunk and swung them into her mouth. Bits and pieces fell to the ground. Violet suctioned them up, thrusting the tip of her trunk against the uneven boards of the dock.

Mr. Christie held a stick with a long handle, like a bullwhip, with a note tied to one end. He inspected the handwritten message more closely. "'Lead me with this,'" he read aloud to the crowd. "Did you hear that, everyone? 'Lead me with this.'"

Cameras flashed. Mr. Christie handed the stick to Mr. Wright, who offered another carrot to Violet in the palm of his hand. The elephant deftly picked it up. Behind her, Hettie felt the heat and crush of the swelling crowd. She looked around for Ferris. He stood on the other side of Violet, awaiting further instructions.

"Let's see her do a trick," called a boy from somewhere.

"Don't be an eejit," Ferris yelled. "Poor animal has been on a ship for almost a month."

"Where did she come from?" asked another young boy.

"From the wilds of Ceylon," Mr. Christie said proudly. "I'm lucky I got her."

"How much does she weigh?" an older man asked. "Looks like she could crush someone to death."

"Three thousand pounds," Mr. Christie responded, "and she isn't going to hurt anyone. Remember, our animals are about entertainment, not stirring up fear."

"According to the paperwork, she weighs three thousand four hundred and eleven pounds," Mr. Wright added. "A little below average."

Hettie took a few steps closer and stared at Violet. Her circular feet were bordered with half-moon nails. The elephant's tail, with a paintbrush-like tuft of hair, swished from side to side, and her large-lidded sepia eyes popped a bit wider. Mr. Wright lifted the stick in front of Violet, and Hettie noticed the elephant's eyes following the end of it. Hettie imagined her older sister, Anna, standing beside her, whispering into her ear, *She's your elephant. She's the one for you.* Violet was about five feet tall, smaller than the Clydesdale horses Hettie used to ride with her father along the rolling knolls of the Cavehill in north Belfast.

"Steady feet," Mr. Wright said in a neutral voice. "Steady."

He raised the stick higher, and Violet slowly started to lift her front feet from the ground. Soon, she stood only on her hind legs, strong and unmoving like the columns of an ancient building. Her broad torso cast a shadow. The faction of reporters positioned themselves in front of the crowd and aimed their lenses up at Violet. Light bulbs went off again.

"That's my girl," Mr. Christie said, revealing a wide smile. "My number one girl."

He clasped his hands together as if in prayer.

"You can visit Violet at the Bellevue Zoo on the Antrim Road," Mr. Christie declared. "We're open every day. Rain or shine."

"There, there, Violet," Mr. Wright said as the elephant shifted on her hind legs.

He lowered the stick, and Violet returned to all four feet. The crowd whistled and clapped.

"Show us the way, Wright," Mr. Christie said, tipping his hat.

"Up the Antrim Road?" Mr. Wright asked, patting Violet on her side.

A cloud of dust rose from the deep folds of her skin. With the end of her tail the elephant swatted the spot that Mr. Wright had just touched.

"Up the Antrim Road," Mr. Christie repeated with zeal.

He shook hands with Mr. Wright and the ship's officer. Then Mr. Christie gave a wave to the layers of enthusiastic spectators before making his way around to the rear door of the polished Ford Prefect Saloon that Hettie now noticed had been waiting for him all along. The driver closed Mr. Christie's door and seated himself behind the large steering wheel. With a mechanical sputter, the car disappeared into the thrum of the dockyards. Violet raised her ears and unfolded them like two large fans. She released another trumpet call and nudged her forehead into Mr. Wright's chest.

"Easy, lovely," he said softly, patting her side again. During her time at the zoo, Hettie had noted this about Mr. Wright: He often spoke with more kindness to the animals than he did to people. "We're gonna take you home."

Mr. Wright lifted the stick in front of Violet's trunk and guided it forward. Violet stomped her feet against the dock, flurries of dust flying up around her legs. Then she lowered her head and proceeded to follow the curled end of the stick. Her movements were slow and gentle. Hettie walked to the right of Violet while Mr. Wright and Ferris stayed on the left side of the elephant.

"Everyone, give Violet some room," said Mr. Wright.

The crowd parted as Mr. Wright led Violet away from the steamship. Ahead, the cranes of Harland & Wolff were visible amid the sprawl of warehouse hangars and buildings now devoted to producing military vessels, aircraft, and tanks at an ever-increasing rate. Before Hettie's father, Thomas, enlisted in the Merchant Navy, he had worked in the assembly shops of Harland & Wolff for more than a decade. One afternoon, seven years ago, when Hettie was thirteen, Thomas had brought her to the shop where he had worked as a joiner. He gave her a tour of a gantry, where one of the larger ships was under construction. What she remembered most vividly of that afternoon was the deafening sound of the countless machines in persistent motion and how the vibrations shook the concrete floor, traveling up into her legs. It felt as if her entire body were rattling along at the same clip as the propulsive machines. Then her father led her into one of the gantries where the colossal skeleton of a hull in progress was obscured by a high tower of scaffolding;

a dozen men stood at varying heights, welding, which sent up sprays of sparks into their faces.

Violet whistled, the high-pitched sound returning Hettie to the important task in front of her. She positioned herself behind Ferris, to the left of the elephant, with the buckets clutched in both hands. Violet's forehead was flecked with pale spots, like a scattering of petals. A fine coat of dust veiled the bony curve of her broad back. Whiskers peppered her chin. She swung her trunk like the needle of a metronome.

"People, let this girl through," Mr. Wright said in a booming voice.

The crowd stepped aside, creating a wider path for Violet as she walked by. Mr. Wright directed her along the Sydenham Road, which intersected the dockyards and munitions and shipbuilding factories. Clouds of smoke spilled from the redbrick chimney stacks. A young boy pushed a wooden handcart piled with onions, eggs, vegetables, and burlap bags of rice and flour, and three dockworkers hauled oversize pieces of lumber. A half dozen Royal Navy officers, clad in their distinctive mess dress uniforms and dazzlingly white waistcoats, paused to take in the curiosity of Violet and the small parade that followed her. Hettie felt the cold, briny air flush her cheeks.

Together they crossed over the Queen's Bridge. The morning sun brightened, creating a carpet of reflections on the river's uneven waters. As the procession neared the middle of the bridge, Violet veered toward the right; then the elephant lowered her head and trotted into a knot of pedestrians heading in the opposite direction.

"Oh, Mummy," cried a young girl.

The mother whisked the child up into her arms and stepped out of Violet's path.

"Don't let him bite me," said the girl, tears trailing down her cheeks.

The mother glared at Mr. Wright who blew into the brass whistle that hung around his neck.

"Ferris! Hettie!" he yelled. "Where are you?"

Hettie dropped the buckets onto the bridge, ran to Violet's side, and pushed her foreleg with both hands. Her skin was rubbery and rough to the touch, and she smelled of manure and rotten eggs. Hettie shoved the elephant with all the weight and strength that she could summon. Ferris positioned himself near the elephant's rear, pressing against her hind leg. Hettie could see the sinewy bulge in Ferris's forearms as he attempted to guide Violet toward the middle of the bridge.

"Come on, Hettie," he said, his breath ragged. "Help me."

Violet trumpeted, and Hettie felt the vibrations of her call through her fingertips, up the length of her arms, and into the center of her chest. Hettie pushed harder against Violet. The elephant's acrid smell made her feel momentarily nauseated and weak. Hettie gathered herself—and pushed again.

"Violet," Mr. Wright said in a calm voice. "We're crossing the bridge, not jumping off of it."

The elephant stretched her trunk over the bridge's railing, and for a moment Hettie was nervous that Violet would somehow step over it and plunge into the strong currents below. She leaned farther into the elephant. The flash of a photographer's camera blinded Hettie. Sweat collected along her hairline.

"Will you bloody stop it," she whispered.

"Come on, Hettie," Ferris yelled again. "One, two, three."

Hettie closed her eyes tight and heaved the entire mass of her body against Violet's. She was tall for a young woman, five foot seven, and slender and long-legged, like her sister. Hettie was even a little taller than Ferris, but she wasn't muscular and compact like him. Hettie pushed with more force, and Violet trumpeted loudly again, but she didn't budge. The salty air stung Hettie's eyes. She thought of her father and what he'd say: *You hear me. Give it all ya got, girl.* Suddenly the elephant turned away from the railing and trotted toward the center of the bridge.

"Excellent, Miss Quin and Mr. Poole," Mr. Wright said. "Brilliant, my friends."

He waved the stick in front of Violet's eyes and she followed him across the bridge, her trunk swinging like a velvet rope.

"Miss Quin, the buckets," Mr. Wright barked. "Don't forget the buckets."

Hettie turned to see that the buckets had rolled across the wide expanse of the bridge, carrots spilling over the rims. Pedestrians kicked them farther to the side, sending the bundles into the river. Hettie ran to the railing and spotted several carrots floating, like miniature buoys, on the metallic-gray surface. Anxiety pinched her chest. She grabbed the buckets and caught up with Mr. Wright, Ferris, and Violet, who were now walking along Oxford Street, passing the familiar pumping station that sat on the banks of the River Lagan. Hettie marched right behind them, keeping her attention on Violet and her swaying tail.

At the northern end of Oxford Street, they walked diagonally across the bustling square that fronted the Customs House. Near the stairs of the imposing Victorian building, two men, dressed in dark suits and wool scarves, stood on short wooden boxes and debated the prospects of a German invasion: One fervently supported the war against the Fascists and proclaimed Churchill as "our great leader"; the other man, who had an unruly beard, declared that he would welcome the Nazi troops with open arms, that they would drive the British out of Ireland for good and dump the Unionist junta out of Stormont. During the last few years, Hettie had heard many versions of this argument from her father and others. It was challenging to follow all the different opinions except that it was clear no one could agree about what might happen.

"The working-class people of Belfast would be better off if the Germans came. We have nothing to lose," the man with the beard yelled. "The Germans would end discrimination, give us justice. Get rid of the Brits and unite Ireland."

The speaker's cheeks turned roseate. His forehead glistened.

"This war is against the Germans and no one else," the other man yelled, shaking his fist in the air. "They'll enslave us all. Will you please listen to me! We are ill-prepared."

Strangers booed, hissed, and cheered. As soon as the men noticed Violet, though, they suspended their arguments, united for once in their astonishment at the unusual spectacle of an elephant lumbering across the square. Ahead, on the other side, a band of musicians was performing a folk tune at the foot of the Albert Clock on Victoria Street, the crowned tower leaning vaguely to the left on its sandstone foundation. The whimsical notes of a melodeon, an upright piano, a fiddle, and a double bass stitched the air. A young couple swirled in circles among the parting strangers, their feet moving in synchronized motion on the cobblestoned walkway. Pedestrians clapped along with the music. A ship's horn sounded in the distance. The smells of tobacco, leather, and petrol drifted through the air, scents that reminded Hettie of home and her father.

"Follow me," Mr. Wright repeated to Violet. "Follow me."

Near the end of Victoria Street, Hettie caught sight of the manicured greens and familiar domes of city hall pressed against the dull pewter sky. Usually when she traveled through this neighborhood Hettie was on her father's bike and rarely took in the sights and sounds of street life, but walking along with Violet meant noticing details that often rushed past her in a blur. As they moved farther up the avenue, they passed a congregation of silver-haired men throwing horseshoes on a parcel of dead grass next to a pub. Next, they traversed North Street, which gave way to the Shankill Road, which was bordered with the linen mills that, along with the shipyards across the river, employed many of the men of the predominantly working-class Loyalist neighborhood.

"Steady," Mr. Wright said to Violet as they started up the gradual incline of the Antrim Road. "Steady there, me girl."

Strangers opened the doors and windows of their houses and flats, and gazed down at Violet's slow locomotion. Random sticks and branches snapped under her weight. Some people waved; others stared on in silent awe.

"Miss Quin, the carrots," Mr. Wright said.

Her palms grew clammy.

"They fell into the river, sir," Hettie said.

"Here, Mr. Wright," Ferris said, handing him two carrots. "I have a few."

Hettie glanced over at Ferris, who tipped his cap in her direction.

"Thank you, Ferris," Mr. Wright said, not looking at Hettie.

She forced a smile. As she often did, Hettie felt a complicated mix of gratitude, betrayal, and jealousy toward Ferris. He was always prepared for Mr. Wright's every demand or request, but his diligence and readiness often left Hettie feeling flat-footed and ineffectual—and that Mr. Wright would never see her for who she truly was. She pushed these thoughts away, though; she couldn't afford these distractions this morning.

"Come on, Violet," Mr. Wright said in a gentle voice again.

As they traveled farther up the Antrim Road, Hettie relaxed into her stride. The buildings became less dense, with many of the homes hidden behind walls or wrought-iron fences. A mother shelled peas into a bucket on a stoop. She looked up from the repetitive movement of her hands and smiled at the unexpected marvel of Violet. Schoolgirls played a game of hopscotch on the white-chalk squares drawn on the pavement and sang rounds of "Three Blind Mice": *See how they run. See how they run.* The refrains overlapped one other until the girls saw Violet and paused their song, openmouthed with amazement and glee. Up ahead, a police officer stood at the next intersection. As soon as he spotted Violet, he blew into his whistle—and the elephant started to run.

"Violet," Mr. Wright yelled. "Violet!"

The elephant ran up the Cliftonville Road and then toward the storefront of a greengrocer, and Mr. Wright, Ferris, and Hettie dashed after her. Modest pyramid-shaped piles of cabbages, potatoes, and turnips were arranged on either side of the doorway. Violet trotted up to the vegetables, looped her trunk around one of the turnips, and lifted it into her mouth. Then another. The rest of the vegetables tumbled onto the street, like a stampede of lawn bowls. The police officer blew his whistle again, and the grocer stepped outside his store. His complexion paled.

"What on—" he exclaimed.

Hettie tried to shove Violet away from the produce, but the animal merely swatted her tail into Hettie's face. Then Violet dropped several piles of manure onto the cobblestones. The pungent aroma made Hettie feel queasy. She took a deep breath and tried again, and Violet reared into her, kicking her squarely in the thigh. The elephant's sheer strength pushed her backward into the street as if she weighed absolutely nothing. Pebbles and dirt pressed into her palms. A cold shudder moved through her system. Heat seared her thigh.

Hettie closed her eyes for a second. Starbursts erupted against the dark theater of her eyelids. Violet reared her hind leg again and Hettie rolled out of the way. If she hadn't, the elephant would have stepped on her. The grocer yelled at Mr. Wright, who was on his hands and knees, picking up an armful of potatoes. Hettie held on to her thigh with both hands. The ache in her leg radiated like a beam of a light. Ferris picked up the curled stick and attempted to distract Violet from the bundle of carrots that she now snapped into her soft pink mouth.

"Come on, Violet," Ferris said. "Let's go home."

The elephant's gaze softened and she stepped away from the storefront. Her feet crushed several beets, carrots, and turnips that had tumbled onto the street, the smashed vegetables looking something like a child's finger painting. Hettie stood up gingerly, relieved to find that she still could.

"Brilliant job, Ferris. Take Violet to Bellevue," Mr. Wright said. "Hettie, find a shovel. Clean this mess up!"

Hettie felt her cheeks redden. She shook out her hands as the putrid smell of manure filled her nostrils. Mr. Wright disappeared inside the store and returned with a shovel. He handed it to her without saying a word. Resigned, Hettie scooped up the elephant's manure and deposited it into a trash bin. In vain, she attempted to spit out the foul taste that was forming in her mouth from the persistent smell. Inside the store, she noticed Mr. Wright trying to calm the owner down. The man gesticulated wildly toward the door.

"That elephant," he yelled. "He destroyed my precious produce."

Mr. Wright took out his spiral notebook and began to take notes. He glanced up at Hettie and then nodded, indicating that she should go ahead. She ran to catch up with Ferris and Violet as the pair continued north on the Antrim Road in the direction of the zoo. Her thigh ached and throbbed, but she knew that she needed to keep up with Ferris and Violet, or Mr. Wright might use this as a reason to fire her. After all, if she couldn't do more than shovel shit, what good was she?

"Hettie," Ferris said with a smile. "I thought I lost you. Where's Mr. Wright?"

"Still talking to the owner of the shop," Hettie said, struggling for breath. "That man is not pleased."

"He should be honored that Violet made an appearance at his store during her very first day in Belfast."

Hettie gave a laugh, and Ferris smiled. Hettie quickly realized that it had been a long time since she'd laughed. The past three months had been dulled by the regular visits from extended family, friends, neighbors, and church members. The days and weeks had blurred into each other, and a silent grief seemed to shape most of Hettie's waking hours. With each condolence visit, Hettie sat quietly with her hands folded in the pleats of her woolen skirt, listening to her mother and the other women as their conversation migrated from recipes for fish pie to how challenging it was to manage with the rationing to Mrs. Fitzsimmons's daughter and how she had recently given birth to twins before circling back to the sudden loss of Anna. How much she had accomplished during her brief life—a brilliant student of modern and classical languages, a talented tennis player and a winner of many local tournaments, and later a wife and a mother. Even a few months after her sister's death, it still felt baffling and tragic to Hettie that Anna wasn't any of these things now; she was merely a memory, an ephemeral apparition that came and went at unexpected moments, both when Hettie was awake and asleep. That morning, Hettie kept expecting to spot Anna in the crowd, calling out her name and releasing a sharp whistle with two fingers pressed against her bottom lip, just how Thomas had taught them when they were children.

"Look, Mama," a young boy said, pointing toward Violet and pulling Hettie out of her reverie.

Mr. Wright appeared at their side, sweat streaking his rosy cheeks.

"I convinced the man not to press charges," explained Mr. Wright, wiping his white linen handkerchief against his forehead. "I'll find a way to cover the damages. I'll bet you that he forgets the whole thing by the end of the day. Once he gets a few pints in him, it will be a good story that he'll be telling his chums at the pub."

"He didn't seem like a laughing sort of fella," Hettie said.

"We don't want Mr. Christie to find out about this," Mr. Wright said, glancing over at Ferris and ignoring Hettie entirely. "He wouldn't like to hear that one of his animals is running wild on the streets of Belfast."

"Yes, sir," Ferris said as he guided Violet up the winding street.

Within thirty minutes, they were more than halfway up the Antrim Road. The broken views of the River Lagan and the docks were visible through the overlapping rooftops of the rows of houses. Around the bend, there was the silhouette of the Cavehill with its familiar hump along its forested ridge, looking like the crooked nose of a sleeping man.

Hettie was relieved when the raised letters of BELLEVUE appeared around a corner, stretched across the face of the low concrete wall. They had finally arrived at the zoo. A dozen employees—young and middle-aged men dressed in dull green coveralls and caps—were assembled there. Still wearing his dapper top hat, white gloves, and yellow scarf, Mr. Christie stood at the foot of the grand staircase, a series of fifty steps that led into the heart of the zoo.

"Welcome, Violet," Mr. Christie said, removing his hat and tipping it in the elephant's direction. The small crowd of onlookers snickered.

"I'll take her through the rear entrance," said Mr. Wright.

"Yes, yes," Mr. Christie said, replacing his hat. "Of course."

Violet released another nasally trumpet call. A large flock of song-birds lifted up from the autumnal treetops, the fast beats of their wings sounding like a collective whisper in the morning breeze.

"I hope you enjoy your new home at Bellevue," Mr. Christie said to Violet as he rubbed her speckled forehead. "We are happy to have you here."

The zoo staff gave a polite round of applause as Mr. Wright guided Violet onto the narrow dirt path that traversed the hillside to the zoo's rear entrance. Ferris and Hettie followed. Mr. Wright unlatched the rear gate and together they walked in the direction of the Elephant House. Bellevue had already been open for a few hours, and a hand-ful of visitors—mostly mothers with young children—lingered on the pavements. A volley of shrieks rose up from the monkey enclosure. A dense cluster of pale pink flamingos stood along the border of the lily pond. Up ahead, Hettie saw Wallace the lion stretching his forelegs out and arching his back. Wallace yawned, his tongue lolling from his mouth like a soft pink ribbon. His majestic head swayed with each step he took across the sandy ground. On the far side of the enclosure, Vic-toria, the lioness, slept along with her two cubs in the shifting shadows.

Farther down the path, Rajan, the elderly bull elephant, and Mag-gie, a ten-year-old elephant, stood like watchful guards near the edge of the giraffe exhibition, where the pair had been moved a few days ago. Rajan swung his long trunk high in the air and released a rolling roar. Two of the giraffes poked up their necks, stiff as pipe cleaners, above the trimmed hedges. Since Hettie had started working at the zoo six months ago, Rajan had always been her favorite: He maintained a formidable presence as the largest mammal of the zoo. A sort of king of Bellevue, with all the other animals bowing to him. Rajan trumpeted another cry and this time Maggie joined in his bellowing refrain. Violet flicked her ears up like a pair of small sails.

"What a darling," said Helen McAlister, one of the women who worked at the ticket kiosk. "She's a beauty."

Eliza Crowley, a young woman about Hettie's age who worked in the canteen, stood next to Helen. Eliza wore a soiled apron and her shirtsleeves were pushed up to her bony elbows. Her auburn hair was tied back with a red paisley bandanna, looking like a wild spray of flames. She had a narrow nose and a pointy chin.

"Where's she going to sleep?" Eliza asked.

"Violet is going to live alone for now," Mr. Wright said, lifting the stick a little higher, "until she gets used to her new life here at Bellevue."

Ferris had already explained to Hettie this temporary arrangement: Violet's home was going to be in the Elephant House, a simple twelve-foot-by-twelve-foot structure, with a fenced-in yard and a three-foot empty moat surrounding its enclosure. Rajan and Maggie would reside with the giraffes until Mr. Wright thought it was prudent to bring the animals together. He said it could take up to a year before this might happen, that one had to be careful about timing, or the elephants might not get along and end up attacking each other.

"Won't she get lonely?" Eliza asked.

"Violet will have lots of visitors," Mr. Wright said. "I assure you, Miss Crowley, she'll never be lonely at Bellevue." He unlatched the gate to the Elephant House. "Here you go, Violet."

Violet lumbered through and Mr. Wright followed her, securing the gate behind him. Ferris and Hettie looked on, completely absorbed in Violet until a sound at Hettie's elbow startled her. Hettie spun round and saw that Eliza was still standing next to her, also gazing at the elephant.

During her time at the zoo, Hettie had exchanged a few mono-syllabic greetings with Eliza—and not much else. She had heard from one of the other zookeepers that Eliza had left school at age fourteen because her family needed her to work to keep her younger sisters and brothers fed. Hettie glanced at Eliza for a second and noticed that dirt smudged her pale forehead. Freckles dotted the thin bridge of her nose. Eliza popped a pear drop into her mouth.

"Bloody hell," Ferris said, his eyes widening. "Where'd you get that?"

"Wouldn't you like to know, Ferris Poole," Eliza said. "Want one?"

"Of course, I want one."

Eliza reached into her pocket and tossed a boiled sweet to Ferris and then another one to Hettie. She couldn't remember the last time she had eaten a pear drop. The fruity flavor burst in her mouth. It tasted like the sun and the ocean at once. With the tip of her tongue, Hettie tucked the sweet into the warm pocket of her cheek.

"Thanks, Eliza," Ferris said.

"My brother—"

"That's all right," Ferris said, winking at Eliza. "I'd rather not know."

Eliza smiled a sly smile. The pale yellow of the boiled sweet stained the tight corners of her mouth.

"Back to work, everyone," Mr. Wright said. "We have a zoo to run here."

"See you, girls," Ferris said, tipping his cap. "Thanks again, Eliza."

"He's a handsome fella, don't you think," Eliza said to Hettie as they watched him walk away.

It was the first time Eliza had ever spoken directly to her.

"He's all right, I guess," Hettie said, sucking on the pear drop.

"He likes you, you know."

Hettie defiantly crossed her arms over her chest.

"Why do you think Mr. Wright hired you," Eliza said sharply. "Ferris wouldn't quit asking him. He wouldn't give up."

Despite the delightful taste of the sweet, Hettie wanted to spit it out onto the dusty ground before Eliza's feet. She felt flattered by the notion of Ferris's potential affections, but wanted to believe that Mr. Wright had hired her based on her own merits and promise. Despite not having a significant amount of experience with large animals, she had groomed and fed her uncle's farm animals—the goats, pigs, chickens, and horses. Ever since she could remember, Hettie had preferred animals to people. They were always happy to see her, grateful to be fed and given some attention, whenever Hettie made her weekly visits. The life at her uncle's farm provided a reprieve from her own household, which had revolved around her sister, all her success and brightness. Violet whinnied and lifted her trunk into the air.

"You're the lucky one, you know, being the only female zookeeper," Eliza continued. "I'm stuck washing dishes in the canteen. At least I can still say that I work at the zoo. Men like that, don't you think?"

"It's not something I've considered," Hettie said loftily, even though she had, on more than one occasion since being hired part-time by Mr. Wright. Her fictional conversations with young men always went better when she mentioned her responsibilities for and care of her animal charges. The young man would pepper her with questions and compliments, marveling at how unusual it was for a woman to be a zookeeper, how most girls worked in offices as secretaries or typists, longing to get married, or didn't work at all. In her mind, her future boyfriend frequently visited her at the zoo, told his friends about her, and around Belfast, she would become known as the zookeeper at Bellevue rather than merely Anna Quin's younger sister.

"If I were you, I'd go on a date with dear Ferris," Eliza said. "If you let him touch your private place, I bet he could get you the job of taking care of that elephant."

Hettie spluttered and coughed. Gray spots flickered along the margins of her vision. The ground tipped slightly and then snapped back.

"I'm just telling you how it is," Eliza said. "You need to apply your ambition in the right way. That's the only way you're going to get ahead."

Hettie took the pear drop out of her mouth, holding it between her finger and thumb. Suddenly it no longer tasted sweet.

"I'll take that if you don't want it."

Wordlessly, Hettie handed the sweet to Eliza.

"Thank you very much," Eliza said, popping it into her own mouth.

As Eliza walked away, Hettie clenched her damp fists. What did Eliza know about Ferris? And what did she know about Mr. Wright? Hettie noticed that her shoulders were scrunched up and tried to release them. The pain in her thigh pulsed again. Violet paced across the yard.

"Is there something I can help you with, Miss Quin?" Mr. Wright asked, offering a fistful of hay to Violet.

"No, sir."

"Well, then, attend to your morning assignments, please."

"Yes, sir. I'm going, sir."

Hettie headed toward the aviary where she would fill the assorted feeders with seed and refresh the water troughs for the finches, thrushes, parrots, and macaws. Before she turned onto the pathway, she glanced back at Violet one more time: The elephant was now lying down, her gray legs folded underneath the furrows of her body. Mr. Wright carried a bucket of water in one hand and a leafy bundle of celery in the other. Violet lifted her head as Mr. Wright walked toward her. He broke off a stalk of celery and the elephant raised her trunk, gingerly curling it around the pale green stick. Mr. Wright looked up again.

"Miss Quin," he said. "Have you suddenly become deaf? Return to your work."

Two

That evening, as she often did, Hettie decided to take the long way home—through the Throne Wood to the Crazy Path down to the Antrim Road. If she took the grand staircase to the zoo's front entrance, it was only a ten-minute walk to her mother's house on the Whitewell Road, but Hettie preferred this way, even if it took a half hour longer.

The twilight threw shifting, thin shadows on the pathways of the zoo. Helen McAlister closed up the ticket kiosk, shuttering its accordion face and securing its padlock.

"'Night, Hettie Quin," Helen said, nodding. "Be good."

"'Night."

Alice and Henry, the pair of black bears, wandered across their enclosure. Henry found his way into a puddle and settled his rear in the muddy water. Hettie smiled to herself. Even though the bears were only five and six years old, she thought of Alice and Henry as an elderly couple, like her grandparents on her mother's side, who often bickered but loved each other fiercely. More than once, she had witnessed the bears grunting at each other and batting each other's shiny snouts before they moved into a routine of sniffing and licking each other. Ferris had mentioned how Mr. Wright was hoping that Henry would impregnate Alice soon, and that she would give birth to at least two cubs by summer, and how this event would generate attention in the city, and the public would want to come and see the babies. Hettie couldn't wait.

Off to the right, several of the black-footed penguins warbled as they scampered across the pavement before plunging, one at a time, into their blue-green pool. There were six penguins altogether: Oscar, Clementine, Franklin, Gerald, Marie, and Joy. Hettie was always enchanted and impressed by the penguins' readiness to fling their bodies effortlessly into the pool of water, like fearless children hurling themselves off a high dive. Around the corner, Sammy the sea lion sat on one of the highest boulders, his large eyes dark, lustrous moons.

"'Night, Sammy," Hettie said. "Cheers."

He yapped and growled, baring his jaundice-stained teeth. Up ahead, the shadowy silhouette of the Cavehill emerged over the Floral Hall, the popular dance venue that was also a part of Mr. Christie's Bellevue Zoo & Gardens. During the evenings, the lampposts that bordered the walkways were no longer illuminated due to the citywide regulations that had begun over a year ago because of the war. As she made her way down the path, Hettie passed one of the public clocks standing erect on a patina-green column. The wrought-iron hands read six o'clock. She knew that her mother was likely waiting for her.

Hettie passed through the rear gate and headed toward the Throne Wood and the Crazy Path. Beyond the Cavehill, a strip of pinkish light settled across the western horizon. Hettie followed the looping curves of the path, the graveled dirt giving beneath her worn boots. Stands of beech, sycamore, and pine blanketed the countryside. A gray rabbit hopped through the open meadow before disappearing behind a copse of Scots pines. Above, in the diminishing light, a kestrel cut wide, smooth circles.

On the Crazy Path, Hettie felt transported to another place and time—where it was just Hettie, the wild birds and raptors, the old trees, and the distant calls of the zoo animals. They were calling for her, she felt certain. That an abiding appreciation existed between Hettie and many of the animals, that she was just as important to the animals as they were to her. In the meadow, the bending tips of grasses whistled, and the birds scattered in the open sky. Eventually the winding path met the boundary of her uncle Edgar's farm, where Hettie had spent so much time during her youth. He was her mother's only brother and oversaw the family's twenty-five-acre property. Uncle Edgar was the one who introduced Hettie's mother, Rose, to Thomas when she was eighteen, at Thomas's birthday celebration at the Duke of York Pub. At the time, Rose was working as a nurse in the tuberculosis ward at the Royal Belfast Hospital for Sick Children, but she left her job soon after their wedding and becoming pregnant with Anna, in the same way that Anna left her secretarial position at the solicitors' office, across the street from the city hall, when she became pregnant with Maeve. The men had been on the same club football team, with Thomas playing wing and Uncle Edgar in the goal. This was when Thomas had worked with Harland & Wolff, before he enlisted with the Merchant Navy and left Belfast for months at time. Nowadays, Uncle Edgar stopped by the house to deliver checks to Rose for her modest share of the revenue generated from the farm as well as eggs, milk, and potatoes.

Hettie approached the top of the Antrim Road, where strangers collected at the tram stop. She crossed over to the Whitewell Road and then passed her aunt's grocery store. Aunt Sylvia, a second cousin on her mother's side, lived in an unassuming home directly behind the shop. Four years ago, her husband had left her and their fourteen-year-old son, Charlie. There was no note, no telegram, no nothing. Later, a rumor circulated that Uncle Robert had taken passage on a transatlantic ship bound for New York City, found a job as a locksmith on the Lower East Side, and started a new family who didn't know anything about Aunt Sylvia, the corner store, or Charlie.

Hettie continued down the incline of the Whitewell Road. Red-brick, two-story homes, with slate-gray roofs, bordered the street. Her house, with a hunter-green-painted door and a brass door knocker, sat on the left side. A small apron of brown grass fronted the row house, and evergreen hedges huddled below the kitchen and sitting room windows. This was the house where Hettie, now twenty years old, had lived her entire life. For a majority of this time, the four of them—Thomas, Rose, Anna, and Hettie—had lived together in this house. Now, within the mere space of a year, the size of her family had dwindled to two.

During recent years, Thomas had come and gone to the UK and Europe at least a half dozen times due to his rotating assignments with the Merchant Navy. Inevitably, he always returned home—whether it was a month or six months later—and Rose would accept him with little argument or resistance. This time, things were different. Two weeks ago, Hettie had overheard Rose saying to one of her church friends, Edith Curry, that Thomas had up and left with a young woman who had worked as a stenographer in the dockyards. *A tart with no God in her soul*, Edith had said. *Imagine living such a sinful life!* Hettie understood the velocity at which this sort of gossip would have traveled through their neighborhood and the Upper Antrim Road, and imagined that by now most people knew about Thomas and the reasons for his protracted absence. She hated her father for his infidelities, but at the same time she missed his kindness and companionship and longed for his return home.

As she walked along, Hettie watched several neighborhood boys playing a game of rounders. Makeshift bases were arranged in the street, forming a lopsided circle. Johnny Gibson pitched a hard ball to Albert O'Brien. At least a half dozen boys manned the bases and anxiously looked on as Albert swung and missed the ball and started to run. Hettie recognized all the boys as she remembered when each one had been brought home from the hospital, and then later their christenings and confirmations. Only a few young people around Hettie's age still lived in the neighborhood. Across the street, Eleanor Harte took care of her bed-bound grandmother, and Oliver Finney still lived with his parents, like Hettie, and worked as a message boy for a local engineering firm. Everyone else had moved on.

The boys' eager cheers and laughter brightened the evening. Albert was tagged out at first base. Hettie felt the impulse to drop her leather satchel, join the game, and demonstrate for the boys how to give a ball a proper whack. She glanced over to the window of the kitchen. There her mother stood, peering out the window, and Hettie sighed.

"Johnny, send another one over, will you," yelled Albert. "I'm gonna knock this one all the way to Scotland. You'll see."

Johnny pushed his black-framed glasses up and then stared down at the pavement, as if a good pitch might materialize out of the ground. Eventually he looked up and pitched again. This time Albert managed to make solid contact with the ball and it arced down the middle of the street. He started to run as the other boys scrambled after the soaring ball.

As Hettie stepped inside the house, she heard the clang of metal against metal, and then her mother's reedy sigh.

"Where on earth have you been?" Rose asked from the kitchen. "Your supper's cold."

"Sorry, Mum. Mr. Wright asked me to stay late," Hettie lied.

The smell of vegetable stew drifted from the warm stovetop. Like she often did, Hettie had to resist the urge to slip back into the evening air, away from the suffocating sadness of her mother. Rose clicked on the wireless that sat in the far corner of the kitchen. The rotating hum of airplane propellers filled the room, followed by a commentator reporting the news.

Rose was still wearing her robe and nightdress, just as Hettie had left her that morning. She wondered if her mother had changed and gone outside, then changed back, or if it had been another day of shuffling from bedroom to kitchen to bedroom to kitchen and back again. The staccato voice on the wireless reported on the Battle of Britain and the Luftwaffe's relentless attacks on British convoys, ports, and aircraft factories. Rose wiped her hands on a dish towel and returned the dried dishes to their cupboards.

Things hadn't always been this way: Rose used to carry a measure of levity within her, a kind of expectancy. Despite the rationing, Hettie's mother had put considerable effort into making delicious stews and soups, and the four of them would eat in the dining room, often with the candles lit, bowing their heads together and saying a prayer of gratitude before their conversation turned to the day's events. There was never a shortage of topics. Rose used to become animated when asking questions about their studies and later about Anna's responsibilities at the solicitors' office, about their respective friends from school and church, and about her sister's recent wins and losses on the tennis court. But now the house was largely silent.

"You can go to bed, Mum," Hettie finally said. "I'll clean up."

"All right," Rose said, wiping off her hands one more time. "'Night."

Hettie folded her scarf and placed it on the top shelf of the hallway closet. When she returned to the kitchen, Rose had already disappeared behind her bedroom door. Hettie turned off the wireless. The overhead light shone down on a porcelain bowl of pea-green stew with knobs of carrots and potatoes floating on its watery surface. She could hear the voices of the neighborhood boys in the street. Hettie felt an ache in her chest, a longing to be another daughter to another mother, to be a part of another kind of family altogether, one that wasn't indelibly shaped by grief, betrayal, and abandonment. Hettie had assumed these yearnings would subside over time, but instead, with each week, the absences of her sister and father only grew more tender and sharp.

She heard a crash outside. The ball had shattered a window somewhere. There was silence, and then Mr. Brown's voice rang out in the night. "I know it was one of you naughty boys. I'm going to get you!"

The following morning, Hettie touched her toes to the cold wooden floor of her bedroom. A shiver passed up the length of her calf and deep into the crook of her knee. Her thigh still ached where Violet had kicked her the day before. Hettie lifted the edge of her nightdress and inspected the contusion in the dim light: A faint reef of lavender and yellow stained her skin. It wasn't a pleasant sight, but at least it showed that yesterday hadn't been a figment of her imagination.

In the hallway, Hettie heard the soft padding of slippered feet. There was the click of a light switch and the hiss of the stove being lit. Hettie dressed in her gray wool skirt, white blouse, and beige cardigan, and then grabbed her father's old watch from the top of her dresser and encircled the worn leather band around her wrist.

The kettle whistled. There was the sizzle and snap of bacon in a frying pan. Hettie glanced at the cracked face of her father's wristwatch: It was half past seven. She knew that her mother would expect her to eat breakfast at home, particularly since Rose served bacon only twice a month now, but Hettie was determined to speak with Mr. Wright about Violet this morning and his rounds started promptly at eight o'clock.

Hettie retrieved her navy peacoat and tartan scarf from the hallway closet. She noticed, like she did every morning, two of Anna's old tennis rackets, with the wooden trapezoid frames screwed tightly against their stringed heads, gathering dust in the darkened corner. In the kitchen, Rose stood at the counter, in her robe and slippers, the bony knuckles of her spine visible through the worn fabric of her robe.

"Morning," Hettie said.

"You're up early." Rose didn't turn around from the stove. The bacon popped.

"I have an appointment with Mr. Wright this morning."

"Surely you can eat something before you leave?"

Rose placed a plate of toast with two strips of bacon on the table.

Hettie took a fast swallow of hot tea, grimacing as she burned her tongue. She folded a piece of bacon into her mouth and wiped her fingers on a cotton napkin.

"Here." Rose wrapped two more pieces of bacon in a napkin, slipped it inside Hettie's satchel, and handed her a roll. "We can't let the bacon go to waste."

"Thanks," Hettie said. "Thanks, Mum."

Rose turned her back to Hettie and then ran the kitchen faucet. "There's another opening at the Wichell Legal offices on Linenhall Street. I heard about it from Mrs. Moffit yesterday," Rose said. "Mrs. Lyttle's daughter works there. She says it pays well, better than the zoo, and the other girls are nice and respectable. You know, with your father gone, it would be helpful if you could contribute a bit more to the household."

The kitchen felt small. There was suddenly less air. Despite everything, Hettie missed her father again. If he were still around, he would have been supportive of her new position despite the low salary and meager hours. He would have been optimistic that she would soon be employed full-time and that a higher wage would come with this advancement. Thomas had always encouraged Hettie to pursue sciences and math, and didn't mind when she brought home abandoned animals—cats and dogs and the occasional ferret—while her mother forbade it. Her father had often served as the referee, striking a compromise that the animal could stay in their courtyard, enclosed by its tall walls, until Hettie could find the animal a better home.

"I'm going to be late. Bye, Mum."

Hettie closed the front door behind her. The freshness of the morning air lifted her spirits. The tension in her shoulders loosened. When Hettie reached their street, Rose waved from the front window. Hettie waved back, noticing a trail of suds slipping down the length of her mother's pale, freckled forearm and disappearing into the sleeve of her robe. Hettie glanced at her father's wristwatch again. It was a quarter to eight; there was no time for the scenic route along the Crazy Path this morning. Instead, she hurried up the rise of the Whitewell Road, across the Hazelwood Road, and then across the Antrim Road, entered the zoo's front entrance, and made her way up the grand staircase, skipping the steps two at a time.

When she arrived at the front gate, Hettie nodded to Mr. Clarke, who stood in his usual spot in the security booth at the top of the stairs. Even after six months of part-time employment, Hettie had to show her identification every day when she arrived at the zoo. Mr. Clarke took her identity card and inspected her name and photograph, glancing between the black-and-white image and Hettie more than once. His breath smelled of stale smoke and ale, and his bulbous nose was cross-hatched with tiny branches of broken capillaries. The rumor around the zoo was that Mr. Clarke—a man in his late thirties but who could have passed for decades older—was rarely sober and the only reason he was kept on as an inept security guard was due to the fact that he was a distant cousin of Mr. Christie's. Hettie's face hardened as the seconds ticked by.

"Mr. Clarke, you know who I am."

He returned her identity card. Hettie tucked the card into the interior pocket of her worn satchel.

"Did you hear the news?" asked Mr. Clarke.

"The Germans?" she asked, her heart quickening.

Recently, Hettie and Rose had been listening to J. B. Priestley's weekly broadcast, *Postscripts*, on the wireless. Priestley had mentioned predictions of the remote chance of the Germans bombing Northern Ireland, and then moved into the common debate of whether or not the Unionist government needed to be taking more measures to protect the citizens of Belfast. While she and Rose listened to the broadcast, Hettie had wondered if the Luftwaffe would bomb Belfast before the war was over. There were many arguments for why this attack would never happen: that the city was too remote from Germany, that Hitler had never heard of it, that German bombers would have to cross the antiaircraft guns twice to reach Belfast and this seemed unlikely, and finally maybe Hitler would respect Éire's neutrality and not bomb Northern Ireland either.

Despite all this reasonable rationale, Hettie couldn't stop herself from imagining what an aerial invasion of her city might look like: an infinite series of deafening explosions and spontaneous fires blooming along the nocturnal horizon. In her mind, Hettie never made it to the aftermath of the destruction, to the casualties and injuries enumerated daily in the wartime reports on the wireless. The lost limbs, the lost lives. The roofs of shelters that buckled and collapsed onto innocent citizens. Children, mothers, fathers, brothers, sisters. In Hettie's version, there were no tears or blood on the streets. Instead, the explosions always remained suspended in the air. The attack was always something that illuminated the night sky of Belfast, but never destroyed the sleeping city below.

"No, not the ruddy Germans," Mr. Clarke scoffed. "All this guff about Hitler. Everybody knows he's never heard of this place."

"What happened, then?" Hettie said, doing her best to tamp down her growing irritation with this man.

"George is making more purchases," he said. Mr. Clarke was the only employee at the zoo who referred to Mr. Christie by his first name, and it grated on Hettie every time. "A pair of panthers from a zoo in Turkey and then a small herd of camels from Africa."

"That's grand," she responded, quickly recognizing that these additional animals might require the necessity of another full-time zookeeper on staff.

Mr. Clarke glanced over Hettie's head. A queue of other employees had formed behind her, each carrying a lunch box and thermos, their breath curling into the morning air.

"At this rate, everyone's going to be late," said Mr. Clarke.

"Good day," she said.

Hettie walked at a clip past the enclosure of the two polar bears. Felix and Misty had arrived at the zoo at the same time Hettie had. Mr. Christie had acquired the pair from a circus trader in Florence, Italy, who had captured the animals in their native habitat of the Arctic Circle. Felix was standing up on his hind legs while Misty waded in the pool, her white head, statuesque snout, and pointed ears perforating the indigo water. On Hettie's right, black-masked lemurs leaped from limb to limb, their long tails swinging behind them. One lemur carried a baby in her arms, its fists clinging to her white-furred chest. The other lemurs yipped and cackled as if they were lobbing insults at each other. Harold Gilbert, one of the zookeepers, fed the Chinese water deer, with their prominent tusks on either side of their soft mouths. As Hettie took in the presence of the animals and walked through the familiar surroundings, she felt the assurance and confidence that the zoo often gave her.

When she arrived at Mr. Wright's office, she knocked on the door. As she waited, Hettie straightened her coat and lifted her chin. There was no answer. She pressed her ear against the door and heard classical music playing on the other side. Then came the steady punches of a typewriter, one forceful stroke after another. Hettie rapped her fist against the door again, harder this time. The music ceased.

"Come in."

As Hettie opened the door, Mr. Wright stood up behind his desk and lifted the needle from the shellac record on the gramophone. He wore a short-sleeved undershirt instead of his signature red coat. Tufts of black hair sprouted from the ribbed, rounded collar. It was almost as if he were wearing no shirt at all because Hettie had only ever seen him clad in his ubiquitous uniform. Hettie felt a heat travel into her cheeks. Mr. Wright reached for his coat from a hook and slipped into its sleeves.

"What do *you* want?"

"I have a request," Hettie said, feeling each word in her throat.

"Make it quick," Mr. Wright said. "Chop-chop, Miss Quin."

He buttoned his coat, straightened out the shoulders, and picked up his leather crop. Above a short bookshelf, Hettie noticed a wall calendar: The photograph for the month of October was a cheetah racing at full speed, its paws lifting off the grassy tundra, its spotted body lean, nimble, and fierce all at once.

"It's about Violet."

"My time is in short supply, Miss Quin—"

"I would like to be made a full-time zookeeper," she said, her voice shaking slightly. "I can care for Violet in addition to my other duties."

Without looking at her, Mr. Wright grabbed his fedora from the cluttered desktop.

"May I ask, Miss Quin, what about your performance yesterday demonstrated your ability to care for an elephant?"

Hettie stood taller, with her hands tucked into her coat pockets, as she attempted to locate the height of her spine, the length of her legs that she had just felt a few minutes ago, walking along the pavements of the zoo, but that natural confidence and ease had diminished as swiftly as it had materialized. Instead, during that split second, standing in Mr. Wright's office, Hettie felt small and sad, just like her mother. At moments like this, Hettie was convinced that Rose's sorrow was mysteriously slipping into her, and there was no way to avoid becoming her mother. That as she approached middle age, Hettie would be alone and full of melancholy and grief, too—and there was little she could do to sidestep this kind of unhappy existence. She returned her attention to Mr. Wright and the request that she was making.

"I managed to lead her for a wee bit—"

"Ha!" Mr. Wright said. "It was more like Violet was leading you."

She felt a twitchy spasm above one of her eyes—as if an insect were trapped there.

"I'm not sure if you comprehend the situation," he continued. "Elephants are dangerous animals. Violet might look innocent, but one wrong move and she could crush you to death. Don't forget: She weighs over three thousand pounds. It just happened recently. An elephant charged her trainer during a feeding at the Chester Zoo in Cheshire. The man was dead before he arrived at the hospital."

Sudden. Like Anna. One second, she was prematurely giving birth to a baby girl; the next second, Anna was bleeding and dead. The news arrived the following morning when a doctor from the Royal called Rose at their home. Hettie recollected her mother pressing the black receiver against her ear, her complexion draining of its color, and then dropping the phone onto the kitchen floor as the doctor's tinny, miniature voice continued to travel through the receiver's earpiece. Again, Hettie tried to drive these thoughts away.

"Mr. Clarke mentioned that Mr. Christie is purchasing more animals."

"Yes, this is, in fact, true," Mr. Wright said. "Mr. Christie is making a few more acquisitions."

"So won't you—"

"Excuse me, Miss Quin," he interrupted. "I'm needed elsewhere."

Like that, Mr. Wright was out the door, leaving it open behind him. Hettie stood silently in front of his desk. A few papers and receipts drifted to the floor. She picked them up and studied the pages. Invoices for feed, hay, and fish. There was a telegram from an animal dealer in Greece, confirming Mr. Christie's recent purchase of the panthers. She sighed.

As Hettie returned the papers onto Mr. Wright's desk, she noticed an unfinished letter in the platen of his Remington typewriter. It was addressed to the head zookeeper at the Bristol Zoo Gardens in England. Mr. Wright was corresponding to inquire if his peer knew of any well-respected zookeepers who might be interested in transferring up to Belfast. He went on to say that he realized there were shortages of upstanding young men, given the continuing demands of conscription and the munitions factories, but wanted to ask on the off chance that the zoo director might have any worthy referrals.

Hettie slammed the door to Mr. Wright's office. The lock on the handle clicked into place. She wondered if Mr. Wright had a key with him, but decided that he must, given the oversize brass ring of keys that was always attached to the belt loop of his trousers. Mr. Wright didn't seem like the type of person who would get locked out of anything; instead, he was a man of command and control who was always several steps ahead of everyone else. And right now, she didn't really care if he was locked out of his office. Hettie kicked the bottom edge of the door.

"Damn it," she said to herself. "Goddamn it!"

In the distance, a howl traveled from the wolves' den. She still had the day of chores in front of her. She wasn't going to quit impulsively, as her father might have done. Instead, she would figure out a way to ask again, press for another chance. Up ahead, on the pathway in front of Mr. Wright's office, Jack Fleming, another zookeeper, pushed a wheel-barrow filled with mounds of manure.

"Morning, Hettie."

"Morning."

One of the lions roared, the sound echoing against the treetops. Jack and Hettie exchanged glances.

"Wallace isn't feeling so chipper this morning," Jack said.

The lion unleashed another roar. Together, Jack and Hettie walked down the pathway that led to the lions' enclosure, where several other zoo employees were congregated. Mr. Wright stood in the middle of the enclosure. Wallace reared into one of the far corners. A confetti of hay and dirt flew out as the cat shook his flaxen mane. Wallace's ears were folded back. Hettie noticed a trickle of blood dripping from one of his front paws. Mr. Wright took several steps closer. Wallace swiped his good paw at Mr. Wright. Victoria and her cubs cowered in the opposite corner of the enclosure.

"I know you're not feeling well, Wallace," Mr. Wright said calmly.

He took several steps closer until he dropped his crop onto the ground and cradled the lion's injured paw in his hands. He inspected the dark pads before removing what looked like a scrap of rusty metal. More blood leaked from Wallace's paw, and the lion growled ominously. Mr. Wright held a tattered rag against the injury, exerting a steady pressure for several minutes, as the group of zoo employees stood silently and took in the natural ease and expertise of Mr. Wright's medical attention. It was as if he were treating a harmless dog rather than a dangerous lion. Wallace roared again and nudged his head into Mr. Wright's forearm.

"There, there, my boy," Mr. Wright said, removing the compress.

Wallace licked his paw again and again. The other female and cubs emerged from the cave at the rear of the enclosure. Mr. Wright set down an aluminum bowl of pork trimmings donated by a local butcher, and Wallace and the other cats began to feed.

"Mr. Wright may not be so nice, but he certainly knows his animals," Jack said.

"He's not very nice, is he?" Hettie said, scowling.

"He has his moments of kindness," Jack said, adjusting his tweed cap before returning his grip to the wooden handles of the wheelbarrow. "Anyway, back to work."

Hettie made her way to the women's locker room, next to the staff canteen. The locker room was a tiny, windowless space with six metal lockers painted a muted shade of green, one toilet stall, and a sink with a mirror attached to the cinder-block wall. Hettie changed into her work suit and socks, and slipped on her worn boots. She shut the metal locker door and placed her navy blue knit cap on, tucking the staticky strands of her brunette hair underneath its itchy rim, and stepped outside. Already, the day was beginning to warm up, the sun creating spots of heat along the sinuous pathway. Before heading to the flamingos, she walked to the Elephant House, where she found Violet standing near the edge of the moat.

"Morning, Violet," Hettie said, once again feeling the disappointment of Mr. Wright's response as she took in the animal.

The elephant stood with her tail stiff, her ears pleated against her head. Suddenly Violet turned and trumpeted, and then kicked hard against the iron bars of the fence, sending a loud clang into the air. Hettie gasped and took a step back. She thought about what Mr. Wright had said about how an elephant could easily crush her. She imagined a human skull cracked open, like a watermelon, and the hairs on her arms pricked up. She finally understood how lucky she had been yesterday, to get away with only a bruise.

It was hard to imagine an elephant being so violent. She recalled the first time she had seen one at the circus with her father and sister more than ten years ago. She remembered the audience cheering on a chaotic parade of clowns underneath the swiveling spotlight. The warm air had held the smells of sawdust, sweet honeysuckle, and popcorn. The notes of a wheezing organ filled the enormous tent. Below, in the illuminated ring, an elephant emerged from the wings. Right away, Hettie was entranced by the elephant's dignified and elegant presence amid the frenzy of circus performers. The animal seemed to emit an otherworldly peace. A mystery and a knowingness. Her large-lidded eyes slowly blinked as she stared out at the crowd. A rhinestone tiara had somehow been propped up on her forehead. The ringmaster cracked his long bullwhip, and the elephant shifted her weight from side to side. The man cracked his whip again.

And then, it had happened: The elephant had stepped, one foot at a time, onto a sizable blue ball. The ringmaster lashed his whip again— and the majestic creature stood perfectly still, balancing on the curved surface. Then he slipped a harmonica out of his pocket and raised the instrument up to the elephant's trunk. The rowdy din of the audience grew silent as the animal wrapped the end of her trunk around the harmonica and proceeded to blow, producing a series of uneven whistling notes. The crowd erupted into wild applause. Hettie's father had squeezed her hand, the edge of his wedding ring pressing into her finger, and gave her a wink as he cheered the elephant with the rest of the crowd.

With her head lowered, Violet charged toward the edge of the moat, and Hettie quickly realized that the gentle giant at the circus and the elephant standing in front of her were not one and the same. But even as Hettie took a few steps away from the clearly agitated animal, she knew that she was enchanted by Violet just as much as she was frightened by her.

"Miss Quin," Mr. Wright said. Startled, Hettie spun around. "Aren't you supposed to be with the flamingos?"

"Yes, Mr. Wright—"

"Go on now," he said, uncoiling a rubber hose that lay next to the Elephant House. "No time to waste." Mr. Wright turned on the spigot and sprayed a fan of water along Violet's rounded back. "The Monkey House requires a good cleaning this morning, too."

"Yes, sir," Hettie mumbled.

"And after your break, the Reptile House," he said. "Change the water."

"Yes, sir."

In the distance, Rajan bellowed his familiar call. When Hettie arrived at the flamingos' enclosure, most of the birds were asleep, their black-tipped beaks disappearing into their plump, feathered bodies. The smell of rotten cabbage and manure wafted through the air. She reached for the shovel and bucket that were stored in the far corner of the enclosure, drew it back, and got to work.

As she began to scrape up the birds' excrement, Hettie heard Anna's voice in her mind. *You need to get better at asking for what you want. Nobody's going to do it for you.* She was right. Hettie would ask again. Once the panthers and camels arrived at Bellevue, Mr. Wright would realize he needed Hettie, that she deserved to be treated equally, just like the male employees. She would become full-time, earn a higher wage, and her mother could no longer press her about applying for positions in a typing pool at one office or another. Eventually, she would manage to save enough to find a room in a boardinghouse downtown and move out of her mother's home on the Whitewell Road altogether.

Her disappointment eased and Hettie focused her attention on her chores: the repetitive swings of the shovel, the somnolent birds, the occasional roar of one of the larger cats, the low croaks of the toucanets, and the raucous calls of the macaws with their sweeping feathered tails. At least the animals were reliable and consistent, Hettie thought. Every morning she worked at the zoo, Hettie knew the animals would be there, waiting for her to take care of their basic needs. This predictability gave her days a satisfying order and purpose. Hettie had always known that she was someone who preferred habit to spontaneity. Routine—whether it was school, chores, and later her part-time work at the zoo—provided a comforting rudder to her daily life.

During their midmorning break, Hettie and Ferris met at the canteen, as they usually did on the days when Hettie worked at the zoo. After fetching cups of tea, they sat at one of the worn wooden tables. Handfuls of other employees gathered at other tables, their murmurs producing a steady strum. The odors of boiled potatoes and chopped onions suffused the musty air. An electric heater, with its metal coils glowing amber, stood on the linoleum floor underneath the bank of windows. Ferris sat hunched over his cup of tea. A thick lock of hair curled against his forehead like an upside-down question mark. Hettie looked up and caught sight of Eliza Crowley in the kitchen area on the other side of the large window. She was filling a metal bucket with water. Eliza smiled and winked at Hettie.

"What?" Ferris asked, looking over her shoulder.

Eliza waved at both of them.

"She's a character, don't you think," Ferris said.

"Are you friends with her?"

"Everyone knows Eliza Crowley," he said. "She's a free spirit."

"What's that supposed to mean?"

"Nothing, really."

Eliza retrieved a mop from the supply closet and began to swab the canteen's floor.

"I spoke to Mr. Wright this morning about taking care of Violet," Hettie said, blowing on the surface of her tea.

"And?"

"He said no."

"Ah, Hettie," Ferris said, grimacing. "I'm sorry."

Hettie smiled sadly. "He doesn't like me."

"He's that way with everyone," Ferris said, looking up at Hettie, the creases deepening across his broad forehead.

"If I didn't know you, I wouldn't be here in the first place," Hettie said.

"That's not true."

Hettie made eye contact with Eliza Crowley again. This time Eliza blew an exaggerated kiss in their direction. Hettie turned away, feeling a blush creeping up her neck.

"You gotta believe in yourself a wee bit more," Ferris said. He tapped two fingers against the top of her hand. It felt like a knock at a door, and an imprint of his warm touch settled onto her skin. "Mr. Wright will come around," he said. "Don't worry yourself too much."

Ferris returned his hand to his teacup, and Hettie felt strangely bereft. Hettie considered Eliza's words again. Ever since Hettie and Ferris had known each other, they had always been friends. But if she were being honest, she often felt something more when she was in his company. A soft flare of attraction. A buoyancy of self-confidence because she knew he believed in her. They shared a passion for the animal world, and he respected her intellectual curiosity. They had met three years earlier during a class for high-achieving science students that was held at a local technical school. Hettie was the only girl in the unit. From their fellow students, Hettie had heard that though Ferris had been born and bred in the city, he was mad about animals, and that he lived in a cluttered, smelly flat with his own personal zoo of sorts— two dogs, four cats, two rabbits, even a rat (when he managed to catch one)—and no one else. His parents had died in an automobile accident along the coastline between Portstewart and Portrush five years ago. It had been raining and the wheels of the automobile skidded, sending the couple and the vehicle crashing over a cliff into the churning waters of the North Channel. When Hettie had found that out only a few weeks after meeting Ferris, it had made her even more determined to be his friend.

They were assigned as lab partners. During one of the dissections, Hettie remembered tying a baby pig's translucent legs with twine onto the four corners of a shallow metal tray, its bottom covered in waxed paper, and feeling an energizing, unnerving mix of delight and dread. She felt a degree of pity that the pig didn't have a chance to experience much life (their instructor Mr. Spence had explained that these pigs hadn't even made it out of their mothers' wombs alive), but at the same time, she was eager to slice the poor thing open and scrutinize its slippery insides. Ferris had tested the sharpness of the scalpel's blade against the paper of a notebook with intense concentration. Hettie could tell that he was equally thrilled at the prospect of cutting the pale beast open and getting a closer look at its organs. Since then, the two had remained firm friends.

"What do you have this afternoon?" Ferris asked.

"Mr. Wright asked me to clean the Reptile House."

"Ah, the snakes and the lizards."

Hettie frowned slightly. "Not my favorite task."

Ferris glanced down at his wristwatch. "Oscar and the rest of the penguins are waiting for me," he said. "You know how impatient those penguins can be." He took his last swallow of tea before getting up from the table. "Afterward Mr. Wright is sending me in with the hyenas," he said with a grin.

"Good luck," said Hettie, trying not to let envy edge into her voice.

Ferris pushed through the canteen's double doors, and Hettie looked up at the clock on the wall. She still had ten minutes until she was expected at the Reptile House. She took another sip of her lukewarm tea and found herself thinking about Violet again—the gentle, pendulum-like swing of her torso, the rhythmic march of her footsteps, the agile movements of her serpentine trunk. From a textbook she had read during her studies, Hettie recalled how elephants mourned a lost member of their herd, nudging the lifeless corpse with their feet, smelling it with their trunks. Their grief was everywhere. Drooping ears. Listless tails. Heads bowed to the ground as if they were caught in a trance of religious devotion. Later, the elephants returned to the sites where they had lost their loved ones. An internal compass always guided them back to where they needed to be. Hettie felt a kindred spirit with this particular trait of the elephants—that she carried a similar internal mechanism, that she would always return to where her sister had once been.

Hettie took a last sip of tea and ferried their empty cups to the pass-through that connected the dining room to the dishwashing area. There, Mrs. Carson and Mrs. Flynn stood in front of two-basin sinks, their sagging elbows resting on the rounded edges. Hairnets caught stray strands of their hair, the black crisscross of mesh pressing against their foreheads. A crucifix hung around Mrs. Flynn's neck, its gold producing a glint of light. Hettie recalled how both women had attended Anna's funeral, how the fact that her sister's service was held at a Protestant church hadn't mattered to them. After the funeral, they had waited outside for Hettie. Mrs. Flynn had touched her forearm, and when Hettie looked up, she was startled to meet her glassy, red-rimmed eyes. Now Hettie regarded these women with affection.

"Allo, Hettie," Mrs. Flynn said, looking up and noticing Hettie. "Staying out of trouble this morning?"

"Yes, ma'am," she said with a smile.

"That's what we like to hear," Mrs. Carson added.

"Don't let those boys boss you around," Mrs. Flynn said with a wink. "Remember, you're the one in charge."

"Yes, ma'am," Hettie said again, grinning now.

Taking a few steps toward the door, Hettie heard a raspy cough

44   S. Kirk Walsh

behind her. She turned around to see Eliza Crowley sliding a damp mop across the already wet floor.

"I'm happy to see you're taking my advice," Eliza said.

Hettie blushed. "It's not what you think," she said, glancing up at the clock on the wall. She had five minutes left of her break.

"You shouldn't be a tease," Eliza said sternly. "Boys don't like that—"

Hettie shushed Eliza and glanced over her shoulder, worried that Mrs. Flynn and Mrs. Carson might overhear their exchange. Also, she didn't understand why most women were constantly concerned with matching men and women. Perhaps Eliza didn't have much to think about while washing dishes and mopping the floor, so she concocted these fictional melodramas in her mind. Eliza wiped a strand of fiery hair out of her eyes.

"Anyway, all the boys know that you're more interested in animals than a friendly shag."

"Who said that?" Hettie asked sharply.

"You know, some of the boys."

Just then, through the large picture window, Hettie saw Mr. Wright strutting by, his gait long and officious, and his black leather crop tucked underneath his arm. With a shudder of panic, Hettie glanced up at the clock again and realized she was going to be late. She didn't want to give Mr. Wright another reason to criticize her.

"I've got to go," she said, wrapping her father's wool scarf around her neck and tucking her hands into the pockets of her jacket.

"Eliza, almost done with that floor?" Mrs. Flynn called out from the kitchen.

"Don't forget what I said, Hettie Quin," Eliza said, a smirk pinching her face. "Always make sure you've got a good kiss in you."

Eliza yanked the handkerchief from her head and amber ringlets spilled onto her birdlike shoulders. She playfully thrust her chest forward and arched her spine. Even though she was running late, Hettie couldn't stop herself from watching Eliza. She was short with a sizable pair of breasts under her work blouse and denim apron. She exaggerated the sway of her hips and then picked up her feet higher, dancing fluid circles around the mop. Mrs. Flynn clicked on the wireless in the kitchen, and the tinny sound of a big band tune traveled from its meshed speaker. "It Don't Mean a Thing" was playing, the distinctive sound of the slide trombone riding over the swinging chorus of trumpets, saxophones, and piano. Eliza spun in faster circles, looking as if she might take flight at any second. Her body was nimble and elegant, a blur of motion. Her heels clicked against the floor. Mrs. Flynn and Mrs. Carson clapped their hands. Joy was written all over their faces. Finally, Eliza took the mop's handle into her arms and dipped it toward the floor, her hair tumbling down into a cascade of copper locks. She kissed the wooden handle and then turned to Hettie and winked.

"Bravo. Bravo," the two women cheered. "Bravo, Miss Crowley!"

Hettie had to smile.

Three

On her next day off, Hettie rode her bike to St. George's Market. It was an old black Raleigh bicycle, with a crossbar, that used to be her father's. Inside the Victorian market, diluted sunlight spilled through the reticulated rooftop. Vendors sold produce that wasn't yet in short supply: cabbages, turnips, beets, potatoes, carrots. Oatmeal biscuits and rock buns and soda bread. Families gathered around wooden tables, eating bowls of cabbage soup, and fish and chips served in cones of grease-stained newspaper. Somewhere in the cavernous space, live music was being performed; the twangy notes of a fiddle hemmed the midmorning air. Hettie walked farther down the aisle until she reached the rear of the market. There she found Marguerite, her blond braids trailing down onto her floral smock. A couple of items—soda bread, honey-oatmeal buns, and bacon turnovers—were still for sale on her table.

"Mornin', Hettie," Marguerite said, wiping her hands on her smock. "You caught me just in time."

"Morning." She smiled. "I'll take that one," Hettie said, pointing to one of the loaves of soda bread.

"Perfect," Marguerite said, wrapping the loaf in brown paper. "How's your ma?"

"She's grand," she lied, as she often did when people inquired about her mother.

That morning, when Hettie left the house, Rose had asked how she planned to spend her day off. Hettie had said that she would be volunteering at the Carnmoney Parish, assisting with a clothing donation that was being sorted for the church's orphanage in Derry. The answer had satisfied Rose enough that she didn't ask for any further details. In truth, Hettie had made plans to visit Liam Keegan, Anna's widower, and their three-month-old baby, Maeve, at his family's flat on the Falls Road. She knew that if she had mentioned this to Rose, she would have demanded that Hettie not go, and would have pointed out that the Fall Roads was no place for a young woman to be wandering around by herself and that it would be better if the two of them paid a visit together, but Hettie knew this would never happen, because her mother never traveled into Catholic neighborhoods, even if it meant not seeing her only grandchild.

Hettie handed Marguerite a few shillings, and Marguerite handed her the wrapped loaf.

"Say hello to your ma for me. Tell her I miss seeing her."

"I will," Hettie said, stowing the bread in her satchel. She knew she would say nothing to her mother. "Cheers."

She threaded through the busy aisles and tried to forget about her mother and her persistent sadness, and distracted herself with the offerings of the numerous vendors. Careful stacks of purple cabbages and onions were on display. Tight clutches of radishes, their blush of pink fading into white. Hettie bought a waxed-paper package of black licorice pieces. As she made her way toward the entrance, she popped one in her mouth, and bitterness bloomed on the tip of her tongue.

Near the double doors leading to May Street, an illuminated case was filled with sausage links, ground meat, and select cuts of pork. Despite the rationing, livestock—mostly pigs—were still being slaughtered and sold at the market. Behind the case, a middle-aged man in a blood-splattered apron and a paper butcher's hat stood next to a pig hanging by its feet from an iron hook. The butcher angled his sharp knife into the throat of the pig before carefully sliding it along the underside of the animal's breastbone. The smell of copper and fish hung in the air, making Hettie's nose wrinkle.

"My God," someone said. "Hettie Quin."

Hettie turned around and her eyes widened as she saw who it was. There, behind the butcher case, stood Samuel Greene, dressed in a blood-soiled apron and a butcher's hat. Despite it being a crisp autumn morning, damp strands of his dark brown hair were matted against his forehead. In his hands, he held a pile of pig entrails on a fresh sheet of butcher paper.

Hettie's mind spooled back over all that had transpired since she'd last seen Samuel. He and Hettie knew each other from the neighborhood; his family lived five streets over, not far off the Antrim Road, but she still hadn't seen Samuel during the last few months. Right after graduation, Samuel had invited Hettie to the pictures. Her friend Lena from school said Samuel had a reputation for asking out lots of girls but never dating one for long. Despite this, her fellow classmates were jealous when the news circulated that Samuel Greene was taking Hettie to the pictures one Saturday night.

Samuel had selected a Fred Astaire/Ginger Rogers movie playing at the Lyric Cinema on High Street, and once they arrived in the darkened theater, he had chosen a pair of seats in the gods. More than halfway through the film, he reached over, unbuttoned Hettie's blouse, and cupped her breast. His touch felt like sandpaper. He slurped and sucked against her neck like a greedy fish. During that moment, Hettie had attempted to settle into the discomfort and the thrill of being the object of Samuel's attention. She had very little experience with men—and tried to convince herself that this kind of physical unease was a natural part of this rite of passage, that she needed to give in to the encounter rather than resist it. Samuel guided her hand onto his stiff penis as he unzipped his trousers and made motions for her to stroke it with vigor. Hettie tried, massaging his member, but she couldn't get a solid grip and then he squirted into her warm palm and along her forearm, and everything smelled like ammonia. *Oh my god*, Samuel whispered. *I'm sorry.* The only thing she could manage to do was excuse herself and run to the washroom and rinse herself off. By the time Hettie returned to the theater, the closing credits were scrolling up the screen, and Samuel stood awkwardly near the entrance. They walked home, Hettie pushing her bike along the pavement, saying very little to each other. A spot of shame burned underneath her rib cage. She didn't know how to express that she had enjoyed their date—despite the unpleasant turn of events—and that perhaps they could go to another picture again soon. But instead, when they parted ways, Samuel merely shook her hand and wished her a good summer.

"I would give you a proper hug but I'm a bit untidy," Samuel said with a grin, glancing down at his bloody palms.

"Still working for your father, I see," Hettie said.

He wiped his forehead with his arm. A smear of crimson marked his cheek. Samuel's father stared in their direction before continuing to butcher the suspended swine.

"I haven't told my pa yet, but I've applied to join the police," he said softly. "Next month I'll find out if I've been accepted."

"Good luck."

"I don't want to be slaughtering animals for the rest of my life, you know. And if I don't work for my father, he'll force me to enlist in the army. I prefer the police. There's less of a chance of me catching a bullet."

Samuel started to arrange the pig's glistening intestines into neat rows next to the already-butchered feet, knees, and cheeks in the case. Hettie noticed his long, agile fingers against the pig's insides and remembered how Samuel used to play piano when he was still in school, and how the teachers had strongly advised him to study classical music but his father had discouraged Samuel's artistic pursuits because he needed his oldest son to work alongside him in his shop.

"Sorry to hear about Anna," Samuel said. "Everyone is—"

Hearing her sister's name still felt like an unexpected sock in the stomach. A salty film leaked into the corners of her eyes.

"I heard she had a baby girl."

"Maeve," Hettie said, looking up at Samuel. "Her name is Maeve Grace Keegan."

"Sorry I wasn't able to make her service," he said. "I tried, but Pa had a special order that day."

It seemed strange to Hettie that she was now talking civilly to this boy, who she knew both so intimately and not at all.

"Still helping out with your mum?" Samuel asked as he continued to arrange the rows of intestines.

Hettie remembered what Eliza had said, that young men might be impressed by her employment at the zoo, and she found herself standing a little taller. "I have a part-time job at the zoo," she said.

"Impressive."

Maybe Eliza Crowley was right about at least one thing, then.

A fly buzzed near Samuel's face and landed on his cheek. "Where did you come from," he said, swatting it away. Blood now smudged his upper cheek.

Hettie glanced down at her father's watch. It was already half past ten, and the Keegans were expecting her at eleven. "I best get going," she said. "I'm late."

"I'll come by the zoo soon."

"That would be nice," she said, feeling her cheeks warm up.

"Good to see you, Hettie Quin."

"You too, Samuel Greene."

She stepped out onto May Street, feeling suddenly cheerful. All right, so it hadn't been *quite* the encounter she had imagined since the last time she saw Samuel, but it had been pleasant enough. The brisk autumn air needled her skin, and Hettie shivered. She reached into her coat pocket, pulling out the scrap of paper with Liam's parents' address scribbled on it: 499 FALLS ROAD. She retrieved her father's bike and headed west on May Street, past the green-grayish domes of the city hall, the clock at the Great Victoria Street train station, and the pair of gilded minarets of the Grand Opera House. May Street segued into the Grosvenor Road, but the traffic was snarled at the intersection; double-decker buses, lorries, taxis, and other vehicles struggled for any sort of progress. Billows of exhaust rolled into Hettie's face as she rode on the narrow shoulder before turning onto the Falls Road.

The last time she had traveled to Liam's parents' was just a week after Anna's service, and the visit remained vague in her mind, because it had occurred when the days and hours had a tendency to collapse into each other. For Hettie, it felt as if the war in England, Poland, Germany, and Italy had temporarily disappeared; the sudden tragedy of her sister's death and the subsequent grief eclipsed the escalating international events. The occupation of France, Belgium, the Netherlands, and Luxembourg, the relentless Luftwaffe bombings of London, and the seizure of the Channel Islands off the coast of Normandy were like the faint rumblings of a distant train—hardly audible and always receding—and therefore didn't penetrate the fog of her daily grief.

Hettie parked the bike against a lamppost. She glanced up at the numbers of the terraced two-story homes on the left side of the road, relieved to see that she was in the right place. On the far corner, Hettie spotted a Royal Ulster Constabulary armored vehicle with machine guns mounted on its roof. She had read in the paper that most recruits to the newly formed Home Guard, which was being raised to protect Ulster if it was invaded during war, had been members of the B Specials, but she also knew the security forces were still being used in the event of republican riots or other civil disturbances. Hettie tightened her arms across her chest as she made her way down the pavement. Tiny pricks of fear emerged along the nape of her neck. A part of Hettie wished that she didn't find the sight of the RUC vehicle alarming, but there was no way around the fact that a flare-up of violence in this neighborhood could occur at any moment, and that it was one of the reasons her mother discouraged her from paying visits to the Keegans.

A mangy gray terrier barked behind a weathered picket fence, baring its sharp, tiny teeth and making Hettie jump. She scowled at it. Hettie liked most dogs, but she didn't like this one. She felt certain he might leap over the fence at any second and lunge right for her. A young man, dressed in an army-green factory uniform, gave a sharp whistle.

"You bloody eejit," he yelled. "Shut the fuck up."

Hettie thought for one wild moment that the young man might be yelling at her. That somehow he recognized she was a Protestant—and the younger sister of the girl who had died during childbirth, the short-lived wife of Liam Keegan—and was aware that everyone in their respective neighborhoods knew that the mixed-faith couple was doomed from the moment they exchanged vows in front of the justice of the peace in Edinburgh. Before their elopement, Anna had asked Hettie to not tell their mother about Liam. She knew Rose would have forbidden their relationship and later their marriage. Devoted to her older sister, Hettie had deflected their mother's questions about Anna's mysterious new boyfriend with non-answers, insisting she didn't know much about him or his religious affiliation. Four months later, Anna didn't return home one evening. Rose had been about to call the police to report her eldest daughter missing when a telegram was delivered announcing the couple's surprise marriage. Sometimes Hettie speculated on whether their father's abandonment had contributed to Anna's impulsive decision to marry Liam Keegan, that perhaps her sister had toyed with the notion of creating a new family, outside their own, one that might provide the corrective measure needed to bring everyone back together. Instead, it did just the opposite.

"Shut your goddamn trap," the man continued. "Do you hear me!"

Hettie realized with a rush of relief that he had been shouting at the dog, not at her. She fixed her eyes on a distant point on the street, her heart beating in her throat. A pile of broken glass had collected in the gutter. A rat scurried through its dull shimmer. The dog ceased barking. Above, between the narrow houses, a clothesline was strung up; the empty sleeves of shirts and the legs of trousers snapped in the breeze. Slogans were painted across a wall on the other side of the street: ARP STANDS FOR ARRESTS, ROBBERY, AND POLICE. And: REMEMBER 1916; WE SHALL RISE AGAIN; IRELAND SOBER, IRELAND FREE.

Hettie studied Liam's address on the piece of paper again even though she had just glanced at it. She made her way to the Keegans' front door and rang the buzzer. A gust picked up the hem of her skirt, pushing the pleated edges against her stockings. Hettie held a hand between her thighs, trying to keep the hem from lifting up again. She felt the quiet tinge of pain from the bruise on her thigh from the other morning of walking Violet along the Antrim Road. Hettie rang a second time. The last thing she needed was for the shouting stranger to turn his attention to her. Mrs. Keegan opened the door.

"Hettie Quin," she exclaimed, taking her arm and guiding her into the flat. "It's gusty out there! Come right in!" Mrs. Keegan wore a faded, rose-patterned apron. The sleeves of her white blouse gathered around her pudgy elbows. Her metallic-gray hair was held in a bun, fallen strands framing her bright, round face. "Liam, my boy," Mrs. Keegan yelled down the darkened hallway. "Liam! Where are you?"

Hettie kept her coat on and stood in the hallway, shifting from foot to foot.

"A spot of tea, love?" Mrs. Keegan asked Hettie.

"Please."

"The baby is sleeping, but she'll be awake soon. Maeve will be so happy to see you."

Hettie smiled politely, but she knew Maeve was too young to remember her. After all, she was only three months old, and it had been more than two months since the last time Hettie had paid a visit.

Together, Mrs. Keegan and Hettie walked down the hallway into the unadorned kitchen with its two-burner stovetop, small oven, narrow sink, and nondescript table with a set of four folding chairs. A linen tea towel embroidered with pale lavender lilacs and winding green stems was draped over the curved neck of the faucet. The towel reminded Hettie of her mother, as lilacs were her favorite flower and scent. Fleetingly, she wished Rose could be with her and have a chance to visit with her only grandchild, but she knew this would likely never happen.

"Let me put on the kettle," Mrs. Keegan said. "I've got a few biscuits somewhere."

"I brought you a loaf of soda bread from St. George's." Hettie rooted through her satchel and gave the brown-paper-wrapped package to Mrs. Keegan.

"Oh, my dear," she said, taking the package from Hettie and placing it on the counter. "How lovely." Mrs. Keegan ran the faucet, filling up the kettle. She lit a wooden match and ignited a crown of blue-orange flames on the stovetop. "Liam," she yelled again, before turning back to Hettie. "Mr. Keegan is working the morning shift at the mill. He's sorry to miss you."

"I'm sorry to miss him, too," Hettie said even though she barely knew the man.

She had met Mr. Keegan on only two other occasions: He was a quiet, heavyset man who moved around the room in a deliberate kind of way. He was about six foot five inches with broad shoulders and a wide face with pockmarked skin, pitted and roseate, and uttered few words in the company of others. She had read about Mr. Keegan once in the newspaper because his older brother had been killed twenty years earlier during the Troubles in 1920. The brother had been a member of the IRA and had been shot by a member of the Black and Tans in County Kerry. Mr. Keegan was interviewed for the twentieth anniversary, and made a few remarks about his brother, the heroics, and the tragedy of it all.

Hettie sat down at the kitchen table as Liam appeared in the doorway. He was tall, like his father, and was dressed in a navy blue work uniform with his name sewn in red thread on the oval patch on the right side of the shirt. His complexion was light olive and flecked with a constellation of dark freckles. His hair was a sturdy shock of dark brown. Having not seen Liam in a few months, she was struck anew by how handsome he was.

"Hettie," Liam said with a grin. "So good to see you again."

Hettie smiled, stood up, and greeted him with a brief hug. He smelled of petrol, cigarette smoke, and damp leaves. It was a pleasant and familiar odor, and reminded Hettie of her father when he came home from a long day at his former job down at the shipyards. She returned to her chair, and Liam gave his mother a kiss on the cheek.

The morning sun sent quivering patterns of light through the window over the sink. As Liam and his mother chatted, Hettie recalled the last time she had visited Anna in this flat, a few days before she passed away. They had sat at this very same kitchen table. Mrs. Keegan had been out running errands, and Liam had just left for his new job at the mechanics' garage on the west side of Belfast. After the front door had slammed shut and the dead bolt slid into position, Anna had stared into the empty hallway that led to the front door. Hettie remembered the relaxed, joyful expression on her older sister's face: The corners of her rose-colored lips were turned upward and her eyes glistened like the moisture of early morning. It was during that moment Hettie had recognized that her sister was in love with Liam Keegan, a fact that she hadn't fully grasped until then. Here was her older sister seemingly caught in a strong undertow of affection and admiration.

"We're glad you made it today," Liam said, bringing Hettie back to the moment. "It's been too long."

Mrs. Keegan placed a blue-and-white porcelain teapot and a plate of biscuits on the table. A funnel of steam escaped from the teapot's spout. As Mrs. Keegan wiped her age-spotted hands on the dish towel, a slight tremor traveled through her stubby fingers. Hettie looked up at her. A sheen of wetness moistened Mrs. Keegan's eyes and she surreptitiously wiped away a tear. Sitting there in the Keegans' stuffy kitchen, Hettie realized that she reminded them of Anna, too. After all, they shared a handful of familial features—green-brown eyes, high foreheads, and slender, lanky frames; this meant that strangers had often confused them for twins even though the sisters were eighteen months apart.

"Have one," Mrs. Keegan said, pushing the plate of biscuits toward Hettie.

The baby began to cry from another room, her gentle wail quickly escalating into a scream.

Mrs. Keegan tutted. "Liam, be polite and serve your sister-in-law some tea," she said. "I'll take care of the baby."

Mrs. Keegan hurried down the hallway. Liam took a biscuit for himself.

"You're famous, you know," Liam said. "Look here."

He slid the folded *Belfast Telegraph* toward Hettie. The headline read ELEPHANT STAMPEDES THE ANTRIM ROAD. There was a black-and-white photograph of Violet and Mr. Wright on the Queen's Bridge, with Hettie and Ferris following closely behind. She smiled, remembering the dramatic morning. The photographer had captured the moment right before Violet had charged to one side of the bridge. In the caption, only Mr. Wright was identified, as the head zookeeper of the Bellevue Zoo. Hettie scanned the rest of the article. The reporter wrote about Violet's arrival on the RMS *Majestic* from Ceylon, the thirty-one-day voyage, how the ship's captain had caught sight of German U-boats off the northwest coast of France and ordered the navigator to change their course, followed by Violet's disruptive encounters on the Antrim Road and how the constable almost arrested the young elephant during her first day in Belfast. Hettie gave out a soft laugh.

"Nicely done, Hettie Quin," Liam said, breaking a biscuit in two.

"You need to come up to the zoo and meet her, she—"

"Eat one," Liam interrupted, edging the plate toward her.

He reached for the pot and filled both of their cups. Tiny dried leaves collected along the porcelain sides as thin veils of steam lifted from the flat surfaces. Outside on the street, a car's engine backfired with an explosive boom. Hettie jumped in her chair, but Liam didn't even flinch at the sound. A breeze rattled the windowpane. A whirling siren could be heard from the street.

"What's her name again?"

"Violet," Hettie said.

"I can't wait for Maeve to meet her," Liam said. "Maybe when she's a bit older you could give her a ride on Violet. Don't you think Maeve would like that?"

Hettie imagined a girl, a smaller version of Anna, riding astride Violet's broad back, rocking from side to side, with Hettie confidently leading the young elephant down the middle of the street. Pedestrians would gather on the road's graveled shoulders and offer up enthusiastic applause and admiration for the majestic animal and the childlike queen making their way down the road.

"I asked Mr. Wright if I could take care of her," Hettie said, her smile fading as she glanced down at the grainy image of Mr. Wright guiding Violet across the bridge. "He said no."

"Ask again," Liam said, his chestnut eyes flickering. "You need to be more persistent."

"I know," Hettie responded, knowing that her sister would have said the same thing. For an instant, she felt the impulse to slug Liam and then ask for a hug. He always reminded her so much of her sister— and it lifted Hettie with joy and crushed her with grief at the same time.

"There, there, Maeve," Mrs. Keegan said from down the hallway.

"Any word from your pa?" Liam asked.

Hettie shook her head and stared into her teacup again. She pressed the rim of the cup against her lips. The tea had already turned lukewarm.

"Let's go and see Maeve," Liam said. "It sounds like Ma quieted her down."

At the end of the hallway, to the left, the door was halfway open. Hettie could hear Mrs. Keegan cooing, and Maeve was no longer crying. Liam and Hettie stepped into the spartan room. Patches of sunlight fell through the single window and the floorboards creaked underneath their feet. Angled shadows of a bare-limbed tree danced against the far wall. A wooden crucifix hung over Maeve's cot, and a strand of amber rosary beads was draped over a corner of a mirror that was positioned above the bureau. A framed black-and-white photograph of Liam and Anna from the morning of their elopement in Scotland stood on the bureau.

"Maeve was a wee bit hungry," Mrs. Keegan said, her eyes brightening. She gently patted the baby's back, and Maeve released a soft burp and gurgle, then grasped for the wrinkled lobe of Mrs. Keegan's ear. She gently removed the baby's fingers. "Your pretty aunt is here to see you."

Mrs. Keegan lifted the swaddled baby toward Hettie, who awkwardly adjusted her arms as she cradled Maeve. "Here, place one hand behind her neck," Mrs. Keegan said. "That way she can see you."

Hettie slid her hand to the warm spot where Mrs. Keegan's palm had been propping up Maeve's head. The muscles and bones of the infant's neck felt fragile like a baby bird's. She fluttered her eyes closed, and Hettie noticed the network of tiny blue veins mapped underneath the baby's flawless skin, a kind of topography of new life.

"This is your aunt Hettie," Mrs. Keegan said softly. "Your ma's sister."

Hettie stared into Maeve's serene face. Her hazel eyes flicked open, and she pursed her lips, suckling the air.

"She remembers you," Liam said, beaming.

Hettie moved her index finger into Maeve's plump fist, and the baby curled her hand around her finger. Her grip was tight and strong.

"See, she misses you," Mrs. Keegan whispered.

The room tilted. Hettie's legs felt like liquid. The morning light illuminated the floor, shimmering here and there, like tiny mirages. Hettie felt the touch of her sister's hand on her shoulder, but then her phantom weight disappeared. Hettie's eyes became glassy again. An itch tickled the tip of her nose. She wanted to reach up and scratch the spot, but didn't want to disturb the baby. A dribble of saliva spilled over the curve of Maeve's rosy cheek, and Hettie felt the baby's heartbeat against her own.

"Oh, dear," Mrs. Keegan said, wiping away the drool with her handkerchief.

"She looks like Anna, doesn't she?" Liam said.

Hettie recalled standing in this room with Anna when it was still unoccupied and looked more like an oversize closet. It was only six months ago, but already it felt as if a full revolution of seasons had passed. Anna had been staring at the empty walls, trying to decide if she should paint them a new color before Maeve's arrival. Hettie remembered how beautiful Anna had looked, standing there in the bare room, her hand perched on the shelf of her pregnant belly. Despite looking alike, Hettie had always considered Anna to be more beautiful. When they went on an excursion together—whether it was to a fish-and-chip shop downtown or the local swimming pool—the eyes of strangers frequently followed Anna. Over the years, Hettie had grown accustomed to this unsolicited attention and felt a small measure of pride when she was in the company of her older sister; it was as if she existed within the orbit of Anna's natural beauty and this somehow advanced Hettie's social station, too. As if, by mere association, Hettie was beautiful as well. She was no longer an ordinary young woman with a scattering of freckles across the bridge of her upturned nose and a head of mousy brown hair. She was Anna Quin's younger sister. Even though Anna had traded in her respectable employment, education, and athletic aspirations to marry Liam, during that moment in the baby's room, Hettie had understood that Anna likely held all of this brightness, ambition, and tenacity inside of her, that by marrying she hadn't changed that much. Anna was still Anna.

"Yes," Hettie said. "She looks just like her."

A gurgle of gas was followed by an overwhelming stench.

"Oh, there she goes again," Mrs. Keegan said, carefully removing the baby from Hettie's arms. "Let me clean her up."

Just like that, the physical weight of Maeve in her arms was gone, and Hettie suddenly missed her niece again. Mrs. Keegan laid the baby down on the changing table. Liam and Hettie stepped into the hallway, the worn floorboards giving with each step. As they entered the kitchen, birds chirped near the windowsill. Liam glanced up at the clock on the kitchen wall.

"I have a meeting before work," he said.

Hettie nodded, avoiding eye contact with him. Anna had told Hettie about Liam's history and beliefs: that he had joined up with the republican youth organization Fianna Éireann and later, when he was eighteen, the IRA, after dropping out of St. Malachy's College and getting work as a stock boy at a local grocery store. Like the speaker on the square, Liam and his friends thought that Britain's current war with Germany should be seen the same way the first one was viewed by the rebel leaders in 1916: that "England's difficulty was Ireland's opportunity," that Hitler had his good points, that at least he could drive the Brits out of Ireland and end a thousand years of British occupation of their country. In any case, they couldn't be worse off than they already were. Liam grabbed his coat and scarf.

"Don't tell my mum," he said. "She doesn't like the idea of me being so involved. It makes her nervous."

"I don't like it either, Liam, you—"

"I'm sure you're aware de Valera only seems to care about Ireland remaining neutral and doesn't give a damn about the North," Liam said, the pitch of his voice rising. "He represses, imprisons, and executes republicans, and isn't even open to the recruitment of Northern Catholics into the Irish Army. We need to train and organize ourselves. No one else is going to do it for us."

Hettie had read about Éamon de Valera and how his ruling party, Fianna Fáil, supported a military policy of Irish neutrality throughout wartime. And then there were the other stories on the wireless and in the papers about how subversive minority groups were critical of young Protestants enlisting in the army, how they were being "suckered by Stuttering George." More than once, she had wondered about these theories and if Liam was concocting conspiracies to support his increasing involvement in the IRA and its questionable activities, but now was not the time to bring any of this up.

"It's nothing to worry about," Liam continued, his tone conciliatory. "Just training and drills. We've set up a boxing ring in the hall on Kane Street. Come and watch me fight again."

Over the last few years, Liam had also developed a reputation as a fleet-footed boxer, defeating a string of opponents in amateur matches throughout the city. When Anna was alive, Hettie had gone to see him fight once, and he had easily knocked out his opponent within three rounds.

"I will," Hettie said, trying to smile.

"Bring your ma next time—"

"You know she won't come."

"Maybe she'll change her mind," Liam said. "Stranger things have happened. Bye, Ma! Grand to see you, Hettie."

Liam leaned forward, slid a strand of hair from Hettie's face, and kissed her on the cheek. His lips felt like feathers, and her blood pulsed in her ears. Then he was out the front door. Cold air slipped its way into the foyer. Mrs. Keegan carried Maeve from the baby's room.

"God bless," Mrs. Keegan called.

"I should get going, too," Hettie managed.

"Such a short visit," Mrs. Keegan said. "Promise you'll come for a proper tea next time." She opened the front door for Hettie and propped up Maeve's arm so the baby waved goodbye. Hettie felt her heart break a little again, taking in the sight of Maeve in Mrs. Keegan's arms. She waved, too.

"See you soon," Hettie said even though she wasn't certain when her next visit would be.

"Love to you," Mrs. Keegan said. "Say hello to your mum." She shut and locked the door.

The sun had come out again. A few auburn leaves floated down from a tree. Still standing on the front step, Hettie replayed her exchange with Liam. What had just happened? Was she attracted to her dead sister's husband? Was she finally admitting to herself that she found Liam handsome, too, and that occasional purls of jealousy, envy, and shame swirled underneath the veneer of her pleasant exchanges with him? Hettie pushed these questions out of her mind. After all, Liam was still her brother-in-law. He was her sister's husband—whether she was dead or alive. And Hettie knew instinctively that there had been something special about Anna and Liam's marriage, how the two had complemented each other's dispositions: Anna was the container of sorts for his boundless spirit, and his rambunctious nature had tempered her daily need for discipline and her relentless competitive drive. Liam and Anna had completed each other, even if it was only for a short period of time. Deep down, this was something that Hettie desired—a companion, a kind of punctuation that would place some finality to her unspoken yearnings, a pure kind of love.

On the street, a group of young boys played a game of catch, and two girls swung a long leather rope. Another girl paused before jumping in and hopping on one foot and alternating onto the other foot. Together, the girls recited: *Charlie Chaplin went to France / To teach the ladies how to dance.* Hettie started to whistle along with the familiar rhyme as she walked to her bike. Out of habit, she reached into one of the pockets of her coat, as she often carried a talisman—a shell or a rock or some other object—in her pocket, something with worn or weathered contours. Instead, she felt the corners of a piece of paper. Hettie took it out and even before she unfolded it, she knew what it was—a list that had been written by Anna over a year ago, items she had wanted Hettie to pick up at the market:

> *rationing of eggs*
> *sack of potatoes*
> *tin of sardines*
> *square of chocolate*

Hettie refolded the piece of paper and slid it into her coat pocket, and rode her father's bike home.

Four

AUTUMN ADVANCED INTO WINTER. THE DAYS WERE SHORTER, the nights longer, and morning freezes regularly stiffened the dead grass in people's yards and in the large meadows along the foot of the Cavehill. Air-raid drills became routine, and the familiar sirens frequently whined across the sweep of the winter sky. A smattering of pedestrians got into the habit of carrying gas masks, the straps draped over their shoulders, each mask folded into its own cardboard box, the instructions glued to its interior lid.

Hettie noticed other changes, too. Onions, cheese, and jams were no longer being sold at Aunt Sylvia's shop, St. George's, and other stores. The *Belfast Telegraph* arrived during the afternoon hours rather than early in the morning and the news was clearly being censored. Walls of layered sandbags surrounded many of the government offices, such as the city hall, the parliament buildings at Stormont, and the Customs House. Air-raid officers had dug trenches around the perimeters of many of the public parks. Civil defense wardens and ambulance workers staged mock incidents with pretend casualties reclined on canvas stretchers and ferried them through the busy streets of downtown and the dockyards.

In the meantime, Hettie spent less and less time at home. Instead, she found other ways to occupy her evenings, often staying late at the zoo after its doors had closed and taking on extra chores in hopes that Mr. Wright would notice her efforts and reconsider full-time employment in the near future. Since Violet's arrival to Bellevue two months ago, Edward Baird, another zookeeper, had been assigned to the elephant's care, but Hettie remained optimistic. She had also checked out a handful of books from the Belfast Public Library about animal husbandry and elephants. She was studying up on the black bears as well, so she might be able to assist Mr. Wright with the birth of the cubs when the springtime came.

On other evenings, when Hettie wasn't at the zoo, she wandered along the lower reaches of the Cavehill or paid ever more frequent visits to the Keegans and spent more time with baby Maeve, since Rose was paying less attention to the nature of Hettie's whereabouts. If Liam happened to be at their flat, it was nothing to her. And as she walked home at night, Hettie had become accustomed to the darkness of the government-mandated blackouts. The terraced silhouettes of the unlit houses against the paler sky. The glowing ends of cigarettes amid the shadowy huddles of men gathered on street corners and in front of pubs and storefronts. The hooded headlights of the cars and lorries. It was like the city of Belfast was meant for the regulated darkness, its industrial landscape disappearing each night as the early-winter sun set. And Hettie felt as if she were meant for darkness, too, that it made being invisible and lonely acceptable, a natural state of being, at least during the evening hours.

Often when Hettie returned home, the glowing seam underneath her mother's bedroom door disappeared as soon as she slipped off her winter coat and locked the front door. During their brief morning exchanges, Rose asked fewer and fewer questions about Hettie's activities, and their daily conversations were limited to a few subjects, such as changes in the weather, the rationing, and the new prime minister,

John Andrews, who had taken over since the recent passing of Lord Craigavon, who had simply died in his armchair while listening to the six o'clock news on a late November evening. After the sudden loss of her sister, this kind of abrupt death no longer seemed alarming or implausible to Hettie. No one—not even the prime minister of Northern Ireland and the leader of the Ulster Unionist Party—was immune to such a death.

One morning during the first week of December, Hettie arrived early for work, as she often did. During the past week, the temperatures had dropped, and snow flurries had gathered in the flat, pewter sky. Underneath her winter coat, Hettie wore extra layers—one of her father's jumpers and one of his long-sleeved shirts to insulate herself against the biting cold. Throughout the morning, Hettie's assignments followed a familiar revolution: feeding the flamingos, the birds in the aviary, and the lemurs (who were making a habit of escaping their cages on a regular basis, requiring Ferris to recapture them again and again). In the afternoon, she had also been assigned to the dromedary camels, cleaning out their bedding and the drain of their enclosure.

After feeding the lemurs, Hettie creaked open the door to the Elephant House. There, inside, she spotted Violet lying on her side. As soon as the elephant noticed Hettie's presence, she stirred to her feet and shook splinters of hay from her boulder-like torso.

"Hey, Vi," she said. "It's me, Hettie."

Violet took several steps toward her, and Hettie patted the elephant on her forehead. Violet lifted up her trunk and opened her mouth, revealing her pink, slippery tongue. During recent weeks, it seemed that Violet had come to expect Hettie's visits; she had become familiar with the sound of her voice and the occasional treats—stale buns and bruised produce that she brought from her aunt's corner store.

"Hungry?"

Violet released a series of chirps, a kind of Morse code of affection. Hettie gently patted her side, and the elephant's fine bristly hairs sprung underneath her fingertips. She stepped back from Violet and took a closer look: Her belly appeared less full. The drape of her coarse skin barely hid the curves of her rib cage.

"We're not feeding you enough, are we?" Ferris had mentioned the other day that Mr. Wright was closely monitoring the amounts fed daily to the animals so the zoo wouldn't run out, and although Hettie understood, it didn't make seeing Violet going hungry any easier.

Violet swung her trunk from side to side, and Hettie peered around the Elephant House for a bale of hay. Cobwebs stretched across the rafters, the morning sun glinting on the gossamer threads. She didn't see any. Hettie made a note to herself to ask her uncle Edgar if he might be able to spare a few extra bales for the zoo. She stepped into the exterior yard and reached into her pocket for one of the turnips from her aunt's shop. The gate slammed shut, and Hettie turned to see Edward Baird standing at the door of the Elephant House with a rake in one hand and a bucket in the other. Edward was a scrawny young man with rusty sideburns that trailed down the sides of his thin, freckled cheeks. His overlapping front teeth were the color of aging newspaper. From her first day at the zoo, Hettie had never exactly taken to Edward. He looked like one of those people who scratched their face and arms too much, leaving behind a broken trail of red welts, and you felt that if you stood too close to him, you might start itching your arms and face, too.

"Aye, Hettie," he said. "What you doing here?"

"Just saying hello to Violet."

Edward smiled at her. "She's a good elephant, isn't she?"

Hettie smiled back, doing her best not to stare at his teeth. "She's lost a bit of weight."

Edward sighed. "Mr. Wright told me not to feed her more than a half bale a day."

"I'm worried about her."

"Talk to Mr. Wright," he said, sounding defensive now. "I'm just following orders."

"I will."

"Good day," Edward said, wiping his brow with one of his work gloves.

Recognizing his dismissal, Hettie closed the gate behind her. She watched as Edward walked over to where Violet stood. He patted her on the side and then nudged his forehead against hers. For a moment, it looked as if the elephant and Edward were held under some sort of mutual spell. Edward closed his eyes and leaned into the elephant's large, lumbering body. Hettie clenched her fists, turned around, and made her way toward the nearby pathway. A tightness grabbed at her chest. She stole one more glimpse: Edward wiped something from his eye, and Violet walked away from him. He retrieved the rake from the ground and began to comb the enclosure's dusty surface. She suddenly felt a warmth toward him.

As she made her way to the flamingos, Hettie passed the polar bears. One after the other, Felix and Misty dove off the stony ledge and swam in circles before lifting themselves onto the pebbled shoreline, climbing to the top, and diving again. The polar bears performed this continuous loop of movements every day, and Hettie never grew tired of watching them. Misty paused at the top and shook her fur, sending out a halo of moisture that sparkled in the winter sun. She growled, stood up on her hind legs, and bared her teeth and dark gums. Her triangular ears perked up as she returned to all fours and dove into the pool again. Felix followed her.

Hettie rubbed her gloved hands together and blew into them. Already, the tips of her fingers ached from the cold. Misty growled again as she pulled herself out of the water, her wet paws slopping against the ice-laced ground, and Hettie forced herself to move on. A minute later, the pink-and-scarlet huddle of flamingos came into view, standing still on their thin black legs. Clouds of air materialized in front of her mouth as she walked along the pavement, greeting Helen McAlister and Mary Robinson, who were opening the ticket kiosk.

Hettie spotted Eliza Crowley walking toward her. A wool scarf obscured most of her face, and in her gloved hand she carried a tin lunch box by her side. For a moment, Hettie wanted to turn around and walk in the other direction, pretend that she had somewhere else to be. Even though she and Eliza were now in the habit of exchanging friendly pleasantries when Hettie visited the canteen for a cup of tea, Hettie had ignored Eliza's advice of going out with Ferris to earn a promotion at the zoo. She still didn't know if she liked him in that way and didn't want to overstep their friendship as a means of advancement. Hettie had also learned from the other zookeepers that Eliza had gone out with Bobby Adair, who also worked at the zoo, and another boy, who worked at a linen mill on the Shankill Road, one week after the other, and had agreed to a romp with each of the young men in exchange for chocolates and nylons they had procured on the black market. She felt like Eliza's business was her business—and knew this was her habit to move from boy to boy for one reason or another—but she was still fretful that if she became better friends with this scrappy, fiery girl, it might tarnish her reputation among her fellow zookeepers.

"You're here early," Eliza remarked.

"I'm always here early," Hettie said, staring at Felix and Misty and avoiding Eliza's gaze.

"How's young Ferris?" Eliza asked.

When Hettie glanced back at her, she saw a flicker of mischief in Eliza's eyes.

"He's fine," Hettie replied stiffly.

"I'm going to go out with him if you don't hurry up."

Hettie finally looked up at Eliza and studied her face. A ring of lavender stained one of her eyes. At first Hettie thought it could be visible hints of fatigue; she knew that Eliza worked two other jobs—one in the foundry at one of the mills and the other for a fruit merchant on the weekends—and often wondered how she found the time to go out with all these young men. But then she realized Eliza had a shiner.

"What happened?" Hettie asked.

"Oh, that," Eliza said, reaching up for her face but not touching it. "I fell."

"It looks like more than a fall," Hettie said.

Eliza lowered her hand. She lifted one end of her scarf to wipe her running nose, causing her scarf to fall away from her face. The bruising discolored most of her cheek, and a few black-thread stitches marked her chin.

"Who did this to you?" Hettie managed, after a few moments of shocked silence.

"No one," Eliza said, wrapping her face up again.

"Eliza, you have stitches," Hettie said.

"My sister took me to the hospital after it happened," Eliza said.

"After what happened?"

Eliza lowered her gaze to the pavement. "My brother has a wee bit of temper," she finally said. "He doesn't like it when I go out with Protestant boys. You know Ellis Johnson? He lives near you, I think, on the Longwood Road. So, when we arrived home last night, Aiden started to punch the lights out of him, and it made me so bloody mad. I mean, what right does he have to hit my date? It was only my second time going with him. I don't even know Ellis, and there's my older brother beating him to the ground. I had to do something."

"Does it hurt?" Hettie asked, looking more closely at Eliza's face.

"My sister said it'll look all right in no time," Eliza said, wrapping the scarf around the lower part of her face again. "That no one will notice."

"Yeah," Hettie said, trying to smile. "I think she's right. You can barely tell."

"Really?"

"Well, not really . . ." Hettie trailed off, unable to tell a full lie.

"Give me your word you won't tell anyone?" Eliza pleaded. "I'm not daft—I know what people think about me around here."

"Of course," Hettie said. "I won't tell anyone."

Eliza gave her a hug, her nose pressing into Hettie's shoulder. Eliza's body felt frail and light in her arms. All bones and sharp angles. After a moment, Hettie hugged her back.

"Thanks," Eliza said with a sudden grin. "Got to get to work. Mrs. Flynn and Mrs. Carson don't like it when I'm late."

"Cheers."

She watched Eliza walk away. There was a slight limp to her gait. She disappeared behind the double doors of the canteen. As she observed Eliza, Hettie realized that she had a fair amount to be grateful for: her job, despite not being exactly what she wanted; her education, even though Rose had demanded that she discontinue her sixth-form studies because they could no longer afford the tuition; a pleasant-enough home, even if it meant putting up with her mother's relentless sorrow and constant suggestions to find more respectable, better-paying employment; and most important, Violet, who was the highlight of her days at the zoo, even though she wasn't allowed to look after her yet. But Hettie was still determined to change that.

During her midmorning break, Hettie met Ferris in the canteen for tea. She didn't see Eliza behind the counter and wondered if Mrs. Flynn or Mrs. Carson had sent her home after seeing the worrisome condition of her face. Hettie cupped her hands around the teacup and blew on its steamy surface.

"How's your morning going?" he asked.

"Fine," she said brightly. "Although there's no hay—"

"Yes, well, Mr. Wright is having to ration more than expected," Ferris said, frowning. "The herring supply is low, too. He asked me to limit the penguins' diet, and he's feeding the pelicans pork scraps coated in cod liver oil."

"I ran into Edward Baird," she said. "He's an odd fellow, don't you think?"

"Didn't you hear the news?"

"What news?"

"His father decided it's time for Edward to enlist. He's being deployed next week," he said. "Elias and Johnny are going, too."

Hettie thought back to that morning, and Edward touching his pale forehead to Violet's took on new significance.

"They leave on Monday morning," he said. "On the first ferry to Plymouth."

Hettie fixed her gaze on the scars and stains on the wooden tabletop. She felt sad, elated, and ashamed. She knew there was a good chance one of her fellow workers would be injured or killed during the coming months. She had already heard countless rumors and stories about soldiers being blown apart on the front lines of combat during the Battle of France—their faces blasted off, their limbs flying through the air, only to be left among the piles of corpses with no proper funeral or burial to mark their passings. On the other hand, Hettie realized this news could give her what she finally wanted.

"Poor Edward," she managed.

"Poor Elias and Johnny, too," Ferris said.

Unconsciously, it seemed, Ferris moved a hand over his heart. During his last medical exam, he had been diagnosed with a faulty valve. Even if he wanted to enlist, it wasn't an option for Ferris. Becoming an air-raid warden in Belfast wasn't a possibility either. The doctor had discovered that Ferris's coronary valve resembled Swiss cheese: a passage of minuscule holes, making him more at risk for a stroke or a heart attack, particularly if he was placed in stressful situations. Hettie was secretly relieved he wouldn't be going off to fight.

The door to the canteen slammed shut and Ferris glanced over at the entrance. Mr. Clarke strode to the counter and held his green thermos out to Mrs. Flynn, who replenished it with hot tea. He screwed on the lid and tipped his tweed cap toward Hettie and Ferris before leaving the canteen.

They sat in heavy silence as they sipped their cups of tea. Hettie felt like she should offer further sympathies for the young men and what lay in front of them. Then there was Eliza and the stitches on her chin. Maybe Hettie should say something to Ferris and see if he knew Eliza's older brother. Instead she said nothing and returned her attention to her hands: Her palms were laced with grime and dirt from her morning chores. A thin scab crawled over one of her knuckles.

"You should talk to Mr. Wright this afternoon," Ferris finally said. "He's gonna need more people. He can't be picky, given the circumstances."

"Thanks," she said, looking up at Ferris, grateful that he was still considering her prospects. "I will."

Ferris swallowed what was left of his tea and stood up from the table. "Let me know how it goes," he said, reaching for his coat and making his way toward the exit.

Hettie took a final sip of tea. It had already cooled down, and the lukewarm bitterness hit the back of her throat, making her grimace. She stirred the dregs at the cup's bottom. Hettie thought of her father again. In this situation, she knew that her father would advise her to not worry about the boys, that the army would take care of its men. She decided that she would heed his advice, even if he wasn't there to give it himself. Hettie carried their teacups to the far window of the canteen but stopped as she saw Eliza standing in front of one of the deep basins. Her scarf was no longer tied around her face, and Hettie was horrified to see that the bruise traveled all the way down to her chin. She looked up as Hettie finally placed the teacups on the counter.

"How are you feeling?" Hettie asked.

"Better."

"Did you hear? A few of the boys are enlisting," Hettie said. "Ferris said it would be a good time to talk to Mr. Wright."

"See, what did I tell you? Getting in with Ferris was the right thing."

Hettie smiled even though she felt the impulse to correct Eliza.

"I bet he says yes," Eliza said wistfully, glancing down at her sudsy hands in the basin. "You're going to be famous. Everyone will know about you. Bellevue's first full-time female zookeeper. I can see it now."

"Thanks," Hettie said. "And *thank you*."

Eliza stared at her. "For what?"

"You've helped me, too."

Eliza took her cup and rinsed it out. "I didn't do anything," she said, winking at Hettie. "Go ahead now. Get what you deserve."

Hettie used the walk down to Mr. Wright's office to gather her courage. From the other side of his door, Hettie could hear his phonograph playing the forlorn, warbling voice of a French singer with the march of brass and strings in the background. She knocked on the door and then opened it.

"Ah, Miss Quin," Mr. Wright said, lifting the needle from the spinning record on the gramophone. "Come in." He waved Hettie to the empty chair in front of his desk.

The blond wood surface was much messier than last time she had been in there, cluttered with invoices, letters, and feeding schedules. Despite the fact that it was now December, the wall calendar still displayed the galloping cheetah from October. On his bookcase, she saw a framed black-and-white photograph she had not noticed before. It was of Mr. Wright dressed in tails and a top hat with an extended whip forming an enormous *S*, looking as if the leather cord was a natural extension of his arm. In his other hand, he held a large hoop festooned with garlands. Across from him, a sphinxlike lion was perched on a barrel. Though Ferris had mentioned Mr. Wright's past life as a lion tamer, she had never seen any evidence of it before. All at once it dawned on her: Mr. Wright was the ringmaster she had seen with her father and Anna over ten years ago.

"His name was Augustus," Mr. Wright said, and Hettie turned to see him gazing at the photograph, too. "I was with one of Mr. Christie's circuses before he moved me to Bellevue. It was our European tour: 1929. He was one of our star attractions."

"I saw the show here in Belfast," Hettie said. "With my father and sister."

He stared at her. "You were there?"

"I remember the elephant," she said, nodding. "She played the harmonica."

"The crowds loved Marla's harmonica playing," he said, looking again at the photograph. He sighed. "Everyone loved Marla."

"Is she still with the circus?"

"Mr. Christie put her down after she attacked a circus hand," he said sorrowfully. "Of course, it wasn't her fault. I had told Aikens more than once not to use an iron prod when trying to guide Marla into her stock car. He didn't listen, and she ended up trampling him and smashing his skull. Mr. Christie shot Marla himself. It was a sad day. I'll never forget it."

"And the circus hand?" Hettie asked.

"He was buried in the town where we were performing," Mr. Wright explained. "Salisbury. Aikens didn't have any family, so there was nowhere to ship the body."

"That's awful."

"Yes, it is," said Mr. Wright, then seemed to break out of a trance. "Anyway, sit, sit. I think I know why you're here."

Surprised, Hettie sat down in the empty chair. The wet smell of hay and manure rose up from the fabric of her work coat. Mr. Wright placed his fedora on the chaotic tabletop.

"I'm assuming you've heard about Elias, Johnny, and Edward?"

"Yes, sir," Hettie said. "Ferris told me."

"Unfortunate fellows," he said. "Hopefully their assignments won't take them to the front lines. The Germans are advancing rapidly in the Ardennes, and they are brutal."

Mr. Wright paused for a minute. He reached for a pencil and a piece of paper, and poised the pencil's tip over the blank surface, but didn't write anything. It looked as if his next thought had vanished and he had entirely forgotten that Hettie was sitting across from him.

"Everything all right, sir?" Hettie asked eventually.

Mr. Wright blinked and then returned his pencil to the desk. "Where was I?" he asked, glancing up at Hettie.

"The boys," she reminded him. "Their enlistment."

"Yes, yes," said Mr. Wright, clearing his throat. "After some consideration, I've decided to bring you on full-time. That said, I'll be keeping my eye on you, a sort of probationary period of at least six months, until you've proven that you can manage. Understand?"

"Yes, of course," Hettie said, her words rushing together. She couldn't believe it—what she truly wanted was going to happen.

"Will your mum be able to get along without you? I know it's been a difficult year for your family."

Hettie assumed that Mr. Wright was referring to the loss of her sister, but also wondered if the stories of her father's abandonment had made it up to the zoo, and she worked hard to maintain a smile on her face. "My mum is keen for me to be working," Hettie said, her palms becoming moist. "She doesn't need me anymore."

Rose hadn't said this exactly. Rather, she had mentioned in passing how she was growing weary of the McMullen sisters and their regular visits, and wondered aloud if maybe it was time that they all moved on. The elderly sisters were longtime members of their congregation, and had been assigned to the Quin household by Reverend Mills. The sisters dressed in slate-gray wool coats and dull white blouses with white pearl buttons, and gray skirts that hung down to their thick ankles. Their pale faces, moonlike foreheads, and flat, gray eyes looked vaguely familiar to Hettie, like the faces of strangers she might accidentally bump into on the busy pavement or in one of the crowded aisles of St. George's Market.

"Don't you want to speak to her first?"

"She'll be pleased with the news, I know it," Hettie said firmly. She folded her hands into her lap and sat up straighter. She almost felt as if she might dissolve into laughter and tears; she hadn't been this elated in years. Now she might be able to save enough money and begin looking for a room at a women-only boardinghouse downtown. Finally, she could strike out on her own. Underneath all of this, Hettie felt a scintilla of guilt for her strong desire to leave her mother, but she swiftly pushed it away. After all, Rose didn't need her anymore.

"What areas will you be charging me with?" Hettie asked.

"The camels, flamingos, the aviary."

Mr. Wright paused for a moment, and Hettie felt crestfallen that he hadn't mentioned the young elephant as one of her assigned charges.

"And Violet," he finally added.

"Grand," she responded, feeling a rupture of joy bursting throughout her.

"Any questions?"

"No, sir," Hettie said, standing up. "Thank you. I appreciate it, sir. When do I start, sir?"

"Next week," he said, and then paused. "When the boys are gone. And remember, I'll be keeping tabs on you."

"Yes, sir."

Hettie reached for the glass knob of the door. Mr. Wright returned the needle of the gramophone to the record that spun on the turntable. Hettie stepped outside, and the melancholy music filled the office again. Before she closed the door behind her, she heard Mr. Wright singing along with the French lyrics, his sonorous voice harmonizing with the recorded voice of the female singer. Hettie was both surprised and impressed by the mellifluous quality of Mr. Wright's song. She never would have guessed that he had such a beautiful voice.

Before returning to her late-morning assignments, Hettie stopped by the Elephant House, where she spotted Violet outside, wandering along the perimeter of the moat as young children stretched their arms in her direction. Hettie made her way through the Elephant House and into the enclosure. The elephant moved closer to the multitude of hands. The children released a collective ooh. As Hettie took a few steps closer, Violet's attention remained fixed on the gaggle of children— the girls dressed in white socks and black shoes, and double-breasted coats over their flannel dresses, and the boys clad in woolen trousers, navy blazers, and snug caps. With bright eyes, the children awaited the young elephant's next move.

Hettie reached for a turnip in her pocket. "Violet," Hettie called, clucking her tongue. "Treat."

The elephant immediately turned to look at her. She remembered Mr. Wright's cautionary tale about the elephant attacking the circus hand, but despite Violet weighing more than three thousand pounds, Hettie didn't think there was much chance that the elephant would ever try to hurt her. The closest act of aggression she had witnessed was on the morning of Violet's arrival in Belfast, when she had scared the greengrocer. Violet trotted toward her. The cold, hard ground crunched beneath her feet. She opened her mouth and her tongue lolled like a drifting slip of paper. Hettie laughed and tossed the turnip underhand and the elephant caught it squarely in her mouth. The schoolchildren cheered.

"Bravo, bravo," someone said from the other side of the enclosure.

Hettie looked up, astonished to see Liam Keegan standing a short distance from the loose assemblage of children. Instead of wearing his usual work clothes for the garage, he was dressed in his Sunday best: a two-piece charcoal suit with a flat cap. Maeve was in his arms. It was the first time he had paid a visit to the zoo since she started working there, and Hettie was surprised how pleased she was that he had made the trip up the Antrim Road. He motioned for her to join them on the other side of the enclosure and Hettie threaded her way through the Elephant House.

"Brilliant to see you," she said. "I got some good news today. I've been offered a full-time position. I start next week."

"Congratulations," Liam said. "I knew it would work out. Everything always takes a little extra fight."

Hettie nodded, her face breaking into a wider grin. "If all goes well, I should be able to save enough money to move into my own place by summer."

"She's a beauty, Hettie," Liam said, glancing up at Violet.

"Not as much as this little one," Hettie said, leaning toward her niece in his arms. "Hello, Maeve."

Maeve smiled, the soft corners of her mouth curling up.

"You're my sweet girl, aren't you," Hettie said, looking up to catch Liam's eye, but he was still staring over her shoulder at the elephant.

"What brings you to the zoo?" Hettie asked.

"Do you want to hold Maeve?"

"Let me wash up," she said, glancing down at her dirty hands.

Hettie walked into the Elephant House and scrubbed her hands under the cold tap water in the grimy porcelain sink next to the supply closet. When she returned to Liam, he moved Maeve into her arms. From between the folds of the cotton blanket, the baby stared up at Hettie. Maeve's cheeks were rosy and her long black lashes fluttered. "It's your first trip to the zoo, isn't it, sweet girl?" Hettie said.

Maeve babbled, raised a fist, and tapped Hettie on the nose. Hettie laughed and held Maeve more closely, relishing her warm weight in her arms. It felt like their bodies were meant for each other, with Maeve's head nestling in the shallow crook of her forearm. Maeve's heartbeat was her heartbeat, her breath Hettie's breath.

Here was infinite love, here was infinite joy, here was infinite kindness, all within this small bundle of flesh that was also her own blood. At the same time, a sorrow overlapped with this love, the loss of her sister forever imprinted onto Maeve's features.

"We have some news," Liam said, looking up at Hettie. "Later next week we will be moving to a relative's farm. As a part of the evacuations."

Hettie was stunned by what Liam had just said and felt the weight of Maeve more viscerally in her arms.

"Where?" she finally managed.

"Just north of Newcastle," he said.

"For how long?"

"Don't know, really," he said, shrugging. "Ma asked that we stay for a wee bit."

"Do you think the Germans are going to bomb Belfast?" Hettie asked, worry seeping into her voice.

"It's for Maeve's sake, Hettie," Liam said. "I need to follow Ma's wishes. After all, she's the one taking care of the baby."

While they were talking, Violet had lumbered into the far corner of the enclosure and folded her legs underneath her body.

"You take good care of Violet while we're gone," Liam said. "We'll return soon."

"All right," Hettie said hesitantly. She kissed Maeve on the forehead, breathing in her scent of talcum powder and vanilla. And she returned Maeve to Liam's arms.

"Say goodbye to your ma for us," Liam said.

"I will," Hettie said, her words caught in her throat. "I'll tell her."

She didn't know what else to say. She leaned forward and gave both Liam and Maeve a hug together, and for a moment they were a trio. The baby chattered, blissfully unaware of what was going on around her. Liam lightly pecked Hettie on her cheek. Then they broke apart, and Liam walked away, with Maeve in his arms, through the winding pathways of the zoo, past the aviary and the flamingos and the penguins, past the ticket kiosk and down the steps of the grand staircase, through the front entrance and across the busy lanes of traffic of the Antrim Road, to the closest tram stop, where they would wait for the next tram that would eventually deliver them to the bottom of the Falls Road, a short walk away from the Keegans' flat. Hettie felt paralyzed. Another part of her sister was gone, another part of herself was gone. Underneath all this grief, Hettie didn't want to admit to the stirrings of affection that she felt toward Liam.

Violet lifted her trunk and released a trumpet cry, startling Hettie out of herself. Hettie walked back into the Elephant House and hung a bucket up by its handle. At the door of the structure, she ran right into Edward Baird.

"Oh," Hettie said, stopping herself before bumping into his chest. "I didn't see you."

"I suppose Mr. Wright told you?"

"Yes . . . I'm sorry."

"Hopefully, Churchill will take care of the Germans before I see any serious action," he said, his bottom lip quivering.

Unsure what to do, Hettie took a step closer and gave Edward a hug.

"Father says it's going to be grand," Edward whispered into her shoulder. "He says a uniform can work miracles. I'll return home a different man."

"You're just fine the way you are," she said, taking a step back from Edward. "But your father's right: Everything's going to be all right."

Edward wiped his tears away. "Thanks, Hettie."

"I'll take good care of Violet while you're gone," she said with a smile.

"I know you will," Edward said. "Everyone knows you're a fine zookeeper. Just like the rest of us."

A tingling moved into her arms and hands.

"Thank you," she said. "Thank you for saying so."

As she watched him walk away, Hettie realized that, just for a second, she had forgotten about Maeve and Liam, and how they were going away, too. Suddenly she felt another sweep of loneliness. The air, the ground, the light. It all held a slightly different quality, one that was more hollowed out and empty.

Two weeks into December, the sky took on a perpetual gray. Instead of an autumnal shimmer, the slopes of the Cavehill were largely barren, with the exception of the hunter-green huddles of pine trees here and there, and irregular patches of snow checkerboarding the knolls and hillsides. Snow fell and melted, and fell and melted again. The outlying roads were slushy and slick.

It was the end of the workday. Despite the fact that the zoo was still open, only a few visitors lingered. A handful of black umbrellas bloomed over strangers' heads as the freezing precipitation began yet again. The sun set earlier, around half past four, and the visitors left the zoo as the diminishing daylight left the sky.

Mr. Wright was doing his best to enforce the blackout restrictions. The lampposts that dotted the pavements were no longer illuminated after dusk, and the large windows of the Floral Hall and other buildings around the zoo were properly fitted with standard-issue blackout shades. In the meantime, big bands from Northern Ireland, Ireland, and England still performed at the popular dance hall. Ferris had invited Hettie more than once to join him and the other zookeepers for a night of dancing and live music, but she had repeatedly declined, worried that her fellow workers might take her less seriously if they had a chance to see her in a frock and makeup, just like the other girls. And besides, she still didn't know how she felt about Ferris, and she didn't want to give him the wrong impression.

It had been only two weeks since Edward Baird's departure, but Hettie had already fallen into an effortless routine with Violet, checking on the elephant several times a day in between her other responsibilities and chores. Hettie turned on the spigot of the rubber hose attached to the rear of the Elephant House, and a wet puddle pooled on the ground. Hettie lifted the hose up and an arc of water sprayed against Violet's speckled forehead. The elephant shook her head and produced a soft whistle.

Hettie sprayed the stream into Violet's mouth. Droplets of water fringed the fine whiskers on the elephant's chin. The early-evening light broke through the gunmetal bank of clouds and lit up the curve of water. Violet lifted her trunk, and Hettie trained the bend of water a little higher. Violet shook her body, releasing a shower of wetness in all directions. Several drops landed on Hettie's cheek. Tiny footprints of coldness against her skin. Hettie laughed with delight.

As she worked, the freezing rain turned to flurries. Snow accumulated on the bare limbs of beech and sycamore trees. A long-eared owl gave out its low, breathy call. The next time she looked up, Ferris was standing near the door to the Elephant House, and she smiled at him. The amber glow of his cigarette moved from his mouth to his side, and then up again, like the faint trail of a comet.

"Good evening, Hettie Quin," he finally said. "How are you on this fine evening?"

"Just finishing up."

Hettie clucked her tongue again, and Violet walked through the gate and found her usual spot in the Elephant House, settling into the far corner. The horizontal slits of the overhead vent threw shadowy stripes against the elephant's skin. Ferris reached for Hettie's cheek and wiped something away. A warm sensation filled in the spot that Ferris had just touched. Hettie turned around and took in one more glimpse of Violet, whose body was now almost completely obscured by the darkness of the Elephant House.

"Mr. Wright told me that he is pleased with your work with the animals so far," Ferris said. "He's happy that things are working out."

"I'm pleased to hear he's pleased," Hettie said with a smile.

"Are you heading home?"

"In a minute."

She secured the gate leading to the enclosure, and then together, Ferris and Hettie walked along the pathway that led to the zoo's front entrance. But when they reached it, Hettie was dismayed to see that Mr. Clarke had already locked the gate for the night.

"Don't worry, we can go over the wall," Ferris said, leading Hettie to a spot that he assured her was easy to climb.

They both found effortless purchase and pulled themselves onto the wall's flat ledge. Silently, Hettie and Ferris sat there, taking in the view of the Antrim Road, the grand staircase, the intricate network of paths and darkened enclosures, and the distant rounded facade of the Floral Hall that overlooked the zoo. The newly fallen snow left the surface of the Antrim Road and its cobblestones smooth and perfect, like the flawless frosting of an elegant cake on display in a bakery's storefront. Amid the darkness, the zoo—and its numerous inhabitants—looked like a quiet, monastic refuge, where an inherent order and system guided its daily way of life. Then the roar of one of the lions broke the spell.

"It's lovely," Hettie said.

"It is lovely, Hettie Quin," Ferris said, and Hettie turned to find his unflinching gaze on her face. She lowered her eyes to the snowy pavement below their dangling feet, glad that he wouldn't be able to see her flushed cheeks in the darkness. She looked up at him and took in his azure eyes, still fixed on her. She wondered what exactly Ferris saw: If he still considered her as the girl he'd met during their biology class or if he viewed her differently now—more grown-up, mature, and capable, with her time at the zoo, and all that had changed in her life since they first met as lab partners. And at the same time, she wondered what she saw when she looked at him.

"I have something for you." Ferris reached into the pocket of his coat and pressed something small, round, and smooth into Hettie's palm. She opened her hand. It was a snail, its inward concentric swirls spiraling to the middle of its pearly iridescent shell. Its body and rubbery antennae appeared to be tucked inside its carapace.

With a smile, Hettie recalled the Saturday morning several years ago when Ferris took her to visit the fishmonger at St. George's Market. This had been one of Ferris's favorite activities before he began work at the zoo: he would request the entrails of the gutted fish and dissect the innards for snails and other live organisms in the fish's digestive tracts. At first, Hettie found Ferris's recreational pursuit to be odd and eccentric, but then after she agreed to meet him one morning at the market, she began to understand the pure satisfaction of this kind of scrutiny. On the cracked pavement in front of Ferris's building, they discovered a handful of shiny snails inside the intestines of the cod and tilefish. Each shell held a perfect spiral, and their rubbery antennae waved blindly in the air. Hettie remembered being amazed and delighted by the small creature's remarkable resilience—how it could go from being swallowed, traveling through the fish's digestive system, and eventually released from its bloody guts, and still be alive and breathing.

"From my special collection," he said, sounding nervous at her silence.

"Thank you, Ferris Poole," Hettie said finally, closing her fist around the shell and carefully stowing it in her coat pocket. "That's very kind of you."

"Remember everything that snail has been through," Ferris said with a grin.

"I'll take good care of him," she said. "I promise."

"I hope so," he said.

Hettie heaved herself to the other side of the wall and landed on her feet. Ferris followed.

"I should be getting home," Hettie said.

"Good night, Hettie Quin," he said. "Cheers."

Ferris gave her a soft peck on the cheek and Hettie watched as he made his way down the Antrim Road toward the tram stop. There was a subtle swagger in his step. A levity. An exultation. He tipped his tweed cap in her direction before he rounded the corner. Hettie chuckled to herself, as if she had just been told a good secret.

"Cheers," she said softly. "See you."

Hettie walked across the Antrim Road and then turned down the Whitewell Road. For the first time in a long time, she felt unburdened, light and buoyant as if her entire body might magically lift off the pavement and float above the neighbors' rooftops. She noticed that the tips of her ears and fingers were cold, almost numb, but yet she felt warm, like a furnace, and strangely alive. Farther down the street, about a half dozen neighborhood children frolicked in the falling snow. From a distance, Hettie could identify many of the children by the sounds of their voices: There was Johnny Gibson and Albert O'Brien. And Martha Reynolds and her older sister, Lizzie, who lived on one side of the Quins. Rodney Dawkins and his older brother, Jack, who lived on the next street over. And Lily Brown, who lived with her grandfather on the other side of Hettie and her mother. (Her parents had died of tuberculosis within three months of each other.) The children weaved in and out along the street, trying to catch snowflakes on their tongues. Their faces were aimed toward the slow-motion whirl of snow, their arms outstretched on either side of their bundled bodies, looking like an erratic formation of airplanes circling the night sky.

"I got one," Lily Brown yelled, her long chestnut braids flying from the wool rim of her bright orange cap. "I got one."

"Me too," Johnny Gibson said.

"Me too," two other children screamed in unison.

Their voices rose and fell, and rose and fell again. In her pocket, Hettie ran her finger over the smooth curve of the snail's shell. It felt as if the snail contained a store of electricity, a tangible shock. Across the street, Mr. Brown called for Lily; apparently it was nearing her bath time. Lily ran toward her grandfather's house. The other children loped through the snow. A car's engine rumbled over the rise that led to the

Antrim Road. Faint ringlets of smoke drifted up from several chimneys. Hettie unlocked the front door of her house. Its interior warmth mingled with the coldness outside.

"Hello," Hettie called. "Mum?"

There was no answer. Hettie walked down the darkened hallway and peered through the crack of Rose's bedroom door. There she found her mother asleep in bed, an Agatha Christie paperback splayed on her chest like a pitched tent. Rose hadn't changed out of her clothes and still wore her lace-up shoes and woolen stockings. Hettie walked to the side of her mother's bed and loosened the laces and slipped her shoes off. Then she untied the opaque floral scarf she was still wearing and gently slid it from Rose's neck. As Hettie pulled the blanket over her mother, Rose stirred.

"Hettie," she said. "Is that you?"

"Let's get you to bed, Mum."

"Where's Anna?" Rose said, her voice weighed down by sleep. "We mustn't be late for church. We can't be late."

"Shush," Hettie whispered. "Sleep."

"Write your father," she said, a quiet urgency underneath her drowsy words. "Tell him to come home. Tell him we need him."

Hettie folded the wool blanket over her mother and placed the tattered paperback on the bedside table. Rose's feathery inhales and exhales filled the room. She deposited her mother's shoes on the floor, next to her bed, and paused at the door and took in the melancholy sight of her sleeping mother, wondering how things could have unfolded to this moment where her father and Anna were no longer a part of their daily lives. How had things gone so wrong? Hettie soundlessly closed the door behind her and then sat in her usual spot at the kitchen table. Her mother's half-empty teacup sat on the tabletop; a tannic ring stained its porcelain interior. Hettie would wash it up later.

She retrieved the snail from her coat pocket and placed it next to her mother's cup. A bluish-gray iridescence reflected the overhead light.

The swirl was perfect, one circle traveling seamlessly into another. The snail's body was still hidden inside its shell. Hettie folded her arms on the table and laid her head on her arms. Her eyes felt heavy, her muscles stiff. After a few moments, she opened her eyes and stared at the shell and then closed her eyes again.

Outside, the children continued to play. Their lively voices supplied a sort of invisible embroidery to her half-dream state. Hettie's eyelids fluttered. Violet was sleeping in the Elephant House. There was the cry of a monkey. Ferris's steady gaze fell upon her. The swirl of snow spun down from the sky, a vortex of silver and darkness. And the smooth curve of the snail's shell. It was all there—and then it wasn't. The parrot in the aviary was calling again. *Who is that? Where have you been? Where are you going?*

Five

WHEN HETTIE RETURNED HOME FROM THE ZOO ONE EVENING in early March, her mother had laid out a single place setting at the kitchen table—an empty bowl, a cloth napkin, and a spoon. A note on the table read: *Bingo at social club, cabbage stew on stove, bread in the bread box, be home by half past seven. Mum.* Hettie was quietly pleased to see that Rose had gone out for the evening with a friend. It was a rare occurrence these days. On the kitchen table, her mother had also left a stamped letter for Hettie. The return address was *Liam Keegan, Newcastle.* It was the first letter he had sent since the Keegans moved there in early December. Hettie's hands shook slightly as she tore the envelope open.

Dearest Hettie,

We arrived safely in Newcastle, and we have been settling into the pace of life here. There is a beach that we hope to visit when the weather warms up in the late spring. My uncle's farm sits on two acres and he keeps horses, goats, and chickens. Even Maeve is helping out with the morning egg collection. She loves the animals.

Pa stayed behind in Belfast because the foreman at the factory couldn't guarantee that his job would be waiting if he left with us for a spell.

How's the zoo? And how's your brilliant charge? Is Violet staying out of trouble? Come & see us. We miss you. Particularly Maeve. Write soon.

Warmly,
Liam

A key jiggled in the front door before it pushed open. Rose stepped inside. Hettie folded up the letter, slipped it into the pocket of her cardigan, and flattened out the pages of the newspaper in front of her. Rose leaned through the kitchen door, still wearing her overcoat.

"You're home," her mother said.

"Did you win?" Hettie asked, glancing up from the newspaper.

"You know, a few games," she answered. "Did you eat something?"

Hettie nodded. "How did Edith do?" she asked.

"She wasn't there tonight," Rose said. "Her son and his family are visiting from Cornwall. They were lucky to get travel permits to come north. Alistair's working for his wife's father down there, managing his mining company."

Hettie remembered Alistair Curry from school. He had almost failed Latin and Anna had helped him with his translations of Caesar and his victories during the Gallic War. She remembered Anna talking about Alistair, how he had an acne problem that left his forehead a field of tiny scabs and how he had tried to kiss Anna during one lesson but she managed to push him away. This was long before Anna had begun dating Liam Keegan.

"How's that elephant of yours?" asked Rose. "What's her name again?"

"Violet. Her name is Violet," Hettie said, surprised by Rose's curiosity. It was the first time that she had expressed any interest in Violet. "She's even gained a wee bit of weight, despite the rationing."

"I'm assuming that's where you're spending all of your time these days."

Hettie nodded warily.

"Mr. Wright keeps you busy, does he?" Rose asked.

"He's charged me with—" Hettie lifted her eyes from the newspaper's front page to tell her mother more, but broke off as she realized that Rose was already walking down the hallway.

The illuminated crease under her bedroom door appeared, and then, within a few minutes, it was gone again. It was as if the two of them existed in separate spheres and somehow they were no longer related by blood. Instead of mother and daughter, they were merely acquaintances with little in common except their street address and surname. An ache lodged just below her collarbone, and Hettie pressed two fingers against the knot of pain and tried to rub it away. She attempted to convince herself that it was better this way, that she was free—untethered—and could come and go as she wished with little question or complaint from her mother. Hettie slipped Liam's letter from the pocket of her cardigan into her leather satchel and finished her now-cold meal in silence. As she rinsed out her bowl in the kitchen sink, Hettie promised herself she would visit the all-women boardinghouse on the Limestone Road and see if there might be any rooms available in May.

The following morning, Hettie, Ferris, Bobby Adair, and Daryl Griffiths were sitting in the canteen after a staff meeting, during which Mr. Wright had briefed them on the week's duties. The rest of the employees were already filtering through the double doors, the collective din of their voices receding from the canteen.

"We're going to hear the singer Stella Holliday Saturday night," Ferris said to Hettie, not quite meeting her eye. "You should join us."

"Aye," Daryl said, playfully slugging Hettie in the arm. "You need to come out. Have fun for once. You work too hard."

Hettie glanced at the stares of the young men around the table and then into the bottom of her teacup. The heater in the far corner of the canteen rattled and clacked before discharging a steamy hiss. A sudden itch surfaced on her earlobe. Hettie reached for her ear, pinching the soft pad of flesh. She looked up at the canteen's pass-through, thinking she might see Eliza Crowley, but she didn't see her anywhere.

"Come on," Ferris said. "You *have* to say yes this time."

Hettie looked up at him, and Ferris finally looked at her, giving her his best smile.

"All right," Hettie said reluctantly. "Okay."

"See, I knew she'd eventually come around," Ferris said, winking at Daryl and Bobby. "What did I tell ya?"

The four of them got up from the table and carried their empty cups to the pass-through. Eliza appeared from the rear of the building, the screen door smacking behind her.

"It will be a brilliant time," Ferris said to Hettie. "I promise."

"Cheers," Eliza said, placing their cups in the porcelain basin.

Ferris and Bobby exchanged glances.

"Aye," Bobby said, a blush moving into his round cheeks. "We're all going to hear Stella Holliday on Saturday night—"

Eliza glanced over at Hettie. Her chin had healed up, and the spot where she had stitches was no longer immediately noticeable, but if you looked closely, you could see the slightly raised scars on the tip of her chin.

"I'm supposed to watch my younger sisters, but let me ask my mum."

"Terrific," Bobby said.

"You going, too?" Eliza asked Hettie.

"She is," Ferris answered for her.

Hettie handed Eliza her teacup. Their fingertips grazed each other's, and Eliza smiled. Hettie zipped up her work coat and wrapped her father's scarf around her neck.

"Off to the camels," Hettie said.

"To the penguins," Ferris said.

The four zookeepers pushed through the double doors and went their separate ways.

On Saturday night, Hettie waited in front of the Floral Hall while the buoyant notes of the big band floated through the oversize doors. Though the hall had been opened five years, Hettie had attended only a handful of dances there while Anna had always been a regular at the popular hall. Her sister had been an elegant dancer who attracted the attention of others as she glided across the dance floor with her partners throughout any given evening. This was how she had met Liam Keegan on a crisp summer night, and the two of them became an item on the dance floor, drawing the stares of strangers with their fluid, graceful movements and undeniable chemistry.

Flutters of nervousness batted in Hettie's stomach as she continued to wait for her friends. Clutches of well-dressed individuals—young and old, country people and city people—made their way up the steep slope from the tram stop on the Antrim Road. Even though it was early March, traces of spring pulsed along the outer rim of the evening air. Her nervousness seemed to transform into excitement: She couldn't remember the last time she had heard a live band and gone out dancing. Months and months ago. Hettie tapped her foot in time with the music. Trumpets, clarinets, and flutes converged into one syncopated sound, its forceful rhythms riding into the night and generating an infectious energy all its own.

"Hettie," someone said from behind her. "Is that you?"

She turned around, and didn't quite know how to feel when she saw that it was Samuel Greene. He looked different from the last time she had seen him at St. George's Market in the autumn. Like he was taller, or older, or a combination of the two. He wore a navy suit, a pressed white button-down, and a black tie. Fresh comb marks lined his oiled brown hair. When he smiled, his white, square teeth almost glowed. Instead of stepping out of a butcher shop, he looked as if he had just left a formal wedding party or an important business meeting.

"Samuel Greene," Hettie said. "Good to see you."

"You too," he said. "I was hoping we would run into each other again."

He reached for her hand, leaning forward and placing a surprising kiss on the top of it. Hettie awkwardly drew her hand back.

"Are you still working with your father at St. George's?" she asked.

"I'm with the police now," he said, running his fingers through the sleek side of his neatly coiffed hair. "Training at the RUC depot in Enniskillen, but the sergeant says that I've been assigned to a special branch due to my mental sharpness and expert marksmanship skills. I'm at the top of my class."

"That's grand," Hettie said. "Your father must be proud."

"It took him a while to get used to the idea of me leaving the shop," Samuel admitted, "but when he discovered that I scored such high marks on the entrance exam, he became more supportive."

Hettie noticed a tiny piece of white tissue, like a rosebud, stuck to the side of Samuel's neck, just above his shirt collar. For a moment she wanted to reach out and touch it, tell Samuel that it was there, but she didn't. He patted the pocket of his jacket and retrieved a lighter and a package of cigarettes with the familiar logo of the brawny sailor emblazoned on its side. He offered one to Hettie. She shook her head no.

"I'm full-time now," she said after a short pause. "I'm taking care of a young elephant named Violet."

"Always knew you'd be up to brilliant things one day, Hettie Quin," Samuel said, lighting his own cigarette and releasing a trail of smoke from the corner of his mouth. "Going to hear Stella tonight, are you?"

Hettie nodded. "Waiting for a few friends."

"Excellent," Samuel said, following the group of young men he had arrived with. "Promise me that you'll save me at least one dance, will you?"

Hettie nodded again.

"Brilliant," Samuel said. "Cheers. See you inside."

"Cheers."

A subtle percolation of elation rose in her chest. Perhaps Samuel Greene was a finer young man than she had originally judged him to be. Hettie smoothed out the front of her double-breasted coat. It was light blue with leather buttons, and had been Anna's. Underneath the coat, she also wore one of Anna's dresses, a salmon wool frock with an empire line and a grosgrain bow punctuating its high waist. Rose had told Hettie more than once that the dress fit her perfectly and Anna would have loved to know that she was wearing it to a concert at the Floral Hall; until tonight, she had resisted. Hettie plucked pills of wool from the front of the skirt and then smoothed it out with her hand again. For a moment, she felt just as pretty as her sister had been.

But then, just as quickly, she felt ugly and awkward. The satin slip of the dress stuck to her wool stockings, producing starbursts of static electricity. Hettie had borrowed a tube of her mother's lipstick without asking, slipping it into her coat pocket before leaving the house, and then applied it in the bathroom of the women's locker room at the zoo before walking up the hill to the dance hall. Now the lipstick felt like clumsy paint on her lips. Instead of enhancing her appearance, the reddish-brown smear on her mouth only made her feel like a sad version of someone else.

Hettie stood a little straighter, determined to enjoy herself. *Live a little, you know*, she heard Anna say in her mind. *It'll do you some good.*

More stars appeared above the Belfast Lough. A ship bellowed its horn. Despite the blackout regulations, the lighthouse on the Lough still swiveled its beacon of illumination so incoming cargo ships and freighters could make a safe passage through the shallow waters and rocky coastlines of the harbor. From where she stood at the Floral Hall, Hettie could see the lighthouse on the distant point, its predictable revolutions of light circling across the expansive sky. She reached into her small handbag and retrieved a tissue, dabbing the corners of her mouth before crumpling it up and tucking it inside her purse again. Finally, she spotted Ferris walking up the steady rise with Jack Fleming, Bobby Adair, and Daryl Griffiths behind him. Hettie wondered where Eliza Crowley was.

"Sorry we're late," Ferris said, his breath ragged.

Each of the young men wore a pair of woolen trousers and a blazer over a button-down shirt. A wrinkled red bandanna peeked out from the breast pocket of Bobby's coat. Ferris wore an old navy-and-maroon-striped tie from his former school. Daryl's shirt was rumpled and untucked. The small band of them looked more like lonely boys on leave from boarding school than fellow zookeepers who worked with her on a daily basis. Ferris gave Hettie a hug and then a peck on her cheek. The side of his neck smelled of cologne—a pungent cross between anise and pine trees. It was a heady aroma, but he had used so much it made her gag slightly.

"Has the show started yet?" Bobby said, glancing toward the entrance.

They stepped inside. The warm air of the hall's interior pushed at Hettie's face as the brisk breeze from outside fingered her shoulders. The front foyer was painted a tangerine orange, as if the walls held their own particular brand of sunshine. As Hettie remembered, the dance hall was vibrant with its cerulean-blue walls. Gold-leaf trim trailed along the top edge of the immense room. Three elaborate chandeliers hung from the high ceiling. Since her last visit over a year ago, blackout blinds had been fitted onto all the plate-glass windows that lined the art deco building, with patches of brown paper and crisscrosses of industrial tape concealing any potential leaks of artificial light.

They paid the admission to an elderly couple behind a card table with a roll of blue tickets and a tin box. Along one side of the hall, white cloths were draped over a series of circular tables. Simple arrangements of red and white carnations sat at the center of each one. Schoolgirls stood behind one of the tables, selling glasses of punch and bottles of Club Orange and lemonade and packets of biscuits and crisps. Already the ballroom was halfway full. Hettie scanned the room for familiar faces, but didn't see anyone she knew. A prickle of anxiety traveled up her throat. She coughed into her fist, praying the discomfort wouldn't mount into an extended coughing fit. Hettie glanced around the dance hall again. There, standing next to one of the tables, she spotted Samuel amid his circle of friends. They smoked cigarettes, chuckled, and whispered to each other. She noticed that Samuel was staring at her. As their eyes locked, he lifted his glass in her direction with a cheeky grin. Hettie turned away, somewhat flustered.

"Let me take your coat," Ferris offered.

"Thank you, but I think I'll keep it," Hettie said, draping it on the back of a chair.

"Pretty frock, Hettie," Ferris said with a grin.

"My—" She stopped herself. "It's a hand-me-down."

"Looks like it was made for you," he said appreciatively. "Something to drink?"

"A Club Orange would be lovely, please."

"Yes, ma'am."

Ferris made his way across the dance floor. As she waited for him, Hettie found herself hoping that Samuel would notice her standing alone and come over so they could resume their conversation. She could tell him how well she was doing in her job. Despite the rationing, Violet had gained about eighty pounds—and Samuel would be impressed by her husbandry skills, particularly during such challenging times. She was more than the first female zookeeper at the Bellevue Zoo; she was a natural when it came to animals—and she was being paid a reasonable salary, not quite equal to the other zookeepers', but a good salary nonetheless. Compared to the other girls from her school who were already married and having their first or second children, she was making something of herself. And Hettie wanted to ask Samuel about his older brother, Daniel. She had remembered that he played sports, too—football—and had traveled overseas to Europe before the war started. She had heard that he had enlisted with the Royal Air Force over a year ago and was now flying fighter planes somewhere in northern Africa.

"Hey, Hettie."

She turned around to find Eliza Crowley standing next to her.

"Eliza," Hettie said, smiling. "There you are. I was looking for you."

Eliza wore a black-and-white-polka-dot dress with a bow tied at her narrow waist. The tightness of the satiny fabric accentuated her large breasts. A soft pink rouge colored her cheeks and a light blue eyeshadow fanned out from the corners of her eyes. Her flame-like curls tumbled down onto her shoulders. In the dim light of the dance hall, Hettie couldn't see the scar on her chin.

Eliza tapped a cigarette out of a package and lit it in the corner of her mouth before releasing a long exhale, like the extended note of a song. It was the first time Hettie had ever seen Eliza smoke.

"Convinced my older brother to babysit," she said. "He owes me, you know."

"You look beautiful," Hettie said.

"I like your frock, too," Eliza said, her eyes traveling from Hettie's feet to the top of her head, "but that lipstick looks wretched. Come with me."

Eliza took her hand and led Hettie toward the cloakroom crowded with young women. Eliza's thin fingers felt cold between Hettie's. The narrow room was stuffy and smelled of floral perfume and cigarette smoke. Several girls jockeyed for space in front of the rectangular mirror on the far wall. An elbow nudged into Hettie's side. There was warm breath against her neck. She took a step closer to Eliza.

"Here," Eliza said, "give me your mouth."

Hettie turned toward Eliza, squaring her shoulders and doing her best to stand up straight and still. Eliza moistened a tissue with her own spit and then wiped it against Hettie's lips. Her breath smelled of garlic and cigarettes, and Hettie had to fight against the instinct to wrinkle her nose.

"Where did you find this *unfortunate* color?" Eliza said.

"It's my mother's."

"Rule number one," Eliza said, winking at Hettie. "Never wear your mother's lipstick."

She wiped Hettie's lips once more before fishing out a couple of tubes of lipstick from her purse.

"Rule number two: Say yes to every dance," Eliza said, reaching for Hettie's hand. "Here."

Hettie spread out her hand, like a starfish. Women crowded around them. A mist of perfume grazed Hettie's cheek. The high-pitched laughter of young women felt like it held sharp edges. Eliza drew three marks of lipstick on Hettie's hand: a fuchsia pink, a vibrant red, and a deeper shade of red.

"Number three: Whenever a young man tells you a joke, laugh, even if it's daft," Eliza said, pointing to the vibrant red. "This one. It will make you look sophisticated, more mature."

An unfamiliar joy stirred in Hettie as Eliza gently pinched the rounded point of her chin, stared intently into her eyes, and carefully shaded in Hettie's lips.

"Press your lips together like this."

Eliza slowly rubbed her lips together and plucked them apart. Hettie mimicked the movement of her mouth.

"Beautiful," Eliza said, with a smile of victory. "Look for yourself."

Hettie weaved her way through the throng of girls and studied her own reflection in a corner of the mirror. Eliza was right: She looked much better with this shade of lipstick. Her eyes looked a little brighter and her freckled complexion glowed. It was as if she had changed her entire outfit. Instead of feeling frumpy and spinster-like, she felt beautiful and tall and assured, as if she had grown at least two inches in the last few minutes.

When Hettie returned to Eliza, effusive with gratitude, she was applying her own lipstick, a soft pink, and waved away Hettie's attention.

"What are friends for?" Eliza said, beaming. "Ready?"

Hettie nodded, and Eliza threaded her arm through Hettie's and together they returned to Ferris. He handed two bottles of Club Orange to Hettie and Eliza, paper straws bobbing in their narrow glass necks. The soda's sweetness made Hettie's cheeks smart and picked up the corners of her mouth.

"Eliza," Ferris said. "Look at you."

"Good evening, Mr. Poole," she said.

"You dress up nice."

"Why, thank you."

Suddenly, a wave of jealousy and shame rolled through Hettie. She wondered if Ferris found Eliza more beautiful than her. Hettie pressed her lips together and gently smacked them apart again. Eliza winked at her. The bandleader, clad in a black-and-white tuxedo, took his position in front of the big band, tapping his baton against a music stand. The chandelier lights were dimmed further, and a spotlight was thrown on the bandleader. Another man, also dressed in a tuxedo, approached the microphone that stood to the left side of the elevated stage. He tapped the head of the microphone, his touch amplifying throughout the hall.

"Ladies and gentlemen," he said, hitting the microphone's head again. "Your attention, please."

The voices of the crowd softened.

"I'm pleased to introduce Bert Ambrose and his magnificent orchestra, along with Stella Holliday," he said. "They are on tour—and we're fortunate to have them in Belfast tonight."

Ambrose dramatically raised his hands and launched into the first number. From where she'd been hidden in the wings of the stage, Stella Holliday stepped into the spotlight. She wore a shimmering chartreuse dress, with formal white gloves stretching up her arms. Her wavy sienna hair cascaded onto her shoulders. Her lashes were long, her lips a brilliant red. Hettie was startled and mesmerized by the brightness of Stella Holliday's physical presence; she had never taken in a woman who was so elegant and arresting at once.

Hettie glanced over at Eliza. She was already on the dance floor with a boy Hettie didn't recognize, his arms wrapped around her thin waist, her auburn locks flying from her diminutive shoulders. Other couples moved onto the floor, and Hettie surveyed the crowd again for Samuel. She didn't see him anywhere. As the music's tempo picked up, more dancers joined in.

"Shall we?" Ferris asked.

"All right," Hettie said, feeling relieved that she wouldn't be left alone on the periphery of the dance floor, as she noticed that Samuel Greene had already found himself another partner for the first song of the evening.

Ferris took her soda and placed it on a table.

"I haven't danced in a long time," she warned.

Ferris laughed. "Just like riding a bike, you'll see."

He took her hand and led Hettie through the crowd of whirling couples. Hettie closed her eyes and felt the thrumming beats of the bass and the shiny sounds of the trumpets inside her chest. She opened her eyes. Ferris stepped on her toe as he attempted to lead her.

"Sorry," he said. "It's been a wee bit since I danced, too."

He held her hand more tightly and stared down at their feet.

"Let's begin again," he said. "Follow me. Quick, quick. Slow, slow."

Ferris took two short steps and then slid his feet together. This time, Hettie stepped on his foot.

"Sorry," she said. "I'm not very good at following."

"We can do this," he said, his wide grin twitching with a hint of panic. "Again."

This time, Hettie was able to follow as if there were a magnetic force somehow guiding the movements of their feet. As they made their way around the floor, Ferris smiled at her.

"See, I told you."

Before Hettie knew it, they were a part of the collective movement of the dance floor, like a murmuration of a large flock of swallows circling in one synchronized motion. For a moment, she felt as if she were being carried away by something, something that she couldn't exactly name. Ferris guided her around the floor until the number came to an end.

"Another," Ferris said, extending his hand to Hettie.

She felt pleased that she had managed to find her own feet on the dance floor, and that she wasn't as clumsy as she'd thought she would be. Ferris was right: It was like riding a bike, how one's muscle memory returned with very little thought. Instead of requiring effort, it was fluid and easy, producing an unexpected freedom and happiness. Hettie laughed to herself as she gripped Ferris's sturdy hand. Together they danced five numbers in a row before taking a break. As she sat down to watch the others and Ferris went to get her a drink, Hettie felt both energized and fatigued. She noticed Eliza dancing with a man on the other side of the floor; he was older and dressed in a pinstriped suit. A shadow of whiskers covered his chin and lower cheeks. Eliza threw back her head and laughed. Hettie recognized the tune: "Anything Goes."

Ferris returned with two cups of punch. "Thirsty?" Ferris asked, offering Hettie one of the cups.

She took it and drank it down greedily. "Thank you," she said after she had finished.

Hettie looked around and felt the steady force of her heartbeat as she spotted Samuel walking toward them. A cigarette was tucked be-hind one of his ears.

"Looking sharp out there," Samuel said to Ferris.

"Do I know you from somewhere?" Ferris asked.

"I was a class ahead of you at the Academy," he said. "You don't remember me? Samuel Greene."

"Samuel, right," Ferris said absently. "Of course."

"You didn't complete the last form, did you?"

"No," said Ferris, somewhat defensively. "I took a job with the zoo instead—"

"I'm working with a special division of the RUC."

"Sounds important."

"Sure beats enlistment."

For a moment, Hettie wanted to disappear as Samuel and Ferris made small talk: What would they think if they knew that she was attracted to both of them in different ways, but couldn't make up her mind who she had stronger feelings for? Would the two men think of her differently? Ferris was certainly more kind and thoughtful, but she found Samuel more attractive and charming despite what had taken place between the two of them at the cinema several months ago. Hettie willed herself to stay calm. After all, this was what she imagined Eliza would advise her to do in this type of situation: *Never let them know what you're feeling.* The problem was that Hettie didn't know exactly what she was feeling herself. The band launched into another number, "Put Your Arms Around Me, Honey," with its slower, swing-set tempo. The couples swayed more closely together on the dance floor.

"What do you say, Ferris," Samuel said. "Let me dance one with Hettie."

Ferris looked up at her for a second, and furrows deepened along his forehead. "Be my guest."

Samuel extended his hand, and Hettie glanced uneasily at Ferris.

"Go ahead, Hettie," Ferris said with more conviction.

Samuel took her hand and led her out to the middle of the crowd. Stella Holliday sang: *Put your arms around me, Honey, hold me tight.* Her sweet voice reached up to the tiered chandeliers.

"Who's the lover boy?" Samuel asked, placing a hand on her hip.

"He's not my boyfriend," Hettie said quickly, then cursed herself for being so obvious. "We work together at the zoo."

"What's he in charge of?"

"The hyenas, penguins, and sea lions," she said, "but we help each other with everything."

"I hear Mr. Wright is quite the character," he said. "That he enjoys a good tussle with the lions."

"Where did you hear that?"

"I have my sources," Samuel said with a wink.

"Well, he was a lion tamer with the circus before he came to Bellevue," Hettie said. "Mr. Christie is lucky to have him. He's remarkable with the animals."

Samuel didn't reply as he shifted his attention to the subtle movements of their feet. Hettie found it easier to follow his lead than Ferris's; somehow her feet responded to his agile steps as he guided her around the crowded dance floor. His hand felt like worn velvet in hers. Samuel moved in more closely. His pant leg brushed against the fabric of her sister's dress. His cologne reminded her of the scents of freshly chopped wood and worn leather. It reminded her of her father. She leaned her cheek against Samuel's shoulder and closed her eyes.

At the same time, Stella Holliday's song transformed the vast room into something warm and intimate. Her voice lit up the air. Hettie imagined walking along a serpentine path of soft cushions, and somewhere, toward the end, she expected that she would find her sister. After the number, the band ceased playing. Bert Ambrose announced that Stella Holliday and the band would be taking a short break between sets. Samuel's gaze held Hettie's for a protracted moment. She felt a temporary storm on her senses, with his attention being at the center of it.

"How about some fresh air?" he asked, his voice intentionally casual.

A buzz shuddered down her forearm and into the palm of her hand, exactly where Samuel was holding it. "Lovely," she had said before she knew it.

Samuel folded his fingers into Hettie's and led her outside. Several band members stood on the front steps of the Floral Hall, smoking cigarettes and chatting. Stella Holliday, in her elegant, floor-length dress, its silky fabric hugging the robust curves of her body, also stood outside. She laughed with one of the band members.

"There she is," Samuel whispered to Hettie. "Everyone loves her."

Stella Holliday laughed again, lifting her pale chin and placing the cigarette between her red lips. Her presence radiated a glow, and the band members were like moths all trying to gather closer to her. Samuel retrieved his package of cigarettes and offered one to Hettie.

"Thanks," she said, accepting a cigarette this time.

Samuel placed the cigarette between her lips, and she leaned into him as he lit it with a sterling silver lighter. Though Hettie rarely smoked, she managed to inhale and exhale with ease, and the harsh taste of nicotine bloomed in her mouth. After lighting his own cigarette, Samuel clicked the hinged cap of his lighter shut with one swift motion of his wrist. He took a deep inhale and smiled at Hettie. Thin threads of smoke lifted up in front of her face.

"You should know better than saying such off-color comments about my husband," Stella Holliday was saying, tapping her cigarette ashes onto the pavement. "He works for the government, you know. He could have you arrested." The evening breeze scattered the powdery residue into the darkness.

"Her husband is an important Irish diplomat in Rome," Samuel whispered to Hettie. "They travel all over the world. Or they did, before the war."

Hettie stole one more glance at Stella Holliday as she took another draw of the cigarette. The deliberate curves of her body resembled the smooth, perfect lines of a statue sculpted by an Italian artist from another time and place. Her dress gave off an otherworldly shimmer. She glanced down at her own dress; even though it was Anna's, it still felt childish and drab next to the cosmopolitan sophistication of Stella Holliday. Hettie wondered how old Stella was and what age she had been when she and her husband had married, and if she had given birth to any children.

"Isn't she something," Samuel remarked.

Hettie nodded. The growl of a bear could be heard in the distance. Hettie knew it was probably Andy, standing up on his hind legs in his enclosure not far from the foot of the hill.

"The beasts are out tonight," said one of the band members with a snicker.

"I prefer the beasts, you know," Stella said, laughing softly and then tossing her cigarette onto the pavement and grinding out the ambers with the heel of her shoe. "We all know animals are more predictable than men." She laughed again, and the band members joined in.

"Five more minutes, Malcolm," called a man from the dance hall.

"Be right there," one of the band members said. "Ready for the next set, Stella?"

"What an exceptional night," she said, staring out at the darkened landscape of the city and its port. "Belfast will always be my favorite city."

A cool breeze swept across the veranda. Hettie wrapped her hands around herself, chafing her arms to warm them up. Samuel moved suddenly and for a moment she thought he was going to offer her his jacket. But he just rooted through the pockets of his blazer, producing a scrap of paper and a ballpoint pen.

"Mrs. Holliday," Samuel said, stepping toward her. "Can I have your autograph?"

"My autograph?" she scoffed. "What a ridiculous request!"

"You're famous," Samuel said, with a burst of charm. "Everyone knows you."

"I wouldn't go that far."

Stella Holliday took the piece of paper and pen from Samuel, and scribbled her name in two sweeping loops.

"Here you go, young man," she said. "Now scram and enjoy the rest of your evening."

"Thank you," Samuel said, taking her hand and kissing it briefly, making her laugh. "Thank you very much, Mrs. Holliday."

"Stella!" yelled the man at the door again.

The singer disappeared into the hall.

"Look at this," Samuel said, staring down at the autograph. "I'll fetch a lot for this, particularly in Dublin."

"You're not going to keep it?"

"Of course not," Samuel said. "Why would I want to keep it when I could exchange it for chocolate or coffee on the black market?"

Notes of music drifted through the doors. Hettie had heard that smuggling between Northern Ireland and Ireland had become epidemic—everything from butter, tea, coffee, and chocolates to engagement rings and nylons. But she'd never known for certain until now.

"Don't pretend like you don't know about the black market," Samuel said. "How are we supposed to get anything up here—"

"But you work for the police," she said. "Won't it jeopardize your position?"

He gave a derisive laugh. "You'd be surprised who's doing what around here."

The band was now performing at full swing again. Stella Holliday's voice rose above the swelling rhythms.

"Shall we?" Samuel asked, offering his arm to her.

Hettie intertwined her arm with his, and together they walked up the steps of the Floral Hall. The dance floor was already crowded again, and she couldn't see Ferris or Eliza anywhere. But a moment later, as Samuel leaned into her and pulled her body into his, she no longer cared where her friends were. He softly hummed along with the music.

For a second, she was reminded of Thomas and his whistling around the house, how his high-pitched notes used to stitch the day-to-day atmosphere of their home. Hettie let herself sink farther into Samuel's arms.

"May I?" Ferris interrupted, startling her and making her blush that he had seen her with Samuel.

"Just one dance," Samuel said, stepping away from Hettie. "Then she's mine again," he added with a wink.

Stella Holliday and the band seamlessly moved into the next number. Ferris guided Hettie away from Samuel in one swift motion. When they started dancing, his tight grip pinched her fingers.

"Ouch, Ferris," she said. "You're hurting me."

"Where did you go? I couldn't find you." He looked mutinous, and a bolt of defiance made Hettie lift her chin and meet his eye.

"We met Stella Holliday."

"You talked to her?"

"Samuel introduced himself and asked for her autograph."

"He's always in the right place at the right time, that Samuel Greene."

Hettie didn't mention anything about how Samuel had said he was planning to sell Stella Holliday's signature on the black market. She didn't think Ferris would approve. The tempo of the next song was slower, and the couples on the floor whirled in measured circles as Stella crooned. Near the front of the stage, Hettie spotted Samuel with a tall, fair-skinned woman clad in a form-fitting lavender dress. Her wavy blond hair flowed down between her narrow shoulders. Samuel held her close and whispered into her hair. The young woman's cheek rested against the side of his face. Envy sliced through Hettie.

At first, she didn't recognize the young woman and wondered if she was from Belfast or if she had traveled from outside the city, perhaps from one of the smaller towns farther north or west. This particular show with Stella Holliday was an event, after all, and people traveled far distances for such a performance. Then, as Hettie took a longer look, she realized that the young woman dancing with Samuel Greene was Colleen White from school. They had been in the same class together for a year when they read the great novels by Dickens, Hardy, the Brontë sisters, and Jane Austen. Throughout the class, Colleen had always provided the right answers for their teacher, Mr. Swann, when he asked questions about specific characters' conflicts and motivations, about plot, and about overarching themes related to gender, class, and religion. Colleen never had a shortage of insightful commentary about the classic novels and their famous characters and their memorable motivations, whereas Hettie's thoughts and words often got caught somewhere up in her brain, where they remained until she took the time to set a pen to paper and arrange her ideas in some sort of coherent and understandable manner. Now Samuel stared up at Stella Holliday onstage before returning his gaze to Colleen White.

Hettie shifted her attention to the overhead chandelier, with its four tiers of crystals, looking like a cloud of tears. She tried to locate the buoyancy of Stella Holliday's voice again, but it was as if her voice were no longer there—that it had somehow dissolved—even though Hettie could, of course, hear her as she sang the final refrain of the song. As the band concluded the number, the audience clapped and whistled and demanded another. Despite the fact that Hettie had just been standing outside, she felt hot and uncomfortable.

"One more?" Ferris asked.

Before she could answer, the band commenced the high-spirited "Exactly Like You."

"I need to use the loo," Hettie muttered, and dashed off before Ferris could respond.

As she arrived at the entrance of the cloakroom, Hettie's eyes were drawn to Samuel and Colleen again. The couple danced with grace and self-possession, as if they had danced to this exact number many times before. On the illuminated stage, Stella Holliday stood in her

glittery yellow-green gown, her full-length-gloved arms and hands extended out on either side of her body like a pair of wings, as if she might
take flight at any second and soar amid the trio of chandeliers and out
the double doors of the Floral Hall, down the steep, wooded slope of
the Cavehill, above the slumbering animals of the zoo, and over the
darkened buildings of the city and the industrial docks before gliding
over the Belfast Lough and into the blackness of the Irish Sea. Hettie
believed that Stella Holliday could go anywhere she wanted to, even
though she still stood onstage with her outstretched arms in front of the
stand-up microphone.

The cloakroom was crowded and musty. There was a line for the
three stalls, but it was difficult to tell who was waiting for the loo and
who was vying for a coveted spot in front of the mirror. Girls handed
lit cigarettes back and forth. A flask was passed overhead. There was
a harsh cackle. Hettie searched the room for Eliza, but didn't see her
anywhere. She pulled at the neck of her sister's dress. Suddenly, it felt
tighter. After waiting her turn, Hettie returned to Ferris on the perimeter of the dance floor.

"Here," he said, handing her another cup of punch.

Ferris leaned against Hettie and loosely draped his arm across her
back. Hettie stood more stiffly as Samuel and Colleen continued to
dance near the stage. The trumpet section joined the melody, standing
up from their chairs and swinging their flared brass mouths in time
with the music. Despite the accelerated tempo, Colleen continued to
rest her head on Samuel's shoulder. It looked as if they were caught
inside the invisible sphere of their own story where no other characters
existed; there was no other plot except for their unexpected meeting
and instantaneous mutual admiration. Hettie swallowed the rest of her
punch in a few swift gulps. A pain near her right temple started to
throb. Hettie glanced at the clock that hung over the main entrance of
the hall. The gilded hands read ten o'clock. It was getting late, and Hettie's thoughts turned to the early morning she would have the next day.

Despite everything, Rose and Hettie regularly attended the eight fifteen Sunday service at the Carnmoney Parish. Ever since Anna's death, Rose had preferred it this way, because there were always fewer congregants in attendance at the earlier service, making for fewer chances for someone to mention Anna or ask about Thomas and his whereabouts.

"Mr. Wright's here," Ferris shouted over the music.

"Where?" Hettie asked, her attention still fixed on Colleen and Samuel.

"Over there," Ferris said, pointing across the room. "Look."

Hettie peered across the dimly lit hall. At first, she found herself looking for Mr. Wright in his familiar zoo uniform with his red double-breasted coat and black jodhpurs. Instead, here on the dance floor of the Floral Hall, Mr. Wright looked like another person altogether, like a distant brother who might have flown in from Zurich or Rome for a lavish ball or an urgent business matter. He was dressed in a blue serge suit with a yellow bow tie. Instead of wearing his usual fedora, his chestnut hair was slicked back, all gloss and shine. A young woman was on his arm. She wore an orange floral dress that dropped to her knees and matching high heels. A stack of copper ringlets was elegantly piled on top of her head, and she wore bright red lipstick.

"Mr. Wright," Ferris said, waving a hand over his head. "Mr. Wright."

Despite the loud music, Ferris managed to catch their boss's attention. Mr. Wright marched across the floor as if he were leading a parade, the woman staying in step right behind him. When he arrived where they stood, Mr. Wright broke into a smile, and a gleam flickered in his eyes. Hettie felt like it was the first time he was truly pleased to see her.

"Well, look who we have here," Mr. Wright said, vigorously shaking Ferris's hand and then turning to Hettie. He grasped her hand, crushing her fingers a bit, and she had to work not to wince at the pressure. After he released it, Hettie shook her hand out by her side.

"I thought I spotted Jack Fleming and Bobby Adair earlier," he said.

"They're around here somewhere," Ferris said, surveying the crowd.

"And I ran into Eliza Crowley on our way in," he said. "She was just leaving. It looked like she had found herself a respectable fella."

Eliza left already? Hettie thought with a dart of annoyance.

"This is Agnes Berns," Mr. Wright said, motioning to the woman at his side. "She works at Copeland's linen mill off the Shankill Road. Ferris and Hettie work with me at Bellevue. They take care of some of my animals."

"How lovely," Agnes said. "Frank speaks so highly of the zoo—and his people."

It took Hettie a few seconds to understand whom Agnes was referring to, because it was the first time she had ever heard someone call Mr. Wright by his first name. At the zoo, Mr. Wright was always Mr. Wright.

"Agnes hasn't made it up to the zoo yet," he said. "Hettie here takes care of our new young elephant."

"How wonderful," Agnes said. "I remember reading about her in the newspaper. She sounds like quite the elephant."

"She is," Hettie said, a warmth spreading in her chest. "She's remarkable."

Mr. Wright moved his gaze to the bobbing sea of dancers on the floor.

"Such an important job for a young woman," Agnes added.

Ferris winked at Hettie, who smiled with delight. Without saying another word, Mr. Wright and Agnes slipped into the continuous movement of dancers. Once again, Mr. Wright surprised Hettie: He was a very good dancer. He led Agnes across the polished floor, and the other couples parted for the impressive pair. For a moment, it felt as though the glow of the spotlight rested on Mr. Wright and Agnes rather than on Stella Holliday.

"Did you know he could dance?" Hettie asked Ferris.

"I had no bloody idea," Ferris said, his arms crossed over his chest and a grin spread across his face. "Look at him."

The couple twirled in fluid, measured circles, their feet sliding together and apart at exactly the right beats. Mr. Wright lifted his hand up in the air and Agnes traveled under the arc of his arm before effortlessly landing into his sturdy embrace.

"There's a lot more to Mr. Wright than what we know," said Ferris enigmatically.

"What do you mean?"

"He's a man who carries a lot of unspoken stories," Ferris said. "Doesn't he strike you that way?"

Hettie nodded in agreement. She had never thought of Mr. Wright's aloofness in these terms, but in some ways, it seemed as if Mr. Wright might be more like her father than Hettie had first recognized, that he wasn't the type of man to reveal his true character to the people around him.

The song ended, and the band and Stella Holliday segued into another upbeat tune. The dancing pairs whirled across the floor with more distinctive, quick movements—and Mr. Wright and Agnes Berns became a part of the collective pulse of the crowd. Hettie touched her lips, remembering the red shade of lipstick that Eliza had applied earlier. She wondered if it still looked all right, and then wondered where Eliza had gone with the gentleman. The young woman on the other side of Ferris nodded toward the dance floor and extended her arm for him. He glanced over at Hettie.

"Go ahead," she said. "It's all right."

Ferris nodded toward one of the other young men standing on the floor's perimeter, suggesting that Hettie find herself a partner, too.

Then she felt a tug on her elbow and turned around, pleased to be confronted with Samuel Greene. But then her smile faltered. His ruddy complexion glistened and his slightly bloodshot eyes looked as if he had just been weeping uncontrollably. Samuel leaned into her and whispered in her ear. She smelled whiskey on his breath. His words lost their edges underneath the music. Colleen White stood next to him, swaying, with a vague expression on her face, her vacant eyes seemingly fixed on some indiscernible point on the other side of the hall.

Samuel grabbed Hettie's hand. He temporarily lost his balance, one foot fumbling over the other, but then regained his composure as he led her, stumbling, to the front entrance. His palm felt warm and soft in hers. The nocturnal air pressed against her cheeks as Samuel started down the slope in the direction of the zoo.

"Where are we going?"

"I want a tour of your zoo," he said. "A formal introduction to your elephant."

"What about Colleen White?"

"She won't miss me," Samuel responded. "I promise you."

Samuel gripped Hettie's hand more tightly as they continued down the hill. The song of Stella Holliday faded behind them. Hettie felt slightly rattled and unsure about walking down to the zoo with Samuel. He adjusted his grip and threaded his fingers in between hers.

"Hettie Quin, Belfast's first female zookeeper," he said proudly. "It has a good ring, don't you think?"

Hettie managed to find more buoyancy in her step. Samuel flashed his familiar smile. She recalled Anna's advice—*Live a little, you know. Have some fun.* Perhaps this wasn't such a bad idea after all. Even though the temperature had dropped, Hettie no longer felt cold. Then she realized that she had left behind Anna's coat hanging on one of the chairs in the dance hall. She cursed silently and made a mental note to fetch it afterward; her leather wallet was tucked inside the deep pocket of the coat. Rose would never forgive her if she lost Anna's winter coat that her sister used to wear to church when they went together as a family on Sunday mornings.

Samuel and Hettie reached the pathway that circled toward the sea lions, the aviary, and the polar bears. One of the sea lions released a whining peal and then flapped his clumsy flippers together. A flock of parrots squawked, their dazzling green feathers hidden within the shadows of the aviary. One of the birds repeated: *Good night. Good night. Good night to you.*

"Good night to you, too," Samuel said, saluting the parrots.

The carpet of stars brightened the sky. Twigs and dead leaves crunched underneath their feet. For a moment, Hettie forgot about Colleen White, Ferris Poole, Mr. Wright, Agnes Berns, and Eliza Crowley.

"Where to, Harriet Quin?"

The only other person who called her Harriet was her older sister, and Anna resorted to the formal name only when she had grown frustrated or impatient with Hettie, whether it was for leaving dirty dishes behind in the kitchen sink or wearing one of her favorite blouses or skirts without asking. That said, the use of her formal name brought a measure of inherent intimacy, as if Samuel might know Hettie as well as her older sister had, even though he didn't.

"Which animals do you want to see?" Hettie asked.

"You decide," Samuel slurred. "After all, you're the zookeeper."

Hettie decided on the polar bears first even though she knew there was a good chance that the pair might be sleeping. Surprisingly, the bears were awake when they arrived at the edge of their enclosure.

"Meet Felix and Misty," she said. "Felix and Misty, meet Samuel Greene."

Felix pawed the air before diving into the dark pool. Splashes from his submersion grazed her cheek. Samuel reached over and wiped the wetness from her skin. For a second, it seemed as if his intoxication had drained away and he was the version of his former sober self that Hettie had encountered a few hours ago in front of the Floral Hall.

Samuel took a step closer to Hettie and kissed her on the same spot on her cheek. "Felix got you." He kissed her again before breaking away and staring at the polar bear again. Felix was now climbing to the top of the boulders. Hettie touched her cheek with one hand and then glanced over at Samuel. He smiled at her. A quiet shiver traveled across her shoulders. He kissed her again on the cheek, and Hettie turned so his lips grazed hers.

"What's next?" asked Samuel.

"The giraffes," Hettie said, leading the way.

Above, there was a deep flutter of wings. Then a shriek. Stella Holliday's silvery voice drifted through the darkened treetops, and the sounds of the big band dissolved into the hillside. Hettie imagined Stella Holliday standing onstage in front of the shiny rows of trombones and trumpets, and the tuxedo-clad musician sitting behind the small city of drums. Samuel and Hettie arrived at the giraffes. The animals stood silently in the far corner of the enclosure, their long yellow necks barely visible in the darkness.

"They're asleep," Hettie said.

Suddenly Rajan appeared, like a large mountain looming over the horizon, with the shadowy loop of his trunk swinging from side to side. He released a low rumble, its vibrations traveling through the ground like a peal of thunder. As Rajan lumbered closer to the edge of the en-closure, Hettie could see the migration of pale spots across his forehead. Maggie followed closely behind him.

"Who do we have here?" asked Samuel.

"Rajan, our bull elephant," Hettie said. "He weighs a little over thirteen thousand pounds."

Maggie walked several feet closer and reached her trunk through the wrought-iron bars. The end of her trunk wandered like the hand of a blind man.

"This is Maggie," Hettie said. "She weighs about eight thousand pounds. Came from an animal dealer in Italy."

Maggie shifted her weight from one foot to another, her large ears folded against the sides of her head. The elephant chirped and wheezed. Hettie knew that Maggie was expecting to be fed. Hettie spotted a bale of hay sitting on the pavement for their first feeding of the morning. She walked around the edge and tore several fist-fuls of hay and extended the bundles toward Rajan and Maggie. Both elephants walked closer and retrieved the hay from Hettie, tucking the tufts into their cheeks and grinding away at it with their dia-mond-shaped teeth.

"Looks like you have what they want," Samuel said with a chuckle.

The tip of Rajan's trunk suctioned Hettie's hand. She reached for another fistful of hay. The bull elephant swiftly deposited it into his mouth and then kicked his foot against the bars of the enclosure. The loud clang made Hettie jump, then laugh nervously.

"Hello, big fella," Samuel said, taking a step closer to Rajan. "You can't hurt anyone, can you?"

Rajan released a deep roar. Hettie and Samuel took a step back, and the giraffes lifted up their heads, crossing their necks, like a pair of winding vines.

"Where's your elephant?"

"Follow me."

Samuel walked beside Hettie, humming to himself. He paused by one of the benches, retrieved a flask from his coat pocket, and took several swallows before wiping his mouth off with the back of his hand. Without saying anything, Samuel extended the flask in her direction. The silver side caught the moon's reflection. Even though Hettie didn't like the taste of alcohol, she accepted the flask from Samuel. The liquor scraped against her throat; it tasted like rust and fire.

"Stole it from my pa's liquor cabinet," Samuel said. "He'd kill me if he knew."

Hettie took another sip. Then a third. It now tasted warm, like a spot of sunlight. One of the sea lions cried. Hettie imagined Sammy perched on the highest rock, training his whiskered mouth toward the star-filled sky.

"This way," she said, taking Samuel by the hand.

Ahead, the outline of the Elephant House came into view. A flock of birds lifted up from the nearby stand of trees. Off in the distance, the black bear growled. Samuel took another sip from his flask. Hettie opened the gate that led into the Elephant House and then tried the door. It wouldn't give. It was locked. Hettie felt for her coat pocket and the metal teeth of her keys, and remembered again that she had left Anna's coat up at the hall, along with her keys and wallet.

"Vi," Hettie yelled. "Are you in there? Violet."

"Hey Vi," Samuel joined in. "Where are you?"

The elephant trumpeted.

"That's my girl," Hettie said to herself. "There she is."

Violet released another trumpet call and kicked her feet against the dusty ground.

"Stay here," Hettie said to Samuel.

"Don't you have another kiss in you?" Before she could say anything, Samuel leaned toward her and his lips met hers once more. His kiss felt hard and soft at the same time, like a bruise was forming on the far corners of her mouth.

"Let me go around," she said. "I'll let you in."

A buzz intensified behind her eyes. Violet released another trumpet call. Hettie walked around the periphery of the Elephant House and then along the strip of dirt that separated the gray concrete building from the three-foot moat. She slid closely against the concrete wall. Moisture dampened her dress. One of her feet slipped, but she managed to regain her footing. Gripping the bars, Hettie rounded the corner of the Elephant House and stepped onto steady ground. She opened the gate and stepped inside the musty structure. Samuel was right behind her.

"Where is she?"

"Shush—" Hettie whispered.

In the dark corner of the Elephant House, she spotted Violet. She lay in the corner of her stall, which took up half of the structure's interior. A thump hit the ground, and then a gurgling cut the air. That night, the modest house felt even smaller and tighter, and it smelled dank and dirty like an abandoned basement that rarely saw light. Hettie felt a stirring of unease in her stomach, but she told herself it was just the alcohol.

"She doesn't smell so good, does she?" Samuel said.

He unscrewed his flask and took another swig before offering it to Hettie again.

"No, thanks."

Strands of hay crunched underneath Violet's feet as she walked toward Hettie. She extended her hand, and Violet threaded the tip of her trunk through the opening of her stall's wooden boards and tapped Hettie's palm.

"Hey, Vi," she said. "It's me. I wanted to introduce you to a friend of mine."

The elephant released a soft whinny before kicking one of her hind legs against the stall.

"Feisty, isn't she?"

"She needs to get to know you first, that's all," Hettie said.

"Always a sound strategy," Samuel said.

Suddenly Samuel shoved Hettie, pinning her shoulders against the far wall between the supply closet and the washbasin. Violet trumpeted. In one swift gesture, Samuel slipped his lips on top of Hettie's and plunged his tongue into her mouth. It was warm and wet, and squirmed with the force of a snake. He tasted like cigarettes and whiskey. Although startled, Hettie did her best to kiss Samuel back. After all, she liked him, she was attracted to him, she wanted him to kiss her rather than kissing Colleen White. Samuel bit down on her lower lip, and Hettie tasted the metallic twinge of her own blood. She heard Violet's tail switch against the gate that led to her stall. Hettie pulled away from Samuel, her hand at her mouth. She felt traces of wetness.

Violet was now huddled in the far corner and dropped a puddle of runny manure. Samuel lunged after Hettie, toppling her through the gate into Violet's stall, and onto the hay-strewn floor. She cried out, alarmed, and, for the first time, was truly scared. When she looked up, the elephant's foot stomped right next to her head. Rage surged within Hettie, and she quickly stood up and shoved Samuel. He lost his balance and tumbled through the gate, too.

"Is this how it's going to be?" Samuel said, pulling himself up and wiping his hands off on his trousers. "I thought you liked me—"

"We should go now," Hettie said through her teeth, too angry to say anything else.

She pushed past Samuel, opened the door of the Elephant House, and waited for him on the pathway. He leaned against Violet's stall and lit another cigarette. Hettie stared at him: His features had seemingly rearranged themselves so he looked like an ominous stranger; an ugly grin spread across his face and a menacing look seemed to possess his eyes. Her stomach turned. She felt disgusted and embarrassed. How could she have been so stupid? Why would she have thought this time would be any different? Samuel Greene wasn't truly interested in her—or Violet or the other animals. He was just another arrogant man, looking out for his own desires and wants. He didn't care about her. He was never going to complete her. Perhaps the truth was that no one was ever going to complete her, no one would ever be able to fill the gully of loneliness and sadness that seemed to be deepening inside her ever since Anna's death.

"You didn't give me a proper introduction to Violet."

"Another time, I think," she said stiffly, wanting nothing more than to be at home sitting at the kitchen table with a warm cup of tea and listening to the late-night news on the wireless with her mother. "Let's go, we shouldn't even—"

"Why not now," he said, ignoring Hettie and stepping inside Violet's stall. "We're here, aren't we."

Violet kicked against the metal chains that hung from the gate—and the stall gate swung shut on its own.

"Come on, girl," Samuel said. "Let me get a better look at you."

For a second it seemed as if Violet would ignore him just as completely as he'd ignored Hettie, but suddenly she lowered her head and charged toward him in the small space of the stall. Samuel barely managed to step out of the way.

"Jesus Christ," he said, his voice an octave higher. "What's wrong with her?"

"Nothing's wrong with *her*," Hettie yelled. "Now get out."

But again, Samuel disregarded her; instead, he lifted the leather crop that hung on the wall and waved it in front of Violet. "Maybe this will make her listen," he said, snapping the crop in the air.

"Stop it, Samuel," Hettie said, a panic whirring in her belly. "I'm warning you."

He snapped the crop again; this time, closer to the elephant.

"I've heard about you and Violet," Samuel said. "That you spend all your waking hours with this elephant. That you're becoming one of those freak people who can only get along with animals. That you haven't been right in the head since your sister."

Another violent wave of rage rolled through Hettie, and she tackled Samuel onto the floor and swung at him, hitting him squarely in the nose. Somewhere in the back of her mind, she could hear her father cheering her on: *Go on, Hettie! Show him what you're made of!* The knuckles of her hand ached, but adrenaline hurtled through her system. Her limbs felt tingly and light and electric. It was the first time that Hettie had ever hit anyone in her entire life—and she'd be lying if she said she didn't take pleasure in it. She got up and shook off the splinters of hay from her sister's dress.

Violet took a few steps closer and suctioned her trunk along Samuel's cheek. Blood trickled from his nose.

"Get away from me, you fuckin' elephant," he said, knocking Violet's trunk away. "Knock it off."

Violet continued suctioning along his face. Samuel kept trying to bat Violet away, but wasn't successful.

"Make her stop—"

Hettie clucked her tongue. "Go outside," she ordered Violet, opening the door that led to the yard.

Violet lumbered through. Samuel stood up, studying the crimson smears on his fingertips before turning to Hettie again.

"You crazy bitch," he said. "You made me bleed."

"Get out," she said, her voice ice-cold. "Now."

Samuel stormed out of the Elephant House and up the pathway that led to the Floral Hall. Hettie watched him walk away as the evening breeze brushed against the hem of Anna's dress. Its soft pink fabric was speckled with mud and dirt and one of the sleeves was torn. Hettie felt victorious, defeated, and furious all at once, and now Rose was going to be furious with her, too. The thin hairs on her arms stood up. Hettie could still hear the distant voice of Stella Holliday as Samuel disappeared into the darkness, but the magic of the singer's song was diminished now. Behind her, Hettie heard the soft rumble of Violet's call. She walked outside into the yard and patted the elephant on her side.

"I'm sorry, Violet. Rule number one," Hettie murmured, "don't ever trust young men." Violet nudged her forehead into her arm.

"I wished I had a treat for you," Hettie said. "I promise I'll bring you one tomorrow."

She led Violet into the stall and secured the gate before locking the door to the Elephant House. As she got closer to the entrance of the Floral Hall, Hettie spotted Colleen White standing there with her hands wrapped around her opposite elbows. Her pale, translucent skin and lavender dress seemed to glow in the dark. The night breeze pressed the silky fabric of her dress against her slender figure, giving her rounded breasts and petite waistline more definition.

Samuel Greene made his way up the steps and took Colleen into his arms. They embraced and then Colleen stepped back as she held his face tenderly, inspecting both sides as she wiped away the blood near his nose with a handkerchief. Hettie could see that Samuel was beginning to tell Colleen a story, a story about the zoo and meeting a young elephant, but Hettie was certain that the story had nothing to do with her, that he wouldn't even mention her name.

Six

Mr. Wright announced that the zoo's spring cleaning would take place on April 1, and the premises would be closed to the public so the keepers could complete a thorough scrubbing of the enclosures as well as washing and grooming of all the animals. When the day arrived, the staff gathered in the canteen at eight o'clock sharp in the morning. Mr. Wright cautioned everyone that it was going to be a long day and they shouldn't expect to be done until around seven in the evening, at the earliest. Hettie didn't mind putting in a long day at the zoo; at least it gave her a sense of purpose versus the free-floating melancholy that she often experienced at home.

Hettie sat next to Ferris at their usual table in the canteen, despite the fact that some abstract aspect of their friendship had vanished since that Saturday night at the Floral Hall three weeks ago. It felt as if they were no longer in each other's corner, quietly rooting each other on. Since that evening, Ferris had stopped asking Hettie to meet for their midmorning cup of tea. He had stopped coming by the Elephant House. In fact, he barely made eye contact with her when they encountered each other on the paths around the zoo. Hettie tried to convince herself that this unfortunate change in their relationship didn't matter to her, that her time and energy were now occupied with more important things—and perhaps all this was for the best. At the very least, it left Hettie less distracted and more focused on the day's tasks in front of her. But still, when she gave Ferris a small smile and his eyes just slid past her, she felt a spark of hurt in her chest.

Hettie, of course, knew there were far greater concerns: Before the staff meeting, some of her fellow zookeepers were talking about how the Stormont government had entered an understanding with Éire to share information about enemy aircraft crossing over the border and coastline. Andrews and his cabinet were becoming increasingly fearful about aerial raids on the city and its industrial port, given its steady production of military vessels so critical to the English war economy. Starting earlier in the year, the Luftwaffe had been attacking the United Kingdom more regularly, especially the critical ports in Glasgow and Plymouth, and many of these attacks were taking place on evenings of a full moon. Hettie kept her attention on Mr. Wright at the front of the canteen.

With a clipboard in hand, he rattled off everyone's assignments. Ferris would be charged with the sea lions and the llamas. Not surprisingly, Hettie had been assigned to Violet and the camels.

"For some of the enclosures, there are special instructions of where to place the animals while you're cleaning," Mr. Wright added, striking his pencil against the top edge of his clipboard. "Please check with me, and I will advise you of any special measures. We certainly don't want to lose any of our animals today, do we now?"

The staff murmured to each other, and a few others chuckled.

"This is no laughing matter," Mr. Wright said sternly, standing tall in his polished riding boots. "We all have an important job to do today."

Though Hettie had seen Mr. Wright several times since Stella Holliday's show, she still had a difficult time matching up Mr. Wright, the head zookeeper of Bellevue, with Mr. Wright, the silver-footed dancer on the crowded floor of Floral Hall. The two still didn't seem like the same man.

"Well, everyone," Mr. Wright said, tucking his clipboard underneath his arm. "Let's get to work. I'll be cleaning out the lions' enclosure and then inspecting the other areas, so please don't hesitate to find me if you need me. Also, I wanted to let everyone know that Mr. Christie and his sister, Josephine, will be paying us a visit on Friday morning. Given this upcoming visit, I want the zoo in tip-top shape, particularly since this will be the first time that Josephine Christie will be visiting our fine establishment. Let's be on our best behavior and make Mr. Christie proud."

Hettie looked up at the canteen window, expecting to see Eliza, but she wasn't there. During recent weeks, Hettie had seen very little of her. When she had asked Mrs. Carson about Eliza's whereabouts, she said that Eliza had been sick lately and needed to stay at home. Hettie wondered if her friend was all right, particularly after what had transpired with her brother over Ellis Johnson back in December. Hettie made a mental note that if she didn't see Eliza within the next week, she would pay a visit to her home and see how she was doing.

As the staff meeting concluded, the wooden legs of chairs scraped against the linoleum floor. Hettie thought back to a newspaper article she had recently read about Josephine Christie—about her older brother and the zoo, how it was a family-run operation that they had inherited from their father, who had died unexpectedly of an aneurysm at age fifty-nine. That George Christie had taken over the family business ten years ago, at age twenty-five, and never married. Now his younger sister (by seven years) was joining the business since her recent engagement had been abruptly broken off and George needed another family member to share in the growing responsibilities. Next to the article in the *Telegraph*, there had been a photograph of the two siblings: The brother and sister looked alike, sharing dark features, chiseled chins, high foreheads, and pooling dark eyes. Josephine wore a floor-length dress and a tailored coat, its sleeves bordered with bracelets of lace, and the carved handle of a folded parasol hung from her arm. She looked sophisticated and smart, a woman who had seen many places and met many important people.

"Why are Mr. Christie and Josephine visiting?" Hettie asked Ferris as they got up to leave the canteen, thinking it might be a good way to engage Ferris in small talk.

"Didn't you hear?" Ferris said sharply. "The Christies are moving the elephants to Sweden."

Hettie gasped. "Sweden?"

"You should know by now this place is something of a halfway house for Mr. Christie's animals," Ferris said as they walked along the path past the polar bears, still not meeting her eye. "Nobody stays here for long."

Without waiting for her response, Ferris started to jog down the path toward the enclosure of the llamas. For a moment, it felt as if he were running away from Hettie and would never stop. He ran faster, his arms swinging. She kicked her foot against the graveled pavement, knocking the metal leg of a bench.

"Ouch," Hettie said quietly to herself.

Ferris disappeared around the bend. It felt as if she had just stepped through a trapdoor and tumbled into her own sadness. Up ahead, Mr. Wright stood near the door of the Elephant House. Hettie silently prayed to herself that he wasn't about to share the news about Violet's imminent departure to Sweden. Maybe Ferris was wrong.

"You can find the bottles of oil in the supply closet," Mr. Wright said. "Make sure Violet gets a generous coat after her bath."

"Yes, sir."

"I'll be grooming Victoria and Wallace."

"Yes, sir."

As Hettie stepped inside the Elephant House, she chose to focus on the lack of proof for what Ferris had said and on the task directly in front of her. Yes, maybe Ferris was wrong. Maybe she had nothing to worry about. After all, it was a beautiful April morning. The sky was blue and cloudless. Hettie shook out her shoulders, trying to dismiss her interaction with Ferris. Violet paced the width of the enclosure. Hettie gathered the hose from the side of the house and unspooled it.

"Good morning, Vi," she said.

Hettie filled the bucket with water and soap. She clucked her tongue and then whistled a soft whistle. Violet took several steps toward Hettie, swinging her tail.

"After our bath, Mr. Wright wants me to rub you down," she said. "That's gonna feel grand, I bet."

Hettie went into the Elephant House and retrieved the box of neat's-foot oil and placed it along the exterior wall of the house. She turned on the spigot for the hose, picked up its short brass mouth, and sprayed Violet's broad side. Water ran down her skin like the forks of rivers traversing a series of low valleys. Hettie lightly tapped Violet's left rear foot with the riding crop and the elephant lifted it up, and she washed away the clumps of manure and dirt from the shallow ridges of her footpad. Afterward, Hettie aimed the arc of water toward Violet's forehead and then sprayed it into her mouth. The elephant raised her head and curled her trunk high into the air. Her pink tongue slipped out, making the elephant look like a giddy clown. Droplets of water clung to her long black lashes and to the soft hairs that stippled her chin. With the yard brush, Hettie scrubbed the top of Violet's head and then around her ears. Swirls of suds gathered on the elephant's skin.

"You're so good," Hettie sang softly as she scrubbed along the high ridge of the elephant's back. She took up the hose again and rinsed away the suds. Violet shook her head, sending out a halo of moisture.

"You got me," Hettie said with a laugh, wiping away a spot of wetness from her cheek with her forearm. She sprayed along the elephant's back. Violet lifted her tail and defecated onto the ground.

Hettie tutted. "Vi, not the best timing, you know." She retrieved the shovel from the supply closet, and the wheelbarrow. A few flies began to hover around the steamy pile. Violet swung her tail against her back and issued a soft whinny. Then the elephant knelt to the ground and rolled like an eager puppy. Hettie shook her head, unable to keep herself from smiling indulgently. Small clumps of dirt and splinters of hay collected, like magnets, on the elephant's back. Hettie rinsed Violet off one more time before rubbing her coat down with the neat's-foot oil. It smelled like petrol and decaying fish. Hettie scrunched up her nose as she applied a generous layer.

From the Elephant House, the other animal enclosures were obscured by the stands of Scots pines and the gradual slope that led to the foot of the Cavehill. Despite this, the energy of spring cleaning was palpable in the air. Winter was officially over. Signs of spring had arrived. Hettie whistled to herself as she massaged Violet's coat. With each swipe, the elephant's skin turned a darker shade of gray. Hettie leaned farther into each stroke. A growl traveled from one of the other enclosures. A flock of starlings took flight and circled high in the cerulean sky, producing an impressionistic swirl of specks before breaking apart again.

All of a sudden, several people sprinted past the Elephant House. One of the animals emitted a loud cry, and the starlings frantically circled again. In a nearby paddock, the macaques and baboons screamed and shrieked, hopping along the sides of their cage, gripping the metal diamonds of the fence and shaking it as if they were caught in a feverish trance. A sea lion roared. Hettie replaced the bottle of oil in the supply closet in the Elephant House and ran toward the commotion.

When she arrived at the sea lion enclosure, a dozen of her fellow workers already stood along the waist-high chain-link fence that encircled the exhibition, gawking at the large oval pool in the middle. As she followed their gazes, Hettie gave out a barely audible cry. Sammy had pinned Ferris against one of the boulders and was lunging for his shoulder. A stream of blood trickled down his arm and polluted the water. It was a surreal scene, like a child's cartoon, this wrestling match between Ferris and the sea lion—and it looked as though Sammy was winning.

The rest of the sea lions huddled together on the opposite side of the enclosure, mewling and nudging their whiskered noses into each other's slippery bodies. Mr. Wright stood at the pool's edge and ripped off his coat. Several brass buttons popped loose and wheeled into the water.

"Sammy!" Mr. Wright yelled. "Get off now!"

Sammy dragged Ferris, limp like a rag doll, into the pool—and there was little Ferris could do. Sammy bit into his left shoulder again. Ferris hollered and tears rolled down his freckled cheeks. Within seconds, Mr. Wright managed to find firm purchase on Sammy and pried his slick body off Ferris. Then Mr. Wright grabbed his crop from the pool's edge and snapped it in front of Sammy's scowl. His silver whiskers shivered as he displayed his rows of sharp teeth.

"Jesus Christ," Mr. Wright yelled. "Get back where you belong!"

After what felt like hours, Sammy finally retreated to the far corner of the enclosure, growling all the while, and the rest of the sea lions quietly slipped into the pool. Bobby Adair and Jack Fleming rushed to carry Ferris out of the pool. His arms and legs were slack, but he was still conscious, his eyes wide open, taking in what was going on around him. Blood stained the shoulder of his uniform. The dull flat red was becoming deeper. The zookeepers carefully placed him onto the patch of dead grass near the exhibition's entrance. The color had drained from Ferris's face, and his complexion was a pale shade of blue.

"Call the doctor from my office," Mr. Wright ordered Jack Fleming.

Hettie kneeled down beside Ferris and held his hand. He gripped her fingers lightly and gave a small smile.

"Oh, hey, Hettie," he said wearily. "It's you."

She smiled weakly, tears brimming in her eyes. "Does it hurt?" She immediately felt embarrassed for asking such a ridiculous question.

"Sammy knocked a wee bit out of me."

"I would say so, yes."

"He has quite the set of teeth on him, that boy."

Mr. Wright knelt next to Hettie and staunched Ferris's wound with his handkerchief. Spots of perspiration dampened his shirt. Mr. Wright's breathing was labored.

"The doctor's on the way."

"I'm sorry, Mr. Wright," Ferris said. Blood leaked through the wrapping of the handkerchief. "I lost my footing. Before I knew it, he was on me."

"Please, son," Mr. Wright said. "It was an accident. And Sammy. That's the first time I've seen him display such horrendous behavior. I don't understand it."

They all looked over at Sammy. He was licking off traces of Ferris's blood from his satiny coat, and Hettie shuddered. The other sea lions continued to keep their distance from him.

"Let's bring Ferris down to my house," Mr. Wright said to Bobby and Hugh, "and the doctor can examine him there."

Mr. Wright hoisted Ferris's uninjured arm around his shoulder. Hettie stood up and wiped her palms on her trousers. Ferris's blood had dripped onto her hands and now the deep crimson color stained the thigh of her trousers. She stared across the pool to where Sammy now reclined. He beat his foreflippers and arched his back, his chest robust and full, his pointed mouth trained toward the blue sky. Sammy released a throaty bark before diving into the pool. He swam in fluid circles before slipping out of the pool again and finding a high perch on the largest boulder.

Hettie recalled the advice that Mr. Wright had given her when she first started at the zoo last year. "It's inevitable," he had begun. "You're going to develop relationships with these animals. They are going to be responsive to you. Do your best not to become attached to them. Remember, they are animals. Most of these animals were wild and savage at one point in their lives, and at any time they can return to their natural, violent ways."

Hettie remembered thinking that Mr. Wright was being overdramatic in his words and delivery, and though his warning could certainly hold true for lions and bears, she couldn't imagine Violet or even lethargic Sammy hurting anyone. But on this early April day, Sammy had proven Hettie wrong. Here, along the concrete lip of the pool, the fresh puddles of blood and beige shreds of Ferris's uniform provided tangible evidence of Mr. Wright's words of warning. If it hadn't been for Mr. Wright's quick action and herculean strength, Sammy could have killed Ferris.

Along with the other employees, Hettie returned to her assignments for the reminder of the day. She still had to finish up with the oiling of Violet's coat and then move on to the camels. As she walked back to the Elephant House, the festive spirit of the zoo had vanished. Hettie was worried about Ferris and wondered if he was going to be all right. Would he need stitches? Would he be sent to the nearest hospital? Hettie wanted to believe that none of these animals were capable of such harm, and Ferris would swiftly recover from his injury and all would be forgotten, but she knew that this was naive thinking, in the same way it was naive to think that her father would ever return to their home on the Whitewell Road. On this spring day, Hettie somehow understood this fact more deeply than ever. In her mind's eye, Hettie saw him curled over a half-empty glass of whiskey at the neighborhood pub, his fingers gripped around the glass, as if he were caught in a fugue-like prayer. Just as many of the animals were by nature savage and dangerous, her father was by nature a drunk, a cheat, and a liar.

Violet stood near the center of the yard, and as Hettie walked toward her, the elephant chirped. The paintbrush end of her tail twitched. Somehow the elephant looked different—a little more dangerous, a little less trustworthy. Hettie tried to push these thoughts from her mind and focus on the duties in front of her. She retrieved the neat's-foot oil and rubbed it on the rear quarter of Violet's back leg. She concentrated on the circular motions of her hand against the elephant's rutty coat. Immediately, Hettie felt more relaxed, her fears dissipating in the weak

April sun. No, Violet would never hurt her, and she would never hurt Violet. Every time Hettie stroked the elephant's skin, a strange sensation gathered underneath her fingertips. A congress of electricity. Dynamic and static at once. The elephant chirped again.

"It's all right, Vi," Hettie said softly, applying one more coat of oil. "I'm here."

The staff assembled at the zoo's entrance at nine o'clock on the morning of the Christies' arrival. Mr. Wright stood in front, wearing a suit and bow tie rather than his familiar uniform. Hettie found a place next to Ferris, who stood on the periphery of the other employees. Despite only two days having passed since the episode with Sammy, Ferris looked like his former self, except he was a little stiff in his movements and a few scratches decorated the right side of his face. His left arm was positioned in a simple cloth sling against his abdomen. A young man with an accordion stood next to Mr. Wright.

"Remember, happy faces," Mr. Wright announced to everyone. "Positive attitudes, everyone."

A four-door Ford Prefect Saloon drove up the Antrim Road and pulled up beside the zoo's entrance. A chauffeur exited and opened the rear door of the shiny car. As Mr. Christie, dressed in his usual pin-striped suit, stepped out, Mr. Wright signaled the accordion player, and the musician began to perform a polka tune. Some of the employees tapped their feet to the music. The accordionist picked up his tempo and started to dance in time with the infectious music.

Mr. Wright shook hands with Mr. Christie as his sister stepped out of the vehicle. Josephine wore a shapely navy dress, a matching pair of high-heeled pumps, and a stylish pillbox hat. A deep shade of red lipstick colored her full lips. Hettie noticed that she was wearing a pair of sheer blue nylon stockings, an item that could no longer be purchased in Belfast. Mr. Wright greeted Josephine Christie. After he had exchanged a few words with Josephine, Mr. Wright asked the musician to cease playing.

"George and Josephine Christie," Mr. Wright announced. "The staff and zookeepers of Bellevue Zoo."

Mr. Christie bowed to the group, and Josephine gave a curtsy. Mr. Wright brought his hands together, and everyone followed his lead, enthusiastically clapping as if they were in the crowded terraces of a football match watching a leap-of-faith punt down the field that had just resulted in a last-minute winner. Mr. Christie's face brightened as he gazed beyond the group and up the slope of the grand staircase. Josephine opened her fan with a fluid snap of her wrist, fluttering the folds near her sharp chin despite the fact that the April morning air held a lining of coolness.

"Thanks to all of you, the Bellevue Zoo is a sensational success," Mr. Christie said. "This can't be said about other zoos in the United Kingdom. Our visitor attendance is up. It has already doubled this season. Clearly, you are taking excellent care of my animals." He looked over at Mr. Wright with a generous smile. "I look forward to speaking to each of you this morning as Josephine and I make our way around the zoo."

"Back to work everyone," Mr. Wright said.

About an hour later, Mr. Wright escorted Mr. and Miss Christie into the dusty yard of the Elephant House and introduced the brother and sister to Hettie. Nervousness beat against her chest, and a subtle tickle rose in her throat. Hettie hoped that she would be able to impress the siblings and that they would decide to keep Violet at Bellevue. Mr. Christie asked Mr. Wright for Violet's recent statistics of weight and height, and how much she had grown during the past six months, since the last time he had seen her.

"About a hundred pounds, sir," Mr. Wright said, "and she has grown about a half foot taller."

"Despite the rationing?"

"She arrived here a bit on the thin side," Hettie explained, a quiver in her voice. "I don't think her keepers fed her very well on the ship."

"Happens," Mr. Christie said, shrugging. "Sailors don't know the first thing about animals. Three weeks ago, I had two ostriches arrive dead at the Southampton docks after being shipped from northern Africa. Of course, I'm suing the shipping company for the destruction of my property."

"Georgie, how could you let that happen," Josephine said, glancing at her brother.

"The ship had to flee a U-boat," Mr. Christie said, holding his hands up defensively. "The sailors forgot about the birds in the hold. What can I say?"

"Why didn't you tell me about this?"

"I'm very impressed with Violet," Mr. Christie said, clearly keen to move the conversation on. "To be honest, I don't understand how you managed the weight gain."

"Farmers have donated hay and vegetables," said Mr. Wright.

"Georgie," Josephine said, "do we really need to bother with all these details? I mean, look at this lovely elephant."

They turned their attention to Violet, who was now strolling the perimeter of the yard. The late morning light threw dappled shadows against Violet's skin, which still held a deep hue from the oil rubdown earlier in the week. She looked graceful and dignified, her slow locomotion amplifying her stately presence.

"Over the past year, Josephine, our concern has invested in many animals," Mr. Christie continued, studying the small notebook that he held in one hand, a yellow pencil in the other. "These numbers are critical. With the wartime rations, it can be a challenging feat to feed all of the animals."

"Look at her," Josephine said again. "Such a sweet creature."

Hettie pressed her lips together, hiding her own smile.

"How old is Violet?" Josephine asked.

"Three years old, we think," Hettie answered. "We don't know her exact birthdate. Her mother—"

"Still a baby," Josephine interrupted, staring at Violet as she paced the outer ring of the enclosure. "Remember when Papa took us on safari through the wilds of India and we got to ride the elephants with the mahouts. Remember the Bengal tiger. He had just devoured that gaur. Only twenty yards away from us. It was absolutely spectacular."

"Josephine, we don't want to bore Wright and Miss Quin with our tiresome childhood adventures."

"No, please do, sir," Mr. Wright said. "We'd love to hear about the elephants in India."

"It was just one of the many trips that Papa brought us along on," Josephine continued. "He was looking to purchase a few more animals and ended up buying a cheetah and a pair of lions. Whatever happened to those animals, Georgie?"

"Father put the lion down after what happened in Colchester," he said.

Josephine's face crumpled. "Poor Mr. Drummond. His poor wife and children."

Mr. Wright and Hettie exchanged glances.

"Let's not go into that, Josie," Mr. Christie said, writing another scribble in his notebook. "That was a long time ago."

"Certainly," Mr. Wright said in a clipped voice.

"He was a good man, Mr. Drummond," Josephine continued.

"Violet represents a fine specimen of Asian elephant," Mr. Christie said, glancing down at his notes in his pad again.

"Miss Quin and Violet have developed a bit of a rapport," Mr. Wright added. "All the children love to come by and say hello to Violet. She has become something of an attraction here at Bellevue."

"Good work, Miss Quin," Mr. Christie said, flipping a sheet over in his notepad.

For the first time that morning, Hettie felt a sense of ease slip through her. Mr. Christie had said that she was doing her job well. He seemed to respect her as a zookeeper. Josephine liked her, too. Perhaps Violet was no longer in danger of being transported elsewhere.

"Let's not fritter our time away, Wright."

"Of course," Mr. Wright said, retrieving his pocket watch and glancing at its face. "You and Miss Christie have a train to catch to Dublin later on this evening. Shall we—"

"Georgie, listen to Mr. Wright for once," Josephine said, tapping Hettie's shoulder. Her fingertips felt like the delicate wings of a bird beating against her. "We should hire more women, like young Hettie Quin—whether there is a war going on or not."

Hettie glanced over at Miss Christie. She smiled at her like an old friend, and then gave her brother a sharp stare. Mr. Christie studied his notes again.

"Let's proceed with Maggie and Rajan," Mr. Christie said without looking up at his sister.

"Miss Christie, have you met Maggie and Rajan before?" asked Mr. Wright.

"Georgie, listen to me—"

"Dear sister, I heard you. I wrote it down," he said, exasperated. "More female zookeepers."

Josephine Christie winked at Hettie, closed her fan with one fast motion and tucked it into her purse. Even though it was a simple movement, it looked as though she had just performed a magic trick.

"After visiting with Violet, I think we can agree that she's a valuable asset to Bellevue," she said.

"Josephine, we'll discuss this later—"

Hettie looked over at Violet. The elephant stood near the edge of the moat. A young family—a husband and a wife and two girls dressed in matching dresses and coats—had gathered on the other side. The father held one of the girls in his arms as she stretched her hands toward the elephant. Violet extended her trunk and touched the girl's fingertips. The child squealed, and her younger sister hopped up and down.

"Mummy, Mummy," the sister said, excitedly. "I want to meet the elephant. I want to meet the elephant now."

Hettie bit into her lower lip to stop it from shaking. It didn't seem possible that they could ship Violet away.

"Keep up the good work, Hettie," Josephine said gently, extending her hand.

"Thank you, Miss Christie," Hettie replied, stumbling momentarily over her words. "Thank you for everything."

For a moment, Hettie didn't want the Christies to leave. She wanted to tell Mr. Christie how grateful she was to Mr. Wright for hiring her full-time and how he was an excellent boss and ensured that Hettie was always staying on top of her daily tasks, and that if Mr. Christie promised not to ship Violet to Sweden, Hettie would work overtime, taking on whatever extra responsibilities Mr. Wright would like her to perform, even if it meant cleaning out the foul-smelling cages of the fruit bats and lizards. And she wanted to ask Josephine if she might be returning to Belfast anytime soon, and if so, perhaps Hettie could show her around the city, take Josephine to high tea at the Grand Central Hotel, and for a visit to St. George's Market, and then over to the shipyards, so she could see where the famous *Titanic* was built, and then maybe they could conclude their evening by taking the tram up the Antrim Road to the Floral Hall for a night of live music and dancing. Josephine appeared to be the sort of woman who might enjoy a day like this, and then Hettie could show Samuel Greene that she no longer needed to stoop to his standards. By the end of their evening, Hettie would have told Josephine the story of Anna, Liam, and Maeve, and Thomas and Rose, and how she, Hettie, was exactly where she belonged. Now she had Violet, and the elephant seemed to set the world on its right axis and align things in such a way that nothing else mattered. Despite her father and her sister being gone, Hettie was doing better than ever, thanks to Violet and her other charges at the zoo. Didn't Josephine agree, that animals had this power? The ability to enchant and delight during the toughest of times. She was certain that Josephine would concur: Hettie was doing a brilliant job despite the recent setbacks and losses in her life. That she was a grand example of what could be— rather than of what was left behind.

"Wright, lead the way," Mr. Christie said, tugging Hettie out of the rapid whirl of her thoughts.

"It was a pleasure to meet you, young lady," Josephine said, taking Hettie's hand again. Hettie had lost track when Josephine had let go of her hand the first time. "Keep up the wonderful work."

"Yes, Miss Christie," Hettie said.

"Josephine," she said firmly. "Call me Josephine."

A flush of warmth seeped into Hettie's cheeks.

"Yes, Josephine," Hettie said. "Thank you, Josephine."

Mr. Wright, Mr. Christie, and Josephine proceeded up the pathway. The sisters and their parents were gone now, but Violet continued to stand next to the fence. She swung her head in Hettie's direction and lifted up her trunk. Hettie reached into her pocket and fingered a remaining carrot. Violet ambled toward her, and Hettie tossed the carrot into the elephant's mouth before rubbing her gently behind the ears.

"That's my girl," she said softly. "You'll always be my girl."

As dusk approached and the zoo was about to close, shards of the setting sun filtered through the budding treetops. Since the Christies had left the Elephant House, Hettie had attended to the rest of her duties. She kept expecting Josephine to come and find her, to say goodbye one last time, but she never returned. Instead, the day merely followed its perfunctory rhythms and routines.

Outside the camel enclosure, Hettie clomped her work boots against the pavement. One of the camels released high-pitched bleats while the other quietly chewed cud, its thick rubbery lips and large teeth moving in slow motion. According to Mary Robinson, the Christies had departed at half past one. In the meantime, Mr. Wright hadn't sought Hettie out to let her know if Violet was going to be transported or not. She decided to take this as good news.

As she locked the gate of the camels' enclosure, Hettie heard a distant metallic crack and pop. The artificial sounds echoed in the twilight. With a lurch, Hettie realized that it was the discharge of a bullet. There was a second pop, followed by a dissonant chorus of wailing. Hettie ran toward the sounds and arrived at the enclosure of the black-footed penguins. There were six penguins in all, and three of them lay still, like miniature torpedoes, against the pebbled border of their oblong pool.

At first, Hettie saw only their peaceful bodies with their distinctive markings—the black feet, the single black stripe and flecks of black along their broad chests, and the black masks. But as she looked more closely at the still birds, she was able to discern them from each other: Clementine, Marie, and Franklin lay on the pavement. It was easy to tell the birds apart, because those three were much smaller than Oscar, Gerald, and Joy. Clementine also had a black star-shaped spot near one of her flippers. Hettie stared at the penguin's unique mark before she began to notice pools of blood spreading underneath Clementine's body. Her eyes smarted. Mr. Wright stood on the other side of the pool, still dressed in his dapper gray flannel suit and bow tie, with the butt of a rifle pressed against his shoulder and the eye of the weapon aimed at Oscar, the penguin with a black collar across his neck. Oscar scuttled across the pavement. Mr. Wright took another shot. Gerald and Joy brayed as they rocked from side to side, extending their flippers as if they were about to embrace each other.

There were two more shots, and bile traveled up Hettie's throat. Mr. Wright lowered the rifle and wiped his forehead with his pocket square. It looked as if he had been punched in the stomach, and he was doing his best not to give in to the agony. The rims of his eyes were red.

"Why is Mr. Wright doing this?" Hettie asked Bobby Adair, who was standing next to her, even though she already knew what Bobby was going to say: During the past month, there had been many discussions about how to divvy up the herring rations—how much would go to the sea lions and how much would go to the penguins and the cranes and the egrets. Hettie had just assumed that Mr. Wright would find a way for all the animals to be properly fed.

"The penguins were on their way to starving," Bobby said.

"Mr. Christie gave the orders just before he left the zoo," Jack Fleming added.

"That's not right," Hettie said, still unable to believe the scene that had played out in front of her eyes. "How did he know they were going to starve?"

"Either the sea lions or the penguins had to go, and Mr. Christie decided that he was more willing to part with the penguins. He said that when the war is over, the penguins will be easier to replace."

Ferris entered the enclosure and collected Clementine and deposited the bird into the rear bed of a lorry. Despite his injured shoulder, he managed to perform this duty with no indication of pain or discomfort. A tear rolled down from the corner of Hettie's eye. At the same time, she felt a flash of anger. How could Josephine Christie have allowed this? Perhaps Hettie had misread her—perhaps Josephine was more concerned about the destruction of property rather than the actual welfare of the animals, and maybe economics had entered into Josephine's demand that her brother hire more female zookeepers because the salaries of women amounted to cheaper labor and lower costs for the concern's overall bottom line.

Ferris loaded the remaining dead birds into the lorry. Mr. Wright handed the rifle to one of the other zookeepers and let himself out of the enclosure. The chain of events still seemed implausible to Hettie. None of it added up. Just a few hours ago, they had stood in the center of Violet's enclosure, discussing how the animals were the Christies' top priority. When Hettie glanced down the path, Mr. Wright's dark gray figure had already disappeared around the bend. Ferris gunned the lorry's engine and then drove away, and Jack Fleming rinsed off the concrete border of the penguin pool. Some of the blood washed away, but several irregular shapes still stained the pavement.

When Hettie glanced down the pathway again, Eliza Crowley was walking toward her. She carried her tin lunch pail in one hand and a thermos in the other.

"I just heard about the penguins," she said. "What a nightmare."

Hettie stared at the now-empty enclosure. "The Christies ordered their execution," she said, still in a state of disbelief.

"Did you get a chance to meet Josephine Christie?"

"I did," Hettie said. "They came and met Violet. She was approving of my work, but now I don't know what to think."

"It's a shame," Eliza said, shaking her head. "I always liked Clementine and Oscar. Such a lovely couple."

"Where have you been lately?" Hettie asked.

"Sick."

Hettie studied Eliza more closely. Her wool coat was pulled tightly over her body, and the curve of her abdomen looked slightly more pronounced. Eliza's cheeks were rosy and radiant, as if she had just sprinted from somewhere; a few stray strands of her red hair tumbled into her cherublike face.

"Are you pregnant?" Hettie asked with hesitation.

"Of course I'm not pregnant," Eliza said. "What do you take me for? Jesus Christ, Hettie, I thought you liked me. I thought we were friends."

"We *are* friends," Hettie said defensively. "I just haven't seen you since Stella Holliday. And I heard that you left with some fella and then you haven't been at work for the past few weeks, and some of the other zookeepers were talking—"

"You know, you shouldn't believe everything you hear," Eliza snapped.

Hettie lowered her gaze to the pavement.

"I'm actually leaving," Eliza said, more gently now. "That's why I came to find you—to say goodbye."

"Goodbye?" Hettie said, looking at Eliza again.

"My mother asked me to take my younger siblings farther north, up to Cushendall. To her sister's. It's not that far, but it's definitely safer. Not much chance of bombs dropping up there. The government has been trying to get children to evacuate to the countryside, you know. For once, I think they're right. Hopefully, it will only be for a month or so. Mr. Wright said I can have my job again as soon as I get back. I'll miss you. I never knew the zoo was such a good place."

At that moment, Hettie realized that the two of them hadn't spoken since her run-in with Samuel Greene, but at the same time, it felt like that incident no longer mattered, with the executions of the penguins and now Eliza's departure from Belfast.

Before Hettie knew it, Eliza had put her arms around her. Her embrace was solid and firm. Hettie smelled cigarette smoke and floral perfume knitted into the fabric of Eliza's coat. She leaned into her friend. Tears gathered in her throat. She wasn't sure if her tears were over the executed penguins or Eliza Crowley's abrupt departure. Her sadness felt neither here nor there; instead, it felt like a colossal coral reef of melancholy, and that it didn't matter which direction she swam in, she would always run into it. Eliza released her.

"Maybe we can write each other?" Hettie suggested.

"Sure, we could do that," Eliza said. "You can let me know how things are going with Violet and the boys." She took a piece of scrap paper and a pencil out of her purse, wrote down an address, and handed it over to Hettie.

"Write me first," Eliza continued, "and then I'll have your address."

"I will," Hettie said with a smile. "And I'll be here when you return."

Eliza took Hettie in her arms again. When she first met Eliza that morning of Violet's arrival, she had never imagined that she would develop such fondness for this odd girl with flame-red hair who knew how to swing her hips and pick out the right lipstick. Hettie's heart ached in that strange way that it ached for Maeve and Liam. For a moment, Hettie wanted to ask Eliza not to leave, to stay at the zoo and in Belfast, but she knew this was an absurd request. Despite everything, she knew that Eliza's family came first.

"You take good care of yourself, Harriet Quin," Eliza said, stepping away.

"I will, Eliza Crowley," Hettie responded. "You too."

The next afternoon Mr. Wright stopped Hettie outside the Camel House. It looked as if Mr. Wright had aged a decade. Pale lavender half-moons hung underneath his eyes, and deeper wrinkles fanned out from their corners. His trousers hung loosely at his hips; his shoulders seemed to be permanently hunched, as if a cinder block of regret sat on his shoulders, his gaze cast perpetually downward.

"Do you have a minute, Hettie," he said, approaching her on the path.

"Of course, Mr. Wright."

"The Christies were impressed with your care of Violet." Mr. Wright hesitated for a moment and glanced over at the bench in front of the Camel House. "Maybe it would be best if we sat down—"

"Is everything all right, Mr. Wright?" Hettie asked, sitting down next to him and trying to control the tremble in her voice. "Did I do something wrong?"

"No, you're doing an excellent job. Like I said, the Christies were quite impressed."

"Impressed? But they ordered the execution of the penguins," she said. "They don't seem to care about the animals at all."

Hettie rocked on the bench, her hands tucked underneath her

thighs. Her soiled gloves sat next to her. She was waiting for Mr. Wright to reprimand her, for speaking out against the Christies and what had happened to the penguins. She glanced up. A rash had traveled along his neck from the bright red collar of his coat. Mr. Wright paused before he spoke again.

"Hettie, I don't need to tell you this: The execution of the penguins was a very difficult decision for everyone. No one wanted to do it, but sometimes we have to carry out horrific tasks for the overall welfare of the zoo. I know Josephine is sympathetic to the animals. She is on our side," he explained, his voice gathering momentum. "And with Mr. Christie, as long as I've known him, he has been a successful businessman who has made the right decisions so that his circuses and zoos continue to thrive. We wouldn't have the zoo—nor all of the animals—if it weren't for George. You'll see, as you get older, everything is a negotiation, everything is a compromise, and sometimes this means you have to let go of what you care about the most."

Hettie looked up to see that Mr. Wright was staring at her. A tenderness seemed to replace his fatigue. Mr. Wright placed his hand over Hettie's and squeezed it. She was surprised by the smooth, warm touch of his palm against her skin. She had expected that his hand might feel rough and calloused from his endless work with the animals.

"I'm sorry, Mr. Wright," she said.

"There, there, Hettie," he said. "We were all upset, but we're all recovering, aren't we?"

They sat in silence for a moment.

"Is there something else?" Hettie asked.

"Well, there is something else."

Hettie felt the impulse to stand up from the bench, to leave Mr. Wright there, but she forced herself to remain sitting next to him.

"I wanted to talk to you about the Christies and their plans for the elephants. As it turns out, they are planning to transport Violet within the next two months," Mr. Wright said, looking up at Hettie. "They want to get the elephant troupe together for the circus that's now touring Sweden and then will go to India after the war."

Hettie felt a flood of panic and dismay. "She's too young," she argued. "She hasn't been trained for the show. Why would they want to take her? You've seen the families, one of the reasons they come up to the zoo is because of Violet and her way with the children."

"Mr. Christie is married to the idea of using our three elephants and shipping them to Sweden by the beginning of the summer."

"What about the war?" Hettie asked, trying a different tack. "It's not safe."

"That's why he chose Sweden, since the country is remaining neutral for the time being."

"I thought you said Josephine Christie is sympathetic."

"She doesn't want to see Violet moved," Mr. Wright said. "Josephine's going to ask her brother to reconsider, maybe see if he could purchase another elephant from a circus or an animal dealer elsewhere."

"Do you think that's possible?" Hettie asked, lifting her eyes to meet Mr. Wright's solemn gaze.

"I'd say it's fifty-fifty."

Hettie stared at the stand of birch trees on the other side of the pathway, right next to the Camel House. Their branches were just beginning to leaf. Black rooks and two jays, with their striking pinkish hues, flitted in the treetops. The camels slept in the corner of their enclosure, their long legs folded underneath their sandy bodies.

"Between Josephine and me," Mr. Wright said, "we're going to do everything in our power to try and keep Violet at Bellevue. I'll promise you that."

He squeezed Hettie's hand again and released it. Beyond the thickets of evergreen bushes, the plaintive calls of the peacocks filled the air. The Rhesus monkeys swung from branch to branch in the enclosure next to the Camel House. Their howls collided with the cries of the peacocks. One of the camels stood up, sucking in his muscular nostrils, and then released a low moan.

"I know Violet has been a helpful diversion for you," Mr. Wright said.

"Diversion?"

"Your sister's unexpected death," he said gravely. "How long has it been now?"

Her voice caught in her throat, and unexpectedly she thought she might cry. What normally would be an easy question became challenging to answer—and Hettie had to do the arithmetic in her head.

"Nine months," she finally responded.

"Not that long."

Another silence settled between them. The rooks and jays continued to dance on the overhead branches. For a moment, the trees looked shiny, as if their new leaves held some sort of internal illumination, but then they turned dull and flat again. Hettie's vision blurred, and she wiped her eyes.

"You know, I had a brother once," Mr. Wright finally said, staring into the distance. "We were fraternal twins. I was born just a few minutes after Nicholas. When we were older, he always introduced me as his younger brother."

Hettie looked up at Mr. Wright. His face was etched with creases of weariness. His hazel eyes had become glassy. The mating calls of the peacocks grew louder and more persistent.

"The peafowl are lively this morning—"

"What happened to your brother?" Hettie pressed.

"We fought in the same army unit during the last war," he said, and then paused before continuing. "Nicholas was next to me in the trenches. It was the second day of the Battle of Arras. We were outside a village in northern France. It was raining. It was cold. I remember the tips of my fingers were numb and blue. I couldn't feel the trigger.

Gunshots flew over our heads, one barrage after another. I remember thinking that I enjoyed the whistling sounds of the discharged bullets. It sounded like a rare species of bird, one that I never heard before. It was an irrational thought—verging on delusion. Here the enemy was, trying to kill us, and I was pondering the musicality of firing bullets. The next time I looked over at Nicholas, he was crumpled up next to me and blood was leaking onto his uniform."

In a nearby evergreen hedge, a dove sang its hollow song.

"When I went to check his pulse, it had already stopped," Mr. Wright said.

Hettie sat, transfixed. As Mr. Wright had been talking, she was transported to her sister's hospital room again. Rose was uttering a litany of prayers, a slipstream of barely spoken words, over Anna's body. Her sister was merely a corpse with a sheet draped over the length of her. Torpid, heavy, and rigid. Her spirit had already left several hours earlier. Gone, released right out of her. The wisps of her breaths extinguished forever. And Liam was there, too, explaining how the doctors couldn't stop the bleeding, how it had happened so quickly, how she went from living, from giving birth to their daughter, to suddenly dying.

But Mr. Wright was speaking to her, and Hettie wrenched herself back to their conversation. "I'm sorry," Hettie said, attempting to convey the gravity and depth of her sympathy with her words. "I'm so sorry for your loss."

She felt embarrassed to hear this platitude come from her own lips. Hettie remembered friends, acquaintances, extended family members, and strangers expressing this exact sentiment again and again during the reception after Anna's service, and how the condolence had quickly lost its meaning. The words became a continuous loop of emptiness. She recalled the faint haze of the church's community room that hovered between the ceiling and the dense crowd of mourners, a collective miasma of warmth, musty body odor, and grief. Everyone was there, but she still had felt alone.

"That's kind of you, Hettie," he said, removing his fedora and resting it on his lap. "It's been more than twenty years now, but I still feel his absence every day."

Up the pathway, Rajan released a trumpet call from his enclosure.

"With your sister and everything," he said, and then paused again. "I wanted to let you know."

Hettie looked up at Mr. Wright. A tear slid down the side of his face. He didn't try to wipe it away. Instead, it stopped at the edge of his black-stubbled cheek.

"Right after the war, I started working with animals," he continued. "They saved my life, in a way. I wanted you to know, there is a way back from the grief. You just need to give it time."

He placed his hand on Hettie's hand again. Then, after a moment, he lifted it, leaving behind an imprint of warmth.

"Thank you, Mr. Wright."

He smiled for the first time as they stood up from the bench. Mr. Wright leaned forward and gave Hettie a hug. Her body tensed at the surprise of Mr. Wright's embrace, but then she allowed herself to relax temporarily into his arms.

"I just thought you would want to know the status of Violet," Mr. Wright said as they parted, "given how much time and energy you're devoting to the elephant."

Hettie looked up at Mr. Wright again. There was a little more life in his eyes.

"I'm still planning on your assistance with the birth of the black bear cubs," he said, businesslike again, reaching into the breast pocket of his jacket for a notepad, similar to the one that Mr. Christie carried with him. "Alice is coming along well. She's due the first week in May."

"Yes, sir," Hettie said. "I'm looking forward to the birth."

"Don't you need to tend to the flamingos before heading home for the evening, Hettie?"

"Yes, sir," she said. "Good night, sir."

"Cheers," he said, tipping his fedora before replacing it on his head. "Cheers, sir."

Mr. Wright made his way toward Maggie and Rajan's enclosure around the bend from the Camel House. On the other side of the camels was the exhibit for the red deer. The small herd gathered near the shallow pool. A fawn, born just a few weeks ago, hungrily nursed from her mother's swollen teat. Droplets of milk hung, like fragile icicles, from her eager mouth. Again, Hettie heard Rajan's distinctive cry.

Seven

ON THE EVENING OF APRIL 7, HETTIE WOKE SUDDENLY IN THE middle of the night. Her bed swayed. At first she thought she was still asleep, caught inside a dream where she was asleep on a thin cot inside the deep belly of a ship. The wind wailed. The waves smacked against the sides of the ship. Then Hettie sat up, startled. The panes of her bedroom windows rattled. Outside, a cat yowled. Then in the distance, something pattered. As if sheets of heavy rain were hitting the roof of their house. Hettie opened and closed her eyes. Phantom bursts, like the downy fists of dandelion seeds, exploded before her eyes. Then the ghostly apparitions faded into the darkness of her bedroom. There was a loud clap and clatter, like a fierce thunderstorm.

During the past six months, there had been over twenty false alarms, and Hettie assumed this might be another. But then there was no mistaking what was taking place: Hettie heard the distinct unsynchronized drone of distant planes. Shells erupted, shaking the doors and windows. Only then did the air-raid sirens start to wail their song—horizontal and continuous, spreading in all directions. The lament was everywhere. She turned on her bedside lamp and glanced at the clock that sat on a table. It was a quarter past midnight. She slid into her slippers, threw on a cardigan over her nightgown, and ran outside.

A full moon illuminated the night sky, its pearlescent beams throwing long shadows across their courtyard. Strands of Hettie's hair fluttered in the breeze. There was a machinelike patter followed by a series of loud, concussive explosions, both deafening and distant. Some of the explosions were unmistakably and alarmingly close. A field of yellowish orange lit up the sky over the harbor and east Belfast. A dog barked. Something was burning. Neighbors called out to one another. Rose appeared at the rear door.

"This isn't a practice drill," Rose said, her gaze fixed on the pyrotechnic horizon.

A string of percussive thumps trailed another eruption. Hettie ran through the house and out the front door. Their neighbors—Mr. Reynolds, Mr. Brown, Mrs. Lyttle, and Mr. Moffit—stood, as though they were in a football huddle, in the center of the street, dressed in their nightclothes and robes, their necks craned toward the peculiarly colored sky. It was smoky, yellow, and red. Some rushed forward to get a better view.

"They're bombing the docks," Mr. Reynolds said, pushing his spectacles up the narrow bridge of his nose. "Look at that: The bombs are lighting up the port. It almost looks like daytime. There's a really massive fire down there somewhere as well. They must have hit the timber yards."

Hettie stared up at the sky again: The Lough was partially visible through the darkened stands of trees and the overlapping rooftops. Plumes of smoke and fire rose toward the roaring sky. Bolts of fear lit up her insides, and her breath shortened. She couldn't believe what she was seeing.

"It's Harland & Wolff shipyards and Shorts' aircraft factory they're after," Mr. Brown said.

The distant sound came much closer, and suddenly a loud explosion shook the windows of her house. Panic drove Hettie forward, and she began to run toward the Antrim Road and the zoo.

"Wait," Mr. Brown called. "Where are you going? I wouldn't go to the shelters if I were you. We're better off in our homes than in those stinking concrete coffins."

Hettie ran up the rise and turned onto the Antrim Road. She ran until she reached the trail that bordered the fields that led to the Crazy Path. As she ran, Hettie remembered the cautionary story about Nellie Smith, how a year before, a drifter, a man no one knew, had raped Nellie while she was walking along the Crazy Path at dusk, and Hettie ran faster still. The sound of exploding shrapnel thrummed in the sky, and then the distant pop of machine guns. Hettie's ribs ached. A cramp stitched her side.

Up ahead, she could finally make out the rear entrance to the zoo. She turned the key in the padlock and unlatched the gate and made her way along the familiar pathways to the Elephant House. Sammy released a whining peal and flapped his flippers together. A flock of parrots squawked. Another explosion lit up the sky.

This is the apocalypse, the apocalypse, the apocalypse is coming, screeched one of the parrots.

At first, Hettie didn't see Violet as she stared into the Elephant House, and she feared that Violet might somehow have escaped. But then a flare illuminated the sky, and Hettie spotted the elephant at the rear of the structure. She reached for the metal gate, and it creaked shut behind her. Violet kicked her foot against a loop of metal chains that hung from the fence, creating a forceful crash. Hettie jumped. Violet's lumbering figure loomed in front of her.

"Easy there," Hettie said, her voice trembling. "It's me, Vi."

Violet lifted her trunk up into the air and issued another throaty cry, and her reddish-brown eyes glinted in the light of a flare. The elephant began to pace the width of the enclosure. A stream of diarrhea traveled down Violet's rear leg and splattered onto the dusty ground. A mechanical purr charged the night sky. Hettie walked closer to Violet. Liquid splashed and stained the rounded toes of her slippers. Her ankles felt wet, the ground sloshy and foul. Hettie tried not to breathe, but still the odor of shit hit her nostrils.

"It's all right," Hettie said, doing her best to steady her voice. "Everything is okay."

Hettie took a few steps closer to Violet, whispering her name and saying that all would be well even though she didn't believe it herself. Hettie reached behind one of Violet's ears and gently rubbed it. Another explosion erupted above the treetops. One of the lions roared. Something rattled in the darkness. Viscous dung cascaded onto the already-moist ground.

Then for a moment, the explosions receded. It grew quiet. The air smelled like smoke and ash. Hettie looked up at the sky, but no longer could see the moon. She searched the Elephant House for something to feed Violet. Thankfully, she had left behind a bundle of carrots in the supply closet. She broke one off and extended it toward Violet. The elephant took the carrot in the agile finger of her trunk and deposited it into her mouth. Hettie gave Violet another one.

"Maybe the worst is over," Hettie said, glancing over at Violet. "Maybe we're safe now."

Manure decorated the elephant's rear legs, and puddles of dung covered most of the dusty enclosure. Hettie walked to the side of the Elephant House and uncoiled the hose. She turned the spigot on and water spilled out of its socketed mouth. Violet wandered over to the newly formed puddle of water and started to lick it up.

"Thirsty girl," Hettie said. She picked up the end of the hose and sprayed an arc of water into Violet's mouth. Her long pink tongue lolled as the water hit her throat.

Suddenly a silhouette appeared at the door of the Elephant House, and Hettie jumped before realizing it was Mr. Wright. Despite it being the middle of the night, he was still dressed in his customary outfit of a bright red coat, black jodhpurs, and a beige fedora. He held his riding crop in one hand.

"Hettie, what are *you* doing here?"

"I was worried about Violet," she said, glancing down at her muddied nightgown, slippers, and cardigan. "The bombs, they scared her."

"Violet and everyone else," he said with a laugh. "Bloody Germans. So much for those fools who said that Hitler had never heard of Belfast."

Hettie touched her hand against Violet's forehead. The elephant released a soft cry.

"Do you think it's over?" Hettie asked.

"Let's hope so," Mr. Wright said, surveying the puddles of diarrhea around the yard. "Go home. I can take care of the animals."

"I don't mind staying for the night," Hettie said. "At least until Violet is settled."

"Suit yourself," Mr. Wright said. "I'm going to complete the rest of my rounds. Come and find me if you need me."

"Yes, sir."

Mr. Wright walked through the Elephant House, and his red-jacketed figure disappeared into the darkness. Hettie began to spray the surface of the enclosure, the force of the water washing away the puddles of dung. Violet tapped her trunk against Hettie's forearm. She inspected the spot that the elephant had just touched. A moth, with orange-tipped wings, hovered above her shoulder. Its tiny body was there, and then it wasn't. Violet let out another trumpet call, unfurling her trunk and then curling it back up again.

By the time the all-clear sirens sounded at four fifteen in the morning, Violet was calm and settled. She followed Hettie into the Elephant House and found her usual spot in the corner of her stall. Before returning home, Hettie hosed down the exterior yard one more time. The sun still hadn't come up yet as she made her way out of the rear gate and down the Crazy Path.

When Hettie arrived at the Whitewell Road, several neighbors were still congregated in the middle of the street, talking excitedly about the rumors they had heard and the news that was being reported on the wireless. What had made the biggest impression on them was the two massive explosions at the very end of the raid, just when they thought it was over. According to Mr. Brown, one of the Luftwaffe bombs had destroyed the grain silo and a large portion of the Rank Flour Mill near Pollock Dock. He had heard that it was struck by a parachute mine. Apparently a second one had landed on the rooftop of the fuselage factory of Harland & Wolff, demolishing its main building, which covered four and a half acres, and sending pieces of metal and steel into the streets. There was still no word about the potential number of casualties, but the neighbors seemed to agree that there were bound to be some, especially among the men working the night shifts in the harbor area. As she listened to all this, Hettie felt dazed at the scale of the destruction and her night spent at the Elephant House.

When Hettie eventually stepped inside their house, she was relieved to find Rose sitting in her nightdress and bathrobe at the kitchen table, drinking her morning cup of tea and listening to the news. The corners of her mouth hung low. She tapped the end of a glowing cigarette into a nearby ashtray and took a deep breath in. Though Hettie knew that her mother had smoked in her twenties, she had never seen Rose with a cigarette. She looked like a different woman, one who was younger and older at the same time. Rose released a rill of smoke from her thin lips.

"You all right?" Hettie asked tentatively.

"I was worried about you," Rose said, staring up at Hettie and crushing the end of her cigarette into the bottom of the ashtray. Her eyes looked empty and distant. "You can't just run off like that and not say where you're going."

"I went to the zoo," Hettie said. "To make sure that Violet was all right."

"Of course, Violet," her mother said, her voice edged with bitterness. "Always Violet."

"She was scared," Hettie explained. "I needed to calm her down."

Her mother stood up and embraced Hettie. "I'm just glad you're home again."

"Sorry, Mum."

Rose rubbed Hettie's shoulder with one hand. The circular motion of her touch generated a spot of warmth on her back, and she could feel the knots of tension unfurl in between her vertebrae, releasing both a pain and a tenderness.

"Look at you," her mother said, taking a step back. "You're a mess."

Hettie glanced down. Her mother was right: Splatters of dung and mud soiled her nightgown and slippers. She stared at her hands. Dirt filled the creases of her palms, and grime was pressed underneath her fingernails.

"Go and wash up," Rose said, nodding toward the hallway bathroom. "Give yourself a warm bath. We have water."

Hettie made her way to the bathroom at the end of the darkened hallway. The air-raid siren still vibrated inside her chest. Then she felt the phantom tip of Violet's trunk on her forearm again. As she turned on the faucet, Hettie stared at her own reflection in the bevel-edged mirror. Shadows of soot and mud looked like a kind of topographical map on her skin. She rinsed her face again, watching the spiral of dirt and water disappear into the sink's perforated drain. She thought about Maeve and Liam in Newcastle and hoped the Germans hadn't bombed south of Belfast, too. She thought of Liam's chestnut-brown eyes, the subtle angles of his cheekbones and sharp chin. Hettie shook her head and then rinsed her face again, and rejoined her mother in the kitchen for a cup of tea as they waited for the next news update on the wireless.

Later that morning, after Hettie checked on Violet at the Elephant House, she encountered Ferris on the path as she made her way to the aviary. Streaks of soot decorated his cheeks. Without saying a word, Ferris gave Hettie a hug.

"I'm glad you're all right," he said, releasing her. His eyes were bloodshot, his hair disheveled, as if he had just tumbled out of bed a few minutes earlier.

"You too," Hettie said.

"Holy God, what a night."

"Have you been to the docks yet?"

"I rode my bike to the other side of the Lagan, near the city hall."

"Do they know how many people died?"

"There's no official word," Ferris said with a sigh. "Harland & Wolff and Ranks got hit hard, and then a number of homes near the docks. Hundreds of incendiary bombs fell on the lower Newtownards Road and a few landed on some houses. The police and the fire brigade are still trying to determine the damage and get the fires under control."

They were silent for a moment.

"At first I thought it was a thunderstorm," Hettie said.

"Could you see the bombs being dropped from your street?"

Hettie nodded, sweat moistening her palms at the memory. "The whole sky lit up."

"A few of the windows shattered in my flat," Ferris said.

Mary and Helen were rolling up the collapsible metal face of the kiosk. They both nodded as Ferris and Hettie walked by.

"Good morning to you," Helen said. "Glad you're both safe."

"You too," Ferris said, tipping his cap.

Mr. Wright approached Ferris and Hettie. His face was bright, his eyes were clear.

"Hettie, you made it home safely."

"Yes, sir," she said. "How are all of the animals doing?"

"Turns out that Rajan could feel the vibrations of the planes coming before the bombs were even dropped," said Mr. Wright with a grin. "Such an extraordinary creature, he is."

"How could you tell?" Ferris said.

"He was pacing and trumpeting before I heard the drone of the planes," Mr. Wright explained. "A friend of mine who's one of the top experts on elephants says that they can hear a lorry coming at least ten minutes before it arrives. These animals constantly amaze me. They know so much more than we do." He retrieved his handkerchief and dabbed his forehead.

"And the sea lions and the bears?" asked Ferris.

"As far as I know," Mr. Wright said, "everyone is intact. We are very lucky."

"I heard from a policeman that there were never more than eight or nine bombers overhead at any one time, but the damage was far greater because of all of the combustible materials in the factories and warehouses," Ferris said.

"I'd say it's all speculation at this point," Mr. Wright said, flipping his pocket watch open and glancing at the time. "I'm going to do a quick walk-around, and then we'll be gathering for a staff meeting in the canteen at half past the hour."

"Yes, sir," Ferris and Hettie said in unison.

Mr. Wright walked briskly up the incline of the Cavehill toward the enclosure of the polar bears.

"He's chipper this morning," Ferris commented.

"Probably relieved that no one was hurt," Hettie said.

They walked toward the canteen as the other employees made their way along the multiple paths of the zoo. The morning breeze carried the scents of blooming lilacs and burning smoke. Many of the staff were already gathered in the canteen, and an energy took over as people exchanged their respective accounts from the night before. As Hettie listened, she noticed that many of the stories followed a similar trajectory of waking up to the falling bombs, not knowing what was going on, and then trying to determine the severity of the attacks and whether they needed to seek cover in one of the city's shelters. So far, no casualties of family members or close friends of zoo employees had been reported, she was relieved to hear. There had been a close call with an uncle who worked the night shift at Harland & Wolff, but he had stayed home because he had come down with a fever.

Mr. Wright blew his whistle. Everyone fell quiet and scrambled to find seats at the tables. Without further delay, he updated the staff on what had happened the night before.

"At first there were wild rumors that there were a hundred and fifty casualties," said Mr. Wright, "but it looks like the actual figure will be far less than that."

Relieved whispers circulated throughout the room.

"It might be as low as twelve or thirteen victims, mostly men who worked the night shift at Harland & Wolff," he continued. "The timber merchants McCue Dick burned completely to ashes and the fire spread to the neighboring premises, lighting up the docks. Unfortunately, they lost two men. We are still awaiting further confirmation."

Amid Mr. Wright's announcements, the conversations among Hettie's fellow workers grew louder. Despite the bombing and the casualties, everyone appeared to be in optimistic spirits: Their city had been attacked, but had managed to endure the violence relatively unscathed. The bombing had mainly been confined to military targets around the docks, which was what had been expected, and the civilian areas had largely escaped damage. Some felt if that was the worst

Hitler could do, then Belfast would be all right. It felt like they—and the city of Belfast—had been fortunate. So far, at least, they had been spared.

"I did a round of the animals this morning, and all our charges are doing quite well," Mr. Wright went on, his hands tucked in the pockets of his jacket. "The cheetahs and lions were a wee bit rattled. Despite getting overexcited, the lemurs didn't escape. Rajan, Maggie, Violet, Wallace, and the whole lot of them, they are in good spirits. I have plans to speak with Mr. Christie by telephone this afternoon. I will reassure him that all is well at Bellevue and that we are watching over the animals."

Mr. Wright studied the pages of his notebook and then looked up again.

"Resume your assignments as usual," he said. "The zoo will remain open for visitors today. We're not going to let the Germans close our doors and deprive the public of our animals and the necessary diversion that they offer. I'll be in touch with any further updates."

At lunchtime, Hettie and the rest of the staff reconvened in the canteen. During the second meeting, Mr. Wright confirmed that thirteen individuals had been killed, with the twelve civilian deaths occurring in the dock area. One of the antiaircraft gunners had been killed when a shell exploded prematurely. According to Mr. Wright's sources, bombs had been dropped from a squadron of Heinkel He 111 aircraft for just over three hours. He reported that about five hundred German aircraft had bombed multiple cities throughout the United Kingdom on that same evening, including Birmingham, Liverpool, Bristol, and Coventry, but that Clydeside had been the main target. Hettie wondered where her father was now, if he had been in any of those cities the night before and if he might call and see how they were doing since Belfast had been struck. Then she found herself thinking of Liam and Maeve again, and fretting about their welfare.

"The Floral Hall will remain open, too," Mr. Wright said, referring to his recent phone call with Mr. Christie. "Margaret Dolan will be performing, and later in the week, on the evening of Easter Tuesday, Stella Holliday will be returning for an encore performance."

Amid the cheer that went up at this announcement, Hettie and Ferris exchanged glances. For Hettie, it felt as if that early-spring evening at the Floral Hall had happened a long time ago, as if the days and nights possessed a protracted quality, stretching out seamlessly into months rather than just a few weeks. Because of the bombing and her preoccupation with Violet, she had almost forgotten the unpleasantness with Samuel Greene and her sudden flying fist.

"Maybe we can go and hear Stella Holliday again," Ferris said, looking up at Hettie.

"I have a wedding to attend that night," she said.

"No worries," Ferris responded. "We'll see Stella next time."

"Yes, next time," Hettie said with a smile even though she was relieved to have another obligation that evening. She didn't want to endure another evening at the Floral Hall any time soon.

That morning, Rose had received confirmation from her cousin Frances that her son's wedding would still be taking place. With the government and Prime Minister Andrews encouraging Belfast's citizens to resume daily life as usual, Frances had notified guests that the ceremony and reception would go on as originally planned. Her eldest son, Matthew, was getting married to his sweetheart, whom he had met in the church choir over seven years ago. Hettie had tried to convince Rose that there was no need for her to attend, but her mother left no room for discussion. She said the extended family had shown up for Anna's funeral, and Frances had paid them multiple visits, bringing loaves of wheaten and soda bread, using her rationed eggs and butter rather than saving the precious goods for her own table.

"Proceed with your duties," Mr. Wright continued. "If you have any concerns, let me know."

That evening, as Hettie sat in the courtyard paring carrots, potatoes, and turnips for dinner, she heard the telephone ringing from inside the house, and Rose answered. She heard her mother utter a few *huh-uh*s followed by *Did you receive our telegram about Anna?* Then there was a silence and a few more exchanges. *I think they've gone to the countryside with his family. I don't know if they will be returning.* Rose's tone shifted into something more neutral. Almost businesslike. *Not to worry*, she said. *We're fine.* And then finally, *Yes, I'll tell her. Yes. Yes. Goodbye.*

Rose hung up the phone and appeared in the doorway. She wiped her hands on a stained tea towel. A degree of peace and sadness seemed to have settled into her mother's eyes and lips. Rose continued to wipe her hands on the towel even though they were already dry.

"That was your father," she finally said.

"Where on bloody earth is he?" Hettie asked.

"Norwich."

"When is he coming home?"

"He said the Merchant Navy needs him," Rose said, sitting down on the concrete step. "Now isn't a good time to leave."

"Do you believe him?"

"No," Rose said flatly, "I don't believe him, but I don't think that matters so much anymore."

"Did he ask about Anna? Does he even know about Maeve?"

"He said he was sorry that he didn't make it home for the funeral," Rose said, her voice low. "He was very sorry about that."

"Did he ask to speak me?" Hettie asked, even though she already knew the answer.

"He sounded hurried, as if someone else was waiting to use the phone—"

"He's not coming home this time, you know," Hettie interrupted, her words sharp and acerbic. "He's never coming home." She felt an impulse to throw the bucket of peeled vegetables against the brick wall of their courtyard or to throw her fist against the hard surface.

"No, I don't think he is coming home." Rose lowered her gaze to the pavement littered with vegetable peelings and then looked up at Hettie. A clarity seemed to sharpen Rose's features.

Hettie realized that it was the first time her mother had admitted that Thomas wasn't returning home, that somehow she had stepped out of the ever-present fog of her grief into the reality of her life: Her oldest daughter was dead; she was estranged from her only grandchild; and her husband of twenty-five years was gone. Despite the undeniable grief of all this, Hettie found she felt strangely relieved to finally know that her father would not be returning home.

"We're going to be fine," Rose said with an unfamiliar steadiness in her voice. "We don't need him."

Hettie dropped the broken carrots into the bucket.

"I'm sorry, you know, about Anna and Liam," Rose continued.

"It's all right, Mum," Hettie reassured her.

"I wanted a certain kind of life for your sister and her baby," Rose said, wringing the towel in her hands. "I wanted Maeve to be raised a certain way."

"You don't have to explain."

"Have you heard from the Keegans? How are they getting along?"

"Liam found himself a job with a local mechanic. His uncle keeps a small farm. Chickens, goats, and horses. Maeve is happy there."

Her mother nodded and responded, "I'm glad they're getting along."

As they sat in a compatible silence, a pair of jays crisscrossed through the early evening. Mr. Reynolds's dog yipped on the other side of the courtyard's brick wall. The pair of birds flew higher and higher until they disappeared beyond the treetops of budding leaves and into the watery, half-lit sky.

"Are you done?" Rose asked after a few minutes, nodding toward the two remaining turnips on the pavement.

"Almost."

After dinner, Hettie and Rose listened to the six o'clock news on the wireless. As they sipped their cups of tea, the commentator reported on further updates about the recent bombing. A parachute bomb had destroyed a fuselage factory; he didn't say where, but everyone in Belfast knew it was Harland & Wolff. Another bomb had fallen on Alexandra Park Avenue, he said, leaving behind a fifteen-foot crater in the middle of the road. But, he added gleefully, none of the surrounding row houses had been damaged and not a single window had been broken.

"The government is certainly trying to keep up morale with their reports," Rose commented.

"Wouldn't we better off knowing the extent of things?"

"There's nothing to be done about it."

Rose clicked off the wireless.

"Pick some rhubarb, will you?" her mother said. "I'm going to make a pie for Aunt Sylvia."

"Yes, Mum."

As Hettie stepped into the courtyard, she had almost forgotten that the following day was Easter Tuesday. It had always been a holiday that they had celebrated as a family—attending the morning service followed by an afternoon meal of roast beef, potatoes, gravy, and Yorkshire pudding. When Hettie and Anna were young, Rose used to put together elaborate straw baskets laden with dyed hard-boiled eggs, chocolate eggs, caramel creams, and multicolored sugary buttons on rolled sleeves of paper, and then hid the baskets in hard-to-find spots around their house. Anna had always saved her Easter stockpile, parceling out a couple of pieces to herself each day, while Hettie would eat her share of sweets within two or three sittings, often leaving her with a stomachache and an envy for her older sister's remaining store.

Hettie picked several stalks of rhubarb and a handful of lettuce, and rinsed the vegetables under the spigot attached to the house. Diluted dirt ran over her fingers as she washed the rhubarb one more time and took it in to her mother in the kitchen.

"Thank you, my sweet girl," Rose said with a smile.

Hettie smiled back at her mother and sat down at the kitchen table with her, refilling their cups of tea. Rose busied herself collecting and measuring ingredients for the pie. Hettie absentmindedly reached into the pocket of her trousers and fingered the edges of something smooth. She took the object out of her pocket. It was the snail that Ferris had given her back in December. She had forgotten that she had slid the snail into her pocket a few days ago; until then, she had kept it in a small pot of soil in their courtyard. Hettie positioned it on the kitchen table and stared at the concentric circles of the mollusk's design. The evening light struck the shell, intensifying its pink iridescence before its smooth surface became flat again. The snail's antennae tentatively emerged from its chamber and waved in the air. She smiled to herself. The snail extended its dark neck and wriggled its antennae farther. Hettie retrieved a few leaves from a celery stalk in the larder and placed them next to it, and it began to munch away on one of the leaves. Though it was logical that the snail would be hungry, Hettie was quietly amazed by the rate at which the snail devoured the leaf.

"What you got there?" Rose asked from the sink.

"Oh, nothing," Hettie said.

The creature glided onto the next leaf and began to gnaw a hole through it.

"A snail," Rose said, looking over her shoulder.

"He's hungry," Hettie said with a grin. "Can't you hear him eating?"

"Of course I can," Rose said with a soft laugh before returning her attention to the ingredients on the counter.

Hettie continued to watch the snail eat the remaining leaves and as her mother made her rhubarb pie. The comforting sounds of domesticity took over the kitchen: the occasional sound of water running from the tap, the whisking of ingredients, the dough being worked against the counter. Outside, the neighborhood children's voices materialized as they started up another game of rounders. There was the whack of the bat against the ball. The boys cheered one another. After the snail finished eating, the creature returned to the safety of its shell.

On the following day, Easter Tuesday, Rose and Hettie rode the tram back from the wedding, which had been held at Sinclair Seamen's Church, not far from the Customs House and the river. They had felt some apprehension traveling to and from the city center for the wedding. Air-raid warnings had rung out on each of the previous four nights, a sure sign that German aircraft had been spotted overhead. Also during the week, army units had been moving searchlights into position in different parts of the city, and had also installed crude stoves in the harbor area, which belched out thick smoke to obscure the Germans' aerial views of the city. It even seemed that the police and the troops on patrol were more vigilant and more anxious. Certainly, more people were carrying gas masks. The smell of burning still lingered faintly in the air. A Union Jack fluttered in the southwesterly breeze at the top of a flagpole next to the Customs House. As the tram traveled through the heart of the city, Hettie noticed longer queues than usual at the bus stops. Most of the shops were closed for the public holiday, and some of them had their windows boarded up. The Great Victoria Street railway station looked to be busier than normal. She wondered whether people were taking advantage of their day off to go on day trips, or if they were fleeing the city altogether in expectation of another air raid.

In other parts of Belfast, daily life persisted. At St. Paul's Parish on the Falls Road, a surge of congregants lined up for confession with the priests, far greater numbers than the usual seasonal upswing. In the meantime, football fans filled the terraces at Celtic Park and cheered as Celtic defeated Linfield by three goals to one. A new James Cagney picture, *Torrid Zone*, played at the Ritz Cinema. Some teenage boys gathered on the banks of the River Lagan, not far from Shaw's Bridge, hoping to catch a salmon or a trout for tea. A shower of rice and confetti was tossed in the wake of a bride and groom outside the Carlisle Memorial Methodist Church. Evidently, Hettie reflected, as she and her mother rode the tram, the citizens of Belfast were taking to heart the prime minister's advice of carrying on.

In an effort to maintain peace on the streets, annual republican demonstrations—which usually took place every year to commemorate the 1916 Easter Rising—had been banned in Belfast that day. Hettie had heard on the wireless that thousands of people had gathered in Dublin the day before for a military parade and a rousing speech by de Valera, himself a volunteer commandant during the Easter Rising, commending the heroics of the men who fought during the six-day rebellion. Despite Liam's views of de Valera, Hettie wondered if Liam had made the train trip from Newcastle to Dublin to be a part of the celebration and as a way to remember his father's brother. At the same time, she wondered if Liam's involvement with the republicans would bring him back to Belfast sooner than later; certainly he would write to Hettie and let her know if he was returning anytime soon.

Hettie and Rose disembarked at the Upper Antrim Road. The skies had cleared and the mid-April sun was lowering, sending thick bands of coral pink and lavender along the western horizon. There was a mild breeze. In the flower beds of some of the row houses, the delicate petals of yellow and bluish-purple crocuses were beginning to open. A jaundiced tinge still clung to the spring air.

"Did you see Lily Jamison at the reception?" Rose asked as they made their way to the Whitewell Road. "She's recovered nicely from her broken engagement with Walter Hollis. What a dreadful thing he did, breaking things off by post while he's fighting with the forces in North Africa. Her dress was quite pretty, don't you think? And the bride, I wonder where the family managed to find that beautiful lace? It must belong to her mum or grandmother."

A rare levity percolated in Rose's voice. It had been a long time since Hettie had witnessed this kind of lightness in her mother. It seemed as if her veil of melancholy had finally lifted, allowing room for her former, livelier spirit to return. She wondered if it was thanks to attending a relative's wedding—instead of a memorial service—or receiving the phone call from Thomas. Even though there was still loss, it was now a defined loss rather than an ambiguous one floating between here and there. Instead, her grief had rearranged itself into something concrete and tangible so that Rose could move on rather than continue to wait for her husband who was never going to return home.

She looked younger, too, dressed in her navy blue dress with a knitted shawl draped over her shoulders. For the wedding, she had worn her mother's gold brooch of a simple bow on the neck of her ruffled collar. Her round cheeks gave off a pinkish glow.

"Matthew looked like a regular gentleman," Rose said. "So grown-up."

Hettie stared in the direction of the wooded slope of the Cavehill. The buds of cedar and beech trees had begun to unfold their light green leaves, making the zoo's pathways and enclosures less visible from the road. She was curious how the day had gone at the zoo; despite the recent bombing, Mr. Wright was expecting increased attendance. It was a tradition in the city to visit the Bellevue Zoo on the bank holiday for a family day out. Hettie was disappointed not to be there. With the gates now locked for the night, she imagined the lemurs and the monkeys quieting down; the parrots, parakeets, and peacocks singing their distinctive songs; and the lioness and her cubs curling up against one another in their den. Night was coming, and all the animals were settling in for the hours of darkness ahead. For a moment, Hettie wished she could be with Violet at the Elephant House—and away from her mother and her enthusiastic chatter about Matthew's wedding. Despite her mother's liveliness, Hettie still felt a hint of judgment, a kind of unspoken message of the absence of a relationship and a future of marriage and children in Hettie's life. No matter how well she and her mother were getting along, there would always be a tension riding underneath their pleasant exchanges.

She still didn't know how to find the words to express to her mother that this kind of conventional life wasn't going to happen for her, this wasn't her ambition. Instead, Hettie hoped to remain Violet's zookeeper as long as the elephant lived, and then perhaps later, she would travel to other zoos throughout Europe and the world, and meet other elephants and other female zookeepers. Over the years, she would become known as an expert of elephants, as her understanding of the sophisticated social behavior of the extraordinary mammal would continue to grow. Hettie would become a sort of elephant angel. An expert, like Mr. Wright. People would seek her out. People would want to know her. She would no longer be alone.

"Hettie, are you listening to me?" Rose asked.

Hettie started. "Sorry, Mum," she said. "What were you saying?"

Rose glanced at her. In the pocket of her coat, Hettie touched the curve of the snail that Ferris had given her. Its smooth surface felt both soft and hard.

"You look peaked," Rose said, sounding more worried than annoyed.

Hettie hesitated before admitting: "I was thinking about Violet."

Her mother took Hettie's free hand in hers and gently squeezed it. A warmth traveled up the length of Hettie's arm and into the bony ridge of her shoulder. Rose released her grip as they turned onto the Whitewell Road. Now that the sun had set, a blanket of stars started to emerge across the vast sweep of the Belfast sky. On either side of the Whitewell Road, the scattered windows of the terraced houses were dark except for an occasional careless light casting a beam despite the blackout. The moon was three-quarters full. Up ahead, a beaten tin can was positioned in the middle of the road. More than a half dozen children were standing in a row behind the can.

"One, two, three," Johnny Gibson yelled before kicking it down the center of the street.

The can hurtled and clanked against the road before finally arriving at a standstill a few feet away from Rose's and Hettie's feet. Johnny ran toward them with all his might. He was dressed in his holiday clothes—wool short trousers, a tie loosely knotted at his neck, and a white button-down, its sleeves crumpled up to his freckled elbows. He pumped his fists on either side of his stout body until he reached the can, collected it, and returned it to its upright position. Then he began to count to ten. The other children dispersed into hiding places—behind a hedge of evergreens, in the low branches of an ash tree, inside the empty dustbins at the end of a graveled driveway.

"Eight, nine, ten," Johnny yelled. "Ready or not, here I come—"

Rose and Hettie exchanged smiles as they continued to walk down their street. One of the children released a series of hoots from his hiding spot, then there was a shrill scream. Johnny had found Lily Brown hiding in the rear seat of her grandfather's car.

"You cheated."

"Did not—"

"I'm going to tell my grandpa—"

"Cheater—"

"Mum—" Johnny Gibson cried. "I did not."

Inside, Rose and Hettie settled into their routine of listening to the wireless with their evening cups of tea. The news program with the commentator William Joyce—popularly known as Lord Haw-Haw on account of his sneering, snooty voice—came on. His nightly propaganda broadcast *Germany Calling* played on the English-language German station out of Hamburg. Hettie had heard Joyce's program before and also had read about the commentator in the newspaper; he was attracting a growing audience because of the universal suspicion over the government-censored news on the BBC. At the beginning of the show, Joyce exuberantly reported on the Luftwaffe's successive string of bombings in British cities, including Coventry, Tyneside, and Birmingham. He repeated how just a few nights before, on April 11, Bristol was attacked again in what was being called the Good Friday Raid. With unconcealed exuberance, Joyce stated that over a thousand people had been killed and countless homes and other buildings had been destroyed as a result of the Luftwaffe's aerial attacks on the city.

"I'd rather listen to something else," Hettie said. "Why do we listen to this rubbish, anyway?"

"Sometimes it can be helpful to hear both sides," her mother said evenly.

A crackle of static interrupted the show, and then Joyce's menacing voice resumed. "Germany calling, Germany calling. There will be Easter eggs for Belfast."

"Perhaps you're right," Rose said, and without further hesitation, she dialed the wireless to her favorite classical music station, the BBC Home Service. Hettie recognized the familiar notes of Bach's *Goldberg Variations*, the piano chords alighting into a whimsical melody of flying leaps and dramatic plunges.

"By 'Easter eggs,' he meant bombs, didn't he?" Hettie asked.

"He talks about an attack every night," Rose said calmly. "No one takes William Joyce seriously."

Hettie stared through the darkened window over the kitchen sink. She could still hear the children's voices in the street.

"No, you're it!"

"You're it."

"I don't want to be it again. It's not fair!"

"Yes, it is!"

"One, two, three, four, five," the children yelled, their joyful voices converging into one sweet, discordant song. "Six, seven, eight, nine, ten!" The can was kicked again, hurtling down the road.

"I'm going to turn in early," Rose said. She stood up from her chair, leaned over, and gave Hettie a kiss on her forehead.

Hettie couldn't remember the last time her mother had kissed her good night. Despite Rose's lightened mood, Hettie was still surprised by the comfort and kindness of it all, how this sort of affection had returned to her relationship with her mother, that they were now a family of two—mother and daughter—and through everything, they had emerged a little more resilient than what Hettie had thought was possible.

"Good night, Mum," she whispered, squeezing Rose's hand.

Hettie sat at the kitchen table and took in the sounds of the night. The children's rising and falling voices. The tin can careening down the street. The distant horn of a car. A cat's sorrowful meow from one of the neighbors' backyards. Finally, a mother called for her children. Several of the boys and girls said good night to each other. The second hand of the clock over the doorway ticked loudly. The black cotton drapes over the kitchen window weren't fully drawn, and a moth fluttered against the illuminated glass, beating its powdery wings as it attempted to draw closer to the glow. The sight of the insect reminded Hettie of the night when she'd been at the zoo with Violet during the bombing, and the orange-winged moth that had somehow found its way into the Elephant House.

The moth zigzagged, knocking its tiny body against the glass of the kitchen window. Again and again and again. Hettie clicked off the overhead light and then sat for a few more minutes and sipped the rest of her tea. The remaining neighborhood children called good night to each other, their innocent voices ringing out in the evening until finally silence took over the Whitewell Road—and the moth vanished.

Eight

ON THAT NIGHT OF EASTER TUESDAY, THE SOUND OF SIRENS stirred Hettie from sleep yet again. Within a few minutes, though, the short, imperious cries ceased, and an eerie silence veiled the night. Hettie sat up in bed. She heard her mother padding down the hallway. Rose poked her head into Hettie's bedroom.

"I'll be right back."

Rose disappeared, then Hettie heard the front door slam shut. She got out of bed and slipped into a cardigan, socks, and shoes. Outside, her mother stood at the end of their walkway, her arms tightly crossed over her chest, staring up at the unchanged sky. Other neighbors lingered. It appeared to be another false alarm. Relief spread through Hettie like a drink of cold water on a hot day. She wanted to believe that the Germans wouldn't be returning so soon, that Hitler had more critical targets to hit in England. At the same time, this thought made her feel sick to her stomach; she wished no one had to suffer under the wrath of the barbaric dictator. The evening breeze kicked up and then died again, and Hettie shivered. Rose returned to the house and fetched two cups of warm tea. They stood on the street with their neighbors.

"I can't believe they would fly up here again, especially on such a cloudy night," Mr. Reynolds said, lighting a cigarette.

"Did you hear Haw-Haw on his show?" Mr. Brown said. "He was predicting another attack."

"Belfast would no longer exist if we believed every word that traitor said," responded Mr. Reynolds.

Together, they watched the sky and sipped their tea. After about a half hour, Hettie heard the same unsynchronized drone of the German bombers that she had heard the week before. An odd calm possessed the sky despite the fact the collective drone was growing louder. Hettie bit into her bottom lip. She didn't want to believe what she was hearing. Within seconds, their splintered, mechanical purr occupied the night. Everyone looked up, knowing that the sound indicated the approach of low-flying planes. This time, they were arriving in massive numbers. The sky lit up. The city's newly arrived searchlights pierced the darkness. Hundreds of flares dropped from the Heinkels, illuminating the horizon like a summer's day. A loud, concussive explosion echoed against the Cavehill. Silvery parachute mines began to float down like diaphanous ghosts wandering through the night sky.

The buzz and whir of aircraft engines grew even louder; now they were overhead. An *ack-ack-ack* penetrated the explosions. Amber bursts emerged along the edge of the night. The ground shook. Some of the bombs whistled as they fell. The deafening sounds and explosions accelerated, overlapping like fast-moving riptides, colliding and collapsing into one another again and again.

People ran in all directions, some with their pets, to shelters or to the homes of relatives or friends. Others found refuge under kitchen tables, in cubbyholes under the stairs, or in the rooms that held the family's holy pictures. Air-raid wardens and rescue workers scurried toward their posts while soldiers and airmen took up their positions behind antiaircraft guns.

"Go to the shelter on Atlantic Avenue," Rose yelled over the increasing din. "Run, my sweet girl, run!"

Hettie turned to her mother and hugged her.

"I have to go to the zoo," Hettie said.

And before her mother could say anything else, she ran along the street. The vibrations traveled through the soles of her shoes, up her legs, and into the center of her chest. Fear radiated throughout her limbs. Hettie saw strangers congregating in the middle of the streets, their necks craned skyward, their hands clasped over their mouths. The red sky was all around them, disturbing and hypnotic at once. Hettie continued to run. Other people surged up the Antrim Road toward the Cavehill to seek refuge in the shadowy ditches, hedgerows, and caves there rather than fleeing to the city shelters because of the rumors that the structures might not provide adequate protection when the bombs began to fall.

As she flew past, Hettie heard snatches of strangers' panic.

"The Germans. The bloody Germans."

"They're coming for us. They're going to kill us all."

"Holy mother of God."

"The goddamn IRA," screamed an older man, and she saw him shaking his fist into the smoke-filled air. "They put the Nazis up to this. They've lit lights and fires to guide their path." Hettie hoped this wasn't true.

More and more people emptied out of their houses onto the already crowded streets, but Hettie turned away from the chaos and onto the Crazy Path, and ran faster. The sky lit up again. Heat traveled into her limbs. A terror rushed along the narrow slope of her shoulders. Hettie reached for deeper breaths. Flames raged in the sky. Frantic shadows danced against the dense forest wall. It felt as if the whole world was on fire.

"Run, run, run," Hettie repeated to herself.

She pushed her legs harder, running as fast as she ever had in her life. Suddenly she was back with Anna, when they were young and would race across the manicured playing fields of the Academy, the wet blades of grass biting at her bare ankles, the morning dew brushing against her cheeks. Somewhere on the pitch someone blew a whistle. The sisters' legs stretched underneath them, their fists pumping at the sides of their slender frames, and Hettie felt a shimmer of joy for a moment. But as the sound of bombs rent the air, she came back to the horror of her surroundings. Tears stung the corners of her eyes. Flames licked the night. *I don't want to die,* she said to herself. *Please don't let me die. Please don't let Violet die. Please don't let my mother die.* The ground shook again.

Hettie ran toward the zoo's rear entrance as the sky lit up again. She unlocked the padlock and flung the gate open. At the Elephant House, Hettie found Violet pacing the yard. As Hettie slowed to approach the elephant, her ribs aching from the run, the acrid smell of fresh dung hit her like a slap in the face. Violet released a deep guttural cry.

"I'm here, Vi," Hettie said softly. "I'm here."

Light gathered and scattered in the sky. Hettie heard the continuing drone of aircraft. Dozens of bombers were up there now, and they all seemed to be approaching from the northeast, along the shores of the Belfast Lough, and flying directly over the Whitewell Road. Hettie rubbed Violet absently behind one of her ears. The elephant's skin felt cold and clammy. She rested her cheek against Violet's heaving side and rubbed the elephant behind her ear again, speaking softly to her, the way that Thomas used to whisper to Hettie when she couldn't fall asleep when a thunderstorm rolled over their neighborhood. Only then did she notice the wall of animal cries and howls that surrounded the Elephant House. It was different than the other night. Louder. Fiercer. And it came from all sides. Like everything was escalating to another level, another volume, another rung of fear, another circle of violence.

As Hettie listened, the fine hairs on the nape of her neck stood on end. The animals' calls gained more definition. The growls of lions and leopards. The roars of the black bears. The cackles of the hyenas. The shrieks of the monkeys and baboons. The brays of the sea lions. The squawks of the toucans and macaws. It was as if a call and response were taking place between the animals, and the shadows and darkness transformed into its own sort of mythic cathedral with all its devout congregants praying in their distinctive tongues at the sacred altar of their greater animal god with hopes of reaching a higher state, a higher consciousness, so they could endure this suffering of higher proportions. They were singing, singing to something.

Hettie closed her eyes—and prayed. She prayed for her mother. She prayed for Violet. She prayed for Maeve. She prayed for Liam and for Ferris. She prayed for her father. She prayed for Johnny Gibson, Martha and Lizzie Reynolds, Lily Brown, Albert O'Brien, and the other neighborhood children. She prayed for Mr. Wright. She prayed for Eliza Crowley. She even prayed for Samuel Greene. She prayed for Anna. And then she prayed for herself, that she would wake up and experience another morning. The calls of the animals soared into a vortex of cries and screams while the Germans continued to bomb Belfast. All of it was breaking upon Hettie—the horror, the sadness, the loss—at once.

Violet released another terrified cry. With her hand still resting on the elephant's side, Hettie felt the sound travel along Violet's rib cage. She knew that the other animals' cries were making the elephant more agitated, but there was nothing to be done. In fact, there was little she could do about anything. Her city was being destroyed. Her sister was dead. Her father was gone. Hettie folded over her knees and lowered onto the dusty yard of the Elephant House, and rocked on her heels. *Help me. Please help me. Someone, please help me.*

Something slipped inside Hettie. A vague, sharp grief. The ground shook again. Her knees felt watery and weak. It felt as if she were breathing in tiny shards of glass. Everything hurt. Violet released another loose stream of diarrhea against the ground. The wings of birds flapped wildly. Monkeys rattled their cages. The wall of sound was infinite and continuous. Hettie willed herself to stand up and retrieve the rubber hose attached to the side of the Elephant House, but when she turned the spigot, no water trickled from its brass mouth.

"Fucking brilliant," Hettie said to herself. "Why aren't you working?"

"Hettie! Is that you?"

It was Mr. Wright. He stood outside Violet's enclosure, peering in at Hettie in disbelief. He was dressed in his pajamas, a red cotton jacket and trousers bordered with white piping, and a pair of wellingtons that were tucked into the legs of his pajama bottoms. Hettie had forgotten that she was still wearing her nightclothes, too.

"I'm afraid the damage is far greater this time," Mr. Wright said.

"There's no water," Hettie said, holding up the end of the dry hose.

"They might have hit the waterworks." Fiery bursts of yellow and orange bloomed over the treetops, and Mr. Wright glanced up at them, his eyes wary. "Come with me, we can check on the lions and polar bears," Mr. Wright said. "It won't take long."

Hettie glanced over at Violet. She was now lying on her side on the hay-strewn floor of the Elephant House. Hettie didn't want to leave her, but didn't feel she could say no to Mr. Wright. "Stay there, Vi," she said. "I'll be back."

Hettie followed Mr. Wright up the footpath that led to the lions' den at the upper reaches of the zoo. The higher they walked, the more discernible the Belfast Harbor became, with the rising flames dancing along its distant edges. The moon was no longer visible, obscured by clouds of black smoke. The drone of airplanes was punctuated by the staccato pops of the antiaircraft guns.

Then Hettie heard the lilting notes of a big band, and she paused for a moment. Amid the falling bombs and the calls of the frightened animals, the music sounded alien and peculiar, as if it were from another world. It seemed impossible that something that embodied beauty and grace could exist right now in this city, in this zoo, in the Floral Hall.

Hettie followed Mr. Wright up the gradual incline to the front steps of the venue. Several buckets of sand and water were lined up along the facade of the building. Just like the Saturday night that Hettie had seen her, Stella Holliday was backed up by a big band of trombones, trumpets, flutes, violins, and snare drums. The performer's mellifluous voice floated out the double doors.

"She is still singing," Mr. Wright said, walking up the stairs to the hall. "I can't believe she's still singing."

Together Mr. Wright and Hettie stepped inside. The Floral Hall was half full. Stray clutches of strangers danced near the stage, swaying like unmoored ships at sea. The teardrop-shaped lights of the chandeliers were dimmed, looking like the leftover embers of a fire. Hettie felt she had entered a dream, crossed over a threshold into another reality, where citizens weren't dying and homes weren't being destroyed and the sky wasn't on fire. Instead, it was only Stella Holliday and her extraordinary song.

"She says she's gonna sing until the bombs stop falling," said a man who stood by the entrance. "Lots of people ran for the shelters, but I think it's safer here. Listen to her. Look at her."

The stage's perimeter was aglow with hurricane lamps, the flames fluttering within their transparent chimneys. Standing before the diffused light was Stella Holliday, dressed in a sapphire-blue gown that dropped luxuriously to the floor. She sang deeply, her hands folded over the center of the chest, her eyes closed. Despite all that was going on, Hettie felt held by the dimly lit hall, by Mr. Wright standing right beside her, and by Stella Holliday's ethereal voice.

I'll be seeing you / In all the old familiar places.

Stella Holliday's full red lips grazed the stand-up microphone as her honey-hued voice was amplified through the oversize speakers that sat on either side of the elevated stage. Hettie thought Stella looked as though she were dedicating every cell and fiber of her body to her song as she moved into the final refrain.

I'll find you in the morning sun / And when the night is new.

Hettie glanced over at Mr. Wright: He appeared to be caught in a trance, as he watched Stella Holliday. His expression was open and full of melancholy, joy, and exaltation. He mouthed the lyrics to the song.

I'll be looking at the moon / But I'll be seeing you.

The floor of the hall shook with more force, but Mr. Wright didn't flinch as he continued to sing along with Stella Holliday. The chandeliers swung. There was another explosion. Several people ran for the door, clenching their bags and coats, ducking their heads. Truly afraid now, Hettie tugged on Mr. Wright's sleeve, but he didn't respond. Another eruption rocked the ground. Instead of staying by Mr. Wright's side, Hettie followed the other people outside the Floral Hall.

Despite her mounting fear, she couldn't stop herself from wanting to witness what was taking place in the city below. Hettie stood at the top of the short flight of stairs, and looked out.

Belfast was a city of flames. Streets, homes, churches, factories, stores. All of it burned and burned and burned. There was a rain of ashes and soot. Everything felt light and heavy.

Hundreds of civilians were losing their lives. Many were being crushed in the air-raid shelters, the unsturdy structures collapsing from the explosions of the parachuted land mines, the sea-green canopies inflating with air and smoke, floating onto rooftops, with the clockwork mechanisms detonating twenty-five seconds after landing.

Walls fell. Concrete roofs tumbled down.

Legs and arms were crushed. Feet were mangled.

A chaotic opera of screams and cries rose into the red sky.

Later, Hettie would learn that the Atlantic Avenue shelter was hit by a parachute mine that caused the roof to collapse, killing most of the people who had found refuge there. A young woman who had fled the Floral Hall to get to the shelter only minutes before she was killed instantly. A mother of two young girls was trapped by the shelter's crumpled roof with the lifeless young woman lying across her legs, bits and pieces of her brain stuck to the mother's stockings. The mother thought, *I'm going to die tonight. I'm going to leave my girls behind without a mother.*

The mother's seven-year-old daughter peered through the cracks of light and listened for her father's voice. Right before the blast, a man in a uniform had yelled, *Hit the ground! Get down on your tummies!* As the girl lay still underneath the rubble, she thought about the enormous balloons she had seen suspended in the sky right before her family ducked into the darkened tunnel of the shelter, how the barrage balloons resembled gigantic floating pigs without legs, their silver bellies pressing down from the night sky. *What are those pigs doing up there?* she thought more than once. *Who is going to feed them?* And then the pigs had begun to sing, a metallic twanging, like the plucking of a wire.

The girl was worried about her mother and her sister and how her Easter dress and Easter gloves were getting dirty and her best Sunday shoes were pinching her toes. Her ankles hurt, and pebbles pressed against her cheek. It smelled of pungent urine. The girl thought of the song that everyone was singing right before the room started to fall and disappear. *Roll out the barrel, we'll have a barrel of fun. Roll out the barrel, we've got the blues on the run.* How blue-orange flames had flickered and danced in the little oil lamps scattered throughout the cave-like space. How she had been standing at her mother's knee, her mum sitting in one of the hard chairs, her soft hand resting against her girl's lower back. She longed for her mum's touch now. She longed for the collective song of the strangers.

Across the street from the city hall, in the clerical office of an insurance company, a young man who had been recruited as a firewatcher by his employer, equipped with two buckets of water and sandbags, wasn't quite sure what to do with either once the bombs started to fall in rapid succession. It was impossible to discern if the explosions came from the falling bombs or from the antiaircraft guns attempting to take down the enemy planes. The noise was deafening, unbelievable. The young man and his fellow watcher took the stairs to the building's roof. Even at the top, they could feel the vibrations from the falling bombs. In the distance, his co-worker pointed toward north Belfast, where fires raged across the residential neighborhoods, and the young man wondered if his home on Duncairn Gardens, where he lived with his father and mother, was still intact.

Earlier, before the first bombs fell, a dockworker had walked over to the Percy Street shelter to entertain his friends and neighbors with his melodeon. This was his nature—to entertain others. After a few hours of playing, the man had returned to his two-bedroom house, and as he fell asleep he thought how lucky it was that his three sons and wife had evacuated to the countryside near Lisburn four days before. A few minutes later, one of the bombs hit a nearby roof and sent a large piece of concrete up into the air; upon falling, it landed on the man while he was sleeping in bed, killing him instantly.

In the Clonard Monastery, situated off the Falls Road, Catholics and Protestants filed down the steep steps into the ornate crypt below the monastery's high altar. Together, people sang the familiar hymns "O God, Our Help in Ages Past" and "Nearer, My God, to Thee" as the mills and docks burned throughout the late hours of the night. All fervently prayed and sang hymns. Catholics murmured recitations of the rosary, the smooth amber beads running through their weathered fingers, till their voices were hoarse and their throats dry. They prayed together for the bombing to end—and for the morning to come quickly. They prayed for their souls.

But during that moment on the evening of April 15, 1941, Hettie knew only about the endless display of detonations and the sweet, sophisticated voice of Stella Holliday. She thought about Ferris and Samuel. Was Samuel patrolling the streets and guiding civilians to safety? Was Ferris at home with his band of animals? Were both men still alive, even? And what about her mother? Had she stayed at home? Or was she standing in the street with their neighbors? Had she taken cover? Or was Rose seeing right now what Hettie was seeing—that Belfast was an inferno?

A rim of flames burned along the far edge of the Antrim Road. With all the rolling billows of smoke, it was hard to determine where the fires began and ended. Another explosion erupted. This one was closer, and a kick of fright nearly pushed Hettie over. She ran. Someone yelled, "Hit the ground!" but she ignored them, racing down the steps of the Floral Hall, down the darkened pathway that led to the heart of the zoo and Violet's enclosure. There, inside the Elephant House, Violet was pacing and squealing piteously. Hettie cast around for a way to comfort the poor creature. She reached into the pocket of her coat and was surprised to find a leftover sweet bun. The spongy bread was flattened and moist. Hettie placed it in her open palm, and the elephant swept the roll up with her trunk and dropped it into her mouth.

The concrete structure shook again. The bombs were now falling along the upper reaches of the Antrim Road, falling ever closer to where Hettie and Violet cowered in the darkness of the Elephant House. Hettie briefly considered going to find her mother, but decided that it would be safer to wait out the attack with Violet. She hoped to God that Rose was all right. A part of Hettie wished she had never left her mother's side and the other part of her was grateful to be with Violet, knowing that the elephant might remain safe and secure as long as Hettie was with her.

She arranged her coat on a mound of hay and lay down, closing her eyes. The boiled wool of her coat smelled of smoke, mold, and Rose's lilac perfume. A sadness and terror traveled up from her gut and moved into her chest before spreading into her throat and finally pressing into her eyes. Hettie tasted salt in her mouth. There was another explosion somewhere, and she heard the creak of Violet's swinging trunk. The elephant folded onto her legs, and her rear landed with a thump on the damp, hay-covered floor. Hettie felt a modicum of relief, seeing that Violet was going to try to rest amid the chaos. Outside the enclosure, Hettie heard the loud braying of the other animals: the parrots, the monkeys, and the lions. She pressed close to Violet's rounded back and draped her arm over the elephant. Violet released another soft trumpet call. Hettie reached her arm farther over the elephant's broad side. Violet's rubbery skin pressed against her cheek.

Hettie heard the distant cry of a child. *Where's me mammy? Me mammy?* An ambulance raced down a road, its rooftop siren howling. There were the metallic pops of gunfire, like a long belt of firecrackers being ignited at once, one after another. Heat played against her cheek. She forced herself to focus on the rise and fall of Violet's breathing against her stomach. She closed her eyes again.

The continuous whine of the all-clear signal sounded at about five o'clock in the morning. Waking from a fitful doze, Hettie lifted herself up from the grimy floor of the Elephant House and wiped the loose strands of hay from her coat and nightgown. She looked over at Violet. The elephant was still lying on her side, sleeping. A pall of yellow smoke hung in the air.

Hettie made her way down the path to Mr. Wright's house, hoping she would find him there. Without knocking, she creaked open the door to find him sitting behind his messy desk. A single burning candle was anchored to a puddle of dried wax on the wooden surface. Mr. Wright attempted to tune in his wireless. Only static was coming in. He smacked the side of the wireless with the palm of his hand.

"Goddamn this daft machine," he said. "God fuckin' damn it."

Mr. Wright hit the side of the wireless again; this time harder, then looked up.

"Oh my heavens, Hettie," he said, shuddering in fear. "I didn't see you there."

He stood up from his chair and hugged her for a long time. For a moment, Hettie thought she might slump into his arms, lose all faculty of her muscles, but she managed to stand still and take in the warmth and comfort of his embrace.

"Where did you go? We were at the Floral Hall, then you disappeared," Mr. Wright said, an urgency riding in his voice.

"I was worried about Violet."

"They hit the gauge line near the front of the zoo, but I think that's it," he said. "Is Violet all right?"

"A wee bit rattled."

"My wireless won't work—"

"Are the rest of the animals safe?" asked Hettie.

"Surprisingly, yes," said Mr. Wright, his eyes brightening. "None escaped. None got shocked to death. To tell you the truth, it's a miracle. I think the Bellevue Zoo is going to come out of this a lot better than the rest of the Belfast." He looked out the window of his office. "I'm afraid it doesn't look good," he said, and then sighed, trying his wireless one more time. "At least we can be grateful that all the animals are safe. How about your mother and father?"

"Well, my mother—"

Hettie broke off as the sound of a voice crackled from the wireless. Mr. Wright's eyes widened as the two of them listened to the report.

". . . death count is still not known, but a high number of civilian casualties are likely. Though the city's defenses functioned well, and military personnel and civil defense workers showed great courage and fortitude, some neighborhoods sustained considerable damage. Several shelters in the city were struck. Clearing-up operations have already begun, and civilian morale remains high."

"My mum," Hettie said, panic flooding through her. "I think she went to the Atlantic Avenue shelter."

"Oh, Hettie," Mr. Wright said, looking up at her. "Maybe it was one of the shelters that wasn't hit."

Ignoring Mr. Wright's half-hearted attempt at reassurance, she ran out the door and along the zoo's central pathway and down the grand staircase, out the front entrance, onto the Antrim Road. There was a red glow in the sky, especially over north Belfast. Shattered glass crowded the pavements and gutters. Water gushed from broken pipes. Half-burned papers from businesses in the city center had swirled up in the hot air of the fires and littered many of the streets. Relief turned to dismay when she saw that Aunt Sylvia's store was merely a blackened skeleton. Heaps of ashes had accumulated along its foundation. A tattered OPEN sign bounced against the remaining wooden doorframe.

Hettie slowed, struggling to take shallow breaths, and peered inside. Her eyes stung, and she closed her mouth against the taste of smoke and burning. Charred cans of tomatoes and tins of sardines and broken jars of pickles were strewn about the aisles. Puddles of pale green juice were leaking out onto the floor. Hettie didn't see her aunt anywhere and hoped that she had made it safely to one of the luckier shelters.

Up the street, three storefronts over, Mr. Gordon stood near the door of his hardware store, holding a cardboard box of candles that he was distributing to passersby.

"Mr. Gordon," Hettie called. "Have you seen my aunt?"

"I'm sorry about her store," he said. "It's barely standing."

Hettie felt a flicker of frustration, and had to work to maintain an air of politeness. "Yes, it is. Have you seen her? And my mother, Rose Quin?"

"I'm sorry, I haven't," he said. "Here, take this." He held out a candle to her. "Might be useful."

Hettie took the candle, feeling guilty now that she had been annoyed with him. She thanked Mr. Gordon and slid the candle into her coat pocket before heading down in the direction of the Whitewell Road. The early-morning sun began to slice through the thick yellow smoke.

Astonishingly, her house appeared to have been untouched by the night's bombing. As Hettie walked toward it, she could see that the windows were still intact, that her house looked exactly the same as when she ran off to the zoo. Unfortunately, some of her neighbors were not as lucky. Homes closer to one of the seats of explosion endured catastrophic damage. The entire facade of the Finneys' house had collapsed, and all its rooms were exposed to the street: There was a mattress with a tangle of sheets and blankets in one of the bedrooms, and plates and glasses were still arranged on the dining room table. Edith Curry's house had lost its roof. Most of the windows had been broken at the Hartes' and the Browns'. Some of the houses farther down the road were still on fire. Desperate wardens and rescue workers urgently roamed the stricken homes in search of survivors. Hettie felt her heart lurch. In the middle of the street sat a singed couch with a majority of its cushions missing. A Mickey Mouse gas mask with large circular eyes and a pale pink flap over the nose was left behind on one of the couch's arms.

Hettie strode up the front sidewalk of her house and burst through the door. "Mum!" she yelled. "Mum, are you here?" She tried the light switch in the front hallway. It didn't work. "Mum," she called again. "Where are you?"

With her heart beating loudly in her ears, Hettie rushed down the darkened hallway to Rose's room. Her mother's bed was unmade, and her bathrobe lay in a crumpled pile at the foot of the bed. Her lamp had tumbled to the floor, and the frosted light bulb had shattered into countless pieces. She sat down on the edge of her mother's bed, as she felt like her equilibrium might give way at any second. Hettie tried to convince herself that Rose had likely sought out safety elsewhere, and it wouldn't be long before they would be reunited.

Hettie steadied herself as she stood up and walked into her own bedroom and changed into a skirt, blouse, and cardigan. Then she went into the bathroom to rinse off her face, but forgot that the water was no longer running.

"Holy God," she mumbled. "Holy Mother of God."

She felt like crashing her forehead into the metal head of the faucet. Perhaps this self-destructive act would somehow relieve the overwhelming pain that was swiftly taking shape inside her. What if Rose was dead, too? Hettie could barely hold on to the thought. It didn't seem possible. Her family had already split in half during the past twelve months. If her mother didn't make it out of the shelter alive, the Quins would be spoken of only in the past tense—*That unfortunate family, so many tragic losses*—in the same way that her city would be spoken of in the past.

Hettie tried to shake her thoughts loose. Surely her mother was all right. Surely she had found a safe hiding spot with a neighbor or at the church hall. Hettie was probably just letting her thoughts run away from her. She looked up into the oval mirror above the porcelain sink and saw that streaks of soot and ash ran like dark veins across her face. A scab extended along the bridge of her nose. She touched the abrasion lightly with her fingers, then harder, but felt nothing.

Outside, Hettie found her father's bike leaning against their house. She pushed it along the Whitewell Road and then up the hill to the Antrim Road before hopping on to it and navigating the numerous obstacles of rubble, broken concrete, and shattered glass. Near the rise in the road, Hettie spotted Mrs. Lyttle from down the street and rode toward her. Creases of ash lined her forehead, and her eyes were red-rimmed and fatigued.

"Mrs. Lyttle, have you seen my mum?" Hettie asked.

"Last time I saw her was last night," she said. "She tried to convince me to go to the Atlantic shelter, but I didn't want to go."

The elderly woman began to shake and cry, lifting her glasses and wiping her eyes with a soiled handkerchief. Hettie placed a hand on her shoulder and then took the frail woman into her arms. Mrs. Lyttle felt like a bundle of dry sticks. As she gently rocked the sobbing woman, Hettie thought about what the wireless commentator had said about the city's shelters, and prayed that the structures had offered true protection against the bombs.

After a minute or two, she stepped away from Mrs. Lyttle, got on her bike, and continued her trip down the Antrim Road. Its tarmac surface was covered in mud, debris, ash, and water; it was slippery and treacherous. Burned-out buildings bordered both sides of the street; their charred shells looked precarious and fragile, as if they might topple over at any second. Tattered bed linens and curtains fluttered from the bare limbs of trees. Stringy roots of a tree protruded from a crumpled roof. Union Jacks poked up from random piles of rubble and ashes, snapping in the morning breeze. Hettie felt as if she were caught in some sort of ghastly nightmare.

Up ahead, she noticed a few women handing out tea in stained, chipped mugs and sandwiches to the continuous waves of strangers heading north on the Antrim Road, fleeing in panic from the city. The most fortunate traveled in cars, but some were on bicycles. Many of the people gripped overstuffed suitcases, baskets, and other parcels, and the hands of trailing, tripping children with bewildered expressions. A few pedestrians pushed along wheeled prams with bedclothes and other belongings strapped to their metal frames. Most were covered with soot, ash, and mud. Some were bloodstained and badly injured. A man walked by with an extra pair of shoes sticking out of his coat pockets. One woman wandered aimlessly up the street; to Hettie's horror, it looked as if the woman was carrying a dead baby in her arms, the infant's complexion a shade of pale lavender and her eyes unmoving and expressionless.

"Bottle," the woman desperately asked. "Does anyone have a bottle? I need a bottle for my baby."

An older woman stepped out from one of the intact houses and placed her arm around the mother's shoulder before carefully lifting the baby out of her arms and kissing the infant's forehead and then drawing the cross over the small body. Wiping several tears away, Hettie continued south on the Antrim Road, swerving around mounds of broken glass. When she glanced down Duncairn Gardens, Hettie noticed that entire rows of homes were obliterated. Despite all the visible destruction she had witnessed, it still felt unbelievable to Hettie that so much of her city could be destroyed. It was as if she were riding her bike through the streets of another city, another landscape entirely, one that didn't seem to resemble Belfast. It reminded her most of the photographs and films she had seen of towns devastated by shelling on the Western Front during the First World War.

Eventually Hettie turned onto Atlantic Avenue. A group of firemen were gathered around an enormous mass of rubble that used to be the shelter. They were removing large pieces of concrete and tossing aside bricks; some of the pieces were so massive and heavy that they had to be winched up. One of the firefighters was carrying a dismembered arm to the bed of a lorry. Slippery muscles bloomed from the limb and scrubs of auburn hair flecked the lifeless knuckles. Hettie noticed a gold wedding band was still on the hand. Another fireman carried a foot with a dirty sock. Hettie's stomach pitched. She gagged and bile rose in the back of her throat. Another man tossed a pair of ash-covered shoes into the metal lorry bed.

Mum, she said silently to herself. *Where's me mum?*

Hettie pushed her bike toward one of the firemen with a shovel. "Excuse me," she said. "Sir. Can you help me?"

The fireman, dressed in heavy canvas overalls and work boots, looked up at her, his eyes haunted.

"Where were the survivors from the shelter taken?" Hettie asked, unable to stop the tears that were streaming down her cheeks.

"We're just digging for remains now," he said. "The bodies are being moved to the city mortuary, and to the hospitals and funeral parlors. Some are being taken to temporary morgues in schools, church halls, and the public baths on the Falls Road and at Peter's Hill. I've been told that all of the unidentified dead will be transported to St. George's, where the public can come and try and find the missing."

"Did everyone—" Hettie started to ask.

"Try the Royal," he said. "A few of the survivors were taken there." Hettie's chest tightened like a fist.

"I'm looking for my mum," she said, stumbling on her words. "I need to find me mum."

"Sorry, miss," he said, returning his gaze to the pile of rubble. "Everyone is looking for someone right now." His shovel scraped against the pieces of concrete. An updraft of ashes swirled into his stoic face.

Hettie mounted her bike again. The front wheel wobbled as she attempted to regain her balance. Pedestrians continued to stream up the Antrim Road. Several strangers called out the names of relatives and friends. Near the corner of the Cliftonville Road, the Phoenix Bar still stood, but it no longer had doors or windows. Rows of patrons gathered along its counter, with smashed bottles and debris at their feet, as they tipped back glasses of whiskey.

Hettie pedaled harder until she turned onto the Grosvenor Road and arrived at the entrance of the Royal. She leaned her bike against the wall. Immediately as she stepped inside the hospital, Hettie was hypnotized by the chaotic scene in front of her. A frenzy of nurses, doctors, patients, and strangers occupied the foyer and the corridors. Injured civilians were splayed out on stretchers; others were slumped in wheelchairs; others lay along the borders of the darkened hallways, sprawled out on the floor. Stretchers were in such short supply doors were being used instead. Two young men carried a barely conscious patient between them, his limp arms draped over their shoulders, a stain of blood spreading from his abdomen, as they headed toward the stairwell. Hettie glanced through the open door of one of the operating theaters and shuddered at the sight of amputated limbs lying on a table. A nurse frantically pressed the button for the lift again and again.

"Lifts aren't bloody workin'," someone else yelled. "Nothing is going up."

"Coming through," another man yelled. "Coming through, people."

A young boy with a blood-soaked bandage wrapped around his head lay, unconscious, on a stretcher. A swaddled baby wailed in a nurse's arms. A paramedic pushed a man with no legs in a wheelchair.

For a second, amid the broken bodies and spirits, Hettie had forgotten who she was looking for. Instead, she felt numb and helpless. A swell of grief rolled through her. She leaned one hand against the wall as she attempted to collect herself. Footprints of blood stained the linoleum floor. A young girl cried for her mother. Hettie looked up, and a pair of nuns, in their nut-brown habits, rushed down the hallway.

Hettie surveyed the frenetic corridor again, trying to locate someone who might be in a position of authority. A nurse with a boat-shaped hat bobby-pinned to her hair and a white apron smeared with crimson walked toward Hettie. She held a clipboard in one hand and an IV bag of transparent liquid in the other.

"Excuse me," Hettie said. "Can you help me?"

"I wish I could—"

"I'm looking for my mum, Rose Quin," Hettie said, grabbing her sleeve and forcing her to stop. "She was at the Atlantic Avenue shelter. I was told some of the survivors were brought here . . ." She trailed off because she couldn't bear to go on.

The nurse stared at Hettie for a second and then out at the

pandemonium around her. She sighed. "Come back in a few days," the nurse said flatly. "That's all I can tell you."

"But I need to find my mother," Hettie cried. "I need to find her now."

She felt compelled to explain to the nurse, get her to understand how her situation might be different from that of other people who were looking for relatives and friends, that her mother was the last remaining member of her immediate family. But then she thought better of it; this nurse probably wouldn't be interested in hearing her story, she had much bigger concerns today.

"Go home," the nurse said gently, patting her on the arm. "You won't find her today."

Then the nurse turned on her heel and left Hettie standing there, watching what felt like her last hope disappear into the mayhem.

"Dr. Loney, emergency amputation in room 105," another nurse yelled.

"We need a stretcher over here. Someone fetch me a stretcher."

Stunned, Hettie wandered back toward the entrance of the hospital. She felt wrung out, like a damp sock, but she knew that she needed to keep looking. She had no choice. With little thought, she mounted her bike and rode eastward, down the Grosvenor Road, and onto May Street and toward St. George's. Despite being so close to the docks, the sandstone-and-redbrick facade of the market looked the same as when Hettie had stopped by last autumn before paying a visit to the Keegans and baby Maeve. The lions still stood regally above the arched doorway, their paws grabbing at the harsh air. A long line of strangers—many of their faces frozen with shock—waited outside the market's doors. Lifeless bodies were ferried on canvas stretchers; some bodies were covered in shrouds, others were not. A silver-haired priest, clutching a Bible and a rosary against his chest, silently nodded at Hettie as he maneuvered his way around her. She managed to follow his black habit through the double doors of the market past the others waiting to gain access.

When she entered, Hettie saw that most of the stalls had been re-moved from the enormous hall. The only evidence of its former state was the rows of tables with their wooden legs pushed up against one of the walls. A rancid stench struck Hettie's face: It was the smell of the city's unwashed poor, and of blood and feces. Hettie lifted the sleeve of her coat to cover her nose and mouth, but its scent of smoke and wet wool didn't do much to mask the smell.

The market's floor was carpeted with bodies. About half the corpses were tucked inside pinewood caskets, a necessary precaution given the high volume of rats roaming throughout the building. The rest lay bare and exposed—they must have run out of coffins. Hettie met the blank eyes of an already decaying corpse, then looked up at the retic-ulated roof of St. George's. Many of its glass panes had been shattered during the bombing. Red Cross nurses, with the familiar red insignia encircling the sleeves of their coats, and clergymen, along with several clutches of people, walked between the lines of coffins with handker-chiefs held up to their faces, lifting the lids one at a time. Personal items were scattered in between the rows. Watches, rings, photographs, wallets. Another priest walked past Hettie, murmuring *Hail, Mary, full of grace . . . / Holy Mary, Mother of God / pray for us sinners . . .* A man dressed in a work suit and wellingtons swabbed the floor. A disinfectant odor mingled with the fetid reek that Hettie feared was the smell of decomposing bodies. An older couple rocked over a dead boy, praying, their words shapeless and soundless. Hettie felt as if her body was going to crumble like a sandcastle at any second.

"Over here," a young man yelled. "I found her."

To the left, there was yet another stack of lifeless bodies—men, women, children. Hettie spotted a woman with the same color hair as her mother lying there amid the dead bodies, but then she quickly noticed the woman's prominent nose and chin and that the deceased woman looked nothing like her mother. Hettie continued to survey the dead that surrounded her. Their dirt-laced complexions were varying

shades of gray green. Their hands clutched nothing. Others were disfigured beyond recognition. Hettie thought of Anna and the last time she
saw her, lying in the hospital bed. The jaundiced shade of her delicate
eyelids. The stillness of her chest. The damp coldness of her fingertips
and her toes. At least her death had been a dignified one, Hettie thought
to herself. At least she and Rose had had a chance to hold Anna's hand
within the privacy and quiet of the hospital room before her shrouded
body was transported to the morgue in the hospital's basement. At least
they had said goodbye.

As she scanned the room, hoping not to see anyone who looked like
her mother, Hettie noticed the navy sleeve and sewn badge of a police
officer lying among the corpses. A grimy sheet was pulled halfway over
another body, revealing a leg missing from the hip and a bloody tangle
of veins, arteries, and cartilage. A tight ball of bile traveled up from the
floor of Hettie's stomach. The image of the dead penguins lying side
by side flickered through her mind—their stiff black feet, the blood
that stained their white under-feathers and pooled onto the pavement.
Hettie stared at the endless rows of bodies and coffins. Some part of
her couldn't look away, but the physical revulsion grew more intense.
Muffled sobs echoed up to the market's rafters.

Hettie ran out and vomited onto the curbside. Strangers' feet
moved around her, paying her no heed as she repeatedly coughed and
retched. Acid seared her throat, and her mouth tasted sour. The smell
of the burning city continued to press against her face. Her ears rang
loudly. Her cheeks were hot. She heaved again.

When she was done, she tried to collect herself and walk in the direction of the river. Her legs wobbled. Her head spun. She leaned her
hands against the wall of St. George's and bent over again. Charred
pieces of notebook paper tumbled across the pavement, and Hettie
reached automatically for one of the crumpled pages. The handwriting looked like a child's. Large, loopy, and lopsided between the solid
and perforated lines of periwinkle blue against the cream background.

All living creatures have square shoulders. Hettie read the sentence to herself again before releasing the burned piece of paper. It tripped down an empty alleyway. She began to cry. She thought of her mother and Mr. Wright and Ferris and Liam and Maeve and Stella Holliday and all the animals at the zoo. She thought of all the dead bodies at St. George's, all the dead and all the injured at the Royal. *All living creatures. All living creatures. All living creatures.*

The nurse at the hospital was right: Hettie should go home. There was nothing for her here. Looking for Rose was a hopeless effort. Hettie knew that she wouldn't be able to find her mother today. She mounted her bicycle and rode slowly through the devastated streets, past the city hall and its manicured lawns littered with broken glass, singed fragments of paper, and loose piles of ashes. Its formerly majestic domed roof now crowned the skeleton of a building, which was barely standing. As she rode up to Carlisle Circus, she saw a steady procession of rats scuttling along the gutters of the Antrim Road; they must have come from the sewers. Her stomach pitched forward again. Hettie turned away and noticed a church without its roof or walls. Only the facade was left, the large arched doorway leading into a hazy veil of nothingness. She cycled around roadblocks, where the streets had been cordoned off, owing to the buildings being unstable and the presence of unexploded bombs.

Hettie continued to climb the Antrim Road. As she pedaled, clouds obscured the road ahead, creating a strange parade of apparitions, shadow people, there and not there. But the people were moving in the thousands, like crowds of football supporters spilling toward their home stadium on a Saturday afternoon, but instead today they were fleeing from their unprotected city. Their collective fear and panic heaved through the streets.

The tinny sounds of a news report came from a wireless perched on a windowsill; the commentator's voice sounded peculiar and distant and full of urgency. The number of casualties was well past five hundred. A boy waved a miniature British flag as he stood by himself. Dried tears stained his round, grimy cheeks. Hettie squeezed her eyes shut for a second and then flicked them open again. The front tire of her bike rocked over a piece of rubble. She gripped the handlebars harder and regained control, but her hands were shaking.

Before she knew it, Hettie was riding onto the Whitewell Road again. The scene had changed little from when she had returned home from the zoo earlier that morning. A police cordon was now in place in an attempt to foil the activities of looters. The singed couch still sat in the middle of the road, but this time a few of the neighborhood children were perched on its damaged arms. Johnny Gibson wore the Mickey Mouse gas mask strapped over his rosy cheeks, his auburn curls poking out from the elastic strap. Lizzie tried to shove her younger sister, Martha, off the couch. Lily stood on the opposite arm, with her fists raised in the air, as though she had just won first place in an athletic competition. A few of their parents were gathered in front of their homes and waved Hettie over.

"You and your mum all right?" asked Mr. Martin.

"I can't find her," Hettie said.

"I hear it's mad around the hospitals and that large queues are forming at St. George's," said Mr. Reynolds, shaking his head. "Utter chaos. I've been trying to find a cousin of mine. It's been next to impossible."

"I went there," Hettie said, breathless.

"Oh dear," Mrs. Lyttle said, holding a hand up to her mouth. "Poor girl."

"I couldn't find her," Hettie said. "There were too many—" She broke off, unable to finish her thought.

"She'll be back soon enough," Mr. Reynolds said after a short pause. "You'll see."

"Go and give your house another look," Mrs. O'Brien suggested. "I bet she is waiting for you this very moment."

Hettie desperately wanted to believe Mrs. O'Brien—that she would walk into the front hallway of their house and find her mother sitting at the kitchen table, with a fresh cup of tea, listening to the news on the wireless and commenting on how Hettie had spent all her time with "that elephant," as usual. Her eyes stung, her throat was parched. Hettie parked the bike along the side of their house, then pushed open the front door with her shoulder.

"Mum," she called tentatively. "Mum, I'm home."

In the kitchen, her mother's blue cardigan still hung over the back of the chair, and her half-empty teacup from the night before sat on the breakfast table. Hettie sat down in her usual spot at the table. A ring stained the porcelain cup's interior. Hettie placed her hands on the tabletop, feeling its cool veneer and tangible solidness underneath her palms. She studied her splayed fingers. Soot and grime lined the edges of her nails. Dirt covered her hands, looking like the crude shapes of seas and continents. She touched her bare wrist where she usually wore her father's watch, only just noticing that it was gone.

Hettie reached into the pockets of her coat and was relieved to find Ferris's snail still nestled here. She took it out, carefully placed it on the table, and studied its infinite swirl and iridescent sheen. She arranged the shell next to her mother's half-empty teacup. Slowly, the snail's antennae emerged from its sturdy chamber. Its rubbery head extended from its opening and stretched along the scarred surface of the tabletop. For a moment, Hettie felt an unexpected elation, witnessing that the snail was still alive. It seemed like a miracle. Perhaps the snail was a good omen for things to come, a sign that maybe Rose was alive and well somewhere.

Hettie lifted herself out of the chair and walked down the hallway. It was still her family's hallway, with the flower-stenciled wallpaper and the familiar geometric pattern of framed photographs from over the years. Anna and Hettie in their matching outfits. Thomas and Rose on their wedding day. Anna posing with a tennis trophy that she had won at the Cavehill Bowling and Lawn Tennis Club. Hettie looked into her mother's bedroom again. Her bed was still unmade. Hettie's stomach felt hollow and queasy. Her bones, creaky. Her joints ached. She thought she might retch again. She moved into her mother's bathroom, lifted the wooden seat of the toilet, and knelt, waiting for her insides to hurl out of her. When they didn't, she leaned her forehead against the porcelain edge. She breathed in the coolness. Still nothing came. Hettie felt she could no longer arrange her thoughts and memories into any kind of logical sense or order. It was too sad and overwhelming.

She willed herself to stand up, to check their enclosed courtyard. The two wooden benches were still situated along the back wall; during the warmer months, Hettie and Rose often sat there after dinner, taking in the changing light of dusk. The courtyard itself was empty except for the buckets of water her mother had filled up a week before, in preparation for exactly this situation. Silently thanking her mother, Hettie rinsed her face, hands, and wrists with water from one of the buckets. With a bar of soap, she lathered her skin and rinsed the soot, grime, and salty sweat away. She was relieved by the simple act of washing her face, how it allowed her to recalibrate to some part of her former self.

Hettie returned to the kitchen and saw that the snail had retreated into its shell. She took the creature in her hand and lay down on the couch in the living room, pulling the ruby-red afghan that Rose had knitted over her shoulders. Hettie placed the snail on the coffee table. The shell rolled across the tabletop and tumbled onto the floor underneath the couch. Hettie was too tired to get up and reach for it. Instead, she closed her eyes, but she couldn't get warm. Her entire body trembled. The metal springs of the couch's cushions pinched her side. She was too spent and exhausted even to adjust the weight of her body to get more comfortable. When she closed her eyes, the couch rocked.

A rusty hinge creaked somewhere. Hettie lifted her heavy eyelids. The door was still closed. A distant siren of an ambulance wailed. A branch tapped against a window. A bird chirped. *Johnny, get off the couch! Come inside this instant!*

"Get off the couch," Hettie whispered to herself. "Get off the couch and go and find your mum."

Her eyes closed again.

"Go and find Mum," she mumbled, even as she felt sleep dragging her down into a dream state.

Outside, a delayed bomb exploded, making her entire body jump. An engine backfired with a definitive pop. Someone's wireless, somewhere, was playing "God Save the Queen."

O Lord our God arise, / Scatter her enemies, / And make them fall.

Nine

A FEW HOURS LATER HETTIE WOKE WITH A START. THE LIGHT was dim. Rain drummed on the windows. She couldn't remember what day it was. Sunday, Monday, Friday. She opened her eyes. Her forehead felt sticky and feverish. She pressed her palm against her cheek. Time held a bent, elastic quality, as if it were no longer linear. The bombs were falling again. One wave of bombs folded on top of the other. There was no way to escape the Germans and the endless drone and destruction of their planes. She closed her eyes. Miniature starbursts exploded behind her eyelids. She waited to feel the vibrations, hear the explosions again. But there was nothing. Only the persistent tapping of rain.

The wiry springs of the couch pressed against the buckles of her spine. Hettie lifted herself up. The room spun. The floor gently tipped. She returned her cheek to the couch's cushion and closed her eyes again. Darkness took over.

The next thing she knew someone was tugging her arm. Hettie opened her eyes.

Ferris stood before her. "Hettie," he said softly. "Wake up. Wake up." She forced herself to focus on him. Ferris wore his familiar old school scarf. Tufts of sweaty brown hair stuck out this way and that. His cheeks were streaked with ashes and soot. Hettie found that she was very pleased to see him.

"You all right?" he asked.

Hettie sat up, feeling groggy and dazed. What was Ferris doing in her house?

"Where's your mum?"

And all at once, it came back to her. "I don't know," she said, her voice raspy. "I can't find her. I don't know where she is."

Ferris stared down at his hands and then at the worn floorboards. "She'll be home soon," he said. "Lots of people are still finding each other."

Hettie sat up.

"You lost something," Ferris said, picking up the snail from the floor and returning it to the coffee table.

"Thanks," Hettie said, taking the snail in her hand and closing her fingers around it.

"How are you doing?" she asked. "Where did you hide?"

Ferris leaned forward, holding his head with both hands.

"I've been up to the zoo," he said. "I saw Mr. Wright."

"Did he tell you about Stella Holliday?" she asked. "How she sang through the night?"

Ferris nodded. "Constable Ward stopped by earlier this morning to survey the damage," he said. "Two parachute bombs hit a row of houses not far from the zoo."

Hettie's mind raced to keep up with what Ferris was saying. "What does that have to do with the constable?"

"The local residents made a formal request that the Ministry of Public Security take no further risks in case the Germans attack again."

"What does that mean?" Hettie asked, sitting up straighter. "No further risks?"

Ferris bit his lip. "The ministry has ordered the destruction of the zoo's most dangerous animals," he said finally.

"Destruction," Hettie said, her voice rising. "You mean the animals are going to be killed?"

"The list of animals was delivered this morning," Ferris said. "The constable and the sergeant will be carrying out the duties today."

"What about Violet? Is she on the list?"

"That's why I came to find you."

Hettie stared at Ferris. A stitching of dried scabs formed a half-moon above his eyebrow. A tear rolled down the side of his freckled face. Hettie reached for his cheek and wiped it away with the edge of her thumb.

"Surely Mr. Wright can stop them," Hettie said. "He won't allow it."

"We should get going," Ferris said, standing up. "We need to go."

Hettie felt drained by exhaustion and propelled by adrenaline. Her mind was reeling and folding into itself. She was torn. She wanted to ride her bike to the hospital again and search for her mother, but also felt compelled to go to the zoo with Ferris and save Violet. After a moment's hesitation, she went into the kitchen. On a piece of scrap paper on the table, Hettie wrote: *dear mum, at the zoo. helping with the animals. come & find me. i love you. hettie.* She slipped into her coat, reached for her satchel, and tucked the snail into her coat pocket. Ferris stood in the doorway to the foyer, and their eyes met for a second before Hettie turned away and buttoned up her coat. She swallowed hard; her throat was a desert, dry and cracked.

When Hettie and Ferris arrived at the entrance, Mr. Clarke wasn't in his usual post at the foot of the grand staircase. The light bulb and the window of the security house had been smashed to pieces. Hettie and Ferris took the steps two at a time. When they reached the plateau in front of the Floral Hall, Hettie saw Mr. Wright standing with his hands clasped behind his back, his eyes fixed on the ground, his broad shoulders slumped. She recalled Mr. Wright from the night before as he stood mesmerized by Stella Holliday and her singing, the intermittent light and shadows of the dimly lit hall playing against his trancelike expression. His eyes had been wet and shiny, full of melancholy and devotion. She thought of Mr. Wright's twin brother, Nicholas, and the Battle of Arras. The flying bullets, the song that he had heard.

As they drew closer, Hettie felt the impulse to run up to Mr. Wright and hug him in the same way that he had embraced her the night before. She wanted to tell him about everything that had happened after she left his office that morning—her ride down the Antrim Road, the persistent stream of evacuees leaving the city, the horrors of the Royal and St. George's, how she hadn't found her mother yet but she was trying her best to stay optimistic that she and her mum would eventually be reunited and all would be well. But as Hettie took in Mr. Wright and his grave expression, she knew better and said nothing.

Mr. Wright was speaking with Constable Ward and Sergeant Miller. Behind Sergeant Miller stood Samuel Greene, looking like an entirely different young man clad in his black police uniform and white gloves. As the men spoke, Samuel made eye contact with Hettie. Deep ridges etched his forehead. Flecks of gray that Hettie didn't remember from the night at the Floral Hall peppered his short sideburns. It appeared as if Samuel was somehow closer in age to Mr. Wright than he was to Hettie and Ferris, that the night of bombing had mysteriously advanced his age by more than a decade. Mr. Wright paused in his conversation with Constable Ward and glanced up at Hettie and Ferris with a glassy gaze.

"This is Ferris Poole and Hettie Quin," Mr. Wright said solemnly. "They're zookeepers here and oversee the care of many of our animals."

"As we already discussed, Mr. Wright, I have no choice but to follow the directive of the Ministry of Public Security. We all know another attack by the Germans is imminent. Next time, the animals could run free and endanger the lives of Belfast's citizens," said Constable

Ward, who also wore a black uniform, the elbows and knees covered with shadows of dust. His mouth was thin and tight, and a delicate mustache sat above his upper lip.

Mr. Wright kept his hands folded behind his back. The constable held a list and began to recite the animals to be executed: the lion, two lionesses, two cubs, the brown bears, the polar bears, the black bears, the wolves, the tiger, the hyenas, the pumas, the panthers, the lynx, and the elephants. Each man carried a .303 Lee-Enfield rifle, with the magazine fully loaded.

"Unfortunately, we will not be able to leave the premises until the directive is carried out," Constable Ward continued. "The government has agreed to pay Mr. Christie and the zoo eight hundred and fifteen pounds in compensation for these losses."

The wind shifted, and the smell in the air became more pungent. It was bitter, like the odor of burning rubber and hair. The parrot in the aviary squawked: *Good morning to you. Good morning to you.* Hettie could hear Rajan's trumpet call in the distance.

"You've made your orders clear," Mr. Wright said finally.

Hettie stared at Ferris with dread and shock. He was looking directly at Mr. Wright. His lower lip trembled, and patches of redness emerged along the length of his neck. A sudden affection for Ferris swept over Hettie. She pinched the soft interior of her palm.

"Shall we proceed," Mr. Wright said in a restrained voice.

Constable Ward and Sergeant Miller nodded. Mr. Wright guided the party to the path that led to the top edge of the zoo. Hettie knew that he was taking the group to the lions' den first. The men followed Mr. Wright with their official gaits and measured arm swings. Samuel Greene slowed down and fell in step with Ferris and Hettie.

"There was nothing I could do," he said, quietly.

"Hard to do anything when the orders come from the ministry," Ferris said.

"If a bomb hadn't fallen in the neighborhood, they might've not issued the directive, but it fell too close to the animals." Samuel was talking quickly, his words running into each other. "How are your families?" he asked. "Did everyone survive?"

"Hettie's still trying to find her mum," Ferris responded. "What about you?"

"I'm sorry, Hettie."

"She'll be home soon," she said with conviction. "I know it."

"We lost our house. It was completely destroyed, but everyone in the family is fine. I was working down at the station during most of the night. It turned out to be one of the safer spots in the city. I heard from Alan Creighton that Colleen White wasn't so fortunate . . ."

Samuel trailed off, his eyes welling up. Hettie thought of Colleen in her lavender dress, her arms crossed over her middle, standing at the front of the Floral Hall on that Saturday night just last month. How Colleen's slender figure had almost glowed in the dark, like phosphorescence, as she called out Samuel's name. Hettie couldn't take in the fact that Colleen was gone, too. It didn't seem possible that she could be dead.

"She was at the Floral Hall. When the incendiaries started going off, a warden told her to hurry on to the Percy Street shelter." Samuel bent his head into one hand and his shoulders shuddered. "Then the constable called me about this," he said, wiping away his tears, "because I scored so high in the marksmanship competitions in Enniskillen. He wants to see if my mark is as good as theirs."

Up ahead, Mr. Wright, the constable, and the sergeant were waiting at the perimeter of the lions' den.

"We best pick up our pace," Ferris said.

A few minutes later, they were standing outside the lions' enclosure. Hettie thought the cubs might be spared because of their size and age, but it turned out that wasn't going to be the case. Silently Sergeant Miller positioned his rifle with the heavy butt pressing against his shoulder. Through its sights he carefully took aim, pointing the grooved barrel toward Wallace, who lay on the floor of the enclosure. His flaxen tail twitched back and forth.

A pop pealed through the air, and the fast-spinning bullet struck the large cat in the chest. Wallace growled and threw one paw up in the air before falling over onto his side. Sergeant Miller shot Wallace one more time. Hettie cupped her hand over her mouth. The other lions circled the wounded cat. His chest was still. Blood pooled by his front paw. Sergeant Miller lifted his rifle again, aimed at Cecil, and pulled the trigger. The cat tumbled onto the ground with a heavy thump. Victoria released a deep-throated howl and barreled toward the enclosure's wrought-iron bars where the sergeant stood. Hettie took several steps back. Warm moisture gathered in her armpits, and it felt as if her bladder might let loose at any second. She looked over at Mr. Wright: He stood erect and motionless in his brilliant red coat. Tears streamed down his black-stubbled cheeks.

"Mr. Greene," the constable said, tersely. "The females."

Samuel lifted his rifle and spent a minute adjusting his aim on the animals. In quick succession, Samuel shot the two female lions. The cubs cried and paced around their fallen mothers. Their cries sounded like the sorrowful cries of human infants. One of the cubs climbed on top of Victoria, nestling his nose into the bloody scruff of his mother's neck. He howled and kneaded his paws into her tangled mane. Hettie felt as though a part of her had died, too. Samuel positioned the rifle and killed each cub with a single shot. The group of officers and zoo-keepers stood there as the sound of the shot rippled in the morning air. Warm tears ran down Hettie's face. Her knees weakened.

"Ferris, we're going to have to bury the animals," Mr. Wright said in an even voice. "I would suggest the field near the top of the Crazy Path."

"Yes, sir."

"The brown bears will be next," Mr. Wright said. "This way."

Rain started to fall, tiny drops splattering against the pavement and tapping against the budding leaves on the trees. A goldcrest, with its vivid strokes of green and bright yellow, flitted on one of the low-lying branches. The brown bear, Andy, was curled up near the granite boulders at the rear of the enclosure. His deep chestnut tail was tucked into the shiny surface of his fur. Constable Ward took a step forward, and the sergeant handed him a rifle. Just as he was aiming at the bear, the animal began to pace nervously before standing up on his hind legs and clawing at the sooty air.

"Come on, Andy," Mr. Wright said with a noticeable quiver in his voice. "It's all right."

Constable Ward drew back the rifle, carefully aimed, and shot the bear in the center of his chest. Andy instantly collapsed to the ground. Ward shot a second time, the bullet entering near the bear's large hind leg. Hettie held her stomach with both arms. Bile tickled her throat. Andy convulsed, frothy saliva gathering in the fine whiskers that bordered his mouth, before finally growing still. Hettie glanced over at Mr. Wright, who stared straight ahead with little expression although tears continued to travel down his cheeks. Hettie prayed silently that she wouldn't retch again, as she had outside of St. George's. Was that just this morning? She felt like she was losing her ability to track time. Instead, it seemed to be circling, a continuous spiral of violence and devastation, one trauma collapsing into another, with no beginning or end. Hettie looked up at Andy again. His pink tongue slipped from the side of his mouth. His eyes were open and still.

The next enclosure was the home of the black bears, Henry and his mate, Alice, who was due to give birth in early May. The pair lumbered across the dusty yard. Alice's abdomen was noticeably swollen, like a large watermelon, and hung low as she walked and then dipped her nose into a bucket of water.

"Alice is pregnant with a pair of cubs," Mr. Wright said, haltingly. "She is due in a few weeks."

"I'm sorry, Mr. Wright," said Constable Ward. "I cannot make any exceptions. Mr. Greene, please proceed."

The bears paced the length of the enclosure.

"Mr. Wright—" Hettie said, her voice strangled.

Ferris grabbed her hand and squeezed it. She looked up at him. He shook his head, and she bit into her lower lip. She tasted her own blood in her mouth. Samuel took a step forward and steadied his rifle on his shoulder. He issued two swift shots, and the bears fell onto their sides, their chests heaving. Samuel took two more, and their large black bodies stopped moving. Hettie wondered if the babies were dead already, if the bullets had entered the placenta, or if they would die slowly from the lack of sustenance from their mother.

"Mr. Wright, should I recruit other men to help with the burials?" asked Ferris, blowing his nose into his worn handkerchief.

"Yes," Mr. Wright said, mopping his forehead. "You'll need at least four men."

Ferris squeezed Hettie's hand one more time and then headed off to the employee canteen. She felt the warm imprint of his palm against her own fingers as she watched him walk away.

Hettie clenched her hands into fists as she followed Mr. Wright and the group of men. If she couldn't stop Violet's death, it was important to her that she be present with Violet when the end of her life occurred, to be a witness when the elephant made her transition from living to dying. After all, she hadn't been able to perform this intimate privilege for her sister, having arrived four hours after Anna took her last breath. At least she could provide this comfort for Violet. Her tears fell steadily. Hettie wiped her cheeks and nose with the sleeve of her coat. The outer rims of her nostrils felt raw and red.

The puma lived in the next paddock. The sleek cat prowled along the ground before jumping up onto the highest rock of the enclosure. He kept his body close to the boulder, as if he were preparing to pounce on his next prey.

"Greene," Constable Ward said.

Samuel stepped forward again and quietly aimed his rifle at the majestic cat. This time, Hettie closed her eyes as she heard the now-familiar pop. *Please, no,* she said silently to herself. *No.* But when she opened her eyes, the cat was lifeless on top of the slate-gray boulder. His powerful body was now limp except for a single paw that briefly shuddered in the air.

"Rajan will be next," Mr. Wright said.

Hettie stood at the edge of the enclosure, staring at the puma. She knelt on the pavement, clasped her hands together, and said a prayer for the dead animal. When she stood up again, Mr. Wright and the officers and Samuel Greene were already at Rajan's enclosure. She walked toward the group even though a part of her wanted to turn around because she didn't think she could take in another act of violence. The enormous elephant was standing in the corner with his broad rear facing the group. Maggie stood next to him, her long tail jerking from side to side. Soft pinks and grays flecked Maggie's forehead. The three giraffes clustered in the other corner, their long necks extended, as they tore at the young leaves of the nearby trees.

Without any delay, Constable Ward lifted his rifle and shot directly at Rajan. The bullet struck the bull elephant's side. Rajan raised his long trunk into the air and gave a loud trumpet call. Maggie retreated into the far corner with the giraffes; the small herd huddled closer together, bowing their necks toward the ground. Rajan began to pace, his flaplike ears pinned to his head, and then jammed his trunk between the bars. A metal chain attached to the enclosure's padlock knocked against the cage, and Hettie flinched. The concussive sound reminded her of the bombs from the night before, as if the explosions were detonating within the muscle memory of her system, a theater of flame-red pyrotechnics and deep vibrations that would always lie underneath her skin. Rajan reared and charged toward the group.

"He doesn't appear to be even injured," Sergeant Miller said with astonishment. "That can't be possible."

"Again," ordered Constable Ward. "Shoot him again."

Sergeant Miller lifted his firearm again, and Rajan released another roar and stood up on his hind legs. Miller rested the rifle against his shoulder and pointed it at the elephant. Hettie turned away. The sergeant made another attempt. Hettie looked back at Rajan. He released another guttural roar, pacing and swinging his trunk wildly.

"We need a more powerful gun for the bull elephant, sir," said Sergeant Miller.

"Mr. Wright, does this surprise you?" asked Constable Ward.

"Rajan weighs over thirteen thousand pounds," Mr. Wright responded, his voice subdued. "To be honest, I thought a rifle would manage it, but it seems, given his sheer size, weight, and determination, he requires something more."

Maggie walked toward Rajan and began to lick the wound near his left ear. Rajan buried his large head into Maggie's side. She continued to clean the blood from his rubbery skin.

"Good God, we need to put the poor thing out of his misery," Hettie gasped.

"Quiet, girl," Constable Ward said sharply.

Hettie stared at Mr. Wright. Tears continued to roll down his blotchy cheeks.

"We'll return with a more powerful gun this afternoon," continued Constable Ward. "Miller, go ahead. Shoot the other elephant now."

"Can we wait until tomorrow?" Sergeant Miller responded wearily. "Perhaps she needs a bigger gun, too."

"Miller, do as I say," Constable Ward said curtly. "Now."

Without another word, Sergeant Miller drew back his rifle again and shot Maggie with three consecutive blasts. The elephant crumpled to the dusty floor of the enclosure. Rajan gingerly suctioned the end of his trunk over Maggie's large-lidded eyes and ears, bowing his head as he whinnied: at first softly, and then louder and louder.

Mr. Wright stepped toward Hettie and gripped her arm.

"Take Violet home," he whispered urgently. "She'll be safe there. Now, go."

Surprised by Mr. Wright's instruction, Hettie did her best to stifle her response, and quietly turned around and headed toward the Elephant House. In the near distance, she heard another distinctive pop of a rifle. Then another. Hettie ran down the winding pathway until she reached the Elephant House. There she found Violet. She stood near the center of her enclosure, tucking a small bundle of hay into her mouth.

"Morning, Vi," Hettie said, her voice trembling. "Mr. Wright wants me to take you home. We can take the Crazy Path. Then you'll be safe—and we can stay there together until Mum returns. And Maeve and Liam, too. And we'll be all together."

Another metallic pop perforated the air. Violet walked toward Hettie and released a series of chirps. Her ears flapped in the morning breeze.

"Let's go," Hettie said, clucking her tongue.

Hettie unhooked the stick with the curled end that hung from a brass hook on the wall of the Elephant House and opened the gate. Its rusty hinges rasped like a waking voice. The elephant shook her head and kicked the gate with great force.

"Vi, what are you doing?" she said, nervous and startled. "Do you want to get yourself shot, too?"

Up ahead, a flock of gray pigeons pecked away at the pavement before lifting into the sky in one symphonic motion. For a fleeting moment, Hettie thought the elephant would refuse to move. But then she started walking, and Hettie breathed again.

"Steady, Vi," Hettie said. "Steady."

Together they walked along the pathway that led to the rear entrance of the zoo. Hettie held the stick not far from Violet's forehead, and the elephant followed as they continued along the curving path that bordered the aviary. Parrots rested in the crooked arms of the trees, and the peacocks congregated in a cluster near the back of the aviary.

One of the parrots squawked: *Good morning! Good morning!* Another bird chimed in: *Where are you going? Where are you going?* Hettie picked up her pace.

"We need to move," she whispered to Violet. "We need to get out of here."

Hettie guided Violet through the gate that led to the Throne Wood and the Crazy Path. To the right, the clearing was obscured by the long shadows of the Cavehill, where Ferris and four other zookeepers methodically dug into the ground. The rusty heads of their shovels swung up into the yellow-tinged air before hitting the field with considerable impact and then hurling tangled clumps of dirt, grass, and roots over their shoulders.

Swing, dig, hurl.

Swing, dig, hurl.

Swing, dig, hurl.

Again and again.

Ferris and Jack Fleming and Bobby Adair and Daryl Griffins and Hugh Mallon moved in unison, as if they were a team rowing the flat blades of a scull together. Hettie and Violet paused at the clearing.

"Ferris," Hettie said.

Ferris didn't look up, his attention absorbed by the systematic movements of his shovel. Hettie glanced back in the direction of the zoo, knowing that the officers and Samuel Greene wouldn't be far behind her once they discovered that Violet was no longer in her enclosure.

"Ferris Poole," Hettie said, louder this time. "Over here."

Ferris finally looked up, pushing strands of hair from his eyes. The other zookeepers stopped their digging and looked up at her, too, and expressions of astonishment opened up on their faces.

"Hettie," he said, looking both relieved and surprised to see her and Violet together on the path. "What are you doing?"

"Taking Violet home. Mr. Wright told me to."

Ferris stared up the path and then at the pile of dead animals before him—the lions and their cubs, and the puma. Pools of blood collected around the edges of their furry bodies. Buzzing flies and bees darted over the carcasses. The smell of rot was beginning to take over the field.

"Go, go," Ferris said urgently. "Before the constable realizes Violet is gone."

Hettie looked over at Violet. In the end of her trunk, she held a tuft of a buttercup flower, its yellow petaled bloom luminous like a bit of sunlight. The rain had ceased, and the overcast clouds still sat low above the rolling knolls of the Cavehill.

"When you're finished here, come to my house," she said.

"Go, Hettie," Ferris said again, nodding toward the Crazy Path. "Before it's too late."

Ten

THE DIRT OF THE CRAZY PATH CRUNCHED UNDERNEATH THEIR feet, as they marched almost in step with each other. Tendrils of smoke lingered in the late-morning brightness. Once they reached the street, Hettie glanced back at Violet, who was a few paces behind her.

"Come on, Vi," Hettie urged. "It's not much farther."

Violet clomped her feet against the street. Down the road, Hettie heard the wardens ringing handbells. This was the signal that it was now safe for the citizens to come out of their houses, as all unexploded bombs had been dealt with and many of the half-demolished buildings were now stabilized. Hettie cursed inwardly: This undertaking would be much easier with fewer people on the streets. Then from the direction of the Antrim Road came the distant whine of ambulances, military vehicles, police tenders, fire trucks, and the lorries of rescue workers. Hettie could also hear the constant murmurs of the crowds of desperate civilians still moving en masse northward and out of the city.

Suddenly, a shadowy weight moved toward her. She looked over her shoulder to see Violet skidding on the gray cobblestones of the Antrim Road. Her front feet were slipping out from underneath her huge body.

The elephant was falling. She was tumbling in midair. Her presence seemed to take up most of the road.

Violet's eyes became more pronounced, wide open, and alert.

Her large ears fanned, like a pair of eagle's wings.

Her long trunk reached into the air.

Hettie jumped out of the way. Her feet slid across the street as she tumbled into the opposite curb. Pebbles and dirt pressed into her slick hands. Her head hurt. Hettie glanced over at Violet: She was on her back, her feet flailing in the air. Hettie jumped up and ran to her side, patting the elephant with trembling hands, checking for injuries and comforting her at the same time. Violet's belly heaved up and down. She trumpeted again.

"It's all right, me girl," Hettie soothed. "It's all right."

She rubbed the elephant's side. She looked around. Despite their presence in the middle of the street, strangers continued to stream along the Antrim Road. She wondered where they were headed: No doubt some would seek refuge for the night in the rounded foothills and fields of the Cavehill. But it was evident that others were evacuating the city altogether, heading toward Carrickfergus, Whitehead, Larne, and beyond that to the Glens of Antrim. An elderly man pointed at her and Violet.

"What are you doing with that elephant?" he yelled. "Police, police. Somebody."

"Get up," Hettie whispered. "You can do it, Vi. You can do it."

Hettie looked at the older man again; he had continued up the road. And thankfully there were no police around. Pain glowed inside her wrist. Heat rose in her chest and sweat dampened the back of her blouse. *Come on, Violet,* she pleaded silently. *I can't lose you, too.* Hettie rubbed circles along Violet's broad side, and the elephant released a soft cry. Several strangers walked around them in the middle of the road.

"Look, Ma," Hettie heard a young boy say. "It's an elephant. It's an elephant on the road."

Hettie felt the shadows of other people fall on them. There was a high-pitched whistle. A charge of fear barreled through Hettie's body that it might be the constable coming after Violet, that she had lost her chance to save the elephant, that soon she was going to be dead, too.

"Come on, Vi," Hettie whispered again. "I need you. I really need you."

A runnel of sweat traveled down her cheek, and Hettie wiped it away. It felt like a rash of pebbles were embedded in the skin of her face. The tips of her fingers tingled. She glanced down at her hand and saw that her fingers were smudged with traces of blood. She wiped her forehead again, and more blood appeared on her fingers.

"Stupid, stupid, stupid," Hettie said to herself, feeling she wouldn't have gotten hurt if she had been paying better attention to Violet. "How could you be so bloody stupid—"

Several more people continued to walk around them, their arms full of personal belongings and cherished items. It was as if the sighting of this unusual pair was customary on the Antrim Road, as if the bombing had recalibrated daily life into a different kind of normal, where anything was acceptable, including a young elephant lying in the middle of a public road during broad daylight. Others cycled past her as fast as they could pedal. An overcrowded bus—with the tired faces of young children pressed against the windows—motored north. An army lorry swept by, its rear rammed full of frightened children with their mothers, many of them clinging onto its sides. A middle-aged woman, still dressed in her tattered nightgown, clutched a large clock in her arms as she trudged up the road.

Violet blinked, and then folded onto her legs and stood up in one fluid motion. Hettie rubbed her eyes. She could barely believe it: Violet was standing again. She flapped her large ears and then shook her entire body.

"Yes, Vi," Hettie said, encouraged that they might make it safely home. "Yes!"

Hettie clucked her tongue again and then waved the stick. Violet followed her across the Antrim Road. The pain in her wrist smarted again. Hettie touched it, gently squeezing her thin wrist. The ache pulsed, like a heartbeat. For a moment, Hettie imagined another scenario that could have just played out: Violet landing on top of her, crushing her with a single impact, her ribs snapping, her back breaking in two, her skull cracking in more than one place, her brain matter splattering against the cobblestones. Hettie trembled at the irony of it, how she could have died being crushed by an elephant rather than by a collapsing shelter or a falling bomb. Hettie thought of Rose again, praying that her mother would be home when they arrived.

"We're almost home."

"What on earth—" an elderly man said, approaching them.

Hettie kept her gaze on the bend of the road that led to the Whitewell Road. A layer of ash coated the leaves of the trees. Passing pedestrians stared at Violet and Hettie while others barely glanced in their direction.

After what seemed like a very long time, they turned down the Whitewell Road. The scorched couch still sat in the middle of the street, which was now half deserted. Scrawled notes were pinned to the doors of some of the vacated houses, letting worried friends and neighbors know that the former occupants had taken refuge in the countryside. Much of the broken glass had been swept up, but piles of debris and rubble were still strewn across the road. Soldiers and rescue workers were combing through the shattered ruins of houses, searching for survivors and exhuming the dead.

From a distance, Hettie's house looked the same as when she had left it a few hours earlier: The front door was still closed, the window above the kitchen sink still darkened with the blackout curtains. As they walked along, Hettie kept expecting to hear the stern voices of Constable Ward or Sergeant Miller, demanding that she step away from Violet so they could execute her. She picked up her pace.

Up ahead, the remaining neighborhood children gathered in the middle of the road. Rodney and Jack Dawkins, Johnny Gibson, Albert

O'Brien, and Lily Brown surrounded a beat-up tin can, then Rodney kicked it as hard as he could, propelling the can into the air before it dropped onto the street and careened into the gutter. Hettie wondered what had happened to the other children—if they had evacuated with their parents or if they were among the masses of unidentified bodies being collected in the impromptu morgues around the city. She decided to believe the former.

Right as the children were about to scatter to their hiding spots, they looked up and saw Hettie and Violet.

"Look," Johnny Gibson yelled. "An elephant. An elephant!"

The others gasped and giggled, then ran toward Hettie, forming a broken circle around Violet. Their faces were flecked with smudges of dirt and scratches, their eyes bright and attentive. Johnny pushed his black-framed glasses up along the bridge of his nose, staring at Violet as if she were a priceless artifact on display behind glass in a museum.

"Is she friendly?" asked Lily Brown. "Will she hurt me?"

"No, she won't hurt you," Hettie said, looking over at Violet. Her ears were pinned alongside her head. "She's just not used to being around so many people."

"Can I touch her?" Johnny asked.

"Quickly," Hettie said, her eyes flashing back down the road. "Rub her forehead. She likes that."

Johnny Gibson stepped closer and carefully extended his hand and touched her forehead with a gentle pat. Violet stood still and spooled up her trunk and released it. Then she swung her tail, swatting Lily Brown on the shoulder.

"She got me," Lily cried, taking a step back.

"She didn't mean to," Hettie said. "Right, Violet?"

This time, Albert O'Brien took a step closer and extended his hand, and Violet suctioned his open palm.

"That tickles," he said with a smile.

"She's hungry," Hettie said, glancing up the road, still expecting the constable or a sergeant to appear at any moment. "I need to take her home. Please do me a favor and don't mention to anyone about seeing Violet. We need to keep her a secret for now."

Johnny locked his pursed mouth with an imaginary key and then tossed it away. The other children nodded.

"She is our secret," Johnny said with a smile.

"Say goodbye to Violet," Hettie said.

"Goodbye, Violet," Lily said.

"Can we visit with her again soon?" Johnny asked.

"Yes," Hettie said, lifting up the crop. "Very soon."

"Goodbye, Violet," Albert said.

"Welcome to the Whitewell Road, Violet," Johnny said with a playful grin. "We'll see you again soon."

Hettie continued toward her house in between the Reynoldses' and the Browns'. She felt the children's eyes on her as she unlatched the gate to their courtyard and then carefully closed it behind the two of them, and she finally breathed a sigh of relief.

Though Thomas had always said he was going to fix up the courtyard, he had never gotten around to it: The area was still no more than a square parcel of concrete with narrow beds of soil bordering two edges. Scraps of nondescript paper and twigs littered the barren yard. Violet stood in the center. Hettie fetched one of the buckets of water that Rose had filled after she had heard the air-raid sirens, and placed it next to the elephant. Violet reached her trunk into the water and sprayed it into her mouth.

On the other side of the wall, the Reynoldses' dog barked. A fine drizzle of rain started to fall again and Violet, fatigued from her recent exertions, lay down on the pavement. Hettie went into the kitchen and collected a bundle of carrots from the larder. Rose's half-finished cup of tea still sat on the table. As she made her way out of the kitchen, she heard a rustling in her mother's bedroom. Then the opening and closing of drawers. Footsteps moved across the floorboards.

Exhilarated by the possibility that her mother might be alive, Hettie dropped the carrots onto the kitchen counter and rushed into the darkened hallway, its walls still holding the shadowy checkerboard of family photographs. The thin bar of light on the floor vanished again, and the metal springs of her mother's bed creaked.

Then Hettie felt a bolt of panic: What would her mother say about Violet being in their courtyard? Surely she would force Hettie to return the elephant to the zoo, where the police would be waiting for her. But perhaps, Hettie reasoned, her mother would understand, due to the unusual circumstances, that it was a temporary arrangement, just until the threat of the ministry's directive had passed. Maybe it would only be a few days, and things would somehow return to normal.

"Mum," Hettie said tentatively. "Mum, is that you?"

No one answered. Hettie walked down the dim hallway toward her mother's bedroom. She slowly opened the door. There, in front of Rose's chest of drawers, a man was bent over, rifling through her clothes, tossing random articles of her mother's lingerie onto the floor and the unmade bed. A crush of disappointment tumbled onto Hettie. She couldn't believe it wasn't her mother.

"Excuse me," she said, her voice trembling. "Who are you? And what are you doing in my house?"

The man wheeled around.

"Hettie!"

"Liam!"

His name caught like a burr in her throat. In the dull half-light of her mother's bedroom, she couldn't quite make out his features. She took a step closer so that she could see him more clearly. Liam's face was unshaven; a dark shadow of stubble covered his lower cheeks and angular chin. A fresh cut extended across his forehead and a lavender bruise bloomed along his right temple; it looked as if he had recently been dragged out of a fight. Despite all this, Hettie felt relieved to see Liam. Perhaps he would be able to help her find Rose. Given his vast network of friends and colleagues in Belfast, he would know who to reach out to, who might know the best way to go about finding her mother amid the chaos of the city.

"Liam, what are you doing here?"

"We were worried about you. Ma was worried that you—"

"Where's Maeve? Is she all right?"

"Yes, yes," he said. "She's still in Newcastle with Ma."

Liam folded Hettie into his arms, and she felt her entire body tremble. She wanted to be held and wanted to pull away from him at the same time. The shoulder of his coat smelled of forest and fire. He gently kissed Hettie on the forehead, and Hettie felt safe and protected for the first time since the bombs began to drop. Finally someone who could help her. Finally someone who could hide Violet from the constable. Hettie relaxed into the sturdiness of Liam's embrace. A parade of shivers marched down her center. Her cheeks began to burn. She felt caught in the riptide of his affection. She couldn't stop herself from responding to his advances. Liam effortlessly moved his mouth over hers. His tongue felt like warm liquid spilling down her throat. Her mouth melted into his. Liam pulled away.

"I thought you might be dead," he said. "My mates said the White-well Road was hit."

"I was at the zoo with Violet during the bombing."

Liam stared into her eyes. "Return to Newcastle with me," he said. "It's safer there. Word around the city is that the Germans are planning to bomb Belfast again soon. Ma is worried about you."

Before Hettie could respond, Liam leaned in and kissed her again. She felt as if she were lost in some strange dream: Here, her sister's widower was kissing Hettie in her mother's bedroom. This sequence of events didn't belong in her life. Despite this, Hettie allowed herself to fall further into Liam's kiss and surrender into her own need and desire. Hettie held Liam with a fierceness that she hadn't known she possessed. Here was a rhapsody of affection. A holy communion of sorts. One that she had little experience or understanding of, but only knew that it held many things at once: lust, love, guilt, shame, passion.

Suddenly all these emotions sharpened into one truth: Hettie wanted Liam. He was the only person who mattered to her. This temporary euphoria eclipsed her dead sister, her missing mother, the executed animals, Violet in the courtyard. Instead, Hettie was caught under the hypnotic spell of Liam—and all that he was. It was both bewildering and thrilling. He pushed Hettie against the bedpost as he slipped his hand under her pleated skirt, moving his hand inside the elastic of her underwear and pressing against the heat between her legs. She released a soft groan. Liam bent onto the bed and caressed her thighs before thrusting two fingers inside her. Her muscles tightened and opened up at the same time. Hettie bit into her lower lip, willing herself not to cry out.

When Liam finally guided himself inside her, it was as if he were the missing puzzle piece that fit into her. In and out. Soft and hard. Pleasure and pain. Hettie wanted to tell Liam to stop—and to keep going. Her body was waking up and resisting, charging and collapsing until it accumulated into a physical crescendo. His nails dug into her forearms as he pushed himself more deeply into her, taking her virginity as his own.

Then Liam released a shudder and crumpled across the length of her body like a deflated balloon. Hettie felt dazed and stunned. The act had begun and ended so quickly. Hettie's gaze lingered on her mother's bedside table: Her simple gold wedding band sat in a porcelain dish, and there was her worn Agatha Christie paperback with its dog-eared pages. Rose was more than halfway through. Hettie's eyes moved to her mother's chest of drawers on the other side of the room. Her small rosewood chest was open. It was a beautifully carved box with decorative inlays of vines and flowering morning glories along its polished sides and lid. It had been a gift from Thomas's mother on the day of their wedding over twenty-five years ago. Several crumpled pound notes littered the tabletop and were scattered on the floor. Hettie looked at Liam: His eyes were closed. His breaths were wispy and long. Suddenly, he revolted her.

"Get off of me," Hettie said, attempting to push Liam away. "Get up."

He flicked his eyes open. "What's wrong?" he asked, confusion tightening his brow.

He turned on to his side, and Hettie slid out from underneath him and collected her clothes and quickly dressed herself. As she buttoned her blouse, Hettie stared at him: He looked like a different person to her. He was no longer her sister's widower. He had become someone else, like a stranger, this man lying in her mother's bed, with clouds of wiry brown hair clustered around his flaccid penis. Her own blood streaked the sagging skin. She thought she might be sick.

He wiped his hand along his member. "Could you get me a wash-cloth?" he asked.

"Get out."

He just sat there mutely as Hettie began to pick up the pound notes from the floor. There, she also discovered Rose's favorite gold brooch that was handed down from her mother—a bow with three small di-amonds nestled into the knot—near the wooden foot of the bureau. Next to the brooch was the snail that Ferris had given her. Hettie had no idea how these objects had ended up on Rose's bedroom floor. She gathered them along with the pound notes.

"You need to leave," she said to Liam.

Without another word, he stood up and zipped his trousers, and quickly slipped his arms into the sleeves of his work shirt.

"Hettie, I'm just as surprised as you are," he said. "I'm not lying."

"Why did you come back?" Hettie asked as she scooped up the rest of the notes and folded them into her mother's chest. "I assume there was another reason, other than robbing us?"

"It's not what you think," Liam said, tucking the tails of his shirt into his trousers.

Hettie sat down on the edge of the bed, attempting to steady herself. The pungent odors of smoke, fish, and her mother's lilac perfume surrounded her.

"I had to return to the city on IRA business," he explained. "The officer commanding my brigade was blown to pieces in the raid. His house on Lincoln Avenue took a direct hit. I had to come back and figure out who will take over his command."

"So, for the IRA," Hettie said, staring at her mother's chest again. Despite everything, she realized she'd been hoping he would say he had returned for her.

"Hettie—"

Her head began to throb.

"Where is Rose?" Liam asked.

Hettie stood up.

"Where is your mother?" he asked again.

"I don't know where she is," Hettie finally snapped. "I haven't seen her since last night. She told me to go to the shelter on Atlantic Avenue, but I was worried about Violet and ran to the zoo instead—and I haven't seen her since."

"She went to Atlantic Avenue," he said, taking another step toward Hettie.

Suddenly everything hit her again—all that had transpired during the past twelve hours: the never-ending detonations of the bombs shaking the ground, the deafening cries of the zoo animals, the song of Stella Holliday that had opened up her soul, the chaos of the Royal, the lifeless bodies at St. George's, the twitch of Wallace's paw as the rest of his body grew still. Outside, there was a loud clang. And then Violet's trumpet call.

"Violet," Hettie said. She couldn't believe she'd been so caught up in Liam that she had forgotten about her elephant. She hurried down the hallway, grabbing the bundle of carrots from the kitchen counter as she headed outside. Liam followed her. What Hettie saw nearly made her faint: Violet stood in the center of the courtyard, and Samuel Greene stood on the far side, near the gate that led to the street, his rifle slung over his shoulder. He straightened his posture and kept his gaze fixed on Violet. The elephant began to pace, kicking her foot against the metal bucket and spilling a pool of water across the pavement.

"Samuel," she said, her voice quivering.

Hettie felt certain he was going to lift his rifle and aim it at Violet in one swift motion. His expression remained still, his mouth a mere line of sadness. Patches of crimson decorated his neck.

"Hettie, the constable is on his way," he said. "You need to take Violet somewhere else."

Hettie thought she must have been hearing wrong. Was Samuel trying to help her? Violet continued to pace the courtyard.

"Who are you?" Liam asked, buttoning up his shirt. "I suspect you're in the RUC."

Samuel said nothing. Hettie noticed Liam reaching for a solid shape in the front pocket of his trousers.

"My name is Samuel Greene. I work for the government," he said. "Hettie, they know where you live, they will be here shortly. Mr. Wright is trying to stall Constable Ward, but I don't think he'll succeed much longer."

A soreness pulsed between Hettie's legs.

"Why don't you just bugger off," Liam said, his hand still in his pocket.

"The Ministry of Public Security ordered the execution of the dangerous animals at the zoo," Hettie said, looking up at Liam and then at Samuel. "And Violet was on the list."

"They're going to be here soon," Samuel said, more urgently now. "They intend to shoot Violet as soon as they see her."

Without another word, Hettie ran inside to her bedroom and quickly changed into a pair of dungarees, a blouse, socks and work boots, and her peacoat. In the larder, she found another bundle of carrots and a few turnips, and in the bread box, a few stale rolls. Before returning to the courtyard, Hettie stepped into her mother's bedroom once more and retrieved her wedding ring, the snail, her lucky talisman, and a few loose bills, folding them and the other items into the front pocket of her trousers. She tucked her grandmother's brooch and her mother's valuables into one of the compartments and closed the rosewood chest securely and slid it underneath the bed, and then arranged several pairs of her mother's shoes in front of it. It wasn't much, but it was all she could do to protect Rose's valuables during that moment.

When she returned to the courtyard, Liam was standing near the garden beds. He had taken out a handgun from his pocket and was polishing its barrel with his own spit and a handkerchief. Samuel Greene stood on the other side of the courtyard, tapping his foot against the pavement. Hettie glanced at both men, and picked up the curled stick from the bench and walked toward Violet.

"Let's go, Violet," she said, then halted as she realized she had no idea where to take her.

"Anywhere but here," Samuel said, almost reading her mind.

"We'll take her to my friend's house," Liam said. "He lives just down the hill."

"Fine," Samuel said curtly. "Just leave. Now."

Hettie didn't have time to consider the wisdom of Liam's plan. She guided the stick in front of Violet and right away the elephant followed her along the narrow pathway that led to the street. She broke another carrot and passed it back to Violet. The elephant curled her trunk around the carrot and slipped it into her mouth.

As they approached the street, Hettie looked up the rise for any evidence of the constable and sergeant. She was relieved not to see the pair. Instead, her neighbors, Mr. Reynolds and Mr. Brown, stood on the curb, talking to each other. They stared up at her and Violet with expressions of amazement. Their eyes were wide open, their mouths gaping as if they were about to break into laughter.

"Hettie Quin," Mr. Brown said. "What on earth—"

"I'll explain later," she said. "If my mum returns, please tell her that I'm taking care of Violet, that I'll be back soon, that I miss her, that I'm safe, that I'm alive."

"Of course, of course," Mr. Reynolds said. "We'll tell her."

"This way," Liam said, walking down the hill toward the Arthur Road.

Hettie embraced Samuel.

"Thank you so—"

"You should go," he whispered. "Take good care of Violet—and yourself."

"I'm sorry," she said, "about Colleen White."

"Go on, Hettie," he said.

Samuel took a step back and repositioned his rifle on his shoulder. As she looked into his face, she realized despite everything that had transpired between the two of them, Samuel was a good man. She hoped she would see him again. Hettie turned around and followed Liam, and Violet ambled after her. Over the modest hill, multiple homes had been reduced to piles of rubble and ash. The Thompsons', the Smiths', and the Longeleys'. Farther down the road, Mr. Wilson hammered away, boarding up the broken windows of his house. In the distance, Hettie heard a whistle. She was certain that it was the constable and the sergeant right behind them, but when she turned around she saw only Samuel Greene standing on her street with his rifle slung across his back.

"This way, Hettie," Liam said.

From the Whitewell Road, they turned left on to the Longlands Road and then down the Church Road. Hettie noticed with some trepidation that they were crossing over into the Catholic section of her neighborhood. Irish tricolors were hanging out from the windows of many of the row houses, and she spotted a republican slogan— ERIN GO BRAGH—painted on one of the gable walls. Hettie surmised that Liam was probably taking Violet and her to one of his friends' houses who was also involved with IRA-related activities. Fear radiated throughout her system as she thought about the gun in Liam's pocket and what had just happened in her mother's bedroom. Hettie turned around and stared up the street. A broken water-main pipe gushed like a fountain into the air. A young boy in velvet trousers waved. A part of Hettie wanted to return home and determine the best strategy of finding her mother, but she knew that if she returned to her house, it was likely that the constable and the sergeant were already there, questioning Samuel Greene. Hettie imagined the officers would question Mr. Brown, Mr. Reynolds, Mrs. Lyttle, and perhaps the children, too. Her stomach turned again. Violet released another trumpet call.

"Easy there," Hettie said. "Easy, me girl."

The elephant reached her trunk up into the air, the loop and curve seemingly forming random letters of the alphabet—first an *S* and then a *U*. Violet appeared to be growing more agitated. Hettie felt in her pocket for something to feed her. She pulled a stale roll out and gave it to Violet. She munched on it and seemed to calm as they continued along the street. A few strangers collected along the curb, taking in the bizarre sight of Violet marching down the road. An enormous crater filled the front yard of one of the homes, making the neighborhood look like a foreign landscape, a place that was no longer welcoming for humans and animals alike.

"Almost there," Liam said.

Suddenly a mangy dog appeared in front of Hettie and Violet. His coat was a ratty gray brown, and there was a pair of bite marks on one of his ears. At first the dog cocked his head to one side, as if he was merely curious about the presence of the young elephant. Then the hairs on the dog's neck bristled. Hettie looked around and noticed several other stray dogs sniffing, combing, and roaming through the yards. At least a dozen or more. Hettie wondered where they had all come from. The dog in front of them began to growl, baring his teeth. He moved closer to Violet's feet and barked. Violet unfurled her large ears and released a hostile cry. Liam turned around. The elephant lowered her head and barreled toward the dog.

"Oh, no," Hettie said. "Vi—"

The dog retreated, whimpering and skittering underneath a broken fence and disappearing into the next yard. Violet still charged after it at full speed and smashed through what remained of the fence, snapping the boards like brittle twigs. Then Hettie heard another crash. Liam ran toward Hettie from the road. The other dogs ceased their scavenging and stared on.

"What the bloody—"

Violet emerged from behind the broken fences, carrying a large turnip the size of a cricket ball in her mouth. Stringy roots with clumps of dirt hung from her mouth. The dog was nowhere to be seen. Hettie pressed her fingers against her temples. Her head throbbed with greater intensity. Her ears started to buzz, as if insects were caught inside them. Meanwhile Violet happily munched on the turnip.

Just then two elderly women stepped outside their homes. Right away, Hettie recognized them from the neighborhood and her aunt's corner store: It was Mrs. Sloane and Mrs. Kilduff. Mrs. Kilduff's silver-and-chestnut hair was tightly wound in a set of plastic curlers, with most of the stiff rollers hidden under a floral kerchief. Blotches of cold cream dotted Mrs. Sloane's pale, wrinkled face. Aunt Sylvia had always been that way, catering to both the Catholics and the Protestants along the Antrim Road.

"That elephant ruined my garden," Mrs. Kilduff screamed, brandishing her wooden cane in the air.

Hettie looked around at Mrs. Kilduff's garden in disbelief. It was clear that much of it had already been destroyed during the bombing. A large crater hollowed out a corner of her yard, and a small dog yapped from the other side of the enormous hole. The other dogs—mutts,

German shepherds, Labradors, and collies—gathered around the gaping hole, standing like a vigilant company of soldiers awaiting their orders. Some wagged their tails, others had their ears pinned back. No longer paying attention to the dog, Violet fed on another turnip she had just yanked from the ground.

"Where did all these dogs come from?" Hettie asked Liam, ignoring the old woman.

Hettie and Liam took in the sight of the burgeoning pack of dogs.

"They've lost their owners during the attacks," Liam said, pausing for a moment, "or they've been abandoned by their owners who have fled the city."

Many of the dogs perked their ears up as they stared at the spectacle of Violet munching on the turnip. A few of them issued sharp barks and low growls.

"That wild animal belongs behind bars. He's a dangerous-looking bastard," Mrs. Kilduff continued. "I'll get that constable to come here, I've heard he's shooting all the animals up at the zoo."

At the mention of the constable, Hettie's chest tightened again. Violet kicked her feet through the piles of dirt and fallen flowers.

"Vi, stop," Hettie said, clucking her tongue against the roof of her mouth. "Stop it."

Liam took the crop from Hettie. "Here, Vi," he said, walking around the rim of the crater. "Let's not create any further wreckage."

"What about my garden! What about my yard!"

"I'm sorry for the damage, Mrs. Kilduff," Hettie said.

"I know who you are," Mrs. Kilduff shouted. "You're Thomas Quin's daughter. Everyone knows about your father, how he cheats and lies. Your poor mother. You're just like him."

Hettie held the stare of Mrs. Kilduff's steely gray eyes. A few wisps of wiry hair flew out from her curlers. Her skin was thin and papery, like a ghost.

"Mrs. Kilduff," she said in a steady voice. "I'll pay for the damages. I'll fix your fence."

Mrs. Kilduff's expression remained blank and empty, but then her face crumpled into tears, and Hettie realized she wasn't angry at Mrs. Kilduff, or even Violet. She was angry at the Germans. She was angry at Hitler. She was angry at the war.

"Hettie, we've got other things to worry about," Liam said.

He was leading Violet toward the street with a pack of stray dogs scampering after them. Hettie walked toward Mrs. Kilduff. The elderly woman stared at her with a bewildered expression. Hettie took a few pound notes from the front pocket of her trousers and handed them to Mrs. Kilduff.

"I'll bring more later, I promise."

Mrs. Kilduff sniffed, accepted the bills, and rubbed her nose with the sleeve of her housecoat.

Hettie sprinted down the road and caught up with Liam and Violet. The dogs followed them, howling and barking as they surveyed the ruins of the street. Liam turned right before heading down a dirt driveway that led to a series of row houses. Hettie nervously glanced behind them. The dogs lingered, now rooting through the charred shell of a neighboring house. Liam opened the gate and guided Violet into the rear area. The courtyard of the row house didn't look much different from her own on the Whitewell Road: a bare square of concrete surrounded by high redbrick walls on three sides. A young, slender man stood near the back door of the house with his arms crossed over his chest and a grin of bemusement on his face.

"Is this your idea of an offensive strategy, Keegan," said the man with a harsh laugh. "A goddamn elephant. What are we going to do with that beast?"

The man started to pace around Hettie and Violet as if he were a vulture circling a plump rodent. Hettie took a few steps closer to Violet, feeling worried again. The stringy roots of a turnip still hung from the corner of the elephant's mouth.

"Sell her on the black market? If we keep that bloody thing, the security forces will be crawling all over this neighborhood in no time looking for her."

Hettie stared at Liam. He walked over to the young man and smacked him against his arm. The sight of her mother's opened rosewood chest flashed through her mind. Why hadn't she tried harder to take all the valuables with her? She fingered her mother's wedding ring in her pocket and glanced at the gate and back to Violet, and wondered if the constable and sergeant might have already come and gone from her house.

"Why don't you ever know when to shut the fuck up, Éamon—"

Liam shoved the man against the brick wall of the house.

"Calm down, Keegan," he said, stepping to the side. "I'm just wondering how the hell an elephant figures into our plans is all."

"I'm trying to help Hettie out here. She's my sister-in-law for God's sake," Liam said, releasing Éamon from his grip. "She works at the zoo. Because of the air raid, the government has ordered all of the dangerous animals to be shot and sent the constable to do it. Bombs fell close to the zoo during the attack, and the locals want the animals put down."

"The constable," Éamon said. "I don't understand."

"I know, I know," Liam said.

Éamon paused and then studied Hettie more keenly. "Aye, I knew I knew you from somewhere," Éamon said, a smirk playing on his thick lips. "You're Anna Quin's kid sister. You look just like her."

Hettie's cheeks reddened. Suddenly she was reminded of the reality that she had just lost her virginity to her sister's widower. She felt guilty, foolish, and embarrassed about what had happened between Liam and her. How could she have been so daft to fall for Liam? Clearly he had been stealing from Rose and the only reason the two of them had ended up in her mother's bed was because he was attempting to cover up his illicit actions. Still, some part of her wanted to believe that their encounter would amount to something greater, that Liam might love her in a more permanent way.

"Tell me her name," Éamon said, his tone becoming more menacing. "The elephant, what's she called?"

"Violet," Hettie offered.

"Violet," Éamon repeated, tightening his circle around Hettie and Violet. "I like that name. How old is she? Where does she come from?"

"She's three," Hettie responded guardedly. "She's from Ceylon."

"An exotic creature from a distant land," he said, and Hettie could practically see the cogs whirring in his mind. "Maybe I'm wrong. Maybe there is a way Vi could assist us in our efforts. What do you think, Keegan?" As he said this, Éamon retrieved a pistol from the pocket of his jacket. Hettie stared at Liam. Perspiration glistened along the top edge of his forehead. His right eye twitched.

"Come on, Éamon," Liam said. "Don't do this. Violet needs a safe hiding place until the constable loses his interest in the zoo and its animals. It won't be long."

"Well, you never know," Éamon said. "We want the constable, and the constable wants Violet. Maybe we could work something out."

"Liam, what is he talking about?" Hettie asked sharply.

Ignoring her question, Liam retrieved a bucket from the side of the row house and placed it next to Violet. She unfurled her trunk and sucked the water into her trunk, and then sprayed it into her mouth. Éamon watched, transfixed, his finger resting on the gun's trigger.

"Poor thing," Liam said. "She's dying of thirst."

Hettie pulled out the last remaining roll from her coat pocket and extended it to Violet in the center of her hand. The elephant swiftly slurped it up.

Suddenly, Éamon pointed his pistol up into the air and fired. Hettie jumped violently, and Violet released a throaty cry.

"What are you doing?" Liam yelled.

"Just testing it out," Éamon said with a deranged smile. "I stole it from my uncle. I wasn't sure if it worked."

"You're a fuckin' crazy eejit," Liam said, taking a step closer to Éamon. "You know what your problem is? You never know when to stop. That's why I had to come back to Belfast. That's why Billy Foyles is dead."

Hettie felt confused. Why were they talking about all this when all she wanted was somewhere to hide Violet for a little while?

Éamon's dark eyebrows furled, and his eyes lit up. He was like a child and an adult, mischievous yet dangerous. Slowly, Éamon turned the pistol's barrel from the sky toward Liam. Hettie held her breath.

"I've never liked you, Keegan," Éamon said.

Éamon walked toward Liam. Hettie looked around for the crop and saw that Liam had leaned it against the wall, near the gate that led out to the street. She retrieved it and slowly started to guide Violet along the narrow pathway that led to the front of the house. Éamon thrust the pistol's barrel against Liam's chest, but Liam just stared him down.

"You've always been the one with the big ideas, but nothing ever gets done," Éamon yelled, the pistol shaking in his hand. "I should have listened to my instincts in the first place. Neal was always saying that Liam Keegan was good for something, but it turns out that you're good for nothing. You're all talk. You don't really give a damn about Ireland. You're never willing to make any sacrifices for the cause. You're using Maeve as an excuse now to run away to the country and do nothing. You don't care what we're doing here in Belfast. You're too concerned with de Valera and his so-called causes."

Suddenly Liam pummeled Éamon alongside his right cheek. Hettie stopped for a split second. She felt as if she were witnessing the violence in slow motion—Liam's arm swinging back and then moving forward with a terrible powerful force, the impact sending Éamon clear across the pavement. A bullet accidentally discharged from the gun, swishing over Hettie's head and piercing the wooden rear gate.

"Jesus Christ," she screamed, ducking down to the ground. "Jesus bloody Christ."

She scrambled to unlatch the gate and started for the street. Violet followed right behind her, swinging her trunk, agitated again after the blast from the pistol. Hettie didn't know where to go. She imagined that the constable and sergeant were still at her house, interrogating the neighbors about her whereabouts. Then she heard another gunshot behind her. The fine hairs on her arms pricked up. Hettie whipped around. There Éamon stood, panting, his pistol still in his hand.

"Hettie and Violet," Éamon said, "where are you going now? Aren't you going to let me help you? I think I can help you."

Hettie swallowed. As she stared into Éamon's eyes, she realized she had run out of ideas. For a moment, she wished that Ferris were here with her, that he could help her decide what to do next.

Then Liam appeared behind Éamon and tackled him to the pavement. More fists flew, and the pistol skittered across the ground toward Violet's feet. Hettie rushed to pick it up. She had never touched a gun before. The handle felt warm and sturdy and solid. Liam threw another forceful punch before standing up, brushing the dirt off the front of his shirt and leaving Éamon behind, limp on the pavement. A thin stream of blood traveled along the side of Éamon's cheek. He looked up at Liam.

"Keegan, this isn't going to end well for you," he rasped. "You're going to be sorry."

Liam spat into Éamon's face, and Éamon flinched, wiping away the spit from his cheek.

"You're a bastard, you know that," Éamon said. "You're a goddamn bloody bastard."

"Come on, Hettie," Liam said, putting his arm around her shoulder and turning her away.

"Don't you worry: I'll call in at the zoo and let that constable know where you're headed. I know where you're going," Éamon yelled, finally pulling himself off the pavement. "You and the elephant aren't going to get away."

"This way," Liam said, and they started walking.

The last glimpse Hettie had of Éamon was of him wiping away the blood on his face with the sleeve of his uniform. He looked like one of the injured patients that Hettie had encountered early that morning at the Royal—bloody and disoriented.

Liam led Violet and Hettie down the hill toward the shoreline, in the opposite direction from the Whitewell Road and the Bellevue Zoo.

"I wish we could return home," Hettie said.

"We can't go back there," Liam said sternly. "The risk is too high."

Violet paused for a minute and sniffed the end of her trunk across the gritty pavement. Tumbleweeds of trash and other debris tripped down the street. Hettie noticed a few wrapped presents buried under a pile of rubble near the concrete foundation of what had until recently been someone's home. Most of the badly damaged and dangerously unstable houses had been taken down by the rescue squads and soldiers, their bricks and masonry roughly scattered over their front gardens. Violet gave out a soft chirp, like a bird or a cricket, and Hettie stroked behind one of her ears.

"I'm sorry, Hettie," Liam said. "I thought he was my friend. I didn't think he'd see Violet as some kind of weapon." He shook his head, looking almost bewildered about Éamon's behavior. Hettie nodded wearily, too exhausted to respond. "I know a better place, I promise," Liam said. "Give me his gun. I'll keep it safe."

Hettie hesitated.

"Really, Hettie. Trust me."

Hettie looked up at Liam: His calm chestnut eyes and his subdued smile seemed to provide Hettie with her only possibility of hope and safety. She handed the weapon over to Liam, and he stowed it in the pocket of his jacket.

The three of them continued down the street in silence. The smell of burning still hung in the air. They passed several more homes that had been diminished to powdery mounds of detritus. Almost every surface of the neighborhood was coated in shifting layers of ash, dust, and grime, as if this place now existed in an ancient time. Personal effects were scattered here and there: a toothbrush, a doll with rosy cheeks and red lips, a Bible with its torn, gold-leafed pages ruffling in the breeze. Ahead, next to an upside-down dustbin, was a woman's blue leather purse with its contents spilled onto the curb. Violet reached for the handle of the purse with the end of her trunk and lifted it up, causing the rest of its contents to fall onto the road. Coins, hairpins, a fountain pen, and a linen handkerchief. Violet shook the purse as if she was looking for something.

"Vi, leave it alone," Liam said.

Strangely, it appeared that Violet had already grown accustomed to Liam and his low-pitched voice. Violet dropped the purse onto the small pile of rubble. As she walked along, the elephant's tail twitched from side to side, swatting away a fly.

Liam led them through the hazy maze of streets until they were walking along a road that hugged the shoreline. The port of Belfast and the enormous skeleton-like cranes of Harland & Wolff were visible in the distance. To Hettie, it felt as if it had been several years since Violet's auspicious arrival at the port, even though only seven months had passed since her walk up the Antrim Road.

"Do you think Éamon will call in at the zoo and speak to the constable there?"

"Don't worry about him," Liam said. "Éamon's harmless."

"He didn't seem harmless."

"Believe me, he won't be calling in at any zoo. He's in serious trouble with the law himself. If he calls, his arse will be thrown in jail for a very long time. That's why I thought we could count on him to help us."

"What did he do?"

"It's up here," Liam said, picking up his pace. "Across the road."

Liam turned left and walked across the two-way street. There was a large wooden gate with an iron knocker in the middle and a doorbell to one side; it appeared to be the entrance to a compound surrounded by a brick wall with tight circles of wire ringing its top edge. There was no sign, no indication of who might reside on the other side of the wall. Hettie worried that it was the address of another one of Liam's IRA colleagues, and that more chaos and fighting would ensue.

All at once she yearned to return home again. She imagined there was a good chance that the constable and his men had already come and gone. Maybe Ferris was now looking for her and Violet, too. Maybe he had run into Samuel Greene again, and he had told Ferris what had happened, that she was looking for a better place to hide Violet until the danger of the constable had subsided. Then, she could go and search for her mother again. She wished more than ever for Ferris's steady presence and trouble-free smile.

Hettie stared up the forested hillside toward the Antrim Road and the zoo. Threads of smoke hovered over the neighborhood. Violet clomped along the pavement. Somewhere in the gray overcast sky a low droning sound emerged. Liam looked up, too. For a moment, Hettie felt certain that parachute bombs would begin floating down, hundreds upon hundreds of them, silvery teardrops accenting the brightening sky, looking innocuous at first but soon delivering another round of massive destruction on her beloved city. She knew this wasn't a rational thought: The Germans attacked only during darkness, never during broad daylight, but she was certain that she heard the sound of an aircraft. It struck her that it was probably on reconnaissance, assessing the damage that the Luftwaffe raid had caused and identifying what targets had been hit. But Hettie also recognized that some degree of her rationality was leaving her, that she was now making decisions from a place deep inside her that she didn't even know existed twenty-four hours ago. The drone of the plane grew louder.

"Come on," Liam said, ringing the bell a second time. "Be here. You need to be here."

Eleven

THE LARGE DOOR SLOWLY OPENED, AND HETTIE WAS SUR-prised to see a pair of elderly nuns dressed in powder-blue habits and white caps step out to meet them. One was short and rotund, and wore silver-rimmed glasses, the lenses perfectly circular like the narrow mouth of a glass bottle. A few black hairs stippled her double chin. The other nun was tall and angular, her cheekbones high and pronounced. A crucifix hung around her neck.

"Liam Patrick Keegan, what are you doing here?" exclaimed the short, bespectacled nun. "I thought you were in Newcastle with your mother and the baby. Is everyone all right? Don't tell me the Germans attacked Newcastle, too."

"Who do we have here?" the taller nun asked, staring at Hettie and Violet.

Hettie patted Violet's flank, feeling the elephant's stiff bristles spring underneath her fingertips.

"I have a favor to ask, Sister Helen," Liam said.

"What is it this time, Liam Patrick?" she said, her hands perched on her hips.

"Let me introduce you," he said. "This is Hettie Quin."

"Anna's younger sister," said the taller nun, peering at Hettie.

Liam turned his attention to the elephant. "And this is Violet," he said.

"Well, I suppose you ought to step inside," Sister Helen said, opening the gate wider so they could walk through the oversize entrance. "It's been a bit mad around here—and I don't want your elephant to get hit by a speeding lorry."

"What a truly awful attack. I wouldn't want to live through another night like that again," the other nun said. "We spent the whole night on our knees in the chapel, but there was no damage here, not even a window was broken. Dei gratia."

When they were all safely inside the courtyard, Sister Helen closed and locked the gate behind them, and Hettie looked around. Just as the nun had said, within the walls of the expansive compound, it looked as if the bombing of the city had never taken place. The pristine courtyard led into a second courtyard, one curved arch answering another, with a series of low-lying gray stone buildings making up the cloistered area. At the rear of the second courtyard, the white steeple of a chapel rose toward the overcast sky. Well-manicured flower beds hugged the walls with vines of blooming morning glories crawling skyward. A large wooden crucifix hung on the side of one of the structures. A fountain— with a statue of Mary standing at its center—gurgled in the middle of the flagstone courtyard. A flock of barn sparrows fluttered in the shallow basin of water, and one of the birds rested in Mary's open palm.

"There we go," Sister Helen said, pushing her sleeves around her dimpled elbows. "Now, tell us what this is all about."

"I have to say this is the first time we've been honored to have an elephant as a guest," said the other nun.

"We're a convent, Sister Evangeline," Sister Helen said. "Not a stable."

"Yes, Sister Helen," Sister Evangeline said with a smile, "but we all know God comes in all shapes and sizes."

As they stood there, a few other nuns emerged from the buildings and the outlying pathways, their feet shuffling under the floor-length hems of their powder-blue habits.

"We're waiting, Liam Patrick," Sister Helen said, her voice stern. "What's your story this time—"

"Hettie works up at the zoo," Liam said. "You might have remembered me talking about her before we left for Newcastle. She is the only female zookeeper."

The fact that Liam had previously mentioned Hettie and her work at the zoo to the nuns produced a small degree of pleasure in Hettie. She did exist within his orbit.

"Well done," Sister Helen said, her eyes reflecting both warmth and scrutiny. "God knows we need more women to lead us these days. Look at the mess the world is in, and it's all because of men—Hitler, Stalin, Churchill, and, nearer home, Craigavon. They're brutal, insensitive, arrogant. They never go down on their knees and pray, and consider the will of God, or think how what they're doing will affect the women, their sisters, wives and mothers, and the wee children."

"Violet is one of Hettie's charges at the zoo," Liam continued. "This morning, Andrews ordered all of the dangerous animals be executed, in the event their cages get bombed and they escape."

"What does that man know, he's an old fool," Sister Helen tutted, glancing at Liam and then turning her attention to Violet. "And what would you like us to do with Violet here?"

Now there was an edge in her voice. Hettie couldn't tell how Sister Helen felt about the presence of Violet in the convent's courtyard—whether she was thrilled by this peculiar turn of events or found the situation objectionable. Sister Helen examined the elephant carefully, walking a slow, wide circle around Violet. When she returned to her original spot next to Liam, she extended her hand and patted Violet on the forehead. The elephant swung her tail.

"The constable and his men are looking for Violet right now because she's on the government's list to be shot," Hettie explained further. "I need to hide her until she is no longer in danger."

During their exchange, ten, twenty, thirty women had gathered soundlessly around Liam, Sister Helen, Hettie, and Violet in the large courtyard. Many of their moonlike faces were pale and translucent, their silver and chestnut strands of hair tucked under the fitted folds of their white caps. Constellations of freckles punctuated their cheeks, foreheads, and chins, their eyes were reflective pools of blues and browns. They stared at Violet with a sense of wonderment and joy. An elephant! In the convent's courtyard!

Sister Evangeline reappeared from one of the buildings with something under her arm. As she drew closer, it became apparent that she was carrying a basket of small red apples. To Hettie, the fruit might as well have been gold. She hadn't seen an apple in over a year; she had almost forgotten that they existed. She wondered how the nuns had managed to get hold of them.

"Sister Helen, do you think we can spare one or two apples for our special visitor? Particularly since a few weeks ago we received a few bushels from our faithful church members."

Sister Helen narrowed her eyes. "One apple," Sister Helen conceded. "That's it, Linny."

"Here you go, lovely," said Sister Evangeline, extending an apple to Violet.

The elephant grabbed the apple nimbly with her trunk and placed it into the triangle of her mouth. Shreds of crisp flesh and red skin clung to the whiskers underneath her chin. Violet squeaked, and her ears flapped. Everyone laughed. Sister Evangeline tentatively reached her hand into the bushel again and offered one more apple to Violet as Sister Helen scowled at her. The elephant dropped the fruit into her mouth before brushing her trunk against Sister Evangeline's arm.

"She's a good girl, isn't she?" Sister Evangeline said fondly.

"That's enough, Linny," Sister Helen said firmly.

Hettie's mouth started to water. A part of her wanted to reach into the basket and grab an apple for herself. She looked over at Liam. He pushed back a thick curl of his hair with the smooth base of his palm. Then Hettie felt an intense itch between her legs. Violet kicked against the ground and clouds of dust billowed around her feet. Several of the nuns stepped back, startled.

"Hettie, make her stop that," Liam whispered from the corner of his mouth. "We don't want to upset Sister Helen."

Hettie rubbed Violet behind one of her ears. "You're all right," Hettie said to Violet. "You're good."

As she rubbed behind Violet's ear, the elephant surreptitiously curled the end of her trunk around another apple and dropped it into her mouth.

"She's a schemer, just like the rest of them," another nun said.

"Linny, please," Sister Helen said sternly. "Put the apples away."

"Yes, Sister."

"How long?" Sister Helen asked Liam, pushing her glasses up the bridge of her nose.

"Until the constable stops looking for her," Liam said. "Until she can return to the zoo safely."

"Days? Weeks?" she asked impatiently. "I need to know. We have only a limited amount of hay and we need it for the goats and pigs. I can't be using our rationings on an uninvited guest who isn't able to contribute to our community."

"Days. A week at the most," Liam answered, glancing over at Hettie, who gave a small shrug.

She hoped Liam was accurate in his assumption. After a few days, she hoped that the constable and his men would have more pressing concerns on their minds than executing a three-year-old elephant.

"I'll ask one of my mates to drop off a supply of hay," Liam said. "I promise, Sister Helen."

"Oh, I've heard all this before," she said, raising her eyebrows. "Is baby Maeve baptized yet?"

"Sister, you know it isn't that simple," Liam said.

Hettie tried to decide what Anna would think if she saw Hettie and Violet and Liam surrounded by this growing group of nuns. She imagined that her sister would laugh and then make a half-hearted joke about how Hettie should have considered becoming a nun herself, how the measured regimen of prayer, work, and meals would have suited her tendency to habitual activities. Instead, Hettie had discovered this kind of routine and ritual at the zoo. As Hettie stared at Liam, she also recognized that this monastic way of life was out of the question because she was no longer a virgin.

"She can stay in one of the empty stables," Sister Helen said at last, and Hettie smiled a broad smile. "And Liam, make sure the additional hay is delivered tomorrow. Sister Linny, show Hettie and Violet to the empty stall in the barn."

Hettie grabbed the crop from Liam and followed Sister Evangeline before Sister Helen could change her mind. The crowd of nuns parted for Sister Evangeline, Hettie, and Violet as the three of them walked toward the stables at the rear of the compound. Hettie took in their faces as they walked by. She was surprised to see that many of the sisters looked around her age, most likely having gone straight from school to the convent. A few of the young women smiled and extended their hands as they walked by, and Violet's trunk grazed their open palms.

"She's a beautiful specimen," Sister Evangeline said, "though it looks like she hasn't been eating enough."

"The rationings," Hettie said in explanation, realizing that she herself hadn't eaten since the evening of the bombing. Her stomach felt hollow like a deep, empty well.

"Despite what Sister Helen said, we have a wee bit of extra hay that we can feed her. She's always trying to make us believe that we have less than we do," Sister Evangeline said. "I imagine Violet could use a good feeding."

"Yes, ma'am," Hettie said, unable to believe their luck that Liam had brought them here. "Thank you, ma'am."

As they turned down a dirt path into the second courtyard, Hettie noticed Sister Helen greeting at least dozen women and children at the convent's front entrance. A young woman knelt before Sister Helen, her shoulders shaking, her dress soiled with dirt and blood. Sister Helen took the woman's hand and guided her up to her feet.

"Many others are coming to us for food and shelter," Sister Evangeline said, noticing Hettie's gaze.

The nun paused for a moment with her head bent, and then traced the sign of the cross over her chest before leading Hettie and Violet to the rear area that housed a modest barnlike structure painted red with white trim, and a dusty yard of wandering chickens and goats.

"Careful," Sister Evangeline said, pointing to the cattle guard near the barn's entrance.

Hettie guided Violet over the parallel metal bars. The elephant seemed to know somehow that the guard was there and stepped gingerly across it. Sister Evangeline slid open the large barn door with the entire weight of her body. The pigs snorted in the pen. Inside, short stacks of hay created a series of rectangular steps that led into the darkened shadows of the rafters. Sister Evangeline led them into a sizable stall located at the end of the musty corridor. Slants of daylight dappled the passageway.

"Violet will be safe here for the time being," Sister Evangeline said. "I assure you that the constable will not be stopping by here."

"How can you be so certain?"

"Trust me," said Sister Evangeline. "No RUC constable is likely to set foot in a Catholic convent."

The nun opened the wooden door to the stall, its rusty hinges creaking. Violet began to rear into Hettie, her large foot almost landing on Hettie's foot.

"Watch it," Hettie said, tapping Violet lightly on the rear.

Violet stepped into the stall and immediately grabbed a bundle of hay with the curl of her trunk and tossed it up onto her back, and then shuddered. Several strands of hay tumbled to the ground, but a loose net remained, like a broken crown resting on her forehead.

"She looks like a queen," Sister Evangeline said, laughing. "The queen of the Sisters of Adoration and Redemption. We've always needed a queen."

"How do Sister Helen and Liam know each other?" Hettie asked.

"Sister Helen has known Liam since he was a wee boy. His father got into some trouble soon after his brother was shot, and needed to leave town. Mrs. Keegan fell gravely ill for a spell, so we took care of poor Liam until his father could return to Belfast," Sister Evangeline said. "Then, as Liam got older, he became more involved with the cause, and now Sister Helen and Liam help each other in different ways."

Just then a pair of nuns walked toward them. "Our midday meal is now being served," one of them announced.

Sister Evangeline scattered handfuls of hay in front of Violet before securing the door of the stable.

"She'll be all right," Sister Evangeline said. "Don't you worry."

As they walked along one of the white corridors, Hettie caught a glimpse through a pair of double doors of a large, cavernous room filled with women and children. Several nuns hurried around the huddles of families, offering bowls of soup while others washed bleeding wounds on arms and faces and carefully bandaged up injuries. A young mother gripped her swaddled baby to her chest; it was difficult to discern whether the blood that stained the baby's blanket came from the child's or the mother's wounds. Hettie felt her heart sink further, as when she'd first set foot inside the mayhem of the Royal.

"So many sad stories," Sister Evangeline said as she continued to lead Hettie down the corridor, "but God is being liberal with his Grace. He allows us to find purpose amid this grave suffering."

Sister Evangeline pushed through a door. The convent's dining hall was crowded with the overlapping voices of nuns and children. There were at least thirty or forty school-age children. They had all been cleaned up—their faces washed and their hair brushed—and dressed in matching uniforms of light blue and white.

"Is this convent also an orphanage?" asked Hettie.

"No, we haven't taken in children for decades," said Sister Evangeline. "Here, sit."

Hettie felt puzzled by the presence of so many children as Evangeline pointed to the far end of the long table, where Liam and Sister Helen already sat. Sister Helen nodded at the empty space next to her. Hettie slid into the spot, and a steaming bowl of vegetable stew was placed in front of her. She took in the welcoming smells of potatoes, peas, and chicken broth. Sister Helen knocked her spoon against her glass and the entire dining room grew silent. She bowed her head and everyone else followed suit. A few children snickered at the end of one table, and Sister Helen glared in their direction. Once they settled down, she commenced to say grace.

"Let us pray," Sister Helen said, raising her voice. "Dear God, look down with mercy on all those dear souls who have lost their lives in the air raid on our city. Please sustain and support their families and friends in these dreadful times, and help those who are hurt to recover from their grievous injuries. *Per Christum Dominum nostrum.* Amen."

Despite it being a Catholic prayer, Hettie felt moved by Sister Helen's blessing. She wanted to believe the tensions between the Catholics and Protestants might subside in the face of the immense devastation. That the entire city of Belfast was in this together. The women and children responded with a collective "Amen." Then the nuns served the children, placing ceramic bowls of vegetable stew in front of them. At the center of each table, there was a plate piled with chunks of bread that were quickly disappearing as a flurry of small hands snatched them up. The dining hall rang with the music of spoons on bowls and the sweet melody of children's voices.

"Help yourself," Sister Helen said, nudging the plate of bread toward Hettie.

She thanked the nun and took a piece. The bread felt like a strange object in her hand. She tore off a piece and ate it. Even though the bread didn't have much flavor, it melted in her mouth. Hettie's stomach grumbled, and she realized how hungry she was. She glanced over at Sister Helen and Liam. They were working away at their bowls of stew, and she proceeded to do the same. The heat of the soup scorched the side of her tongue, but she couldn't resist eating it quickly. Sister Evangeline slid into the spot next to her and tucked a napkin into the neckline of her habit.

"Eat up, everyone," said Sister Evangeline.

Liam winked at Hettie. She smiled at him as she tore off another piece of bread and dunked it into the stew.

"Where are these children from?" Hettie asked again.

"The orphanage on the Ormeau Road," Sister Helen said, casting a broad gaze at the roomful of children. "They were moved from there because it is right beside the city's gasworks, and they were afraid it might be bombed, and their fear was proven correct last night. Only a few walls of the orphanage are now standing."

Their youthful voices and bright laughter filled the air. Several nuns were already gathering bowls, one stacked on top of the other, and the children obediently remained seated at the long tables.

"Isn't that a Protestant orphanage?" asked Liam, frowning.

"Don't look at me that way, Liam Patrick," Sister Helen said, giving him a steely stare. "We're taking care of them until we can determine a safe place for them outside of the city. I've already heard from the headmaster at Downpatrick. He said that he could take half of the girls."

"Downpatrick?" Hettie asked.

"It's a boarding school about fifty miles away," Sister Helen said.

"They will be safer there. I'm still waiting to hear from a few other schools. It's only a matter of time—then they will all be where they need to be."

"Elephants and children," Sister Evangeline said to Hettie. "Everyone deserves a safe place in this city of ours."

Sister Helen clapped her hands, and all the children fell quiet at once. The nun slowly lifted herself up from the wooden table, placing her large hands on the sturdy surface. She threw a long stare across the length of the dining room before raising her hands like an orchestral conductor. In unison, the children stood up from their seats and began to sing the hymn "This Little Light of Mine," their sweet voices converging into one harmonious song. Their innocent voices seemed to elevate the entire dining room, as if everyone was temporarily suspended above the polished floor, no longer attached to either here or there.

Jesus gave me light / I'm going to let it shine.

Hettie felt Liam reach underneath the table and squeeze her bony knee. A shiver traveled along her thigh. Hettie moved her hand underneath the table and threaded her fingers in between his. Once the children concluded the hymn, Sister Helen clapped again and they began to file quietly out of the dining room, one table at a time, until the room was empty and their buoyant voices occupied the courtyard.

"Children shouldn't have to endure the horrors of war, but they do," Sister Helen said, returning to her seat at the head of the table. "These poor wee children are never going to forget the sounds of the planes in the sky—and the scenes of death, destruction, and awful suffering that they have witnessed. No child should ever see that. It will be with them forever."

Another elderly nun came through the door of the dining room. Tufts of gray stuck out from the rim of her white cap, like the gossamer wings of a moth or a butterfly. The nun bent over and whispered into Sister Helen's ear, and then handed her a folded slip of paper before silently leaving the room again.

"It's a message for you, Hettie," Sister Helen said, handing her the folded slip of paper.

Hettie's hands shook as she unfolded the piece of paper. Who on earth knew she was there? She was prepared to read that her mother was dead, but couldn't help but hope that maybe the note contained news that was the exact opposite—that Rose was alive and well and accounted for. The message read:

> *Dear Harriet Quin, Please return to the Bellevue Zoo as soon as possible. The constable is looking for you as he has news to share about your mother. Her identity has been confirmed and he has more details about where she is currently receiving medical attention.*

The message was unsigned. She wasn't sure if she should believe what was written, but felt exhilarated by the prospect that her mother could still be alive. Hettie looked up at Liam and then the two sisters. They were all staring at her, waiting for her to speak. What if the note was fraudulent, written by someone trying to find Violet? What if someone was trying to set her up?

"My mum," Hettie said, her mouth dry and moist at the same time. "They say she's alive."

"Hettie, that's good news," Liam said, reaching for her hand underneath the table again. "Where is she?"

"I don't understand," she said nervously. "Who could know I'm here?"

"What does it say?" asked Sister Helen.

Hettie looked down at the paper again. "That I need to return to the zoo and the constable will be able to share more news about the exact nature of my mum's whereabouts and medical condition," she said.

"Well, it sounds like you need to get yourself to the zoo," Sister Helen responded.

"What will I do with Violet?" Hettie asked.

"Leave Violet here with the sisters," Liam suggested. "Like we already planned."

"Go on," Sister Helen said. "Find your mum. We'll be here when you return."

"I'll come with you," Liam said, standing up from the table.

Sister Helen gave Liam an austere look. "Liam, remember what we discussed," she said. "You need to stay and help with the children. Until tomorrow. That's all I ask."

For a moment he looked as if he were going to protest, but then he lowered his eyes. "Yes, of course," he said, his forehead crinkling.

Sister Helen nodded.

"If it's all right, I'm going to say goodbye to Violet before I leave," Hettie said.

"Please do," Sister Evangeline replied.

Hettie stood up, headed out of the dining room, and walked in the direction of the stables at the rear of the compound. Liam followed her. They could hear the sounds of children playing in the courtyard on the other side of the concrete wall. Then there was a woman's distant cry. A pair of nuns walked past them, carrying a supply of bandages and other first-aid materials, and Hettie and Liam exchanged a worried glance.

When Hettie and Liam arrived, Violet was lying in a corner of the stable. As soon as she detected Hettie's presence at the stall door, the elephant stood up and shook the hay and other debris from her wrinkled sides.

"Hey, Vi," Hettie said softly. "It's me."

Hettie opened the door and stepped inside the stall, and Liam latched the door behind them. Violet nudged her forehead into Hettie's chest. Hettie patted the speckled spots between the elephant's eyes.

"You're doing good," she said. "You like it here, don't you?"

Liam grabbed a fistful of hay from the dusty floor of the stall and held it out for Violet. She snatched the bundle of hay and tucked it into her mouth.

"Hettie, she's going to be all right," Liam said. "The nuns are good people."

Hettie stepped toward Liam and leaned into him. She couldn't stop herself, despite being inside the sacred walls of this convent. It was as if a magnetic force was propelling her toward him. Pleasure and indulgence. Euphoria and intimacy. These were sensations that Hettie hardly knew, and now she was experiencing them in all their depth and dimension. Here was Liam's mouth on top of hers again. Here were his hands, slipping inside her shirt. Here was his touch against her bare belly. He unbuttoned the pearl buttons of her blouse and cupped his hand over her breast, making her shudder. It was happening all over again. Liam dropped his trousers and underpants to his ankles. He pressed her against the door of the stable, and she felt the dull splinters of wood against her buttocks. She smelled the stench of fresh manure, heard Violet's heavy footsteps against the bed of hay. She was already moist and wet, and his penis slipped in easily. The rhythm of Liam's repeated thrusts was answered by her soft cries.

We belong together, Hettie tried to convince herself. *This is meant to be.*

Liam pushed one final time, and she bit into the shoulder of his shirt as they came together. A warm flood of semen dripped down the inside of her thigh. Liam held Hettie closely, and the rhythm of their breaths matched each other, and she felt as if they temporarily existed within a pristine orb of golden light, where nothing could touch them.

"I love you," Liam whispered into Hettie's ear.

"I love you, too," she responded, feeling a rush of tenderness, passion, and lust all at once.

The barn door slid open, and footsteps traveled down the corridor. Violet released a series of loud chirps.

"Bloody hell," Liam whispered, zipping up his trousers.

He wetted his palms in Violet's drinking pail and pressed them against the thick curls of his hair.

"Button up, Hettie," he said with a soft laugh. "Someone's coming."

Hettie fumbled with the buttons of her shirt and then tucked it into the waistband of her trousers. Violet grabbed another bundle of hay and tossed it up on her head.

Just as Hettie succeeded in doing up the last of her buttons, Sister Evangeline appeared at the stall door.

"I brought a few treats for my new friend," she said. In her hands, she held two sweet buns. "Do you think she'll like these?"

Before Hettie could answer, Violet looped the end of her trunk around one of the buns and it disappeared into her mouth.

"I'll take that as a yes," Sister Evangeline said, her eyes brightening.

Violet slipped the second bun out of Sister Evangeline's hand. Hettie patted the elephant's forehead and then glanced up at Liam. His cheeks were crimson and splotchy. She moved her gaze to the uneven floorboards of the barn. She felt if she looked up again at Liam and Sister Evangeline, she might faint. Violet snaked the tip of her trunk around Hettie's thin wrist. She smiled up at the elephant and gently held the end of her trunk, like a hand.

"Thank you, Sister Linny," Liam managed.

"No worries," she said. "I'm honored. It's not every day that I get the chance to care for an elephant."

"I won't be gone long," Hettie said, as much to herself as to Violet. "Only a few hours."

"Go on, Hettie," said Sister Evangeline. "Find your mum."

Hettie gave Violet a final pat on the forehead before Liam walked her to the front gate of the convent. The children had already dispersed from the courtyard. The notes of an organ in the chapel played, and the voices of the children began to join together in another hymn. Liam gently swung open the large gate that led to the Shore Road.

"That was close," he said.

Hettie blushed.

"What does Sister Helen need you to do with the children?"

"Do you remember the way back to the zoo?"

Hettie reflected on the route that they had taken to Éamon's and then to the convent—down the hill from Church to Arthur to Whitewell to the Antrim Road. Even though she felt as if she were as far away as she could possibly get from all that was familiar, it wouldn't take more than fifteen or twenty minutes to walk to the zoo.

"I remember," Hettie said, looking down the road.

A lorry, with its rear compartment filled with crumbling debris and twisted girders, drove by.

"Be good," Liam said, kissing Hettie on the forehead.

Twelve

"I HOPE EVERYONE IN YOUR FAMILY IS SAFE," MR. CLARKE SAID to Hettie as she paused at his security booth at the front of the zoo half an hour later.

"Are the constable and his men here?" she asked.

"They should be returning soon," Mr. Clarke said, flipping open the gold lid of his pocket watch. "Mr. Wright told me that he's expecting Constable Ward at half past the hour."

Hettie glanced at the face of Mr. Clarke's watch. It was ten minutes past three o'clock.

"And your family?" Hettie asked hesitantly. She was uncertain if Mr. Clarke had any family in Belfast. She couldn't recall him mentioning a wife or children by name. All she knew about him was the well-known fact that he was a third cousin of Mr. Christie and that the aroma of whiskey often accompanied him in the modest space of his security station.

"My wife and me wee children," he said, his eyes glistening, "we went to the Clonard Monastery off the Falls Road and hid in the crypt until the bombs stopped falling."

"The monastery near the Royal?"

"That's the one," he said. "I don't think the place has ever invited so many Protestants inside its doors in its whole history. One of the priests stepped forward and gave us absolution during the middle of the night. We didn't think we were going to make it."

"I'm glad you and your family are okay."

"Oh, me too," he said. "I thought that the walls of the crypt might come tumbling down when the earth shook, but she held solid and steady throughout it all. My baby daughter was crying in my arms, but eventually once the bombs stopped, she fell asleep."

Hettie tried to imagine Mr. Clarke, with his pockmarked complexion and whiskey-laced breath, consoling a baby throughout the horror of the bombing. She looked up at him again: His features had softened, and a sheen of wetness dampened his eyes.

"Is Mr. Wright here?"

"You might find him in the canteen."

Hettie proceeded up the staircase and followed the path that led to the canteen. The ticket kiosk was still closed, with its metal face pulled down and locked. Near the end of the path, Sean, one of the maintenance men, methodically pushed a straw broom against the pavement. He held a stand-up receptacle in his other hand as he collected loose bits and pieces of half-burned paper and trash. He gave Hettie a wave before returning to his task. In the bear paddock, a large red ball sat stock-still next to the high wall of boulders. Flies swarmed over a pile of dried, cracked manure. A flock of shiny black rooks pecked at the ground. In the aviary, the parakeets and finches fluttered from branch to branch. Hettie felt an immediate sense of relief at being surrounded by the familiar sights and sounds of the zoo despite the absence of so many of the animals. It allowed Hettie to return to herself—and remember who she really was.

At the end of another pathway, next to Rajan's enclosure, she noticed Mr. Wright and Ferris. Eager to see them both, Hettie picked up her pace. She felt certain that Mr. Wright would know more about the constable and the news about her mother—whether or not the message was true, and if it were true, maybe he would be able to pass along any further news. Hettie still wasn't certain who had sent the note. Maybe it had been Ferris.

As Hettie drew closer, she could see Rajan's enormous body lying against the dirt floor of the enclosure. Hettie started to run. Mr. Wright and Ferris turned around as she approached the enclosure.

"I don't understand," she said, breathless. "Mr. Clarke said that the constable wouldn't be returning until half past the hour."

Ferris and Mr. Wright stood there, staring at the immense body of the elephant, a motionless field of gray. Rajan's eyes remained open and still, and his ears flapped gently in the afternoon breeze. A few crows pecked near his dusty feet, one hopping along the boulder-like ridge of his massive body.

"He died of a heart attack or shock," Mr. Wright said. His shoulders trembled, and sobs rolled up from the center of his body.

Hettie looked over at Rajan again. It didn't seem possible that the bull elephant could be dead, but there he was lying on the concrete area of the enclosure. Strands of hay were strewn on the ground around him, like a subdued nimbus of light. Ferris placed a hand on Mr. Wright's shoulder. It sounded as if Mr. Wright was choking on his own sobs. Tears streamed down Hettie's and Ferris's cheeks as they stood there, silently, taking in the tragic sight of the dead creature.

"We'll bury Rajan's remains over there, next to Maggie," Mr. Wright finally said, looking beyond the far edge of the enclosure. There, up on the hill, was a clearing surrounded by stands of Scots pines. "It will be too difficult to move him over to the Crazy Path with the other animals."

Mr. Wright gave another shudder.

"There's no need to butcher Rajan?" Ferris asked.

"Yes, take what you can," Mr. Wright said with little emotion left in his voice, "and then bury him next to Maggie."

"What are you talking about?" Hettie asked, horrified. Her mind flashed to Samuel Greene's father's butcher stand at St. George's Market—the swine suspended from the iron hook as Samuel's father sharpened his knife, the shiny arrangements of pig intestines behind the glass, the blood dripping along the sides of Samuel's freckled arms.

"We have no choice, Hettie," Ferris said flatly. "If we don't butcher some of the executed animals, the others will starve."

"But—"

Mr. Wright took Hettie's hand in his for a moment and looked at her. Hettie had never witnessed so much sadness in one person's face— the downward tugging at the far corners of his mouth and eyelids, the seemingly permanent trails of tears traveling down his cheeks, the quiet anguish reflected in his dark irises. She thought about Mr. Wright's story about how the animals had saved him after losing his twin brother during the war. She recognized the depth of his pain in accepting that he could no longer save the animals that had been saving him all along. Mr. Wright squeezed Hettie's hand and released it. Then he turned away and walked toward his office.

"Where have you been, Hettie?" Ferris asked when Mr. Wright was out of earshot. "Where's Violet?"

"It's a long story," she said. "I had to find another place to hide her because the constable and his men were on the way to my house—"

"Where is she?"

"She's at the Catholic convent on the Shore Road—"

"You left Violet at a convent?" he asked. "Do you really think that's the best place for her?"

"The nuns are taking good care of her," Hettie said, her voice wavering.

At that moment, a large lorry arrived at the side of Rajan's enclosure. An oversize metal crane and several shovels sat in the rear bed. Ferris nodded toward Rajan and then pointed to the hill behind the enclosure. Bobby Adair and Hugh Mallon stepped out of the lorry and unfurled the chain attached to the crane until it reached Rajan. A pair of pink-hued jays settled on the gray landscape of the elephant's side, pecking at the insects that already hovered over his corpse.

Jack Fleming and Daryl Griffiths also arrived at the enclosure. Two of the men positioned the sturdy belt of the crane across Rajan's broad torso and then his enormous body was slowly lifted up in the air. Suddenly, the crane's engine sputtered, stalled, and then reignited, groaning as it lifted the elephant. Rajan's trunk and feet hung in midair. After several minutes, the bull elephant was maneuvered higher in the air and then was guided toward the clearing. Everyone remained silent as Rajan was lowered to the ground with a definitive thump.

"I had to leave Violet," Hettie said softly. "I got your message about the constable, that I needed to return to the zoo, that he has news about my mother."

"I don't know what you're talking about," Ferris said.

"I thought you sent the message—"

"What message?" asked Ferris.

"Do you know where the constable is?"

"They haven't been here since this morning," said Ferris, "but I know they're still keen on finding Violet. Constable Ward is set on fulfilling the directive of the Ministry of Public Security," Ferris said. "Believe me, I wish this wasn't the case."

"The note said that the constable might know something about my mum."

"I'm sorry, Hettie," Ferris said. "Maybe she's still out there."

Devastated that there was no further news about her mother, Hettie sat down on one of the benches that bordered the path. Across the way was the empty puma enclosure. A few twigs tumbled across the barren, dusty surface. Ferris sat down next to Hettie and rested his hand on top of hers. Together they sat in silence. In the distance, the large mechanical crane whined and creaked.

"It's time for the sea lions' feeding," Ferris said eventually. "Why don't you join me?"

Together they walked toward the sea lions' enclosure. On the way, Ferris paused at one of the storage closets that bordered the path and gathered an empty bucket. As he opened the door wider, Hettie noticed the strips of meat piled on slabs of ice on the shelves. Ferris retrieved an amber bottle of cod oil, poured a modest amount into the bucket, and then placed several pieces of meat in the bottom and doused them in the oil. The meat was slippery and bloody in between his fingers.

"The bears," Hettie said, and then paused as she stared into the darkness of the closet.

Ferris nodded as he dropped a few more pieces into the bucket. Hettie ran to the other side of the path and retched. The pale-green vegetable stew that she had eaten at the convent gushed out of her, and Hettie vomited again at the sight of it. It felt as if her stomach had been punched inside out. When she was certain that she wouldn't retch again, she wiped her mouth with the sleeve of her coat and returned to Ferris's side.

"You all right?" he asked.

"It doesn't seem possible—our animals being fed to one another."

"I know it's not pleasant," he said, "but we're all having to do things that we don't want to do."

Once they reached the sea lion enclosure, Ferris unlatched the gate and they both stepped inside. Sammy stood in his usual pose, perched on the highest boulder, his whiskered nose trained toward the metallic-gray sky. The other sea lions languished on the concrete ribbon that bordered the pool, but they all nudged themselves up by their foreflippers as they noticed Ferris's presence and the strong-smelling bucket in their enclosure.

"Dinner," Ferris announced.

The sea lions stood a little taller as Ferris tossed up pieces of meat that they caught agilely in their mouths, one by one.

"They don't seem to notice the difference," Ferris said, as his eyes followed his careful throws to each animal. Sammy slapped his rubbery flippers together, demanding another piece, and Hettie smiled. "See, they like it."

Hettie reached into the bucket. The meat felt slick and cold between her fingers, and she tried her hardest not to remember where it had come from. She found purchase on a piece and then tossed it to Sammy at the top of the rock. He caught it squarely in his mouth.

"You're right," she said to Ferris.

"Have I ever been wrong?" Ferris teased, keeping his attention fixed on the cadre of sea lions.

"No, you haven't," Hettie said.

Ferris looked up at her, their eyes locking for a split second.

"Hettie, I—"

But then Ferris's gaze seemed to travel beyond her shoulder and down the path toward the heart of the zoo. Hettie turned around. In front of the Floral Hall, Constable Ward, Sergeant Miller, and Samuel Greene appeared. As soon as the men noticed Ferris and Hettie standing in front of the sea lions, they approached them at a quickened pace, walking in step with one another, their rifles slung over their shoulders.

"Miss Quin," Constable Ward said. "We've been looking for you. Where's young Violet? We've already checked the Elephant House and she isn't there."

Hettie didn't respond.

"Miss Quin," Constable Ward said again, "you need to share her whereabouts with us. This is about the safety of the Belfast people. This isn't just about you and your elephant."

"She isn't here," Hettie said, her voice trembling in her throat.

Samuel Greene made eye contact with her. His expression remained neutral, but Hettie could see the worry in his eyes.

"Did you stop by Rajan's enclosure?" Ferris asked.

"Yes, we saw," Constable Ward responded. "What happened?"

"Mr. Wright said it was a heart attack or shock," Ferris said. "We'll never know exactly what happened."

Sergeant Miller rested the heavy butt of his shotgun against the pavement.

"Miss Quin," Constable Ward continued. "You still haven't answered my question. I'm waiting. Where is Violet? I demand that you tell me—"

"Violet died of natural causes, too," Ferris said. "We've already buried her in the meadow along with the other animals."

Ferris and the constable stared each other down. "I don't believe you," Constable Ward said sharply.

Ferris drew himself up to his full height. "I can show you. Follow me to the Crazy Path."

"Fine," Constable Ward said. "Show us the way."

"Constable," Hettie said hesitantly. "Do you have any news to share about my mother? Rose Quin. I think she might've been injured in the Atlantic Avenue shelter and transported to one of the hospitals, but I haven't been able to find her."

The constable stared at Hettie for an extended moment. The shallow lines of his forehead deepened, and his mouth under his thin mustache became hard.

"How on earth would I know where your mother is?" Constable Ward said. "The city and the hospitals are in a state of madness. How could I possibly know the whereabouts of one woman—"

"But you sent me the message," she said, feeling ashamed of the desperation in her own voice. "You wrote that you knew where she is."

"What message?" he barked.

She reached into her pocket and showed the constable the folded note.

"Who sent this?" asked Hettie.

Constable Ward took the piece of paper, studied it, and then gave it back to her.

"I have no idea."

Tears fell down her cheeks.

"I'm sorry, Miss Quin," Constable Ward said, softening his tone. "The reports so far suggest that nearly all of the occupants of the Atlantic Avenue shelter perished. There were very few if any survivors."

Hettie swallowed hard. She felt as if something might slip inside her at any second, that she might lose herself and crumple to the ground. Hettie pinched the inside of her hand again, willing herself to stop crying, to try to not believe what the constable was saying. Sammy dove from the top boulder. Water splashed on the pavement next to Hettie's foot.

"Now, Mr. Poole, please show us to Violet's so-called burial site," Constable Ward said skeptically. "As I have mentioned, we have many other issues to attend to."

"Excuse me," Hettie said.

"Not yet, Miss Quin," Constable Ward said. "Not until we have verification of the elephant's death."

"I need to find my mum," she said, turning toward the path that led to the entrance. "I need to see if she has returned home."

With that, Hettie ran toward the grand staircase and down the long flight of stairs, skipping the steps two at a time, and out the front entrance. The Antrim Road was once more thronged with people unwilling to risk staying another night in the city, and making their way along the footpaths and up into the fields and forested knolls of the Cavehill. Hettie noticed that many of the men were carrying spades over their shoulders. Others carried bags of personal belongings. Others held the hands of crying children.

When Hettie turned onto the Whitewell Road, the damaged couch still sat in the middle of the road. She didn't see any of the neighborhood children. Instead, only Mr. Brown and Mrs. Lyttle stood in front of Mr. Brown's house. They looked like an odd pair there, sharing a cigarette back and forth.

"Hettie Quin," Mr. Brown said. "We've been wondering about you, where you might be."

"Have you found your mother yet?" asked Mrs. Lyttle.

"No, I haven't," Hettie said, staring at her home down the street. The windows were still dark, and the front door was closed.

Mr. Brown averted his stare to the pavement and rubbed the corners of his eyes. Instead of taking the cigarette from Mrs. Lyttle, he lit a second cigarette for himself. He inhaled deeply and released a curl of smoke from the corner of his mouth.

"What is it?" Hettie said. "Have you heard any reports about Atlantic?"

"Yes," Mr. Brown said. "They say no one survived." Mr. Brown paused, sucked on his cigarette again, and then looked up at Hettie. "I'm so sorry," he said.

"Maybe she didn't make it to the—the Atlantic shelter," Hettie stammered. "Maybe she went somewhere else—"

"That could be," Mr. Brown said, placing a hand on Hettie's shoulder. "Maybe you should lie down, get some rest, and then you can make another round of the hospitals and other places where people are identifying family members."

Hettie knew that Mr. Brown meant the impromptu morgues at the Falls Road Baths, and Peter's Hill and St. George's, that these were the places she would most likely find her mother. It felt as if the center of her chest were caving into itself.

"I will," Hettie managed.

"Give yourself a wee rest, young lady," Mrs. Lyttle added.

Just then a number of people filed out of the Gibsons' front door, three houses down. Hettie noticed that all the individuals—young and old—were clad in their church clothes of grays, blacks, and browns. They exchanged hugs and pecks on the cheek. Then Hettie saw Mr. and Mrs. Gibson and Johnny's older brother, Tommy, at the center of the gathering crowd. She surveyed the familiar faces. Many people from the neighborhood stood on the square parcel of brown grass: the Moffits, the McGraths, the Smiths, the Finneys, and others. Many of the children—Albert O'Brien, Lizzie Reynolds, Rodney and Jack Dawkins—who usually played on the street stood next to their parents, their hands folded in front of them, their round cheeks red and splotchy.

"Where's Johnny?" Hettie asked.

"Didn't you hear?" Mr. Brown said.

Hettie shook her head, knowing what they were going to say but not wanting to hear the news.

"Johnny Gibson died, love," said Mrs. Lyttle gently.

Hettie's knees trembled. She thought back to little Johnny playing on the damaged couch in the middle of the road. His kind greeting to Violet. How could he be dead now?

"He and Albert O'Brien went out on their bikes, and as he rode along the road a delayed bomb concealed in the rubble near the footpath exploded. He bore the full brunt of the blast. He was so unlucky—a case of the wrong place at the wrong time."

"Johnny Gibson," Hettie whispered. "No." For a moment, Hettie could see him running away from the toppled-over tin can, his clenched fists pumping on either side of his compact body.

"I know," Mr. Brown said. "It's a horrible loss for his family. I hope his mother survives this."

"Go and lie down, Hettie," Mrs. Lyttle said, holding Hettie's hand and then letting it go. "Poor thing, she's in a state of shock."

Without saying another word, Hettie walked toward her house. Instead of walking in the front door, she crossed the street and joined the dense crowd of mourners. Mr. and Mrs. Gibson stood near the front steps of their two-story home. His arm was threaded through hers, and Mrs. Gibson clutched a stained and worn handkerchief in one hand. It looked as if Mr. Gibson was holding her up. Tentatively, Hettie approached the couple and gave them each a hug.

"Johnny was a brilliant boy," Hettie said as she hugged Mrs. Gibson.

Mrs. Gibson stifled a sob. "He always liked you, Hettie. He often talked about you, how you work with the animals."

Mrs. Gibson continued to hug Hettie, her embrace both strong and soft. Hettie stood still. In her mind, she saw Johnny again and his freckled face and his unbridled enthusiasm for Violet.

"I'll always remember him, Mrs. Gibson," Hettie whispered into the grieving mother's ear. "You were blessed to be his mum."

"Thank you, Harriet Elizabeth Quin," she said. "Thank you."

Mrs. Finney came up to Mrs. Gibson and held her for an extended moment. Hettie stepped away and lingered among the crowd, then felt a little tug on her hand. She looked down to see Albert O'Brien staring up at her.

"Hettie," he said, "where's that elephant of yours?"

"Oh, Albert," Hettie said, kneeling and hugging the boy.

Albert slumped into her embrace.

"She is with the nuns right now," she said, "but I'm going to bring her home soon."

"You promise?" he said. "I want to see her again."

"Yes, you'll see her again soon," Hettie said, reaching into her pocket. "In the meantime, can you take care of another friend of mine?" Hettie presented Albert with Ferris's snail. "Just for a few days," she said. "You'll need to feed him a few leaves every morning and every night. And water, too."

Albert's eyes brightened.

"Yes," he said, cupping the snail in his palms. "I'll take care of him."

"Thank you," Hettie said.

"Does he have a name?" Albert asked, holding the snail between two fingers.

"No, not yet."

"What about Ulysses?" he suggested. "I read about him in school last week. He was a hero and a king who loved adventures. We'll call him Uli for short."

"Perfect," Hettie said. "You take good care of Uli for me, then."

"Yes, Hettie," Albert said, still staring down at the snail in his palms. "Yes, I will."

Hettie made her way across the street. Her house looked the same, except there was a handwritten note taped to the front door. Hettie's heart rate quickened. Perhaps the note offered some definitive news, maybe her mother was alive after all. As she approached her house, Hettie lifted the note from the door, unlocked the door with her key, and closed it behind her. Without taking her coat off, she sat down at the kitchen table, and finally read the note:

Dear Hettie:

It's with great regret that I discovered your mum's body at the Falls Road Baths when I was looking for one of my cousins earlier today. I was told that her body is going to be transferred to St. George's. It would be good if you could visit the morgue at the market tomorrow so you can identify her body and collect any of her personal belongings.

Hettie, I'm so sorry for the loss of your mum so soon after your sister. Please come & knock on my door if you need anything.

Warmly,
Mr. Reynolds

Hettie reread the note, the piece of paper shaking in her hands. She could hardly believe what she was reading. Maybe Mr. Reynolds had gotten another woman's identity confused with her mother's, and therefore this note wasn't meant for her. Hettie's head started to spin.

She lifted herself up from the table and held on to the edge of it. She felt light-headed and dizzy. She held on to the table more tightly.

When her head was clear again, she managed to stumble down the darkened hallway to her mother's bedroom. A seam of light appeared on the floor, making her feel hopeful for a moment. She couldn't remember if she had left the overhead light on or not. Hettie flew through the door, half expecting to see her mother in her own bed. All those months she had felt discouraged and sometimes even sickened by her mother's inability to get out of bed most mornings, and now she would welcome the sight of her mother lying there, with her tired eyes and groggy voice, her hand holding her spot in a paperback mystery. Instead, Rose's bedroom appeared the same as when she and Liam had left several hours earlier. A crumpled tangle of sheets sat in the center of the bed. She could smell the lingering scents of their sex—musty like the smell in the woods after a steady downpour. She reached for her mother's lilac perfume on the bureau, sprayed several squirts into the air, and stood watching the vaporous mist of the perfume disappear in the dim light.

Then Hettie noticed the assorted contents of her mother's mahogany chest and random shoes scattered across the worn floorboards: clip-on earrings missing their partners, tortoiseshell hair combs, a lace handkerchief that used to be Rose's mother's. Hettie began to collect the stray items from floor and realized that several objects were missing. Her grandmother's brooch with the three diamonds nestled neatly in the knot of the golden bow. A pair of pearl-inlaid cuff links. A small, gold-plated engraved clock given to her father by his workmates when he left Harland & Wolff. Dismayed and dejected, she sifted through the side compartments of the polished box. Nothing was there.

Frantically, Hettie examined the cluttered surface of her mother's bureau, opening and closing the drawers several times. Rose's savings were gone. Not a single pound note was left behind. How could she have been so careless? With a shout of fury, Hettie hit her fists against the bureau's surface and started to cry. Maybe a stranger had wandered into their house and looted the valuables and currency while she was gone. Then Hettie remembered the front door had been locked, that she had used her own key to enter the house.

Hettie ran to the door that led to the courtyard. The door was flung open and the gate to the adjacent walkway left ajar. She returned to the house and sat down at the kitchen table. The note from Mr. Reynolds lay there still. Next to his note, she noticed the short message with her own handwriting, telling Rose that she had gone up to the zoo to help out with the animals and that was the best place to find her. It felt as if she'd written the note several years ago.

Hettie pressed the warm heels of her palms into her eyes. She felt the impulse to crawl into her bed and try to sleep her way out of this. It struck Hettie that maybe this was what Rose had been attempting to accomplish with all those mornings and afternoons spent in bed; the weight of the sadness was too much, it was somehow easier to surrender to the melancholy rather than move through the prescribed motions of the day. Hettie blinked her eyes again—and the handwriting above her own came into focus. The brief note was written in a chicken scratch that was difficult to read. She strained to make it out. It was from Liam.

> *Dear Hettie, I'm sorry that I had to do this. It's not for me. It's for the cause. This war is our opportunity to strike. We, in this generation, must fulfill Ireland's destiny. The thousand-year yoke of England's rule must end. We can't give up now. It's about a better future for all of us. You, me, Maeve. I hope you understand. I hope you will find forgiveness for me. Tiocfaidh ar la. Liam*

Hettie swept her arm across the surface of the kitchen table, sending the porcelain teacups crashing onto the floor and shattering into countless pieces. She glanced down at her trembling hands. Her palms were damp and dotted with spots of redness. Everything was piling up, and she felt as if she were being buried under an avalanche; it was tumbling down on her, like a tall shelf of books spilling onto her, their hard edges and solid weight pounding onto her body.

Amid the whirl of her fury and sadness, Hettie sat down at the breakfast table and placed her head against the tabletop. The surface felt cold against her cheek. Her head buzzed. She didn't know what to do. Who could she trust? Who should she turn to? Then somewhere inside, Hettie managed to recall her conversation with Mr. Wright, about Nicholas and the animals. From the hallway, she retrieved a broom and dustpan. Hettie methodically swept up the scattered shards of the broken cups and deposited them into the trash bin. She went out to the buckets of water that Rose had filled in the courtyard prior to the bombing and washed her face and hands, and dried them with a dish towel. From the larder, Hettie gathered the last turnip and a stale roll left behind in the bread box. Without further thought—after all, what was there to think about anymore?—she departed the house and followed the road down through the neighborhood and down the hill to the convent, making each turn as she remembered it. On the other side of the Shore Road stood the large blue gate with the curlicues of wire intersecting the top edge of the wall.

Hettie pressed the bell and heard a melody of chimes on the other side of the gate. She waited. There was no answer. Hettie tried the bell again. Once again, there was only silence. She pressed her ear against the wooden gate, expecting to hear the voices of the young children playing in the courtyard. She hit her clenched fists against the gate and rang the bell multiple times. What if Éamon had found Liam and somehow convinced him that selling the young elephant could contribute to the IRA and Ireland's cause?

Hettie paced in front of the convent. She tried the bell one more time, but still there was no answer. Several cars and lorries passed on the two-way street. Distressed and disoriented, Hettie began to walk along the shoreline road in the direction of the docks. An oncoming car honked its tinny horn as it passed by, and Hettie jumped farther onto the narrow shoulder, lost her balance, and fell to the ground, but she managed to break her own fall. Pebbles and twigs stuck to her palms. She wiped her hands off on her trousers.

When Hettie looked up again, she studied the shoreline, which was visible from the other side of the street. Despite the lingering smoke of the air raid, Belfast Lough was a clear expanse of gray blue flecked with curling whitecaps. A convoy of merchant ships, with Royal Navy frigates and corvettes escorting them, lumbered along the distant horizon. Silver-backed seagulls bobbed in the salt-laced air before one of the birds plummeted into the water and snatched up a small fish with its yellow bill. Looking farther down the beach, Hettie examined the shore more closely. At first she thought she was seeing things: There, near the frothing surf, was a modest audience of nuns, dressed in their blue habits, watching Violet as she trotted in and out of the breakers. Overjoyed that Violet was still with the sisters, Hettie climbed over the short wall that bordered the beach and started to run toward the small group of nuns. As she drew closer, she recognized Sister Evangeline and Sister Helen.

"Sisters," Hettie said. "Sisters. I'm back. I'm here."

Sister Evangeline looked up with a smile. A few stray hairs escaped from the edge of her habit and flew up into her face. "Violet, look who's here!"

The elephant chased the waves into the Lough before running up the steady incline of hard-packed sand as yet another wave pursued her.

"We thought Violet might appreciate a change of scenery," Sister Evangeline explained, holding the curled crop in one hand. "Hettie, you've trained her brilliantly. She follows so well."

Hettie glanced back up at the road and felt some relief, realizing that the shoreline wasn't entirely visible.

"They can't see us from the road," Sister Helen said, noticing her gaze. "I promise, Violet is safe here."

"We thought she might enjoy a swim," added Sister Evangeline, "and we all needed a wee break."

"We should all go swimming," one of the other nuns said.

"Sister Ruth, you know it's not proper for nuns to swim," Sister Helen said.

"At least we can dip our feet in," said another. "Feel the water."

"Fine," Sister Helen said.

Hettie knew what the nuns suggested was ridiculous; it all verged on absurd. With the aftermath of the bombings and the constable and his men pursuing Violet, why would she join this group of women in the sea? But then she thought of her mother. Of little Johnny Gibson. Of Colleen White. Of Rajan and Maggie and Wallace. Of Mr. Wright's brother. Of the hundreds of thousands of lives already lost around the world to this ghastly war and other wars—and of the many thousands who would, in all likelihood, still die during the months to come. And when might the Germans bomb Belfast again? What if this was her last opportunity to feel the bracing salty water against her skin? Despite her better judgment, Hettie decided to bypass caution and remove her boots and socks along with the nuns. The sisters held up the hems of their habits to their knees and edged closer to the breakers. Hettie folded up the legs of her trousers. The water was cold and refreshing. A brisk snap against her skin. Violet threw her trunk through the wave and spouted a shower of water.

"Hey, Vi," Hettie called.

Hettie stepped farther into the waves and watched Violet spray her own back with water. She closed her eyes and felt the salty breeze against her face. She felt a childlike wonderment taking in the bizarre sight of the elephant playing in the sea amid all the loss and chaos. It was like watching a fanciful filmstrip that she had never seen before. Light and levity opened up inside her.

Here is your gift. Here is your elephant, Hettie thought to herself. *Violet is alive. And so are you.*

"Did you find your mother?" Sister Helen asked.

Hettie didn't answer Sister Helen. Instead, she reached into her coat pocket for the stale sweet bun. Right away, Violet started to trot in Hettie's direction, curled her trunk around the roll, and deposited it into her mouth. Hettie took a step closer to her and rubbed Violet's forehead. She smelled like salt and seaweed.

"Did Sister Evangeline take good care of you while I was gone?" Hettie said.

Violet searched her trunk under one of Hettie's arms for another treat. Hettie laughed and gave her the turnip from her other pocket.

"I love you," Hettie said. "I love you so much."

Hettie and Violet touched foreheads before the elephant trotted into the surf again, kicking her feet through the breaking waves. Sister Helen stood next to Hettie and placed a hand against the small of her back. Hettie kept her eyes fixed on the distant horizon, where gray met gray along the far edge.

"The constable didn't have any news, did he?" asked Sister Helen.

Hettie sighed. "He said that very few people survived after the Atlantic Avenue shelter was bombed," she explained, "and then when I returned home there was a note from a neighbor who had identified my mum's body at the public baths on the Falls Road. He said that they'll be transferring her body to St. George's and I should go there tomorrow."

Sister Helen didn't say anything, but moved her hand into Hettie's hand and held it for a long moment. A tear fell down Hettie's cheek.

"At least Violet is all right," Hettie said with a sniff.

Hettie and the nuns continued to watch Violet play along the shoreline. A flock of seagulls continued to bob in the air. Hettie's feet sank into the cold sand as the water rushed around her ankles and then receded. She watched as the shifting tide and sand made her feet disappear.

"Where did Liam go?" Hettie finally asked Sister Helen.

"Unfortunately, he fell in with the wrong people," Sister Helen said firmly. "He listens to me about some things, but not everything."

"He was at my house," Hettie said, her voice dull. "He stole my mother's valuables and savings."

"How do you know it was Liam?" Sister Helen asked. "I heard on the wireless that looters are breaking into the houses all over the city."

"He left me a note telling me so," Hettie said.

"Liam," Sister Helen said with a sigh. "He's gone too far."

"Too far with what?" Hettie asked.

"Liam is a simple man, and he has simple ideas," she said after a pause. "He believes that the Catholics in the six counties are the most oppressed people in Europe, and that the British government and their Unionist lackeys at Stormont are to blame. He would welcome a German victory in England's war. He thinks that it might lead to a united Ireland and a fully independent Irish republic."

Even though Hettie knew all about Liam's passion for a united Ireland, she still couldn't believe what she was hearing. Violet walked over to Hettie and nuzzled her damp forehead into her side, imprinting a fragmented map of wetness on the sleeve of Hettie's coat.

"You have a good swim," Hettie said to Violet. "You like the water, don't you?"

The elephant took a step back and shook her entire body, releasing an arc of moisture, and they laughed, holding their hands up to protect their faces.

"She can stay as long as you want," Sister Evangeline said.

"Thank you, Sister Evangeline," Hettie said.

"I'm sorry about Liam," Sister Helen said. "I'm sorry for what he did. I will do my best to reach him and have your mother's valuables returned to you."

Hettie understood it was highly unlikely that any of the possessions or money would be returned to her. She thought back to the Gibsons' front yard of mourners and Albert O'Brien and his delight over the small gift of the snail. At least Hettie still had Violet, and in a way, taking care of the elephant was restoring some part of herself, a part of herself she didn't know existed until she met Violet on the quayside of Belfast all those months ago.

"I imagine Liam is probably trying to sell everything on the black market right now," Hettie said matter-of-factly. "Her valuables will be crossing the border soon."

"He asked us to collect funds for the republican cause," Sister Helen said, "but this time he's gone too far. He shouldn't be stealing from anyone. It's a sin, and undermines the righteousness of his cause."

Hettie looked beyond Violet, out toward the breaking waves, the weak afternoon sun that was making its way through the gray bank of clouds, and the distant ships hugging the horizon. The elephant trotted toward Hettie, and she rubbed Violet's forehead again. At that moment, Hettie felt a precision and a clarity. She needed to distance herself from Liam and his associations even if he wasn't returning anytime soon. The reality of her situation only sharpened all of this: Her mother was dead, Liam had never loved her, but she had Violet. She was her family now, and Hettie needed to do everything that she could to protect her. She retrieved her socks and boots, and sat down on the sand to slip them back on.

"We're going home," Hettie said, standing up and brushing the sand off her trousers.

Despite the fact that the nuns provided suitable safety and a steady supply of food, Hettie felt compelled to take Violet with her: After all, what if Liam returned? What if Éamon knew that Liam had brought the elephant to the convent? Despite the comfort of the convent, it still wasn't entirely safe. Hettie wasn't sure where she would take Violet, but she knew that she would be able to find a hiding spot until the threats subsided.

"Are you certain you don't want to stay with us?" Sister Evangeline asked. "There are rumors of another bombing."

"We'll return if we need to," Hettie said with a rising conviction in her voice. "I promise."

"We'll be here," Sister Helen said. "I'm sorry again. I'll do what I can."

"We best get going."

Hettie embraced each of the nuns. As she stepped away, she clucked her tongue, and Violet followed Hettie as she focused on the rhythm of her footfalls, each boot sinking slightly into the shingly sand. Then Hettie turned around one more time. The nuns now stood in a circle with their hands joined together and their heads bowed in prayer, their feet bare as the bottom edges of their habits rippled in the breeze. The powder blues of their robes blended into the soft blues and grays of the Lough, creating a single band of color along the eastern horizon.

Thirteen

HETTIE MADE HER WAY UP THE HILL FROM THE SHORE ROAD, Violet whinnying behind her, lifting her trunk into the air. The image of the praying nuns receded from Hettie's mind as they navigated the heavily potholed road. Piles of rubble were still scattered throughout the streets. Random objects appeared on the lawns and the shoulders of the road—a man's lace-up shoe, a cracked teapot, an unopened letter, a lace brassiere. But a growing boldness informed Hettie's gait, and she kept her attention on Violet until they arrived at the Whitewell Road.

As they walked up the incline of her road, she noticed that the Gibsons' front yard was now empty. In fact the entire street was quiet and empty except for the tattered couch still sitting in the middle of the road.

"Come on, Vi," she said, her voice hushed.

The neighborhood was a ghost town. Hettie had heard rumors that in their fear and blind panic, at least half of the city's population had fled from Belfast and sought safety in the countryside, some even going as far as Dublin. All the windows were darkened. Hettie and Violet walked past the Moffits' house, with only its concrete foundation remaining. A few shirts, a pair of trousers, and two frocks hung limply on the clothesline in the backyard. Mr. Brown and Mr. Reynolds stood in front of her house, passing a pocket flask back and forth. When Mr. Reynolds saw Hettie and Violet walking along the road, he slid the flask into one of the pockets of his trousers. He stepped toward Hettie and embraced her.

"I'm very sorry about your mum," he said. "And I'm sorry for the note. I wasn't certain when I might see you again—and I wanted to let you know as soon as possible."

Hettie allowed herself to fall into Mr. Reynolds's embrace.

"Rose looked peaceful when I saw her, I promise," he whispered to her. "She wasn't bloodied, like some of the others."

"I plan to ride down to St. George's in the morning," Hettie said, stepping away from Mr. Reynolds.

Violet released a trumpet cry behind her.

"Hettie Quin and Violet," Mr. Brown said with a soft smile. "My favorite couple." He placed a hand on Hettie's shoulder. "I'm sorry about your mother," he said. "Rose was a fine woman who had been through a lot. I'm sorry her life ended this way. It's not fair."

A tear made its way down the side of Hettie's face. It didn't feel fair. But she knew there wasn't much that she could do apart from ride her bicycle down to St. George's and identify her mother and ensure that she was given a proper service and burial. In her mind's eye, Hettie recalled her sister's burial, watching the gravediggers maneuver Anna's coffin into the ground at Carnmoney Cemetery on the northern edge of the city. Beyond her sister's grave was the vast hillside of the cemetery, row upon row of white marble gravestones lining the slope, like a fixed formation of soldiers prepared for battle. Hettie remembered the three empty plots next to Anna's grave: One of those would soon be filled, and one of them would never be needed. It was only hers, now, that was waiting.

"You're a brave woman, Hettie Quin," Mr. Brown said, his hand still resting on her shoulder. "Don't you ever forget that. There are not many young ladies like you."

"Thank you, Mr. Brown. Have the constable and his men stopped by again?" Hettie asked, glancing toward the end of their street that met the Antrim Road.

"No," Mr. Brown said, taking another long draw from his pipe. "Not since the last time I saw you."

"They haven't returned?" Hettie asked again, hardly daring to believe it.

"They have other worries on their minds," Mr. Reynolds said. "I've heard that they've been tasked with helping the rescue squads search for the dead and the injured in the rubble."

Hettie felt relieved even though she knew her concerns about Violet's welfare were far from over.

"I should get Violet home," she said.

"Yes, yes, of course," Mr. Brown said. "Please let us know if there is anything we can do."

Mr. Brown hugged Hettie, too. She had lived next to the Browns and the Reynoldses for her entire life and had barely ever exchanged more than a few words of greetings with this pair of middle-aged men. Now they were both as dear as beloved uncles.

Violet followed Hettie down the walkway that led to the rear courtyard. Scattered leaves whispered across the pavement. Her mother's garden was thriving in the beds: There was a leafy abundance of rhubarb, lettuce, and radishes. One of the buckets was still filled with water. Hettie retrieved it and placed the bucket in front of Violet. The elephant swung her trunk into the water and then squirted it on top of Hettie's head. Cold water dripped down onto her face and shoulders.

"I know I need a bath," Hettie said, exasperated, "but I didn't need you to give it to me." She wiped away the wetness from her eyes and stepped back from Violet. "That's for you," Hettie said, pointing to the bucket. "Not me."

As if she had understood, Violet filled her trunk with water and sprayed it onto her own back. Then she took a second trunkful and directed it into her mouth. Hettie found the last bundle of carrots from the larder in the kitchen. She made a mental note to herself about retrieving a bale of hay from the Elephant House. She broke off a few carrots and gave them to Violet, who munched on them, dropping one of the carrots onto the pavement. Violet suctioned it up and threw it into her mouth. Hettie sat on the bench that Rose had often sat on when she took her first cup of morning tea. She stared beyond the top edge of the far wall of the courtyard. Already, daylight was starting to diminish.

"Vi, you're going to sleep here for the night," she said. "It's not quite as nice as the convent, but I hope you'll be comfortable."

The elephant dropped her trunk into the bucket again, but this time she tipped it over, spilling the water. A large puddle formed at Violet's feet, and she stomped through it several times.

"Violet!" Hettie exclaimed. "We need to be careful." She carried the other two buckets over to the wall of the house, out of Violet's way. "I'm not sure when the water is going to be turned back on."

Violet trumpeted before lowering onto her side. Bits of dirt collected on her skin as she rolled back and forth. Finally she folded her legs underneath her body and laid her head against the pavement. Above them, a pair of goldfinches, with their distinctive crimson faces and golden feathers, darted through the twilight.

"I'll be inside," Hettie said, patting the elephant on her forehead.

Violet pushed the empty bucket against the pavement with the curl of her trunk, her ears flapping. Hettie made her way into the kitchen and hunted around for something to eat. She was pleased to find some leftover cabbage stew that Rose had made four days before, but the sight also reminded her that this was the last meal she would ever eat that had been cooked by her mother, and again she was almost overwhelmed with longing and loneliness. She heated it up and ate dinner by herself. Out of habit, she turned on the wireless that sat on the kitchen counter. The station snapped into a news report about the Germans' Balkan campaign, their invasion of Yugoslavia, how that country had surrendered unconditionally and was now occupied. Then the reporter moved on to the growing number of casualties and injuries related to the bombing in Belfast. It said that there were several hundred fatalities. Hettie didn't believe the censored news; she had heard rumors that the actual number was well into the thousands. She wondered if her mother was being counted among the dead or if she was still among the unaccounted-for individuals.

When she was finished, Hettie clicked off the wireless, stepped into her bedroom, and changed into her nightdress. As she walked through the house, Hettie turned off the lights, drew back the blackout curtain, and peered out at Violet. The elephant was now lying in the darkened shadows of the far corner of the courtyard. Hettie released the curtain and crawled underneath the covers of her bed. It felt as if it had been weeks since she had slept in her own bed, even though she had been awakened by the bombing just the night before. So much had happened. She listened for Violet's movements and calls. The curtain's edge knocked against the glass pane. Hettie closed her eyes. Tears formed in the back of her throat, and she finally gave in to her grief.

The following morning, Hettie woke to a loud knocking on the front door. For one blissful moment as she sat up in bed, she forgot where she was—and all that had happened. But then it cascaded upon her again, and her shoulders slumped with the burden of her sadness. Hettie glanced out the window to the courtyard and was relieved to see that Violet was still there, standing next to one of her mother's garden beds, yanking young leaves of lettuce from the ground and tucking them into her mouth.

The person knocked again. This time, louder.

"Open up," a man called. "Open up now."

As fear trembled through her, Hettie slipped into the sleeves of a cardigan and walked toward the door, paused, and looked out the front window. There stood Samuel Greene: His eyes were rimmed with redness, and dark stains of blood soiled the front of his uniform. Hettie took a moment to steady herself and then opened the door for Samuel and he stepped inside without a word. Hettie closed and locked the door behind him, and he sat down on the couch in the sitting room.

Samuel said nothing. Instead he just sat there, holding his head in his hands. Stiff strands of his dark caramel hair poked through his long fingers dotted with dirt and dried blood.

"What happened, Samuel?" Hettie asked eventually.

He still didn't answer. Hettie noticed that one of his knees was shaking.

"It's Constable Ward."

"Is he on his way?" Hettie asked. "Do I need to hide Violet somewhere else?"

"He's dead, Hettie," Samuel said, finally looking up at her. "He was shot, killed."

Hettie thought of Constable Ward and his careful aim at Andy, the brown bear, whose meat was now being fed to the other animals. It didn't fully register that the constable could have been the target of someone else's weapon.

"What happened?" Hettie asked, sitting down next to Samuel.

"Liam Keegan shot him."

"Liam—"

She felt a quiver of disbelief. Her stomach turned.

"Yes, your brother-in-law, Liam Keegan," he spat. "The man who was here yesterday, threatening me."

Hettie worried about what was going through Samuel's mind at that very minute: Did he think that she had put Liam up to the deadly task in order to protect Violet? Did he have any idea of what had happened between Liam and her?

"He and three of his IRA mates were hiding in one of the damaged shelters this morning. We were driving down Ainsworth Avenue, about to stop—and out of nowhere, they opened fire on us and then ran away. Constable Ward chased after the men into a house, and there was more gunfire. I ran in just in time to see his bullet graze Keegan's shoulder, but before I could do anything Keegan managed to shoot the constable and he died instantly."

Samuel paused for a minute and stared down at his hands, opening and closing his fingers.

"He didn't even make it to the hospital. The bleeding wouldn't stop." His voice cracked.

"Oh God—" Hettie had no idea what to say. It was too horrific.

"I know you didn't put Liam up to this despite how much you must have hated Constable Ward for carrying out the execution of the animals," Samuel said, his eyes pinching together. "His murder was the work of the IRA. Even after all we've been through, with most of the city reduced to ruins and dead bodies being dug out all over the place, they won't stop." His voice was laced with disgust.

"Where is Liam?" Hettie managed.

"He's in Crumlin Road Gaol," Samuel said, "along with two of his mates. The third one managed to get away. Liam and the two others aren't talking."

"What will happen next?"

"He'll be charged with murdering a policeman. It's a capital offense. If he is found guilty, Liam Keegan will likely be hanged," Samuel said. "It'll be the first hanging of a republican terrorist in the history of this state. De Valera has already executed loads of them in the south. It's the only way to deal with them."

"Executed?" she spluttered.

"He murdered the constable. He killed my boss," Samuel said, glancing down at his trembling hands. "It's an act of absolute treason."

Just then Violet released a soft trumpet call from the courtyard.

"She's here," he said, finally meeting Hettie's eye.

"We returned last night. She slept in the courtyard. I'm not sure where to take her now."

"I don't think you need to worry about Violet anymore," Samuel said. "With the constable's death, the IRA's campaign, hundreds of bodies to be exhumed and buried, survivors to be dug out, I think we have other things to worry about."

"What about the official orders?" she asked.

"The Ministry of Public Security has told us to prioritize rescue work, searching for bodies, stopping looting, gathering intelligence on the IRA and arresting the bastards. The entire force is totally exhausted. We've had practically no sleep. We're run off our feet. We don't have enough men or equipment. We can't cope on our own and are totally dependent on the help we get from the troops. Éire is at the root of it all. There's no doubt that the entire IRA campaign is being armed and funded by the Germans. It's being orchestrated by their embassy in Dublin."

"What do you mean?" Hettie said, her forehead furrowing in confusion.

"Local IRA leaders are supplying intelligence about our defenses and targets here in Belfast to German agents who are based south of the border. They've passed on information about what targets still need to be bombed. They've told them to blow up the bridges over the River Lagan, so Belfast will be brought to a standstill."

"That doesn't seem possible—"

"The IRA is our fifth column. If German troops invaded, they would come out into the open and help them all they could," Samuel said softly.

There was another knock at the door. For a second Hettie prayed that it might be her mother or Liam, even though she knew these weren't rational thoughts. Her mother was dead, and Liam was in prison. She was going to have accept these facts at some point. Hettie opened the front door and felt another ripple of relief.

Ferris stood before her. The sleeves of his work shirt were rolled up to his elbows. Scratches and dirt decorated his forearms. He still wore his old school scarf. She opened the door for him and guided him into the sitting room. Samuel Greene looked up at him.

"What are *you* doing here?" Ferris asked.

"I wanted to let Hettie know about the constable," Samuel said. "That she didn't have to worry about Violet and the government's directive any longer."

"Is it true? Did Liam Keegan shoot Constable Ward?" Ferris asked.

"I was there," Samuel said, his bottom lip shaking. "I saw Liam pull the trigger. He shot him right in the chest."

"Have the IRA taken responsibility for it?"

"That's what's being reported."

"That's unbelievable," Ferris said. "After all the city has been through."

"None of us can—" Samuel said.

A loud cracking resounded from the courtyard, and they all jumped in fright.

"What in damnation is that?"

"Violet," Hettie said, making her way to the rear door.

The two young men followed her. There in the courtyard, Violet stood on her hind legs, her broad torso extended up into the air, and her trunk curled in the curve of a question mark.

"Come down, Vi," Hettie said, calmly. "Come down now."

Violet returned to all four feet and lay down on the pavement. The elephant had torn up her mother's garden beds and eaten most of the greens and radishes. One of the wooden benches along the exterior wall of their home had been shattered into several pieces.

Ferris looked around and smiled weakly at Hettie. "So much for your spring garden."

"It doesn't matter," Hettie said. "It was my mother's, not mine. She won't need it anymore."

Hettie slumped down on the remaining bench—the one that she used to sit on with her mother—and Samuel and Ferris sat down on either side of her. Together, they watched as Violet munched on the scattered greens on the pavement. A strange peace took over the courtyard, the kind of peace Hettie hadn't known in a long time. Despite the death of her mother and Liam's despicable actions, she knew in that moment she would be able to go on and meet whatever came next.

"Ferris, could you take Violet back to the zoo?" Hettie finally asked. "I need to go down to St. George's. They say my mum might be there."

"Yes," Ferris said. "Yes, I'll take her back to her home."

"Let me go to St. George's with you," Samuel said. "I might be able to help."

At first Hettie wanted to refuse Samuel, to go by herself, but she knew that he was right: With his position in the special branch, and given the crowds and chaos at St. George's, he could make the search for her mother easier.

"Thank you," Hettie said.

"We should go sooner rather than later before the bodies are re-moved from the market and taken for burial in the city's cemeteries," Samuel said.

"Let me change," Hettie said.

She went into her bedroom and changed into a clean blouse, a fresh pair of trousers, and a jumper. The hem of her other pair of trousers was still damp from when she'd stood in the waves with the nuns and Violet. She lifted the fabric to her nose and took in the salty scent, and thought of Sister Evangeline and Sister Helen. Inside the pocket, she found her mother's wedding ring still tucked in the bottom corner. Hettie stowed the ring in the front pocket of her clean trousers before returning to the courtyard.

"Good luck," Ferris said.

"Thank you, Ferris," Hettie said. "Thanks for everything."

"Come and find me afterward."

"I will," Hettie said, walking over to the side gate to her father's bike.

She unlatched the gate and turned around and looked at Violet one more time. Ferris stood next to her, feeding her a radish from the garden. Samuel had already made his way out to the street.

"You're a good girl," he said to Violet. "Aren't you?"

Hettie felt something amorphous and sharp grow in her chest.

"You listen to Ferris, all right? Follow his direction," she said, leaning against Violet's front flank. "I'll be back soon. I just need to go and see Mum."

Violet nudged her forehead into Hettie's arm.

"Thank you, Vi," she said, lightly kissing her forehead. "Thank you for everything."

"Don't you worry, Hettie," Ferris said, patting the elephant's side. "She'll be waiting for you at the zoo when you return."

"Thanks, Ferris."

Hettie pushed her bike along the gravel walkway that led to the road. Samuel kicked away the metal stand of his own bicycle. Mr. Brown still stood in front of his house, puffing on a pipe, as if he had never left the spot since the previous evening.

"Hettie Quin," he said. "Where is your Violet?"

"My friend Ferris is returning her to the zoo," Hettie said. "I need to go to St. George's."

"Of course you do," Mr. Brown said, his gaze traveling to Samuel Greene, who held the handlebars of his bike and had one foot on the ground. "I hope to God you find her."

"I pray to God that I do, too," Hettie said.

"The Antrim Road is a mess, but it's still the best route to St. George's," Samuel said.

"All right," Hettie said, glancing back at her house.

Ferris hadn't emerged from the courtyard with Violet. Samuel tucked his RUC cap underneath his arm, hopped onto his bike, and rode up the hill that led to the Antrim Road. Hettie followed him. As she pumped the pedals of her bike, she felt both a palpable strength and a crippling weakness. She kept her eyes focused on the dented rear fender of Samuel's bike as he turned left onto the Antrim Road. Debris and scattered piles of rubble still covered a majority of the street. Pedestrians were still streaming northward along the Antrim Road. An urgent panic permeated the smoke-laden air. A young man pushed a wooden cart of tangled clothes, mismatched shoes, a portrait, and a wireless, its flex dangling over the edge. Women carried bundled blankets. The Phoenix Bar was still serving patrons despite missing its windows and doors.

Several dogs and cats roamed the street, sniffing and digging through the loose rubble. Farther down, not far from St. Anne's Cathedral, Red Cross volunteers handed out mugs of tea and sandwiches. Down another side street, a group of men and women knelt together, reciting Hail Marys. The air hummed with their prayers. Hettie thought of Mrs. Keegan and what would happen when she learned the tragic news about Liam. And now Maeve would grow up with no parents. She wiped her runny nose with her sleeve and tried to keep her attention on the street in front of her.

Before long, she and Samuel were turning on to the crowded

pavement of May Street. They leaned their bikes against the side of St. George's.

"Ready?" Samuel asked.

Hettie nodded. Together they walked around the corner to the front entrance of the market. A pair of army officers stood near the double doors, holding their rifles diagonally across their chests. Samuel went ahead of Hettie. Ignoring the long queue snaking up May Street, he approached one of the doors and reached for its brass handle. One of the officers had spotted Samuel's police uniform and had beckoned him to come forward. Samuel showed them his identity card.

The other officer took it from Samuel and inspected it. Then the man scrutinized Samuel's face and looked over at Hettie. She wondered if he would question Samuel about the news of the constable's death. Or perhaps the news about Constable Ward hadn't circulated throughout the city, since it had just occurred that morning.

"How long have you been in the special branch?"

"Almost a year," Samuel said.

"Is she with you?"

"She is," Samuel said, taking his identity card back from the officer.

The officers stepped aside, and Samuel held the door open for Hettie. They were met by the fetid stench of the dead. The piles of corpses had been removed from the concrete floor of the market, but hundreds of coffins still lined the cavernous space. Some of the lids of the coffins were open; others were closed.

"Excuse me," Hettie said to a Red Cross nurse who was walking by. "Could you help me?"

The nurse paused.

"I'm looking for my mum's body," Hettie said. "I was told that she was transported from the public baths at the Falls Road, that I could identify her here—"

"I'm sorry about your mother," the nurse said, regarding Hettie with sympathy. "It's a good thing you made it in this morning. There's a funeral service being held here early tomorrow. Immediately after that, the bodies that can be identified through religious artifacts will be interred in mass graves—Catholics at Milltown Cemetery on the Falls Road and Protestants in the City Cemetery. A whole fleet of army vehicles has been requisitioned to transport the coffins. Anyway, it's good you're here. Walk around. Take your time."

Samuel and Hettie began to wander among the makeshift rows of coffins. There were far fewer people searching amid the dead bodies than her last visit. Brief notes in white chalk were written on the lids of a few of the coffins: the street corner where the body was found, a general description of the person inside.

girl, brown hair, rag doll

young woman, crucifix necklace, duncairn gardens

elderly man, glasses, missing teeth

Inside one open coffin there was a young boy dressed in his striped pajamas with a worn teddy bear lying by his side. His freckled face was a peculiar shade of gray green. One of his legs was missing, the hem of his pajama pants deflated and empty. As tears welled up in her eyes, Hettie thought of Johnny Gibson and his family again. She wondered where his parents were going to bury him.

"Hettie," Samuel said softly, waving a hand over his head.

She quickly walked to where Samuel was standing. There, next to him, was a coffin with *middle-aged woman, Atlantic Avenue shelter, man's watch* written on its rectangular lid. Hettie felt as if her breath had been knocked right out of her. She crouched down and rocked on her heels. She didn't want this to be true—that her mother was dead, too. Hettie bowed her head in her hands, praying to God for the strength, grace, and resilience to be present for her mother and her death, to provide her with a dignified resting place, just as she would have wanted.

"Hettie, would you like me to open it?" asked Samuel, his hand resting on her shoulder.

She nodded, and he slowly opened the coffin's lid. Hettie stood up. The brass hinges of the coffin were loose, and the lid accidentally smacked against the hard floor.

"Sorry," Samuel said. "I lost my grip."

There was her mother. Her blue-veined eyelids were drawn closed, and her long, elegant fingers were folded over her chest. A laceration and a flowering bruise marked her left temple. Her complexion was pale and gray. She was still dressed in her nightgown and beige overcoat. For a moment, Hettie couldn't stop herself from imagining another set of circumstances, an overlay of a different reality, one where her mother would reach for her hand and squeeze it and her eyes would flick open, and she would utter, like a song, *Oh my sweet girl, I'm sorry about everything you've been through.* And she would lift out of the coffin, and together they would wander through the field of dead bodies in St. George's, out the double doors, and through the smoky, shattered streets of Belfast to their home, where Hettie would make them cups of tea, and mother and daughter would exchange stories about everything that had happened since the moment when they had left each other when the bombs started to fall.

A siren rang in the cavernous space. Someone made an announcement through a megaphone. Feet shuffled by. Hettie opened and closed her eyes—and refocused on her mother: Rose was dead. There was no song. There was no recognition. A shiver traveled across Hettie's shoulders.

"God help me," she whispered to herself. "Help me."

Hettie touched Rose's forehead. Her skin felt cold and clammy. She took her mother's stiff hand into her own. She tried to slide strands of her mother's hair out of her eyes, but they were caked onto her forehead with dried blood and dirt. Hettie knelt down, bowed her head, and prayed. She whispered murmurs of love and forgiveness. She asked that her mother never be alone again. She asked that her mother's broken spirit finally be able to rest. She asked that her mother find the peace and contentment that she had always been looking for.

Grief hummed through her.

It sang.

An aria for the dead.

An aria for the human spirit.

An aria for what her mother used to be.

For her mother's younger self.

Before Thomas. Before Anna and Hettie.

When a different kind of life was in front of her.

Hettie opened her eyes and noticed her father's wristwatch lying across Rose's chest. She took it to her ear. By some miracle, the watch was still ticking. Hettie buckled it around her wrist and listened to its ticking again. Then she carefully slid her mother's wedding ring from the pocket of her trousers and studied it—a perfect circle of gold. For a moment, a shimmer danced along its thin circle in the stale light of St. George's. Hettie kissed it and slipped it onto Rose's ring finger, and then carefully returned her hands into a folded position.

"Let me find someone to help us," Samuel said, standing behind Hettie.

"Thank you."

She sat silently with her mother for what felt like a long time. A stillness and a commotion coexisted in the enormous space—the scuffling of feet around her, the whispering of voices, the clicking of rosary beads moving through strangers' hands, the sloshing mop against the concrete floor.

"Thank you for all that you gave me," Hettie said to her mother. "For teaching me how to love and forgive. I love you. I will always love you."

A nurse with a clipboard returned with Samuel. Hettie stood up.

"Where would you like the body delivered to?" the nurse asked.

"Carnmoney Parish Church," Hettie said. "I'll call Reverend Mills and let him know about my mum."

The nurse scribbled on the sheet attached to her clipboard. "Please sign here," she said, handing the clipboard and pen to Hettie, who took it and signed next to the blank that read NEXT OF KIN. The nurse closed the lid of the coffin. With a rag, the nurse erased the description of Hettie's mother and wrote *Rose Quin, Carnmoney Parish Church, Reverend Mills* on the lid.

"It might take a few days, but I'll make sure that she gets there," the nurse said.

"Thank you," Hettie whispered.

She leaned forward and embraced the nurse. When Hettie stepped back, the nurse was smiling sadly, her eyes glistening. The nurse started down the aisle toward the next family waiting for her assistance. It was a young man, a mill worker, dressed in soot-streaked overalls. He held the hand of a young girl with a red ribbon tied at the end of her long braid. The girl sucked on her thumb as she stared up at the doves that were soaring amid the rafters, their low, mournful coos echoing through the market.

Hettie and Samuel stepped out onto the street. The officers still stood in front of the doors. Samuel gave them a formal salute, and they responded with the same gesture, then he turned to Hettie.

"They need me at RUC headquarters," he said, taking her hands in his.

Hettie nodded.

"I'm not sure what you're planning, but you might want to wait a few days before visiting Liam," Samuel said. "I don't want anyone to draw any strange conclusions about Violet's well-being and Liam's ambush of the constable."

"Yes, whatever you think is best," Hettie said, her words rushing together.

"The court case hasn't been scheduled yet," he said. "It probably won't happen for another month. In the meantime, I think it's all right if you leave Violet at the zoo. No one is going to be looking for her."

Hettie hugged Samuel. He smiled at her and then hopped on his bike and made his way along May Street, weaving his way through the cars, military vehicles, ambulances, lorries, soldiers, and pedestrians that filled the streets and pavements. Hettie stood there watching Samuel ride away until she could no longer see him or his black bike on the crowded street.

Fourteen

THE NEXT DAY MR. CHRISTIE SENT A TELEGRAM, SAYING THAT he and Josephine would be paying an emergency visit to Bellevue by the end of the month to survey the loss and damage firsthand as well as to see how the meat of the executed animals was being distributed to feed the other animals. So far, according to Ferris, the bear meat was being fed to the sea lions and the storks and the herons. Rajan and Maggie were being fed to the foxes, the baboons, and the lemurs. The tiger to the monkeys and the baboons. Mr. Christie said they couldn't afford to lose any more of their charges. This might mean the demise of the zoo, the closing of its doors for good. Mr. Christie also advised Mr. Wright to begin purchasing domestic animals from local farmers to populate the empty enclosures and paddocks until the city allowed him to procure more wild and exotic animals. It might be some time before those kinds of animals would be permitted to reside at Bellevue Zoo again. The government was concerned that yet another attack was imminent, and it might be several months—even years—before city life was restored to its former existence. Mr. Christie also ordered ticket admission prices to be cut in half to attract visitors despite the loss of the more popular animals. He ended his telegram by saying that he and Josephine would be arriving on the morning of April 28 and would spend two days at the zoo.

In the meantime, Hettie met with Reverend Mills and made arrangements for the funeral service and burial of her mother. The reverend mentioned how fortunate Hettie had been to find Rose's body amid the dead of the Easter Tuesday attacks, as many of the deceased had been too disfigured or decayed for identification. At least Rose would be given a respectable memorial, where friends and family could celebrate her life and spirit. Hettie struggled to feel grateful, as Reverend Mills suggested, but she knew he was right. He also recommended that it would be wise to wait at least a couple of weeks with hopes that the city would by then be restored to some degree of normality so extended family members and friends in Belfast and outside the city would be able to attend her service.

Word of Rose's death circulated throughout their neighborhood, and Uncle Edgar and Aunt Sylvia stopped by on separate evenings to express their condolences and see how Hettie was doing. Uncle Edgar reminded Hettie of the monthly revenue from the family farm and that she would be able to count on these funds in covering the expenses of maintaining the house. Now that the water and electricity were working again, she wouldn't need to move. She could stay where she was.

On Wednesday, April 23, Hettie rode her bike down to the Crumlin Road Gaol after work. Given Samuel's advice, it seemed as if enough time had passed for her to visit Liam without generating any sort of suspicion. The jail was situated at the southern end of the Crumlin Road, beside the Mater Hospital and not far from the city hall. The four-story Victorian prison was huge, covering a ten-acre site and able to accommodate five hundred prisoners. Four wings fanned out from a central area, colloquially known as "the circle," and each of the wings had three landings. Its tall watchtower was like a beacon looking over the surrounding devastated neighborhood; much of it had been obliterated during the Easter Tuesday raid. At the prison, two bombs had struck its high walls, but the impact was barely noticeable. Opposite the prison stood the austere courthouse, where Liam's hearing was scheduled for June 2.

When Hettie arrived at the prison's entrance, a mustached, bespectacled security guard behind a metal grate asked if she had scheduled a visit. Given the gravity of his crime, Liam was being allowed only one visitor per week, and these visits had to be arranged ahead of time.

"I'm family," Hettie argued. "Please, sir."

"Are you his sister?" the man asked, studying her features.

"Sister-in-law," she clarified, thinking it would be best to be honest. "He's the widower of my sister."

"Identification card," he demanded.

The man disappeared from his post. Hettie tapped her foot against the polished floor and stared down the long, brightly lit corridor. The voices of men and heavy footsteps echoed throughout the enormous building. She glanced down at her father's watch. It was half past ten.

"We will make an exception today. The next time you visit, you must make arrangements prior to your arrival," the man said, sliding her identification card along the scarred countertop back to her. "A guard will escort you to the visitors' room on the other side of the yard, first floor, to the right. Wait there."

"Thank you, sir," Hettie said, taking her card and returning it to her wallet.

Behind one of the closed doors, a guard, dressed in uniform with a gun and a pair of handcuffs attached to his belt, emerged and stared blankly in her direction.

"Visitor for Liam Patrick Keegan," he said.

Hettie nodded, wiping her clammy palms on her frock.

"Follow me."

They walked down a long hallway with a multitude of doors. Angled transom windows allowed narrow rectangles of natural light to fall onto the floor of the hallway. Hettie kept her eyes on the polished heels of the guard's shoes. Loud clanks echoed in the corridor and she heard the jangling of keys, and then a man bellowed instructions from another floor. An alarm sounded.

The guard opened a door that led to the interior yard, a barren space the size of a football pitch, which was bordered by the wings of the prison, a neat row of warders' houses, and the jail's external walls. The gray bulk of the buildings and walls cast long shadows across the field. The endless circles of wire along the high walls looked like lethal teeth against the bluish sky. Along one section, Hettie noticed over a dozen graves marked by crude crosses; they held the mortal remains of prisoners who had been executed in the prison and buried in its unconsecrated ground. Hettie wondered how many other guards and prisoners were watching her and the guard as they walked silently across the yard, and if Liam could see her from his cellblock. She speculated on whether he would be delighted or disappointed or even indifferent upon seeing her for the first time since their last encounter at the convent on the Shore Road. She felt the heaviness of Rose's death and the strange sensation of hoping that Liam might be pleased to see her. Hettie knew it was preposterous, and she tried to bat the naive thought away.

After they crossed the yard, they reentered the prison compound, and the guard led Hettie into a windowless room. Another guard was stationed behind an empty desk with a newspaper spread open before him. The seated guard was an elderly man with wiry gray hairs sprouting from his nostrils and ears. His large belly hung over his clinched belt, like a puckered balloon. Three tables with chairs were situated in the room.

"Sit there," the guard said. "The prisoner will be here soon."

The other guard at the desk was smoking a cigarette, a pile of mashed-up stubs already overflowing in a glass ashtray. Hettie sat down and opened her mother's Agatha Christie mystery that she had retrieved from her satchel before handing it over to the guard at the front gate. Even though her mind was too unsettled to read, she was relieved she had the paperback in her possession so she could stare at something other than the gray walls of the visitors' room and the elderly guard smoking his cigarette. Another siren sounded in the hallway. The guard didn't flinch. Instead, he licked the tip of a finger and turned a page of the newspaper. He grunted and hummed. Hettie tried to focus her eyes on the words displayed across the cover of her book, but couldn't. The clock on the wall ticked louder. More heavy footsteps echoed down the hallway. She heard the clinking of keys again, and the rasping sound of numerous locks being opened and then closed. There was a volley of male voices.

Finally the door opened—and Liam stepped across the threshold. He was clad in a one-piece hunter-green prison uniform, and his hands were shackled together by handcuffs. His face was pale and gaunt, his vacant eyes lowered to the floor. It looked as if a part of him had disappeared and would never resurface, making Hettie feel as though she was breaking all over again. As soon as Liam saw Hettie, his expression lit up. She stood from her chair, and he shuffled across the room with a prison guard at his side. The guard unlocked his handcuffs, and handed Liam a cigarette and lit it for him. His right shoulder looked stiff, but there was no bandage indicating that he had been struck by the constable's bullet.

"Twenty minutes," the guard said, placing an ashtray on the table, a poof of ashes lifting up and then falling.

Liam nodded and then gave Hettie a wry smile. The end of the cigarette trembled as Liam brought it to his lips and then exhaled. The two of them sat down at the table.

"Hettie," he said. "So good to see you."

Hettie stared into Liam's eyes. Besides the obvious signs of his physical exhaustion, she noticed that there was something different about Liam's expression: A quiet wildness stirred in his features. He tapped the cigarette against the glass-bottomed ashtray. His fingers shook.

"Are you all right?" Hettie asked. "I heard you were injured."

In answer, he reached for his shoulder and held it for a moment as if he were trying to listen for the beat of his own heart. Then he reached for his cigarette again and took another long draw. "I'm surprised you're here," he said, nervousness flickering across his face. "I didn't think you would come."

Hettie remained silent.

"You know, after everything—the note about your mum and Violet, and then your mum's belongings."

"You wrote the note that I received at the convent?"

Amid her nervousness and anticipation, rage rose inside of her. Her cheeks reddened, her palms prickled with perspiration. Liam looked up and stared at her for a moment as if he was attempting to arrange his jumbled thoughts into some sort of coherent meaning. Hettie didn't know what to say.

"I was going to take Violet," he said, "and sell her on the black market to a circus owner across the border. My uncle knew this man, a buyer who was looking for a young elephant for his troupe, and he had agreed to pay a tidy sum, but Sister Helen told me that I couldn't. She wouldn't let me."

He blinked hard a few times, and took another inhale of his cigarette, the end of it shaking from the jittery motions of his fingers. Her temples begin to throb, and an ache settled along the edge of her right eye. As Hettie sat there, staring down at her own hands, she could barely register the depth of his betrayal but also realized that she was no longer surprised by Liam's words or actions, that the IRA's mission was the compass that had been guiding his priorities and morals all along. Nothing else mattered.

"The constable had it coming, you know," he whispered in a hoarse voice. "The other brigade members all agreed with me. I had no choice. I had to do it. We have to break the spirit of the police. In time, the Germans will boot them all out. The Brits are using the war to militarize the six counties. They have tens of thousands of troops here. Next thing you know, they'll invade the South, occupy its harbors, and use them as bases in the Battle of the Atlantic."

"But Liam, what about Maeve?"

He stared at Hettie blankly. It was as if she had uttered the name of a stranger, someone Liam had never met before.

"Maeve, your daughter," Hettie said again, exasperation creeping into her voice. "The daughter you had with my sister, Anna. Or do you not care about her anymore?"

Liam took another long inhale. The cigarette had already burned down to its end. He nervously looked over at the guard reading the newspaper at the desk and then back to Hettie. A barely noticeable twitch jerked at the corner of his lips.

"I can't trust anyone in here," he said. "Even some of the republicans on my wing. You know, Éamon was here. He must have grassed. He never could keep his mouth shut. So they set him free. Let him go. But look at me."

She felt a muddle of rage, fear, and empathy as she considered what this meant for Maeve and her future. Hettie touched one of his hands. He interlaced his fingers with hers. She could feel the quiver traveling from his hand to hers.

"I've always liked your hands," he said, staring down at her fingers. "You have the prettiest hands."

Another prisoner was escorted into the room. He looked to be about Hettie's age, nineteen or twenty. A young woman carrying an infant followed the prisoner. The man started to cry as the woman revealed the baby's face in between the folds of a blue blanket.

"That guy," Liam said from the corner of his mouth. "He's on my block."

The man took the infant into his arms.

"You know, some of the other boys here, they've told me that there are tunnels underneath this place," Liam continued. "They've been dug through all the way underneath and beyond the walls."

Liam stomped one of his boots against the scuffed-up floor. The guard started and glanced in their direction.

"Easy there, Keegan," the guard said.

"I could use another cig," Liam said. "Can you help me out, Smith. Please."

The guard rolled his eyes, walked over, and gave Liam a second cigarette.

"That's it, Keegan," he said. "You hear me?"

"Yes, sir," Liam said, his voice frail.

He failed to light the cigarette on the first, second, and third attempts. Finally, Hettie took pity on him and struck a match and held it up to the end of the cigarette.

"Thanks, Hettie," he said with a grateful smile.

Liam reached into one of his pockets and retrieved a worn deck of playing cards. He began to methodically shuffle the cards as though in a trance as he continued to smoke, the cigarette hanging from the corner of his mouth. The cards slid together and collapsed into each other. Again and again.

"This is all we do here," he said. "Play cards. And then play cards again. There's nothing else to do."

The guard stood up and stepped outside of the room, closing the door behind him. The couple whispered to each other. The baby released a soft cry.

"He's one of the crazy ones, you know," Liam said, nodding in the direction of the young couple. "Tried to off himself the other day, hang himself in his cell. The guards found him just in time."

Liam began to flip over the cards, one by one: the queen of hearts, the ace of spades, the two of diamonds. He stared at the trio of cards before collecting them again and reshuffling the deck.

"Know any games?"

"What about rummy?"

He dealt ten cards from the deck to Hettie and then ten to himself.

"No cheating," he said with a mischievous grin. "I'll know if you're cheating, Harriet Quin."

Liam nudged his foot against Hettie's foot.

"I won't."

Liam crossed his leg, and the tip of his black shoe shook uncontrollably.

"Liam," she said hesitantly. "Are you all right?"

He stared at his shaking foot and then returned his gaze to Hettie. "Have anything good?" he asked.

She gave up trying to get him to talk and instead studied the cards in her hand. Hettie glanced at the red geometric designs on their backs and noticed that several of the cards were marked with Liam's handwriting. He smiled and nodded. Hettie discreetly slid the cards into the front pocket of her coat, and a light danced in Liam's eyes. The guard returned to the room, slamming the door behind him.

"All right, Keegan," he said. "Time's up."

He roughly yanked Liam out of his seat. Hettie felt the bent corners of the tattered cards in her coat pocket.

"Thank you for coming to see me, Hettie," he said. "Say hello to that elephant of yours for me."

It was as if Liam's former self had temporarily returned, as if the old Liam still existed inside the Liam who had lost his mind, and stolen from her, and gone and shot the constable. She wanted to say *Stay*. She wanted to say *Don't go away*. Despite her desires and longing, she knew there was nothing she could do to change the course of things.

"I will," Hettie said, standing up from the table. "I'll say hey to Violet for you."

The guard escorted Liam out of the room, and the other guard held the door open for Hettie.

"Collect your personal belongings at the desk."

Hettie made her way down the long corridor. Once again she heard keys being rattled, and the opening and slamming shut of the multiple doors and gates behind her. At the front area, she retrieved her satchel from the warden behind the grate. Outside, the cool spring air expanded deep inside her lungs. After she pushed her bike a few blocks away from the prison, Hettie reached for the playing cards in her front pocket. Each one held a different message.

I AM PROUD TO DIE FOR IRELAND'S FREEDOM. THERE NEVER WAS A NOBLER CAUSE.

MY HEART WILL FOREVER BE WITH MY BELOVED ANNA. I WILL MEET HER AGAIN SOON.

GOD BLESS MAEVE.

Hettie studied Liam's barely legible writing on the cards one more time before she released them, allowing the cards to fall and trip down the pavement. She stood there silently as the cards drifted away from her. A stranger walking by kicked one of them into the gutter.

Hettie thought of baby Maeve. Her gentle grip on her finger, her cherublike cheeks. For a moment, Hettie's love for Maeve felt immeasurable. Expansive and endless. An entire ocean. It was similar to how she felt about Violet. And then she quickly recognized that they—Ferris, Maeve, Lily, Violet, the children living at the convent, and herself—all had one thing in common.

We are all orphans, Hettie thought to herself.

We are all orphans.

It was like an incantation, a set of ancient prayers, and the four words transformed into deeply felt undercurrents of truth and sadness that eventually settled into the center of Hettie's chest. They had all been left behind, but would be able to survive, even in the most difficult of circumstances.

Once the danger of further German attacks was over, she would travel to Newcastle and see Maeve. She would be a good aunt. She would be a good sister and a good daughter. She would forget what had happened between her and Liam, and regularly visit Maeve and Mrs. Keegan. Hettie hopped on her bike and pushed the pedals with all the strength she could find. She turned onto the Antrim Road and made her way up the hill.

Fifteen

DURING THE FOLLOWING WEEK, THE ZOOKEEPERS STARTED TO ferry in ponies, chickens, and goats purchased from the neighboring farms. In the meantime, Mr. Wright mostly remained sequestered in his office, making appearances only when it was necessary. He had become something of a ghost: his gaze vacant, his voice subdued, his posture slumped. More than once, Hettie had stopped by his office, but he never answered the door when she knocked.

Despite the changes in Mr. Wright and the zoo, everyone attempted to go about their usual business, cleaning out the enclosures and preparing the areas for the new animals. Hettie developed a habit of bringing Violet home each evening, walking along their familiar route of the Crazy Path to the Antrim Road to the Whitewell Road. Despite Samuel Greene's reassurances that the police would not seek out the elephant, Hettie felt better knowing that Violet was within close proximity, day and night. In addition, another scenario played out in the back of Hettie's mind: What if the police's special branch started to draw conclusions about Liam's violent act being associated with the protection of Violet rather than the IRA's mission to unite Ireland and set up a thirty-two-county republic? Given all this, Hettie thought it was worth the risk to have Violet under her care at all times. Surprisingly, Hettie's neighbors were growing accustomed to the appearance of Violet on their street, coming and going, at the end of the day, and in the morning. In addition, the elephant's presence in the courtyard made Hettie's evenings and mornings more bearable now that Rose was gone.

Once the zoo had reopened, it remained largely empty despite maintaining its regular hours of operation. During the evenings, the ornate doors of the Floral Hall remained open, too. Instead of live musicians and singers, a collection of shellac records and a gramophone were positioned at the front of the stage and supplied music. A kind of tinny, distant facsimile of the former big band sound. There were always a few people who were courageous enough to remain in the city and who still had a heart for dancing. Soldiers often turned up, if only out of boredom. There was nothing else for them to do in Belfast apart from drink in its pubs and clubs.

On Monday, April 28, Josephine Christie arrived at the zoo before it opened in the morning. Mr. Christie had apparently fallen ill and wasn't well enough to travel from their office headquarters in London. That morning, as Hettie made her way to the Elephant House with a half bale of hay in a wheelbarrow, she spotted Mr. Wright and Josephine Christie standing in front of the flamingos. Many of the birds were still asleep, perched upon a single leg, their graceful necks and heads curled into their pale pink bodies. Josephine wore a black dress that dropped to her ankles; a transparent charcoal collar of ruffles bordered the edge of her chin. She and Mr. Wright were walking slowly along the pathway, their heads bowed as they spoke with each other.

That afternoon, Hettie busied herself with her usual duties, but kept expecting Mr. Wright and Josephine Christie to appear at the door of the Elephant House. Finally, toward the end of the day, when Hettie was preparing for their nightly walk down the Crazy Path, Josephine appeared. She carried a collapsed umbrella, the folds of tartan cloth gathered together, the curved bamboo handle hanging from her delicate wrist. In her other hand, she held a drawstring bag of black velvet that looked like a magician's bag of tricks. Josephine stepped into the dusty yard of Violet's enclosure.

"Good to see you, Hettie," she said. "Are you doing all right? Mr. Wright told me about your mother. I'm so sorry."

Hettie allowed Josephine to hug her. She still wasn't sure what to say when others mentioned Rose. During recent weeks, grief overcame her at unexpected moments—fixing a pot of tea, exchanging morning greetings with Mrs. Curry on the street, listening to classical music on the wireless. A sudden dilation of sadness would open up inside of Hettie, and warm tears would roll down her cheeks. But then, sometimes the sorrow disappeared just as quickly. At home, she slept in her own bedroom and left the door to her mother's bedroom closed. Each evening, she still kept expecting Rose to join her for a cup of tea on their bench in the courtyard. Even though they had never talked that much, Hettie missed the comfort of their rituals and daily conversations. Nowadays, she took her nightly cup of tea with Violet in the courtyard.

Josephine silently studied Violet across the yard.

"Did Mr. Wright tell you about Rajan?"

"He did," Josephine said, averting her eyes to the dusty yard and then pausing. "What are your plans? What are you going to do now?"

"I'm staying here," Hettie said, "to care for the animals and Violet."

"But the government is urging citizens to evacuate. Women and children, in particular."

"I have to stay," Hettie said. "I want to stay."

"Because of Violet?"

"Yes."

Josephine surveyed Violet's enclosure again. Violet walked in their direction, lifted her trunk up in the air, and opened her mouth, her tongue slipping out and curling up in the air, like the subtle curve of a sly smile. Hettie reached into her coat pocket and handed Violet a broken end of a carrot. The elephant grabbed the carrot with her trunk and tucked it inside her mouth. Josephine patted Violet's forehead and then clasped her hands together, lowering her head as if she were saying a silent prayer.

"Well, I must be going," Josephine finally said, looking up at Hettie. "Apologies for my hasty visit."

Hettie frowned. "I thought you were staying the night."

"Poor George is ill," Josephine said. "My brother needs me."

The shrieks of the monkeys ricocheted across the treetops. Violet answered with a trumpet call. The peacocks and parrots joined in. Then the mournful brays of the sea lions. A growing chorus of living animals, a sort of plaintive ode to what once was. Hettie looked over at Violet, who seemed to be listening, too, her flap-like ears raised in the air, and then over at Josephine, who withdrew a linen handkerchief from her purse.

"Mr. Wright told me what happened with Violet." Josephine paused, and Hettie wondered what version of the story Mr. Wright had told Josephine. Since she hadn't spoken to Mr. Wright, she still wasn't sure what parts of the story he knew.

"How you took her home in order to avoid the ministry's directive," Josephine continued, looking up at Hettie. "How you saved Violet's life."

"That's one way of seeing it," Hettie said.

"I don't understand."

"If I hadn't been so worried about her, I might have died, too."

"I guess you saved each other," Josephine said.

"Thankfully, we did," Hettie said.

Josephine sighed. "I need to return to London."

"Do you need Mr. Wright to call you a taxi to the station?"

"A driver is waiting for me on the Antrim Road." Josephine took Hettie's hand and looked her in the eye. "You're doing good work here, Hettie Quin," she said. "I hope you'll continue with it."

"Thank you."

"I'll be sure to give Georgie a good report."

"Thank you."

"Goodbye, dear Hettie."

Josephine Christie proceeded down the path that led to the grand staircase and the front entrance of the zoo, the lace hem of her black dress trailing behind her. Hettie continued to watch Josephine until her dark figure disappeared down the grand staircase. It felt strange, but Hettie was certain that she would never see this impossibly elegant woman again. That this would be her last exchange with Josephine Christie.

The following morning, Hettie returned Violet to her enclosure after their walk up the Crazy Path. As she walked toward the canteen to fetch a morning cup of tea, Hettie ran into Mr. Clarke. His face was rumpled with distress, his complexion a patchwork of redness.

"Mr. Clarke, are you all right?" Hettie asked.

"Mr. Wright is gone," he said. "He left early this morning."

"On an errand?"

"On the train to Dublin. He's taking the ferry to Holyhead and then the train up to Yorkshire."

"He's going home?" Hettie gasped.

"Yes, that appears to be the case," Mr. Clarke said. "George will be sending a replacement as soon as he can find a suitable head zookeeper."

Mr. Clarke started down the pavement again, but then stopped.

"You know, out of everyone," he said, "I didn't think Mr. Wright—" Mr. Clarke didn't complete his thought, but only shook his head. He continued down the path to his security station.

Hettie made her way to Mr. Wright's office and knocked on the door. No one answered. She heard the recorded voice of a woman singing, but didn't hear Mr. Wright's voice harmonizing along with the lyrics. Hettie checked the knob, and the door slipped open. No one was there. Many of his personal effects had been left behind: The framed black-and-white photograph of Mr. Wright and Augustus was still on top of the bookcase. His gramophone sat in its rosewood cabinet with his collection of albums leaning against one wall. When the French singer stopped singing, the thin needle skipped on the last rung of the spinning record. Hettie lifted the arm of the needle, replaced it onto its elevated position, and turned the gramophone off.

The room was silent. The framed poster from Mr. Christie's Continental Circus still hung on the wall. Its frame was crooked, and a hairline crack traveled across the clear glass face. Loose papers were scattered on Mr. Wright's desk. Hettie sifted through them with hopes of finding some kind of note related to his abrupt departure, perhaps explaining that his hiatus would be only a temporary one, that he would return in a week's time or less. Instead, there was nothing. The short nub of a candle was still anchored to the corner of his desk by a dried puddle of wax. For a second, Hettie saw the dancing flame of the candle against Mr. Wright's ruddy complexion the night of the bombing and then, earlier, his trancelike stare fixated on Stella Holliday as she sang amid the shadows of the Floral Hall, and later his solemn stance as Constable Ward, Sergeant Miller, and Samuel shot the animals one by one.

The door to the office opened. Hettie prayed that it might be Mr. Wright returning for something he had accidentally left behind. Maybe she could convince him to stay. Instead, Ferris emerged from behind the door. He studied the untidy office.

"I heard—"

"Did he tell you? Before he left?"

"No," Ferris said, shaking his head, "but I'm not surprised."

"But—" Hettie started to say, but then stopped. She looked around the office. A piece of scrap paper with Mr. Wright's handwriting drifted from the desktop onto the floor. Hettie picked it up. It was an order for hay, cornmeal, and feed. The date written at the top of the note was October 20, 1940. Hettie held the piece of paper in her hand for a second before letting it fall back down onto the floor.

"I'll ask Jack to come in and clean things up," Ferris said.

He held the door for Hettie and together they walked up the path to the center of the zoo.

"How could he leave us?" Hettie asked abruptly.

"I don't think he wanted to," Ferris said. "I think he felt like he'd disappointed us, so he had to leave."

They stopped in front of the Elephant House. Violet was standing near the end of the wrought-iron fence, lightly kicking her front feet against the dusty ground. Before Ferris walked away, he gave Hettie a hug. She leaned into him, and took in his familiar scents of cigarettes, soot, and manure. For a moment, she allowed herself to feel the solidness and strength of his sturdy arms. She felt his reliability and steadiness, and their mutual respect for each other. All this from his embrace. She rested there for a moment, and then they stepped apart again.

"Tea at our usual time?"

"Yes," she said with a smile. "That would be grand."

Ferris went his way to feed Sammy and the other sea lions. By the end of the day, the rest of the zoo staff had learned about Mr. Wright's sudden departure. Very few rumors circulated about the reasons behind his leaving. Everyone knew Mr. Wright would never recover from the execution of the animals, especially Rajan's death.

As the hours edged toward dusk, Hettie raked the dirt floor of the camel enclosure. At one point she thought she heard the phantom roar of one of the lions and then later the distant cackling of the hyenas. With each one, a tingling traveled through her body. She recalled the decaying carcasses that were now buried in the meadow next to the Crazy Path and the supply of butchered meat on ice in the storage shed.

When Hettie stepped into the Elephant House, Violet gave out a roar into the early-evening sky, which still held a smoky haze and a noxious smell from the fires still smoldering in the city. Hettie clucked her tongue. Violet turned around and walked slowly toward her. Hettie offered the elephant a turnip. Violet opened her mouth, and Hettie threw the vegetable underhand and it landed with a thunk in the elephant's mouth. Hettie looked over at Violet. Tiny pieces of white flesh were caught between the fine black whiskers underneath her chin. Violet touched her trunk into the pocket of her jacket. Hettie reached in and felt for the last turnip.

"How did you know I had one more?" she said, handing the turnip over to Violet.

Hettie glanced down at her father's wristwatch. It was a quarter past eight. She looked up at the sky. Along the western edge of the Lough, the sun was beginning to set, its diminishing rays sending deep ribbons of lavender and apricot against the horizon. Violet walked through the Elephant House, strands of hay crunching underneath her feet. The peacocks in the aviary called out, like the prolonged wail of an infant. Hettie imagined the birds fanning their eye-spotted feathers of iridescent blue, green, and black, strutting back and forth across the width of the caged enclosure. The spring leaves clattered and vibrated in the twilight.

Together, Hettie and Violet walked along the pavement that wound toward the rear entrance of the zoo. As they got closer to the top of the Crazy Path, Hettie turned left and walked until they stood on the far edge of the meadow where many of the animals were now buried. During the past few days, makeshift memorials had emerged across the mounds of dirt. Broken sticks and twigs were tied together with twine and pieces of ivy, forming a series of crosses of different shapes and sizes. Loose bouquets of purple lilacs and bright pink azaleas had been picked and placed in front of many of the homemade crosses. A few lone daffodils were scattered, their yellow trumpet-shaped heads resting on the uneven ground.

A flock of swallows rose from the treetops that bordered the meadow. A swirling mass of what looked like hundreds of birds flew up into the weak twilight of the sky, a synchronized movement of black flecks flowing into one fluid, shape-shifting cloud before the birds returned to the same treetop, momentarily resting on its branches before taking off and circling the watery sky again. Violet gave out a soft trumpet cry. They stood on the top edge of the meadow and took in the changing light and the multitude of memorials for the dead animals as the gathering of swallows lifted up from the treetop once more and circled the expanse of the early evening sky. The elephant gave out another call.

Hettie looked up at Violet before turning around and heading down the Crazy Path. Violet walked in front of her along the sinuous curves of the wide trail, and Hettie followed. Then they traversed the short path that bordered Uncle Edgar's farm and across the Antrim Road. The road was still cluttered with piles of gray rubble. Union Jacks attached to thin poles stood in the mounds here and there, the red, white, and blue snapping in the evening breeze. Together, they turned down the Whitewell Road. The few remaining neighborhood children sat on the burned-out couch in the middle of the road, but quickly ran toward Hettie as soon as they spotted Violet. For a second, Hettie expected to see Johnny Gibson leading the pack, but instead it was Lily Brown running at the front of the group of young children.

"You promised," they sang collectively. "You promised, Hettie!"

"Me first," Lily Brown said, shooting her hand straight up into the air. "You said."

"No, me!" said Albert O'Brien. "Let me go first."

"You remember Violet, don't you," Hettie said, patting the broad side of the elephant.

Hettie extended Violet's trunk and placed it into Lily's palm, and the two of them gave each other a gentle handshake.

"Her skin feels funny," Lily said, releasing her grip and staring into Violet's serene, blinking eyes.

"Her skin is rough to the touch," Hettie said, "but it's also resilient."

"How old is she?" Lily asked.

"She's three years old," Hettie said, "but sometimes she acts older than her age."

Hettie lifted Lily Brown up onto Violet's broad back. The lightness of the young girl surprised her. For a moment, she was reminded of when her father taught her how to ride one of her uncle's Clydesdales when she was seven years old, how to trust the movement of the animal through the act of riding, the swaying back and forth, the graceful locomotion. It was like a new kind of freedom, sitting atop a horse and being able to command his movements. "Pretend you're riding a horse," she told Lily. "Press your legs against her sides so you stay in one place."

"Like this?" Lily said as she attempted to squeeze her short legs against Violet's broad sides. Violet swatted her tail from side to side.

"Exactly."

Hettie walked in front of Violet and clucked her tongue, and the elephant lumbered slowly with Lily on top of her. The other children gathered on the side of the road as Hettie and Violet and Lily made their way up the rise before turning onto the Antrim Road.

"Brilliant, Lily," Hettie said. "You're brilliant."

Lily smiled as she held on to the loose skin of Violet's neck. The neighborhood children formed a procession behind them, along with Mr. Martin, Mrs. Lyttle, and Mr. Brown. In a broken window of one of the houses that bordered the Antrim Road was a cardboard sign that read CARRY ON, BELFAST. A porcelain bathtub, streaked with soot and filth, sat askew on the pavement. Another sign in the rubble warned CAUTION BOMB CRATER. From a wireless that sat in the window of a terraced house, a big band tune played, its notes from trumpets, clarinets, and saxes floating up into the air. Lily waved to the sparse collection of pedestrians who had gathered on the curb. Air-raid wardens, with their black steel helmets and dark blue uniforms, paused to take in the sight of Hettie and Violet and Lily. Hettie whistled softly along with the big band melody.

"I'm the queen!" Lily said with a grin, revealing a missing front tooth. "I'm the queen!"

"You certainly are," Hettie said. "You're the queen of the Antrim Road."

Acknowledgments

Thank you to my editor Harry Kirchner who was the first to say yes to this unlikely pair of Violet and Hettie—and guided my novel along the path to publication at Counterpoint. Thank you to Dan Smetanka for his early enthusiasm and being the next yes that made this novel a reality, and to Kendall Storey for expanding the readership of Hettie and Violet. Thank you to my editor at Hodder & Stoughton, Thorne Ryan, for her thoughtful edits. Also, at Counterpoint, thanks to Wah-Ming Chang, Chandra Wohleber, Alison Forner, and Nicole Caputo. And to the marketing and publicity team of Megan Fishmann, Sarah Jean Grimm, Katie Boland, and Rachel Fershleiser. I'm very grateful to everyone at Counterpoint—and Hodder & Stoughton—for getting behind this novel and championing it to the finish line.

This novel was inspired by the early life of Denise Austin (also known as the "Elephant Angel"), who was the first female zookeeper at the Bellevue Zoo. I first heard about her life when her identity was discovered by the zoo in 2009. Later, after I decided to pursue the idea as a novel, many individuals on both sides of the pond assisted during the writing and researching of this book. Thank you to former curator Ciaran Doran and the late John Hughes of the Northern Ireland

War Memorial Museum in Belfast. Thank you to the Blitz survivors who took the time to speak with me: the late Vance Rodgers, the late Sammy Clarke, and Eithne O'Connor as well as David Ramsey, Denise Austin's last living relative. At the Belfast Zoo, I'm indebted to Zoo Curator Raymond Robinson and Zoo Manager Alyn Cairns for sharing stories of the zoo's history and animals. In addition, thanks to Aidan McCormack of Belfast City Sightseeing for a tour of the city through the lens of the World War II. And thank you to Daryl Campbell and Tina Chong for your hospitality.

I'm enormously grateful to scholar Brian Barton, Ph.D. He is the author/editor of twelve books on Irish history and politics, including *The Belfast Blitz: The City in the War Years* (Ulster Historical Foundation, 2015). This comprehensive volume served as a research Bible of sorts as I was writing and revising the novel over the years. Brian also read drafts of my manuscript, providing detailed feedback to ensure that the novel reflected the historical accuracy of the city, the bombings, and the time period. I will always be thankful for Brian's knowledge, expertise, and kindness. Also, in Ireland and Northern Ireland: thank you to Anne Kennedy, Raymond Robinson, and Ciaran Doran for your helpful, instructive reads of my novel.

Other volumes also imparted valuable insights and details: *The Belfast Blitz: Luftwaffe Raids in Northern Ireland, 1941* by Sean McMahon (The Brehon Press, 2010), *Post 381: The Memoirs of a Belfast Air Raid Warden* by James Doherty (Friar's Bush Press, 1989), *The Belfast Blitz: The People's Story* by Stephen Douds (Blackstaff Press, 2011), *The Emperor of Ice-Cream* by Brian Moore (Viking Press, 1965), *Bad Blood: A Walk Along the Irish Border* by Colm Tóibín (Picador, 2010), and *Say Nothing: A True Story of Murder and Memory in Northern Ireland* by Patrick Radden Keefe (Doubleday, 2019). Thank you to Vanessa Cameron, librarian/archivist at the New York Yacht Club, where I completed further research about the Belfast shipyards and Harland & Wolff. I also made multiple research visits to the main branch of the

New York Public Library. And thank you to Nick Flynn for the permission to include the sentence—*All creatures have square shoulders*—from his memoir *The Ticking Is the Bomb* (Norton, 2011).

For my elephant-related research, I would like to thank Large Mammal Curator Daryl Hoffman and Elephant Manager Martina Stevens at the Houston Zoo. Hoffman and Stevens allowed me to visit the elephants at the Houston Zoo on several occasions. This firsthand experience with the elephants, especially three-year-old Tupelo (at the time), and interviews with Hoffman and Stevens gave me a deeper understanding of the lives and care of elephants. In addition, *How Animals Grieve* by Barbara J. King (University of Chicago Press, 2013) and *Beyond Words: What Animals Think and Feel* by Carl Safina (Henry Holt, 2015) also provided further understanding of the lives of elephants and other animals.

On a summer afternoon in 2014, I met Scott Sellers in front of the Neil Simon Theatre on Broadway while waiting to purchase tickets for the final performance of *All the Way*. Scott recognized my husband, Michael, because he had seen Michael perform in the role of the hustler opposite Derek Jacobi's Alan Turing in the Broadway production of *Breaking the Code* in the very same theater twenty years earlier. Then, we learned that Scott worked for Penguin Random House in Toronto, and our conversation moved between plays, books, hockey, and more over the next few hours. This chance meeting gave way to a friendship, and as I struck out on my own to find a home for this novel, Scott provided mentorship every step of the way. During the contract process, I also received guidance and advice from Nancy Bilyeau, Max Epstein, Andy Bowman, and Tanessa Harte.

Heartfelt gratitude to my mentors, teachers, and friends: the late E. L. Doctorow, Mary-Beth Hughes, Margot Livesey, Lily Tuck, Rick Moody, and Abdi Assadi. Thank you to the following writers for reading my manuscript and providing valuable feedback: Elizabeth Crane, Fiona McFarlane, Margot Livesey, Lily Tuck, Dalia Azim, and Anne

Burt. Thank you to the editorial expertise of Sarah Branham on a later draft of this manuscript. I'm also indebted to Karen Olsson, Dominic Smith, and Elizabeth McCracken for their friendship, feedback, and advice during the writing process.

Love and gratitude to my friends and family who have been cheering me on along the way: the Harte family, Lize Burr and Chris Hyams, Stephen Marshall and Shirley Thompson, Nancy Miller, Karen Christensen and Kathleen Donnelly, Hester and Jim Magnuson, Ted and Melba Whatley, Greg Cowles, Vivé Griffith, Debra Lamberson Young, Clune Walsh III and Natalie Germano, E. Bennett Walsh, Liza Lauber, Lee Ford Walsh, Colleen Dolan Vinetz, Beverly Curtiss Walsh, and John Baird. And a very special thanks to my sister, Ami.

Thank you to the Ucross Foundation and the Virginia Center for the Creative Arts; both residencies gave me valuable time and space to write and work. Thank you to my friends at Austin Bat Cave, St. Stephen's Episcopal School, the Michener Center for Writers, and my students of my nine-month workshop.

My late friend and writer John McNeel served as an enlisted soldier who fought in numerous campaigns during World War II. He saw action in North Africa and southern Europe, participating in some of the war's worst battles, including the siege at Anzio Beachhead. When I still lived in New York City, I spent many hours with John—in his small studio apartment on the Upper West Side and over lunch at Old John's Luncheonette on West 67th Street—and he recounted his experiences as a soldier in combat and as a young boy growing up in rural Virginia. John's stories—and spirit—inspired many aspects of this novel, including Mr. Wright's wartime history of fighting and trauma.

Lastly, I want to thank my husband, Michael Dolan. It has been a long journey to publication, and his enthusiasm and support has been with me all along the way. Michael, thank you for your love, your talent, your creativity, and your inspiration. Thank you for making me laugh—and smile—when I needed it the most. Your love has been a harbor and a home. Thank you.

Discussion Guide

Thank you for reading! We hope you enjoyed S. Kirk Walsh's debut novel, *The Elephant of Belfast*, and found it thought-provoking. Below are some topics to consider and questions to discuss with your book group.

1. During World War II, women finally broke into the workforce as men were drafted into the war. What challenges did Hettie face in becoming the zoo's first female zookeeper? Why do you think advancement opportunities in the workforce were made available to women only in the absence of men?

2. Chapter 4 begins: "Air-raid drills became routine, and the familiar sirens frequently whined across the sweep of the winter sky. A smattering of pedestrians got into the habit of carrying gas masks" (p. 64).

   How was the war represented in *The Elephant of Belfast*? Did danger feel ever-present during your reading? Why or why not?

3. Like Violet, the snail Ferris gives to Hettie endures an interesting

journey throughout *The Elephant of Belfast*. On pages 166–67, we see Hettie and Rose interact with the snail:

> Hettie positioned it on the kitchen table and stared at the concentric circles of the mollusk's design. The evening light struck the shell, intensifying its pink iridescence before its smooth surface became flat again. The snail's antennae tentatively emerged from its chamber and waved in the air. She smiled to herself. The snail extended its dark neck and wriggled its antennae farther. Hettie retrieved a few leaves from a celery stalk in the larder and placed them next to it, and it began to munch away on one of the leaves . . . Hettie continued to watch the snail eat the remaining leaves as her mother made her rhubarb pie. The comforting sounds of domesticity took over the kitchen . . . After the snail finished eating, the creature returned to the safety of its shell.

Animals have long been metaphoric in literature (*Moby-Dick*'s white whale, *The Old Man and the Sea*'s great fish). Discuss what the snail symbolizes to Hettie. What could the young elephant, Violet, represent?

4. Consider the following passage: "During her time at the zoo, Hettie had noted this about Mr. Wright: He often spoke with more kindness to the animals than he did to people" (p. 9).
    Hettie views Mr. Wright in a judgmental light in the beginning but comes to realize they are more similar than they are different. Discuss the choices made by Mr. Wright and Hettie. How might one character be reflected in the other?

5. Hettie has a complicated relationship with both her mother and her father. Though her father abandoned the family, Hettie remembers him

fondly, saying, "If he were still around, he would have been supportive of her new position despite the low salary and meager hours" (p. 30).

Why does Hettie's view of her parents change throughout the novel? How do her experiences inform her outlook on Anna and Liam's marriage and Liam's relationship with Maeve?

6. Hettie finds herself attracted to three different men throughout the course of the novel—Ferris, Liam, and Samuel. What did Hettie learn about herself from her relationships with these three young men?

7. Consider the following passage:

> God knows we need more women to lead us these days. Look at the mess the world is in, and it's all because of men—Hitler, Stalin, Churchill, and, nearer home, Craigavon. They're brutal, insensitive, arrogant. They never go down on their knees and pray, and consider the will of God, or think how what they're doing will affect the women, their sisters, wives and mothers, and the wee children. (p. 245)

How are the women portrayed in the novel in comparison to the men? Are there any reversals? Anything surprising?

8. Discuss the Protestant/Catholic conflict in the narrative. Were you surprised that the Troubles played a role during World War II and the fight against the Germans?

9. Consider the following passage:

> Here was Violet . . . Mr. Wright, the head zookeeper, stood at the foot of the gangplank. Two reporters

appeared by his side and scribbled in their notepads as Mr. Wright kept his gaze fixed on Violet. The elephant hovered, her feet hanging in midair, her flap-like ears pinned against her head. There was another collective sigh as she lifted her trunk and produced a high-pitched whistle. The elephant's cry tumbled over the crowd. (p. 4)

Do you remember your first encounter with an elephant or another wild animal? How would you describe it?

10. Consider the following passage:

Hettie felt she had entered a dream, crossed over a threshold into another reality, where citizens weren't dying and homes weren't being destroyed and the sky wasn't on fire. Instead, it was only Stella Holliday and her extraordinary song. "She says she's gonna sing until the bombs stop falling," said a man who stood by the entrance. "Lots of people ran for the shelters, but I think it's safer here. Listen to her. Look at her." . . . Hettie thought Stella looked as though she were dedicating every cell and fiber of her body to her song. (pp. 181–82)

Music plays a considerable role throughout *The Elephant of Belfast*. Is there a song or singer who you turn to in hard times? Why do you choose this particular piece of music? If possible, play your songs for one another.

11. Hettie Quin is inspired by a real woman named Denise Weston Austin, who was Bellevue Zoo's first female zookeeper. Do you think it makes

a difference in your reading experience that this novel was based on a real person and events as opposed to being composed of wholly fictional characters?

12. Hettie's grief changes throughout the novel, particularly as her private grief about her sister and father is shaped, or informed, by the public grief of the Belfast Blitz. Many readers have connected this theme with their own experiences of the COVID-19 pandemic. What similarities do you see between the two time periods?

S. KIRK WALSH is a writer living in Austin, Texas. Her work has been widely published in *The New York Times Book Review*, *Longreads*, *StoryQuarterly*, and *Electric Literature*, among other publications. Over the years, she has been a resident at Ucross, Yaddo, Ragdale, and the Virginia Center for the Creative Arts. Walsh is the founder of Austin Bat Cave, a writing and tutoring center that provides free writing workshops for young writers throughout Austin. *The Elephant of Belfast* is her first novel. Find out more at skirkwalsh.com.